FOR THE GOOD OF THE UNION

By
Alan Starforth

info@straightfacedpublications.com

www.straightfacedpublications.com

Published by **Straightfaced Publications**
© Straightfaced Publications

Dedicated to my beautiful Grandson,
James Alan Starforth.

CHAPTER 1

***

Colonel General Leonid Klamenkovich stands six feet two inches tall, a large menacing man with arrogant pride as he looks over the Gulf of Finland. Almost hemmed in by the thick ice, a small cargo ship sits further down with Captain Vassilev, a weedy unlikable, overconfident man, standing on the bridge's exterior, chain-smoking himself through a pack of Sobranie Black Russian cigarettes to keep warm.

A blacked-out Mercedes 500 AMG S class travels through the docks of St Petersburg, Russia. It comes to a halt aside Major Rosstof alights into the falling snow that covers the docks as a bitterly cold wind whips off the Eurasian Steppes to cut into everyone unlucky enough to be in its unsympathetic path. Rosstof comes to attention with a smart, intelligent salute, but the general lifts his hand, stopping him from talking, and they walk off a short distance until out of earshot of those not connected to their clandestine organisation. "You were about to say, Major?"

Aware of the violent reputation of his commanding general, Rosstof recomposes himself, "The money has been deposited as arranged, General."

Overcome with greed, Klamenkovich grins and then waves at Vassilev, who enters the bridge's welcoming warmth on receiving the go. "Are we still in contact with the buyer?" he said with straight-faced steadfastness his subordinate is well acquainted with.

"Yes, General. They are requesting more armaments."

Klamenkovich is aware that after the invasion of Crimea in 2014 and its annexation from Ukraine, the Kremlin's intentions to rearm for a full invasion of their southern neighbour and that all arms will be required. "Has Sokolov been in touch?"

"Not for a while, General."

"I'm beginning to feel some heat from the Kremlin, so I need the colonel to up his game and get me the intelligence required."

"I will see to that immediately, General."

His discussion over, Klamenkovich walks off and Rosstof salutes and then gets the rear of the Mercedes to be driven off. With impatience reaching the breaking point to escape the cold, Klamenkovich pulls his overcoat in tighter, then moves to the water's edge as the cargo ship's engine belches black smoke out of her old funnels, and it heads off painfully slow through the creaking ice.

***

Christmas decorations dominate the Marquis of Granby public house in Greater London, with only 20 shopping days to the big day and 26 to the start of 2015. Ridiculously busy, several Christmas parties are going on at the same time with people dancing, drinking and having fun, but not all are in the festive spirit as others only have getting drunk as quickly as possible on their minds.

Unassuming, handsome and middle-aged, even though of late he looks and feels tired and withdrawn, James Ashley sits on a stool at the end of the counter enjoying the solitude as he drinks his favourite relaxant, Newcastle Brown Ale, along with a whisky chaser and grins with the pleasure each mouthful gives. Ron, the ever-dutiful barman, knows through experience that he is craving peace and doesn't venture into a conversation as the ex-soldier's mind is mixed up with long-past traumas that take him into his nightly quest for melancholic inebriation. All of a sudden, the unlikeliest of enemies explodes its irritating fun, but the sound of the party popper overtakes to remind Ashley of a cracking bullet which overloads his sensitivity, and he grimaces at its sound. He glances at Ron, who had courteously looked away in the hope he will believe he hadn't witnessed his harrowing awkwardness, then recomposes his shaken standing as he produces a container of Meperidine pain medication and throws two into his mouth to swallow with a mouthful of the Brown Ale.

"I don't think you're meant to take your pain meds with alcohol, James," Ron said with concern, making Ashley grin discomfited.

"Well," Ashley starts solemnly. "As neither takes away the pain, I can't see the problem."

"Then why take them?"

Well aware that if he wants to function, he has no choice, Ashley grins broadly but decides not to answer, and Ron, seeing his discomfort, decides not to press the issue he knows is disturbing to his friend and customer.

Bright and Westwood, two large well-dressed over powering military types, enter from behind and look around as they aggressively push their way through the revellers toward Ashley.

"James," Ron said for Ashley to look and see him nod toward the men towering above.

Ashley recomposes his tremor to take a sip of his Brown Ale and turn on the stool to look between the menacing men unimpressed as Bright flashes his MI5 credentials to bring a wry, mischievous smile out of him.

"Bright and Westwood," Bright said with an overrated opinion of himself. "Sergeant James Ashley?"

Even though the bar is frequented by many who work for the security services, Ashley had informed Ron he was a nobody working in the city, and the bartender laughs at the use of the rank as the former soldier grins embarrassed and he has to turn away to withhold the need to increase his laughter.

"Wrong man," Ashley gripes to Bright's irritation. "Another bottle, Ron. Nice and cold."

Ron produces a bottle of Brown Ale, takes the lid off, and then places it on the counter for Ashley to top up his glass.

"You know the Yanks believe we like our beer warm," Ashley explains, taking another mouthful. "Never liked it that way myself. The dog has to be ice cold for me, or it's undrinkable."

Bright places his hand on Ashley's shoulder, but he turns to knock it aside, then stands awkwardly to stretch out his aching body, which shows he is still pained from injuries sustained while carrying out his government's bidding. "We need a word with you, Sergeant."

Ashley holds his chest and exhales as he rubs his aching legs to relieve the discomfort that plagues him constantly. "Forget the sergeant shit," he said, giving Ron an awkward grin of discomfort as he sat. "I'm just lowly James Ashley, who happens to be off duty."

"In this game, you're never off duty, and as I'm a captain, I expect to be obeyed by a mere sergeant," Bright condescends as Ashley takes a large lingering mouthful of his Brown Ale to savour the taste.

"That's where you're wrong, Captain," he said, putting spite on the rank. "I'm not in the army, so I don't need to jump when a privileged dick speaks."

Desperate to lash out at the man he has taken an instant dislike to, Bright withholds the urge as Westwood moves to confront but is prevented from doing so by his colleague. "General Shirlow wants to see you!"

Surprised that the head of Section S would want to speak to a desk hound like himself, Ashley says pessimistically. "Why would Shirlow want to see me?"

"It's General Shirlow, Sergeant!" Bright shouts. "And I'm not privy to that information!"

"What?" Ashley said with an overriding urge to use the sarcasm he believes is his greatest weapon. "Such a high rank, and the general doesn't tell you what's going on? You must be well pissed?" he teases. Feeling the derision bite, Bright sneers. "Watch your lip, Sergeant!" "If he wants a drink, he should have come down here. I'm sure Ron would pour him a Pimm's or a glass of tap water."

Ron laughs, but on seeing the stern faces of Bright and Westwood turn on him with intent to harm, he moves off to serve the other customers who have been patiently waiting as they watch the ongoing dispute.

"Look, Sergeant!" Bright adds dismissively calm. "I don't give a shit if you come or not, but I'm not waiting all night."

"Leave him," Westwood interrupts. "He's the one who'll be in the shit."

Bright, the most intelligent of the two, knows it won't go down well if he doesn't deliver as ordered. "There's a car waiting outside, so if you want a lift, you'd better make it now. I'll give you to the count of five," he adds as he moves off, but Westwood remains rigidly staring his anger to Ashley's amusement.

Ashley takes a large mouthful, then lowers his unfinished glass with inevitability and looks at Ron, who shrugs his shoulders, having enjoyed that night's entertainment. "Keep that cold. Hopefully, this won't take too long," he mutters as he pushes past Westwood and limps off for them to exit together.

***

CHAPTER 2

***

The home of the United Kingdom's internal security service since December 1994 sits within the beautiful Neoclassical building of Thames House on Millbank overlooking the River Thames in London between the great bridges of Lambeth and Vauxhall. A mysterious place that, because of its designation gives a sense of disquiet to all who pass with cameras watching their every move with the mistrust of a nation.

Bright and Westwood walk along one of the many corridors, with Ashley limping behind in disbelief of having only left the place two hours prior at the end of that day shift.

Feeling the effects of the brown ale and whisky consumed within a short period, Ashley speaks with intent to lighten the sombre mood. "You two are a real sociable pair," he said but didn't receive a reply, so he continued to annoy. "Have you worked here long? - No. - How long, then? - You can't say. – It's a secret. - Oh, how patriotic to keep this country's dirty washing to yourself."

Bright gives Ashley an anger fuelled glare that shows single-mindedness to cause harm.

"I'm only asking because I care," Ashley carries on with sarcasm that snaps the captain's stoic composure, and he lunges forward, but the highly trained special forces soldier steps aside to make his attacker stumble against the wall. "Are you alright?" he adds sardonically. "I hope you haven't been drinking while on duty?"

Bright throws several punches with increasing anger but misses as Ashley steps aside to make him stumble forward, humiliated.

Ashley grins mischievously, lifting his fists as if waiting for a Victorian boxing bout. "Marquess of Queensbury rules," he mocks as he dances, and Bright recomposes himself and takes several calming breaths intent to carry on his assault. "Come on, Captain. You can't leave that there."

Colonel Jack Caine, a confident, expensively dressed man, had served his country with distinction over the past thirty years at all levels of command through the Welsh Guards, guarding the Royal Family, to active service with the SAS, where he had served in many theatres of war before being assigned to military intelligence which led him on the road to MI5. On hearing Ashley's voice, he exits the side office smiling. "Alright, gentlemen. I will take it from here!" he orders, and the tension quickly calms as Bright and Westwood nod their submissiveness and move off. "How's it going, James?"

Ashley lowers his hands and shakes Caine's with genuine affection for their long-standing friendship. "How do you think?" he moans. "You try and have a quiet drink after a hard day at work, and Laurel and Hardy turn up and ruin it!" he shouts, intent to annoy, but neither MI5 men cares enough to glance back.

Caine takes Ashley's arm and walks him off a short distance. "Are you pissed?"

"No, but if Stan and Ollie hadn't turned up, I would be well on my way."

"I know those two. They aren't to be taken lightly."

"They were pussy cats!" Ashley shouts as he looks to find them gone. "I was only ragging them."

"Straighten yourself out, James," Caine adds seriously. "General Shirlow wants to see you."

"So, Stan said."

"You know he doesn't suffer fools, so you'd better be on your best behaviour."

"What are you trying to say?" Ashley said, laughing. "I've only seen the exalted one once, and as he passed me in the corridor, the wind almost knocked me over."

"Listen, James," Caine adds sternly, hoping his old colleague will act mature for as long as the meeting is to come. "He has two Yanks with him. A general and a colonel."

"This day just keeps getting better," Ashley said, but Caine gave a mischievous wink and intriguing smile that caught his attention.

"I think you'll like the colonel."

"Oh yeah?" Ashley grumbles, gaining a new interest. "How come?"

"Keep in mind they've been waiting a while, so don't expect a good reception," Caine adds, and Ashley stops to question their interest in him, but the colonel has no intention of giving an honest answer. "No doubt someone to save the world. All the Hollywood heroes are busy."

Ashley grabs Caine's arm, anxious about the situation he walks freely into. "What do they want with a desk hound like me?"

"I can't imagine," Caine adds with humour to vex. "But the sooner we go in, the sooner we'll find out."

"Has the general had his car washed lately, or his office hoovered?

"Maybe they need advice on National Security," Caine adds straight-faced as he moves off, leaving Ashley unenthused.

A door adjacent to Shirlow's office opens, and Colonel Soames and Vice Admiral Lawrence exit and move down the corridor.

"Colonel, Admiral," Caine said as they passed, and they nodded their cunning acknowledgement and shook his hand but paid no attention to Ashley, who stared his mistrust until they disappeared.

"Mile End Soames," Ashley said to Caine's bewilderment. "What's a total shit bag like him doing here?"

"Do you mean Colonel Soames?" Caine questioned as his interest increased. "Do you know him?"

"Many years ago," Ashley answers melancholically.

"He's General Shirlow's MI6 liaison. I take it you don't like him?"

"Does anybody?"

Caine nods his agreement. "Forget about him. He's on a deep-cover mission that has nothing to do with us, so your paths shouldn't pass again."

"I can only hope," Ashley said, pleased until his thought process overtook alarmingly. "But answer me honestly," he adds with a mistrusting nervous grin. "Does he have anything to do with me being here?"

"I don't truly know what his mission is, but it can't have anything to do with us as we would need to be informed of such," Caine reassured as he walked off, leaving Ashley unnerved at the thought.

Ashley takes a Kevlar lined hip flask, given to him on the day he was discharged from the Special Air Service, that has the winged dagger motive and the regiments motto of, 'Who Dares Wins' on the front and on the back, the cross hairs of a sniper's rifle and flips it open to take a mouthful of whisky just as Caine turns back to see him.

"Come on, James, that's enough of that," Caine grumbles, and Ashley takes another mouthful, then tucks the hip flask into his jacket.

***

CHAPTER 3

***

Lieutenant General Bartholomew Shirlow, a highly educated ex-Eton, Cambridge and Sandhurst Military Academy graduate and veteran of many conflicts, most unknown to the British populace, sits behind his commanding desk as his eyes shift agitatedly between his uninvited, unwanted American guests who have imposed themselves on his day. He had dealt with the Americans many times throughout his long career but had never taken a liking to them or the way they carry out intelligence which he thought, in his snobby upper-class world, was severely flawed and unprofessional.

Dressed in the uniform of a United States Army Major General, Harold Davison sits chewing hard on an unlit cigar with Colonel Julie Conners sitting to his side on a comfortable leather Chesterfield sofa. Davison speaks with an exaggerated Southern American drawl that grinds through Shirlow's conceited exterior at being addressed by his abbreviated forename.

"Where is he, Bart?"

Even though Ashley's tardiness angers him, Shirlow is more irritated by the American's uncouth mannerisms and snipes his agitation. "It's general, General, and as I have already reliably informed you on several occasions, he's en route, so I must insist you be patient."

There's a knock on the door, and Caine enters, followed by a reluctant Ashley, who stops in the doorway as the tenseness of the room hits, and all eyes fix on his awkwardness and he grins his bewilderment of their interest in him.

Davison vaults to his feet to look Ashley over, unimpressed. "Is this who we've been waiting for, Bart? About bloody time!"

Shirlow rounds his desk to shake Ashley's hand as he feigns interest in a lowly subordinate, only for the American's irritation. "Come in, Sergeant Ashley."

"Sorry to keep you waiting, sir," Ashley said as his eyes fixed on Conners' beauty, and he smiled but gained a look of disinterest.

"Sergeant?" Davison shouts disparagingly. "I thought he'd at least be an officer?"

Everyone in the room ignores his outburst apart from Conners, who coughs in desperate need to laugh.

Shirlow sits and adds courteously to annoy the Americans. "Not a problem, Sergeant; please take a seat."

"No, Sergeant!" Davison belittles. "I enjoy wasting my evenings waiting for a lowly NCO to take the time to visit!"

Ashley is overcome with the need to defend himself, but the two stars on the general's uniform prevent him and he moves uncomfortably to Shirlow's desk as his puzzled glance shifts between Davison and Conners as he sits.

"I have called you here because," Shirlow starts, but Davison cuts him short with bullish exaggerated hand waving.

"Cut the bull shit, Bart, and save the diplomacy for another day and get to the bloody point!"

Shirlow stares at Davison, unable to hide his dislike. "You will have to excuse the general, Sergeant. No doubt you can see he's an American."

"What has nationality got to do with this?" Davison said, playing to type.

"We are all aware of your opinion, General, but your blusterous interruptions don't help!" Shirlow bellows his annoyance, but his words don't phase Davison, who lights his cigar to take a deep draw and blow smoke into the air. "You can't smoke in here, General."

"I don't need to remind you of what's at stake?" Davison argues to Shirlow's increasing disdain.

"No, but we could do without your constant outbursts confusing the matter. I don't need to remind you that I'm in command, do I?"

Davison takes another exaggerated draw on his cigar and exhales a large cloud of smoke to Shirlow's increasing irritability. "No, you don't, General, and that's obvious by the balls up I am witnessing here."

"Oh, and just in case you don't know, it is illegal to smoke in my office, so if you don't mind, please extinguish it," Shirlow gripes as Davison places the cigar into his mouth and chews on the end showing no intention of putting it out. "And even if it wasn't," he adds as his irritability increases. "I wouldn't allow it."

Davison takes another long lingering draw to Ashley's increasing interest as his glance fixes on Conners, but she blatantly ignores him, to Caine's amusement.

Shirlow notices Ashley's attraction to the American beauty. "I see you have noticed the colonel, Sergeant," he said.

Ashley's shuffling discomfort confirms that his initial interest in her has been revealed.

"She's here to assist you."

Ashley looks around in bewildered shock. "Assist me with what, sir?"

Davison walks behind Ashley and slaps him on the back to gain a look of disdain from the Englishman. "Well, Bart, I believe I will take my leave of you."

Shirlow's confused irritation fixes on his American counterpart. "I thought you wanted to be here for the meeting?"

Davison shakes Shirlow's hand with the mutual contempt they hold in each other, then backs to the door. "It's been a long day, so I will leave the rest to you."

"Well, err, I suppose it was good to have met you, General," Shirlow mumbles insincerely, which Davison understands, and Caine opens the door for the Americans to exit.

Amused by the animated actions of the brash, over-the-top American, all in the room look at each other in bewilderment as Ashley laughs but quickly stops in respect of the ranks left in the room.

"I don't believe it. He makes a big deal to be here, then leaves before it starts," Shirlow explains. "Can't say I have ever liked Americans, and this General Davison sums up all colonials to me. Brash, loud, arrogant and overbearing."

In the belief it isn't his place to demean an Allied general, Ashley remains quiet as Caine laughs to Shirlow's nodding agreement.

The General moves to the drink cabinet. "Would anyone like a drink?"

"I'll take a large one, sir," Ashley answers rapidly, catching Caine's unnerved attention.

"Please, sir," Caine said as he moved to Ashley to whisper. "Don't you think you've had enough, James?"

"Because I was called from my comfort zone prematurely, I must say no."

"Remember where you are," Caine adds, concerned. "This isn't the mess in Hereford. The general won't take kindly to your shit."

"I'm afraid I only have single malt," Shirlow said pompously as he lifted a bottle to bring a smile to Ashley. "It's a twenty-five-year-old Dalmore."

"I don't mind slumming it," Ashley said with humour that brought a curious grin out of the general and an indignant shake of Caine's head.

Shirlow pours the whisky, and then hands them over. "To your good health, gentlemen." He raises his glass in salute, and Ashley follows suit taking a large mouthful.

"This is good stuff, General."

Demeaned by words about his favourite whisky, Shirlow gripes. "I would hardly call it stuff, Sergeant. It's a very expensive single malt."

"James wouldn't know the difference between this and dishwater, sir,"

Caine laughs. "Don't allow his unsophisticated northern upbringing to demean such a smooth whisky."

Uncaring of anyone's opinion of him, Ashley adds. "Whisky's whisky to me, and as long as it gets you pissed, who cares?"

Dismayed, Shirlow stares his concern at the roughness of Ashley's attitude with the thought that he has done nothing to inspire him with confidence. "Well, let's get to why you are here, Sergeant."

"I'm looking forward to hearing what I'm volunteering for," Ashley said with sarcasm that wasn't wasted on the officers. "But why the Yanks, sir?" he complains to Shirlow's irritation.

"If you don't mind, Sergeant," Shirlow gripes, and Ashley grins, amused at the effect he is having on the general's sensitive mood. "American intelligence, or should I say the CIA, believe they have picked up on a plot to assassinate their President."

As Ashley listens, he becomes increasingly bemused about the reasoning behind his presence and looks at Caine for confirmation.

"They believe two Russian S40e missiles are being sold to an arms dealer in this country," Shirlow carries on with calm that the situation truly shouldn't warrant. "So, as you would expect from an inferior intelligence agency, they have put two and two together."

"And come up with seven," Caine interrupts to Shirlow's grinning appreciation.

"You've got it, Colonel. I have had it explained to me that their President is due in this country for meetings with the Prime Minister."

"Do we have a date, sir?" Ashley enquires naively, but Shirlow dismisses the newest intelligence officer thrust upon him without knowing his experience or skills.

"I do, but that doesn't concern you or anyone else. That information is still to be released, so we don't know where this alleged attempt could have come from."

"The shit would hit the fan if the Yank President were assassinated on our soil, sir," Ashley adds to ingratiate himself to the officer he knows holds little favour for anyone of his rank.

"Very eloquent, Sergeant, but I have had that pressed home from the highest level and don't require it from the likes of you."

Ashley's enthusiasm wanes as quickly as it had emerged. "I can only apologise, sir," he mutters with derision. "With me being invited to the top table for the first time, I forgot my place."

Caine calls Ashley's name and beckons him to show respect, but the sergeant's attempt at getting a rise out of the general has gone straight over the head of Section S.

"They've come to us with very vague intelligence. They don't know who is buying, who is selling, where or when," Shirlow carries on. "I think it is pure fabrication and a waste of my precious time, but I've been ordered to act on what little I have."

Ashley's curious glance shifts between Shirlow and Caine. "The question that needs answered is why come to me with this, sir?"

"Why come to you?" Shirlow interrupts callously. "You are an operative in the employ of her majesty's government, are you not?"

"I'm a desk jockey with a limp," Ashley explains solemnly, and Shirlow grins with the accomplishment at his thoughts of why he had been selected.

"You are faceless and unknown in the world of intelligence. That's why Colonel Caine believes you are perfect for this job."

Ashley turns his irritation onto Caine, who grins, amused by his friend's disposition. "That just means expendable."

"You and this Colonel Conners are to investigate the intelligence received to dispel it at the earliest."

"The Yank that was with the general, sir?" Ashley adds solemnly as Shirlow's glare shifts between him and Caine.

"I was led to believe you were the right man for the job. Is that not right, Colonel Caine?"

"James is more than capable of carrying this out, sir," Caine explains, and Ashley laughs, bemused by his confidence in him. "It's nothing compared to what he is used to."

"Well, you needn't worry, Sergeant, as I don't take the threat seriously," Shirlow adds as Ashley thinks over the reasoning for his presence.

"So, you're sending me on a mission with this Yank colonel, and you want me to dispel its authenticity before I leave?"

Shirlow downs his whisky with arrogance then moves to pour himself another. "What else could we want you to do?"

"You don't seem interested, James," Caine interjects. "I thought being teamed with a beauty like Colonel Conners would suit you."

Not wanting to look too unenthusiastic, Ashley states coyly. "Well, there's being teamed up and being teamed up, Jack, err, Colonel, but to be sent on a fool's errand on my first mission for the service seems irresponsible to me."

"Irresponsible?" Shirlow growls annoyed that a subordinate is questioning his orders.

"You never had an attitude in the regiment," Caine interrupts, but

Ashley doesn't believe he has a problem. "You were always the first to volunteer."

"That was different. I was a soldier and a great deal fitter in those days."

"You will find most missions around here, as you so eloquently put it, are fool's errands," Shirlow explains with a hint of humour to play down what should be taken more seriously. "We don't always catch the bad guy and have many hours." He pauses to sip his whisky. "Sitting on our rears waiting for the intelligence to show itself."

Having sat in foliage, or a hole in the ground, waiting for a target or intelligence that doesn't always turn up for days, even weeks on end, in many theatres of war around the world, Ashley is aware of the waiting game involved in surveillance and turns to Caine. "Since you recruited me, all I have gained is boils on my arse and a fondness for a life that's a damn sight sweeter without the constant threat of death."

"I understand you sustained injuries in Afghanistan?" Shirlow questioned indifferently, but Ashley didn't like his disability being the focal point of any conversation, and it showed on his tired, alcohol-fuelled face as he turned to Caine for an explanation that wasn't forthcoming. "I am sure it won't hold you back as I fully expect you will have nothing to do but enjoy the beautiful Scottish scenery."

Ashley drains the expensive whisky in one, without tasting anything that would make his working man's pallet impressed by the massive increase in value, then places the glass next to the bottle in the hope of a refill, but Shirlow ignores his obviousness.

"All we want is people on the ground in Scotland just in case someone turns up," Shirlow belittles. "You'll be wasting your highly trained skills, but orders are orders and as I have said these have come from the very top."

"Why Scotland, sir?"

Shirlow nods at Caine for him to move to the wall covered in high-tech surveillance equipment and press a button for the audio to play a muffled voice.

"The missiles are coming, and the President of the United States will be dead soon." There's a little crackling interference. "Dimitri Rossakovich," then the line goes dead.

"Short and sweet," Ashley said, amused. "I can see why the Yanks would be interested."

"That was the second call, and they don't know everything about either of them," Shirlow said to Ashley's confusion. "I had to inform them of the alleged attempt on their President, but that was all."

"Why would that be, sir?" Ashley questioned, but Shirlow had no intention of answering.

"Do you recognise the voice?" Shirlow said, bemusing Ashley as if he could distinguish between a muffled voice and a clear one.

"There's a certain familiarity, but I can't say I do," Ashley jokes sarcastically, but the humour goes over Shirlow's head as Caine shakes his, annoyed. "Maybe if I listen to it another hundred or so times, it may become a little clearer, sir."

"That call was made from a phone box on Hall Street in Campbeltown on the Mull of Kintyre."

"And you want me and this Yank, who outranks me, by the way, to go to Scotland just in case someone wants to make another call," Ashley moans, and Caine nods, amused. "Who was he calling, sir?"

"Now there's the thing," Shirlow adds. "We believe it was the seller of the arms. A Dimitri Rossakovich."

"The name mentioned?" Ashley said with mistrust that instantly turned on the general. "And you know who he is?"

"He isn't known to us," Shirlow adds, embarrassed. "So, it could be a nom de plume."

Ashley looks around, bemused. "A non der what, sir?"

"An assumed name," Shirlow adds condescendingly.

"Surely a nom de plume is used by a writer instead of their real name," Ashley adds as equally condescending. "I think you mean a pseudonym, sir."

Caine can see Ashley enjoying putting the pompous general right but can also see the irritation in his superior officer's eyes. "You are booked on the Prestwick shuttle tomorrow morning," he interrupts to break up the fight of words. "From Glasgow, you will find a car for your drive to Kintyre."

"Scotland's lovely this time of year," Shirlow adds to Ashley's amused irritation.

"Sounds like a nice little holiday, James," Caine said as he held in the urge to giggle.

"And that's all it will be," Shirlow interrupts confidently. "Just go to Kintyre and have a good time."

"And do we have to survey this phone box on Hall Street all the time we are there, sir?" Ashley adds with dread.

"Hardly," Shirlow interjects. "Just book into a nearby hotel and wait just in case another call is made. We've had the box bugged, and you'll be informed of its use in real time."

"It's all on expenses, James," Caine adds, straightening Ashley's face. "Surely you like the thought of that?"

Ever the accountant keeping a tight rein on his section's expenditure, which had been decimated to a meagre percentage of the heyday of the cold war, Shirlow speaks with hindrance to Ashley's smiling expectations. "Within reason, of course. You can't expect the treasury to finance a jolly."

"Of course not, sir. I would hate to think any job perks would come all the way down to the likes of me."

Shirlow moved to his desk and opened a drawer to take out a manila envelope to hand to Ashley. "All you need to know is in there. Hotel, flight tickets, car hire," he said as Ashley opened the envelope to look inside, but the general snatched it back and threw it onto his desk. "Leave your reading for later! There are one thousand Pounds in cash, so you will have to use your credit card for extras, and we will reimburse you later," he adds to Ashley's unease and Caine's added amusement. "But keep your receipts, or you won't get your money back."

"Just in case I add a few pints with my meal without declaring it, sir," Ashley jokes.

"It's been known, Sergeant," Shirlow adds. "I will not tolerate dishonesty."

Ashley grins weakly, but after a glance at Caine, he decides to curtail his humour.

Shirlow moves to the door and opens it as he looks back. "You can leave the rest to us, Sergeant."

"Thank you, sir," Ashley said, disillusioned that he has to cover the expenses and then apply to be reimbursed, which he knows won't be easy in the cash-starved world of British intelligence; then he mumbles his dismissal as he picks up the envelope and exits perplexed to his involvement. He stops to look back as the door closes and shakes his head before limping off as fast as he can to get back to the Marquis of Granby, hoping for a lock-in.

***

With its engine ticking over, a US Embassy car waits at the rear of Thames House as Davison and Conners exit and the door is slammed and locked behind them.

Davison throws the cigar to the ground and then spits into the gutter. "Excuse my bad manners, Colonel," he said, reverting to the normality of his Washington accent as he removed his scrambled egg-covered hat of rank and loosened his tie. "Cigars make me chuck."

Amused at how he had kept up the pretence of the cigar-chomping cliché of an American general for so long, Conners laughs. "You played the part well, sir," she said. "It was just like watching a Hollywood film from World War Two."

"Bloody arrogant Brits!" he snipes. "That Shirlow looks on us as his servant's illiterate half-witted colonial cousins."

"Chewing that cigar won't have taken that thought from him, sir."

"It was worth it if it helped him think he has us in the dark."

"For what reason, sir?"

"That's for you to find out," he explains to her increasing interest.

"Did you notice the sergeant's demeanour, sir?"

"He seemed inebriated, which just adds to my intrigue."

She nods her confirmation. "What intrigues me most is why we waited for him to arrive and then leave straight away without finding anything else about him?"

"I only wanted to see what he looks like."

"And what did you take from that, sir?"

"He looked like a man well picked for the task the Brits have in mind."

"That was my opinion."

"That makes your work harder."

"It makes me look forward to it more, sir."

Davison puts on his exaggerated Southern American drawl. "Now, let's go have a burger, fries and a coke," he said, making her laugh.

They get into the rear of their blacked-out armoured Chevrolet Suburban as the rear doors to Thames House open, and Ashley exits, unaware he is in the sights of the Americans and moves off down the street as fast as his injured legs will carry him.

"And to add to the fun, sir," she adds, pointing at Ashley for Davison to look. "He's disabled."

"That, Colonel, just adds to my intrigue about this whole set-up. Bruce back to the embassy for me, then drop the colonel off where she wants to be."

The driver nods his subservience and then turns the engine on.

"I think I'll go the embassy as well, sir. I get a feeling I need to look at this mission a little closer."

The Suburban pulls off, and as they drive along, they pass Ashley, struggling to keep up his original pace, and Conners stares at him, unsure if he is an ally or an enemy.

***

Caine pours two whiskies and hands one to Shirlow. "What do you think of James, sir?" he enquires but the general's face shows he isn't impressed. "Not good, I see," he adds, and Shirlow shakes his head. "Being the fool's errand, you believe it to be, it would be a waste of resources to use a more experienced operative, and this will give James some experience in the field. What about Colonel Conners?"

"I should ask you. You picked her."

Caine laughs. "From a photograph given by the CIA," he adds, and Shirlow looks bewildered by words he hadn't expected. "They didn't have any agents ready, so they sent me a photo to help me choose."

"Strange way to carry out business?" Shirlow questions.

"I made sure it was done this way as I wanted something that would unnerve James, which is why I named their mission Angel Bait."

Shirlow looks bemused but interested in his operative's reasoning.

"She's the spitting image of Louise, his ex-wife," Caine laughs.

Shirlow grins, unsettled, as he sips his whisky. "If you ever pick a woman to act as my wife, under no circumstances select her on that premise. The thought is enough to give me nightmares."

Caine's laugh turns deadly serious. "Considering we know what else is up there, sir, do you think they will find anything out?"

"I can't see how they could put that and this together, but if it keeps this Davison and the PM off my back, I don't care."

Wanting to change the discussion off his friend being used by the agency at his bequest, Caine decides to talk about something that interests him more. "Are you still intent on retiring, sir?"

"I've been retired for years," Shirlow said with an ironic laugh. "I intend to spend the rest of my days in my garden at Hutton Grange with nothing more to care about other than where my next glass of Dalmore is coming from."

"Anything on the fire, sir?" Caine adds, hoping his retirement will have the same thing in mind.

"A little coal but just enough to keep the cold away and pay for my favourite whisky."

Caine is conscious that after Shirlow's long career in both the military and intelligence services and his high rank, he was in for a bigger windfall than just enough to pay for his whisky, and he lifts his glass for them to clash together in salute. "To a long relaxing retirement."

Shirlow smiles at the thought that has motivated him over the years. "I'm counting the days." He stares at Caine curiously. "Are you after my chair, Colonel?"

"Now it's about to become vacant, I may," Caine adds in jest, him having no ambition to take him further up the chain of command. "You would hate it. It's all politics. I'd rather deal with the KGB than the sycophants associated with Cobra and this bloody government."

"You're right, General," Caine adds apathetically. "I've also been thinking of retiring myself."

"At least you know where you stand with the Russians and Chinese," Shirlow adds, then takes a large sip of whisky. "Do you have anything on the fire?"

"Ashes and embers, sir," Caine adds with reason. "The burnt-out remains of an infantryman's life."

Shirlow laughs and then downs his whisky. "You'd be wasting your time seeking Section S chief as Admiral Lawrence has already been pencilled in for the job."

"He's a good man, sir," Caine said feebly.

"He's been waiting a long time. I need a man I trust to keep things going."

Caine keeps an eye on the man he has never truly trusted. "I thought you didn't like the admiral, sir?"

Shirlow moves to the drinks cabinet to pour himself another whisky. "He's an arse, but he reminds me of myself when I started in this game, so hopefully, he can't be all bad." He laughs clumsily. "A devious shite with no moral compass."

"Surely a prerequisite for the role?"

Shirlow takes Caine's glass to refill. "Let's finish this bottle."

***

CHAPTER 4

***

Special Operations Kintyre, Special Air Service, which abbreviates to SOKSAS or SOK, was set up on the Mull of Kintyre in 1978 by the British Government of the day as a quick reaction force of highly trained Special Forces operatives to be deployed into Northern Ireland to quell any sign of trouble.

Since the Good Friday agreement, also known as the Belfast agreement, had been signed in 1998 and had come into force on the 2nd December 1999, things had calmed in the province and the unit had only been called upon once, but that had turned out to be a false alarm, and they returned to base without landing. Due to the high cost of running the programme and the latter governments' stands on austerity, SOKSAS had been scaled down over many years into a skeleton crew to keep things maintained in case the troubles ever escalated. Their involvement on the mull had been designed to deceive, and no one was aware of any presence other than three Westland Wessex helicopters that sit on the grass helipad, one with its rotors turning, with Lieutenant Thomas sitting at the controls of the four-bladed workhorse that had been retired by the British military in the 1990s but retained for continuity of the programme, and Sergeant Smith at his side.

Dressed in a bright red tracksuit, as if about to go on a run, Kilbride exits one of the hangars and climbs on board the Wessex, and it lifts off on its pre-arranged destination over the North Channel. He looks through the fuselage into the cockpit and hands a piece of paper to Thomas. "We have a new heading," he said, and obedient to the change in flight plans, Thomas nodded as Smith was handed a different piece of paper. "Go onto that frequency and listen for the letters D and R."

Giving Thomas a quick exasperated glance, Smith tunes the radio equally obediently to his pilot.

Major Roger Kilbride is a large athletic man who had served throughout his career in the British military as an officer, starting with the Royal Regiment of Fusiliers before transferring into the SAS on the second and last attempt; he had served all over the world not just in wars but in diplomatic protection roles and was highly skilled in his art.

***

Ten nautical miles south of Port Ellen on Islay, the Inner

Hebrides, Scotland, the Russian cargo ship struggles through the
choppy Straits of Moyle as Vassilev chain smokes his way through a
pack of his Sobranie cigarettes and stares out of the bridge windows
into the dark cloudless night sky. Siminov, his second in command,
stands at the wheel, keeping them rigidly on their pre-ordered course.
"What's the time, Boris?" Vassilev said without taking his eyes off the
stars.
"Nineteen twenty-three hours, G M T, Captain."
Vassilev smiles and then laughs. "You remembered to use local time.
Very good."
"Thank you, sir," Boris said with pride to serve.
Vassilev picks up the radio mike and switches the set on as he looks at
the ship's clock, which shows the time in St Petersburg to be twenty-
one twenty-three hours to confirm his friend's answer. He presses the
transmit button and repeatedly repeats "D. R." until Andropov enters
and turns to see him. "Is it ready, Sergei?"
"Yes, Captain."
"Prepare yourselves!" Vassilev shouts, then repeats his message over
and over into the radio as he waits for the pre-arranged reply.
***

At the height of five hundred metres, the Wessex races at its
maximum speed of 132 miles per hour over the Straits of Moyle.
"I've picked up that message, sir!" Smith said, and showing no
emotion, Kilbride ordered him to return the same message as he turned
to Thomas.
"Get me there as fast as this pile of shite can."
***

Andropov picks up a pair of Russian PNW-57 military night
vision goggles to survey the dark waters outside. "Captain, the
helicopter's approaching."
"You know what to do," Vassilev commands Siminov. "Put me
underneath it."
Andropov picks up a flare gun, and he and Vassilev exit the bridge and
make their way onto the wind-swept deck for Andropov to fire a flare
into the night sky.
***

Thomas sees what at first he believes is a firework being fired
in the distance until it explodes with such brightness; he now knows it
is the distress flare he has been waiting for as it drops toward the water.
"We have a flare burst, sir."

Having expected the flare in a different place, Kilbride shouts, distraught at what could be an absolute ball's up to his plans. "What's its position?"

"Eight to ten nautical miles south of Islay."

"They're in the wrong fucking place!" Kilbride shouts as his irritation increases. "Get me there as fast as you can!"

***

Port Ellen Coastguard station looks out over the vast expanse of the Straits of Moyle and is manned twenty-four hours a day and three hundred and sixty-five days a year as it stands alert for any maritime eventuality.

Looking out the window, a Coastguardsman puts the phone down as a colleague walks up behind. "A flare's been reported, sir" He moves to a wall map to look over with a point. "Approximately ten miles south of here."

"Inform the RNLI to launch."

"What about the chopper?"

"We are only to call one out if required."

The Coastguardsman picks up the desk phone, dials, and waits to connect. "Launch the Ernest and Mary Shaw. A flare has been seen south of Port Ellen in the Straits of Moyle. Keep me informed if the helicopter is required."

***

Smith's attention is taken by a radio message, and he looks at Thomas and then Kilbride, unsure whether to relay the information he has on hand. "Port Ellen Coastguard are on the radio, sir."

"Ignore it!" Kilbride said with calm. "How long to the cargo ship?"

"Two minutes, sir."

Kilbride moves to the side door and opens it for the brisk cold air to enter. "Get me over the cargo deck!"

"They want us to identify ourselves, sir!" Smith shouts, and Kilbride snarls at what shouldn't need explaining.

"Fucking ignore them!"

Smith glances at Thomas for inspiration only to receive a shake of his head to not question the directness of the aggravated special forces commander's order.

***

Vassilev and Andropov stand on the deck next to two containers that have been tightly secured together, measuring six feet by two feet square each. The Wessex comes over to hover, making it hard for them to regain their footing as the down draft and sea wind fight for dominance over them. They brace themselves as the winch lowers for Andropov to grab and fasten it to the containers before moving aside as Vassilev shines a torch upwards to signal the helicopter.

***

Seeing the light coming from the deck, Kilbride lifts the winch, which rises slowly.

"The coastguard is requesting the boat's identification!" Smith shouts, then adds naively. "What about identifying ourselves, sir?"

"Tonight, we don't have an identity!" Kilbride growls. "How fucking long have you been posted to us?"

Even though Smith had been part of the unit for over six months, he didn't know that the major already had a low opinion of him.

The containers appear at the door, and Kilbride pulls them in and across the floor using all his strength. "Get us the fuck out of here!" he shouts as he closes the door with a slam.

"Back to base?" Thomas enquires enthusiastically.

"No!" Kilbride shouts but instantly calms. "Keep to our original destination. Make up the time, and I will buy you both a pint in the mess tonight."

Thomas and Smith look at each other in bewilderment at the major's ever-changing demeanour, but neither intends to take him up on his offer.

***

The Severn class RNLI lifeboat, the Ernest and Mary Shaw, crashes through the Straits of Moyle at its flat-out speed of 25 knots as it heads toward what they believe is a stricken cargo ship lit up in the distance.

The RNLI captain looks out through binoculars. "There's a helicopter moving off!"

"They won't identify themselves!" the radio operator shouts dismayed.

"Why is there a helicopter out here?" the RNLI captain questions, but none of his crew know how to answer. "It looks military." The Wessex flies straight and true into the distance as he twists his neck to look at it through the smaller side windows.

"The ship's captain is on the line," the radio operator interrupts. "He says they have no problems and wants to continue his journey."

The Wessex is now far from his mind; the RNLI captain's thoughts are only for the safety of the cargo ship and its crew. "Get in touch with

Port Ellen," he said uneasily. "Let the decision makers decide the best course of action."

***

The Wessex comes out of the Northern Irish darkness to land in an open field two hundred metres from an old barn that can only be made out in the moonlight. The side door slides open, and Kilbride alights with a bound and moves off without instructing Thomas and Smith, who watch him then turn in tandem into the fuselage.
"What do you think, Smithy?"
"Fuck knows, and fuck cares. The last thing I want to do is get involved in SAS nastiness."
Thomas looks at the silhouette of a windmill on a hill to his right with unease about their situation. "I couldn't agree more."
Not wanting to be overheard, Smith whispers as he looks around tentatively. "I thought it would be an adventure being posted to the idiots, but with all this cloak-and-dagger shit, now I'm not so sure."
"You volunteered?" Thomas jokes, amused.
"And doesn't it show me for the arse I am?"
"We are," Thomas interjects self-consciously. "You don't get transferred to this, you volunteer, but it's a hell of a lot safer than Afghanistan." He ponders his words to come. "It's this flight that does me in." He looks to see Kilbride has disappeared into the darkness. "Dropping into the same coordinates every three days and then having to wait for that arrogant bastard to come back can't be right, but all we can do is as ordered."
"I don't think it's official."
"That's not for us to question," Thomas said frantically to Smith's nervous agreement.
"And we can only thank god for that."
"I'm not sure anything this idiot does is official."
"Then we can't be held accountable," Smith adds, relieved, but Thomas shakes his head, unnerving him more.
"It's always the lowest denomination that takes the fall, and I'm afraid that's us."
Smith looks at the containers with dread and understanding of the lieutenant's words.

***

Well out of sight of Eallach farmhouse, Kilbride moves nonchalantly to the barn, and aware he's not under surveillance, he bangs on the door, which opens slowly to reveal the mistrusting glare of Niall Flynn.

A small, stocky hard man, Flynn had joined the Republican cause due to his hatred of the country that had killed his father, who was a veteran Irish Republican Army commander, in Armagh in 1969, but that hatred had been instilled in him from birth by the bigoted members of his family who still believe in a united Ireland. Having risen to deputy commander of the Armagh brigade after the Good Friday agreement, he could see the IRA were going nowhere, so he resigned to set up his own Republican terrorist group. This was so secret, so as not to get retaliation from the IRA, that they never gave themselves a name, but this also made it hard to recruit members, and he had to stay with the unit he had worked with for many years under the IRA banner. Wanting to take the fight to the British, he knew if he started a small campaign of bombings, he would be found out, so from the start, he endeavoured for the largest of targets to gain the notoriety that members would come looking for him to join.

"There you are, you Fenian bastard," Kilbride snipes, aware it will annoy the Irishman. "I apologise for my tardiness."

Showing no liking or trust for his expected visitor, Flynn snipes back with diplomatic venom. "Welcome to Ireland, Major."

"I've been many times," Kilbride said indifferently. "It's a fucking shit hole."

Flynn opens the door fully but remains in the doorway to prevent Kilbride entering. "I take it you have good news for me?"

"That depends on whose side you're on," Kilbride jokes, but having no sense of humour, Flynn doesn't take kindly to his words and lifts his Webley Mk VI Revolver, left to him by his terrorist father, to point it into the major's face.

"Don't play games with me!"

"Games?" Kilbride said, unphased. "This isn't a game, Mick."

"Then let's get this shit over with," Flynn grumbles with feigned bravado. "Is the missile in your possession?" he questioned, and Kilbride nodded. "Then where is it?"

"I'll be back in three days. Same time, same place."

"Why?" Flynn questioned, bemused by the number of visits.

"Just to keep you informed of all eventualities."

"Then I will look forward to it," Flynn adds, unconvinced.

Aware of the intended slight, Kilbride walks off as Flynn clenches the Webley in his sweating hand, desperate to end the British soldier's life. Robbie exits the shadows behind as he holsters his Beretta M9, and

McInley exits the bushes carrying a Lee Enfield rifle manufactured during the second world war.

"Do you trust him, Niall?" Robbie enquires, appreciative of a negative reply, but McInley answers confidently, believing he is speaking for his commander.

"How can he? He's our enemy."

Flynn lowers the Webley slowly and places it back into his belt. "I'll play along with him until I get what I want," he grumbles. "Then I'm going to kill him like the rabid dog he is."

The sound of the Wessex taking off and flying into the distance echoes that the gathering is over.

"Let's get the hell out of here!" Flynn snarls. "I need a drink."

***

CHAPTER 5

***

Campbeltown on the Mull of Kintyre shows the sad signs of decline from the lofty heights of trawler fishing as a few fishing boats, left from its once mighty fleet, sit tied up along the quay with the unmistakable form of a Russian cargo ship looking out of place to their side. Now a beautiful tourist destination for people worldwide to visit, nobody pays the cargo ship any notice as they pass on their walk through the freshness of the morning air. A bored, tired police officer, having been on guard since the cargo ship's arrival in the early hours of that morning, stands at the base of the gangplank with orders not to allow anything on or off the impounded ship.

Hired for the travel from Prestwick Airport, a Ford Fiesta, containing Ashley driving and Conners in the passenger seat, moves along Hall Street just off the quay as Ashley looks for the telephone box where the call to St Petersburg had been made from. His glance shifts between Conners, in amusement, and the beauty of Davaar Island, which is just visible offshore, but the American ignores him as she keeps her eye on the map on her knee.

Also enjoying the tranquillity of the morning, Kilbride stops to gaze upon the cargo ship in amusement of its capture but catches a glance at the Fiesta approaching and initially paying it little attention, he notices Ashley driving and has to look away so as not to be recognised by the driver he is well acquainted with.

Pleased by his surroundings, Ashley's eyes fix on the cargo ship with its Russian Federation flag flying from the mast, and he breaks hard, forcing the Fiesta into a stalling skid that vaults Conners forward until her seat belt tears annoyingly into her neck. Cars skid behind and beep their impatience, but he ignores their irritation as he stares at the laid-up vessel in bewilderment at its out-of-place presence.
Angered at the pain caused, Conners rubs her reddened neck. "What are you doing, Jimmy?" she complains.

Conscious of the threat to his cover, less than twenty-foot behind, Kilbride moves into a doorway and takes hold of his holstered Glock 19 as he moves with haste to his Land Rover where he has one last look between the Fiesta and the cargo ship as he gets in laughing and drives off.

Ashley restarts the Fiesta and winds down the window to wave his apology as he pulls over to the water's edge with Conners staring her aggravation directly onto him.

"What's going on, Jimmy?"

"The name's James."

"You nearly snapped my neck," she whinges.

"Not Jimmy," he carries on and seeing his irritation, she smiles at having found his biting point so quickly.

"Is that so, Jimmy? Then I will ask again. What the bloody hell is going on?"

Pained after the long drive, he takes out his pain medication and drops two tablets to wash them down with a mouthful of whisky from his hip flask, then alights, followed by the increasingly annoyed American who attempts to keep pace as he moves off.

"What was that you've just taken?" she questioned to his amusement.

"Vitamins," he answers scathingly to her disbelief.

"And the liquid in the hip flask was some form of an elixir, no doubt?" Ashley carries on, and she knows she isn't going to get an answer to that question she reverts to her original query, and he nods towards the cargo ship for her to look, but it doesn't register with her attention.

"Where the hell are we?" she said to his added amusement.

"You had the map. Didn't they teach you to read one in the Green Berets?"

"I wasn't looking at it."

"No wonder we kept getting lost," he adds, but she knows they have travelled on long single roads that would make it almost impossible to lose their way.

"Where are we?" she demands to be given the answer she craves. "Isn't this where we want to be?" she said, pleased to have arrived.

Ashley takes in the quaintness of the quay that doesn't have the same thrill to her as her home in Cape Elizabeth, Cumberland County, Maine. "A lovely place but not as beautiful as St James' Park," he mutters, but she hasn't a clue that the man from Newcastle Upon Tyne, England, is talking about the home of his beloved football team.

"St James' Park?" Conners questions, believing it may be associated to their mission.

"The home of the greatest football team in the world. Newcastle United."

"What state are they from?

"State?" Ashley questions, bemused. "It's in Tyne and Wear."

"In this country? I didn't know they played football here."

Ashley laughs, understanding her confusion. "You're getting mixed up with American handball where those oversized steroid-abusing headcases throw, not kick, a rugby-shaped ball around a field."

"Are you talking about Soccer?" she said to his increasing aggravation.

"No, I'm fucking not! We play football, and you Yanks play handball."

She giggles to herself at his passion for a sport. "So why break so hard?" she questions. "Did you think we were going to miss this grand metropolis?"

Amused by her attempt at sarcasm, he points toward the cargo ship for her to scrutinise.

"You've lost me, Jimmy. What am I supposed to be looking at?"

"Take a closer look, Corporal," he said to annoy, but she didn't rise to the downgrading of her rank as he moved toward the cargo ship with her following. "Notice anything about that ship?" he questions confidently and she looks at the distinctive white blue and red horizontal colours of the flag flying from a mast.

"Other than it's Russian, no."

Looking decidedly more arrogant than he would genuinely want, he adds condescendingly. "Take a closer look."

Frustrated by his increasingly juvenile antics, she takes a pinching hold of his arm. "Let's have a walk, darling," she said, dragging him along. "I mean, we are recently married."

"Soon to be divorced!" he gripes, making her laugh.

"If only I could read minds, I would be able to understand what I am not meant to," she said acerbically as he attempted to break free, but she kept a tight hold as they moved closer to the cargo ship. "Calm down, darling," she adds with the sweetest smile. "We need to look the part of a loving couple."

Ashley laughs as, in his mind, most married couples would not be linked together in any way.

Seeing them getting nearer, the veteran police officer steps in front to stop them. "I'm afraid you can't go any closer."

With New England charm, Conners beguiles. "Why's that, officer?"

The police officer's glance shifts between Ashley and Conners. "I'm waiting for the customs to check it over. I shouldn't tell you, but it set off a distress flare last night, and everything was alright when the lifeboat arrived."

Ashley pulls away from Conners' hold and moves to the water's edge. "What's wrong with that?" he questions as he sizes the cargo ship up.

"In these days of terrorism, you can't be doing that, sir," the police officer explains with authority. "The Coastguard got HMS Bristol, which just happened to be in the Irish Sea at the time, to impound it while enquiries are being carried out."

Ashley looks to see the grey silhouette of HMS Bristol sitting a mile or so off shore.

"The Russian captain wanted to keep going to America but got ordered into port."

Amused, Ashley turns to his American colleague. "They're well-off course."

"Hardly the best route," The police officer said with knowledge. "But the seas were rough last night, so they may have come into the straits for a bit of shelter."

"Where had they come from?" Conners asked for the police officer to deliberate.

"I believe it was St Petersburg, in Russia."

Ashley looks at the large array of radar equipment situated all over the cargo ship as he questions the source of his knowledge.

"A coastguard officer was here for a while, but he left about an hour ago."

Attempting to play down the issue, Conners links Ashley's arm to his increasing aggravation. "Probably got lost in those rough seas. Come on, love; we'd better get on our way. Thank you, officer."

"Enjoy your stay in Kintyre. You couldn't have picked a more beautiful place to honeymoon in."

"Honeymoon?" Ashley shouts shocked, bemusing the police officer by his outburst and playing to the moment; Conners kisses the Englishman on the cheek, unnerving him enough to back off from her reach. "That was several months ago. Now we are here on holiday."

"Well, you make a handsome couple anyway," the police officer adds with a gentle smile. "You look so much in love."

Ashley and Conners look at each other amused, as they walk off, holding in their urges to laugh.

"That ship couldn't have got lost with all that high-tech equipment on," she explains, looking back.

Ashley moves to the water's edge for a closer look at the Russian Cyrillic writing across the rear that can be read underneath the rusting paintwork. "Can you speak Russian?"

"Fluently. Why?"

"Can you make out the name of the ship?"

She moves forward, taking her time in looking over the rear. "Dimitri Rossakovich, Leningrad."

"As I thought," Ashley said self-confidently.

"So, you just needed confirmation?" she said, annoyed. "Leningrad reverted to its original name of St Petersburg in 1991 after the fall of the Soviet Union."

"And Dimitri Rossakovich?"

"No doubt some old Soviet sycophant."

"It's the name said to be the Russian arms dealer," he adds, and she turns her perplexed stare onto him but this is quickly overtaken with contempt as he looks back smiling. "The phone call made from here was to St Petersburg when the arms dealer's name was mentioned," he explained to her with increasing disdain. "That's too much of a coincidence in my book."

"Why wasn't I informed of this?" she argues, but he ignores her contemptuous stare as he produces his phone and walks off.

"Who are you calling, Jimmy?"

"Stalin!" Ashley shouts flippantly as he carries on out of earshot. "He may know why you haven't been informed."

***

Enjoying the tranquillity of the slow day, Caine sits in his office within Thames House when his desk phone rings. He looks at the screen to recognise the number when he answers. "I hope you're not telephoning to tell me you're in Campbeltown, James!"

Ashley grins, amused at Conners, who hasn't taken her betrayed stare off him. "No, but just in case you need to put that into a report, that's exactly where I am."

"Well done, James, you've achieved something at last."

Ashley laughs. "Do you remember the name Dimitri Rossakovich?"

"I informed you of it," Caine snipes. "You haven't been drinking, have you?"

"Not yet!" Ashley answers with the thirst to participate in a few beers. "But did you know there's a cargo ship tied up on Campbeltown Quay that just happens to go by that name, and it's out of Leningrad, which, as your intelligent mind already knows, is back to its original name of St Petersburg."

The line goes unnervingly quiet as Caine shuffles uncomfortably.

"Are you still there?"

"I'm waiting for you to finish," Caine interjects to Ashley's added bewilderment.

"It's waiting to be searched by customs."

Caine's mind races over the best course of action open to him. "We need to get men on board."

"The copper on guard says they are on their way."

"I will speed them up, but I want you on that ship at the earliest. See what you can find out and make sure nothing is allowed to leave."

"I thought that was quite good for my first day," Ashley said with humorous pride. "Don't you think so?"

"Of course, James. I will order your VC now."

Ashley laughs, then turns away so as not to be overheard. "By the way, the Yank's pissed at not knowing about the intelligence you gave me. Any suggestions on how to cope with her?"

"That's down to General Davison to keep his operative informed."

"Does he know?" Ashley questions, concerned, but this only makes Caine laugh, uncaring of such.

"That's down to General Shirlow. Look, James, stay where you are, and I can't implore you enough, don't allow anything to leave that ship." The call instantly terminates to concern Ashley by the actions of the man he trusts, and Conners moves up behind to take him by surprise.

"You have something on your nose, Jimmy," she said, flicking the tip of her nose several times, and he wiped his with his sleeve. "It's shit, Jimmy. Can't you smell it?"

He looks at his sleeve, realises the mockery, and laughs at seeing it clean. "You're just pissed because you aren't in the loop."

Although aggrieved by the apparent slur, she plays down her inner turmoil to not look weaker than the position imposed on her. "I'd rather not be in the loop than have my nose wedged up someone's hoop, Jimmy."

"Keep telling yourself that, and one day you may believe it."

"If brown nosing puts me in your so-called loop and down to your level, Jimmy, I will stay on the outside," she sneers but quickly calms. "By the way, what did Joseph have to say?" she adds to his confusion.

"Ioseb Besarionis dze Jughashvili," she adds in fluent Russian, and he shakes his head, unable to translate. "Joseph Vissarionovich Stalin. I thought history was important to you, Brits?"

"Just of Great Britain," he answers. "All the rest is irrelevant to me."

"Uncle Joe Stalin, you uneducated baboon."

Ashley laughs on understanding where the humour had come from. "I got that when you said, Stalin. He asked if you are enjoying your honeymoon."

"That's clever of him since he died in 1953."

"Thanks for the lesson, but Russian history is just as irrelevant to me as

American."

"So, Jimmy, just out of respect for a fellow intelligence operative," she reasons. "Are you going to tell me why I've been left out of your loop?"

"I wouldn't know," he answers callously, to her dismay.

"I thought we were on the same side?" she mutters, making him laugh.

"And what's so funny?"

"Who put that stupid notion in your head?" he said, moving toward the irritated police officer, who lifted his arms to stop him as an ID was thrust into his face.

"MI5? What the hell does MI5 want up here, sir?"

Ashley points at the Dimitri Rossakovich. "Has anything or anyone left that ship?"

"No, sir, and I've been here since it docked at three this morning."

"Good," Ashley said as Conners walked over.

"What's going on, Jimmy?"

"I've been ordered to board and check the cargo over."

Conners takes her phone out and moves off with Ashley and the police officer watching. "Are you sure you've been given clearance to inform me of this?"

"What's up with her?" the police officer inquired, and Ashley answered with a shrug of his shoulders.

"She's a Yank. Just ignore her."

"Some honeymoon you're having," the police officer adds woefully.

"And I thought police officers were never off duty."

"We ain't on honeymoon. I didn't even know her two days ago," Ashley said as his attention was taken by Vassilev staring over from the exterior bridge of the Dimitri Rossakovich, and he stared back hard enough that the Russian moved off unnerved.

***

CHAPTER 6

***

Fast asleep and snoring, Ashley sits in the driver's seat of the Fiesta as the police officer sits in the rear, wide awake with his eyes fixed on the Dimitri Rossakovich. Carrying two polystyrene cups of coffee, Conners taps on the window, and Ashley comes around to look at his watch before winding the window down.

"Sorry to wake you, Jimmy, have you had a hard day?" she questions, but he doesn't reply.

Although she had only been away twenty minutes, Davison had ordered her to watch proceedings closely. "I take it nothing has happened?" she said, aware of the answer.

"I'm afraid everything goes slow up here," the police officer adds as Conners hands them both a cup.

Amused by the understatement, Ashley laughs. "Slow? I haven't seen anything move yet." He looks between his coffee and Conners. "Didn't you get one?"

"I've had one along with a bacon and egg sandwich and a piece of millionaires cake. It was lovely," she said, moving off refreshed.

"I'm sure it was, but I can't see any more bacon sandwiches or cakes for us!" Ashley shouts, then takes a sip of the coffee but is instantly repulsed. "Ah, no sugar," he whinges as he pours the liquid out the window, making Conners laugh at what was intended.

The sound of police sirens nearing takes their attentions, and the police officer quickly alights to place his cup down and straighten himself out. "Stay where you are!" Ashley shouts. "You've earned a rest."

The police officer smiles at Conners. "Thank you for the coffee." He moves to retake his position as Ashley alights.

With sirens blaring and lights flashing, two police cars race up and then stop on the road next to the Fiesta to block the traffic from the north, which instantly causes a tailback of beeping cars. Two plain-clothed officers alight the first car and four customs officers the second.

"Are you James Ashley?" one of the officer's questions as they shake hands. "I am Superintendent Gardiner of Strathclyde Police, and this is Inspector Forbes of Her Majesty's Customs and Excise."

"I have worked with the security services before," Forbes interjects with pride that isn't reciprocated as Ashley shakes his hand.

"No doubt an unpleasant experience with the added fun of nightmares," Conners said to Ashley's amusement, but Forbes replied with self-importance.

"Actually, it was quite exciting."

Wanting to get on with the job, Gardiner interrupts insistently. "What are we looking for?"

Ever mistrustful of people he doesn't personally know, Ashley's glare shifts between Gardiner and Forbes as he looks for any sign that they are withholding information from him. "Haven't you been informed?"

"Our brief was to get here ASAP," Gardiner answers proficiently. "What do you have in mind?

"Just a thorough search of the ship."

"That's not a problem," Forbes adds. "We were going to do that anyway."

Daunted by the size of the Dimitri Rossakovich and the small number of men at hand, Gardiner looks at Forbes, whose curious stare shifts between Ashley and Conners.

"We thought with the urgency impressed on us you would have an idea of what we are looking for?" Forbes asks insistently for an answer. "Do we have a size or shape?"

Ashley looks at Conners for inspiration but has yet to receive any.

"They need help, Jimmy," Conners said, adding to his discomfort. "You were the one who made the call to Caine."

Ashley doesn't know how much information he can give, and the most straightforward answer would be to put the onus on the American.

"You inform them."

"Hey, I'm here on honeymoon," Conners adds, enjoying her colleague's unease. "What would I know?"

Gardiner and Forbes look at each other, amused by the ridiculous statement.

"Can I ask?" Gardiner interjects. "What does this have to do with the Americans?"

"Nothing," Ashley interrupts with the broadest of smiles. "She's here as an observer come lacky. Just ignore her unless you need a cup of coffee but don't forget to tell her if you want sugar."

"I'm here to observe how pathetic Jimmy is," Conners analyses with glee. "Strangely, he seems to warrant my advice at every turn."

"We are looking for anything out of the usual," Ashley blusters, but neither Gardiner nor Forbes is convinced as they wait for more information.

"That should make life easier!" Conners adds sceptically, but Ashley knows the cards are stacked against them as they move up the gangplank when he realises she hasn't moved.

"Aren't you coming?"

"No, Jimmy, I thought I would wait for you to come back and tell me what you have found," she said, barging past him to Gardiner and Forbes' amusement.

"Bloody Yanks always like to make the grand entrance," Ashley adds as he follows the sound of their laughter.

***

CHAPTER 7

***

Drinking a large glass of Dalmore, Shirlow sits at his desk within Thames House as his intercom buzzes, impatient to be answered. He reaches to open the channel, and his personal assistant's gentler voice comes over the speaker.

"Sir, General Davison is here to see you."

Disinterested in whatever the unbearable American says, Shirlow leans back into his oversized leather chair as he sips his whisky. "Send him in," he said in a reluctant tone that wasn't missed by Davison, who he knows will be standing next to his assistant listening.

Carrying on with his self-enforced role of the clichéd American general, Davison crashes through the door, but Shirlow doesn't stand to greet his unwelcome guest.

"What can I do for you now, General?" Shirlow mutters in a derogatory tone that Davison understands.

"You could start by answering your fucking phone, Bart," Davison barks, his aggravation to Shirlow's humoured appreciation.

"I'm a busy man."

"Is that right?" Davison retorts. "Well, with you not answering your phone or returning my messages, I thought I would look you up to find out what is happening."

"I don't know what you mean," Shirlow condescends, but this makes Davison angrier. "So why don't you tell me why you have disturbed my evening?"

"Then I will start at the beginning. I assume you have heard of the name Dimitri Rossakovich?"

"The ship in Campbeltown? What would you like to know?"

"I heard it goes by the name banded about as the Russian arms dealer."

"Dimitri Rossakovich. I am pleased you came, General," Shirlow said sardonically. "It will save me a phone call."

"Don't patronise me, Bart. You and this Sergeant Ass Lee are withholding information from Colonel Conners and myself."

"I'm sure, Sergeant Ashley," Shirlow said, pronouncing the name with a sneer. "Has informed your operative of all she needs to know."

"I see," Davison said on calming.

"If she feels left out, I will see she is informed of all he knows as soon as I speak to him."

Davison takes a deep breath and then sighs. "This doesn't bode well for Anglo-American relations, Bart. You'd better inform that prick not to withhold information, or there will be repercussions."

Unimpressed by Davison's attempt at intimidation, Shirlow bites back. "I will ensure Sergeant Ashley informs Colonel Conners of all he has discovered."

"But not what he was informed of by yourselves," Davison said as he looked Shirlow over, unimpressed. "And while we are on the subject, I would appreciate it if all information is passed on to me."

"I'm sure your operative will be able to do that for you."

"I'm sure she would, but then I wouldn't be able to compare her notes with yours," Davison said, mistrusting.

Understanding, Shirlow adds condescendingly. "While we are on the subject. I know it's unprofessional of me to assume, but do you think Colonel Conners is up to the job?"

Davison stares his loathing but remains calmer than his character would typically allow. "It was you who picked her from a photograph because of her looks, not because of her ability."

"If that is true, I am unaware and can only apologise for my supposition. I didn't mean to presume she isn't up to the job, but all the evidence confirms my reservations about her ability to carry it out successfully."

Unimpressed by Shirlow's babbling, Davison stares his bewilderment as he debates their true meaning. "You've got an option, Bart. Either give my operator the information she needs to participate as an equal partner or give it to me, and I will pass it on. If not, I will have no other option but to end my cooperation."

"That can only be up to you," Shirlow adds, uncaring of such.

"You say that, but you are making my position untenable and I am sure the President will put it in the strongest terms to your Prime Minister when they meet."

Conscious the PM wouldn't be happy if he didn't cooperate with Britain's greatest ally, Shirlow grins, discomfited. "If you remember, you came to me with this."

"Don't make me feel I made the wrong decision. Do I need to inform you of the questions that will need answering if I carry out my threat?"

Shirlow smiles, defeated, as he realises the repercussions of such an act being carried out. "I will see to it she gets all the information Sergeant Ashley has in his possession, and I will enquire as to why he hasn't informed her."

"We already know the answer to that, Bart!" Davison snipes as Shirlow moves to the drink's cabinet, unperturbed by the slur.

"Let's have a drink to Anglo American relations. I have a fine bottle of Dalmore here," Shirlow said as he went through the motions of getting the glasses and opening the bottle.

"I don't think so!" Davison interrupts with the only thought of leaving the conversation behind. "I prefer my own company when it comes to alcohol, and I have a bottle of Jack Daniels waiting for me in my office."

Shirlow pours himself a whisky and takes a sip. "I was only being diplomatic to enhance our nation's relationship as I also prefer my own company, so if you don't mind, I am sure it is in both our interests to end this awkwardness."

Davison moves to the door, opens it then turns slowly back. "Need I remind you of what's at stake, Bart?" he questions as Shirlow pours another glass of Dalmore and takes a savouring sip.

"I will see to your request at the earliest, General."

"Maybe I will take that drink when this is all over."

For diplomatic reasons only, Shirlow crosses the room to shake Davison's hand. "Maybe then the offer will still be on the table."

Aware that nothing will scupper the CIA's support as they hunt a weapon earmarked to assassinate their President, Davison nods and exits.

***

Two Chevrolet Suburban SUVs sit at the rear of Thames House with their engines ticking over, and two CIA men wait and become increasingly attentive as Davison exits the rear as the door is slammed and locked behind.

"You know what to do?" Davison said as a CIA man opened the rear door of the armoured Suburban for him to get in to be driven off.

The two CIA men move to the second Suburban and get in to drive off and turn in the opposite direction.

***

Disillusioned, Ashley and Conners enter the bridge of the cargo ship, followed by Gardiner, Forbes, Vassilev and Boris, who remains in the doorway as if covering their exit.

Unhappy with the waste of his valuable time and the thought of a long drive back to Glasgow after his unproductive journey, Gardiner criticises with zeal. "All clear, except for two handguns and a rifle!"

"For protection on the high seas," Vassilev explains, but Ashley growls his disbelief and gains stares from all in the room.

"Not going to plan, Jimmy?" Conners said, adding to his discomfort. Gardiner turns to Ashley. "What now?"

"What about secret holds?" Ashley asked, and Forbes shook his head, answering.

"What are you looking for?" Vassilev enquired as his innocent expression shifted, but Forbes interjected, answering Ashley's question. "There are none. When it comes to searching ships, I know what I am doing."

"We should let them get on with their journey," Gardiner said as he headed for the door with Boris stepping aside.

"I take it you are looking for something in particular?" Vassilev presses for information to give to his superiors as he grins lecherously at the unimpressed American.

"We weren't looking for anything in particular, Captain," Forbes answers, taking the role of the diplomat representing Her Majesty's government. "You fired off a flare when you weren't in distress."

"I explained it was an accident. We had lost our way."

"This ship has more electronic equipment on it than the Space X rocket," Conners said, unnerving Vassilev, who knows he can't argue against her point.

"That's a very good English accent," Ashley adds, and Vassilev smiles with what he mistakenly believes is a compliment. "I take it you were in the military?"

"All men do military service in Russia."

"Not all learn to speak perfect English without the faintest sign of an accent," Ashley quickly argues. "I'd say Military Intelligence. What do you think?" he said, turning to Conners.

"Strange career move for someone with an excellent take on the English language to become a ship's captain," Conners answers, then looks around. "Especially a shit bucket like this."

Vassilev desperately wants the attention taken off him but continues his well-versed cover story. "I followed my father to sea."

"I'd think a man with your linguistic talents would be a major asset in today's democratic Russia," Conners interjects with a laugh to his unease.

"The sea was my true calling," Vassilev explains with an awkward self-pitying laugh. "I was conscripted into the army even though I had requested the Navy."

"Bull-shit!" Ashley calls out in disbelief.

Wanting to end his stay on board, Forbes interjects. "That's enough of that." He shakes Vassilev's hand. "Thank you for your cooperation, Captain. I'm sorry we pulled you into port, but I hope you understand our reasoning."

"Apart from the loss of time, there has been no real problem."

"I would assume a ship's time would be precious to its owners," Ashley said but Inspector Forbes interjected with well-versed diplomacy.

"As are good relations between Russia and the United Kingdom."

"Is that why you travel to America with an empty hold?" Ashley continues, but Vassilev doesn't know how to answer his pertinent question. "Doesn't seem good business even for an old communist. Surely you need to make a profit? I mean, fuel isn't free."

"Maybe he's after filling his hold with arms for Russia," Conners interjects to Ashley's grinning amusement.

"We've been called back to Russia by the company," Vassilev quickly interjects.

Ashley holds in his need to laugh. "Which company is that? Kremlin Cargo? FSB Lines? SVR Holdings? KGB Cargo-."

"Alright, Jimmy, the first one wasn't funny," Conners interrupts.

"I could go on," Ashley adds, aware he is annoying all in the room.

"We all got your point."

"You think so?" Ashley said with a smile. "If I'm laughing inside, I think it's funny." He turns menacingly on Vassilev, who shuffles uncomfortably as he acts as if he doesn't understand. "And when I see a face straighten as much as his, I know I have made my mark."

"For the future, Captain," Forbes interrupts, breaking the tension. "Don't set off flares when you aren't in distress. It wastes a lot of people's time and effort. Not just your own."

"No problem, Inspector," Vassilev adds with an awkward laugh. "I always stay within the bounds of the law."

Disgruntled, Ashley shouts as he exits. "I bet you were surprised to see the Royal Navy bearing down on you?"

Conners moves to the door. "Take no notice, Captain. I've only known him briefly, and he hasn't stopped whinging in all that time," she adds, then exits.

***

Ashley storms down the gangplank, followed by Conners, who finds humour in his discomfort.

"Did you find what you were looking for?" the police officer asked, only for Ashley to answer with a vigorous growl and shake of his head as he carried on toward his car.

Conners stops next to the police officer. "Excuse him, officer, he's had a bad day."

Ashley gets to the Fiesta when his phone rings, but as he goes to answer, the RNLI captain approaches from behind.

"Excuse me, but I've just seen you get off that ship," the RNLI captain said, and Ashley turned, annoyed at the interruption, which startled him. "Sorry. I just wanted to find out what happened to the injured man," he adds, backing off, which catches Ashley's attention.

"Injured man?"

"Your phone!" the RNLI captain said as it rang.

"What injured man are you talking about?" Ashley insists to the RNLI captain's discomfort.

"I telephoned several hospitals, but none of them knew anything."

Ashley lowers the ringing phone to his side. "You've lost me, so you'd better start from the beginning."

Intrigued, Conners walks over to see why Ashley is talking to a stranger. "What's going on?"

"I don't know," Ashley said, annoyed by her interruption. "But if you shut up, we may find out."

Ashley's phone stops ringing, and Conners mimics wiping her nose, but he ignores her sarcasm as his interest remains with the RNLI captain.

"You were about to say?"

"Hold on," Conners interrupts. "Who are you?"

"He's RNLI!" Ashley answers to her bewilderment.

"And that's?"

"I'm a lifeboat volunteer," the RNLI captain proudly explains. "Royal National Lifeboat Institute."

"Like your coastguard only on the cheap," Ashley jokes, bringing a smile of acknowledgement out of the RNLI captain.

"Isn't that everything around here?" Conners mutters as Ashley impatiently turns onto the RNLI captain, who is taken aback by the sudden interest in him.

"What about this injured man?"

"I was concerned so that while I was passing, I thought I would enquire about his health."

Getting more impatient, Ashley takes a deep breath. "What injured man are you talking about?" he calls out but instantly calms.

The RNLI captain's bemused glance shifts gingerly between Ashley and Conners. "The man winched off that cargo ship last night."

Ashley's amazed glance shifts between Conners and the RNLI captain. "You saw a man being winched from that very ship last night?" he questions, and the RNLI captain nods. "But the copper said nothing left it."

The RNLI captain laughs awkwardly as if he had done something wrong. "My boat was called to a distress flare fired from that very ship," he adds with a point. "But when we got there, we weren't required. They pleaded to be allowed to carry on, but I informed the Coastguard, who ordered them into port with HMS Bristol's help."

Conners' suspiciously tuned intelligence thinking mind turns onto the RNLI captain. "What makes you think an injured man was winched off?"

The RNLI captain's eyes shift between Ashley and Conners as if he had to convince himself he was speaking the truth. "From what I could see, it was by a stretcher."

"Long and oblong!" Conners adds with a triumphant grin that breaks through her suspicion of being left on the outside. "And this was while at sea?"

"Yes, and as we got closer, I saw the helicopter winching up the stretcher," the RNLI captain adds, then pauses in thought. "Obviously, I must have been wrong. We were quite far off, but when I think about it, it must have been considerably larger than a stretcher."

"And it was dark," Ashley adds, playing down the RNLI captain's account, but Conners interrupts to be more thorough to the intelligence.

"What sort of helicopter was it?"

"I can't be one hundred per cent certain," the RNLI captain blusters. "I love helicopters. I always wanted¬."

"We haven't the time," Ashley interrupts to stop the embarrassed man mid-sentence.

"Sorry. I have a tendency to waffle," the RNLI captain said as he recomposed himself. "I believe it was a Westland Wessex."

"We don't use them anymore," Ashley explains. "And haven't since the nineties."

"It looked like one of the helicopters that fly around here all the time," the RNLI captain explains. "When I think about it, it could have been from Kintyre Oil."

"Kintyre Oil?" Ashley questions. "What the hell is that?"

Amused, they are unaware; the RNLI captain laughs. "It's an oil company based on the mull. They are looking for oil in the Irish Sea which should bring the oil industry to us if they find anything. Mind you, they've been here since the late seventies, so maybe we shouldn't hold our breaths."

"You're waffling again," Ashley gripes making the RNLI captain shuffle uncomfortably.

"I can only apologise for that."

"Carry on but keep to the point!" Ashley insists, determined.

"They use the helicopters between here and Northern Ireland. Suppose they use some radar or sonar to find out where to drill."

Ashley shakes his head in disbelief as his phone rings, and he looks at the screen. "I'd better get this," he adds as he walks off.

Genuinely pleased by the intelligence given, Conners shakes the RNLI captain's hand. "You've been most helpful," she said, but the lifesaving volunteer was unsure what he had done to warrant such praise as he walked off.

"Get his name and contact address!" Ashley shouts, then answers his phone. "Ashley here." He looks around awkwardly.

Conners takes the RNLI captain's name and contact details but keeps her eye on Ashley. "Who's on the phone, Jimmy?" she asks, seeing the concern in his eyes.

"I'm being put through to Shirley O."

Conners looks confused, then, on realising the attempt at humour, she shakes her head unamused. "Do you think the chopper picked up the missiles?" she enquires but he doesn't answer as he keeps his attention on his phone call. "He said a Westland Wessex. One that flies around here all the time. Surely a Wessex is military, but you said you no longer use them."

"I wouldn't know. I'm usually a font of knowledge on who has what, but I seem to be failing these days. Brain dead due to the posting to a desk."

"Another oversight, Jimmy."

"Don't start that. The only thing I know about helicopters is they drop you in the shit, and if you are lucky, they pick you up."

Shirlow picks up the phone on his desk and bellows angrily down the line. "Where the hell have you been, Sergeant? I have telephoned you several times!"

Ashley shook his head in disbelief at the general's arrogant exaggeration, as he'd only missed one call. "Searching the Dimitri Rossakovich, as ordered, sir."

"Did you find anything?"

Ashley moves from Conners, but she keeps pace. "No, but I think I know what happened to the missiles, sir."

"We, Jimmy, we," Conners whispers to his irritation.

"They were taken off by helicopter," Ashley carries on.

Shirlow shuffles, unnerved. "Are you sure?"

"It hasn't been confirmed, but I have a positive sighting of a helicopter winching something resembling a stretcher off the Dimitri Rossakovich last night, but the man reporting it believes the helicopter was a Westland Wessex, sir."

"We don't use Wessex's and haven't for some years now. We use Sea Kings and Merlin's. Do you know what it could have been?"

"I didn't see it, so I couldn't hazard a guess," Ashley adds, perplexed. "Shouldn't be hard for you to find out who flies them these days, sir. Supposedly it flies around here all the time, sir."

"Maybe your information is wrong," Shirlow condescends to Ashley's irritation.

"The identification was made by an RNLI volunteer who is a helicopter anorak. He believed it is part of Kintyre Oil."

Unnerved at hearing the name of a clandestine mission being blatantly spoken over the phone, Shirlow drains his glass of whisky. "Forget about Kintyre Oil and leave this with me, Sergeant. Make your way to your hotel and sit tight. I will be in touch later."

"What about the Dimitri Rossakovich, sir?" Ashley questions as Conners taps his arm, making him turn to her as she whispers.

"Ask why he called?"

"Leave that to me," Shirlow said, and Ashley winked at Conners' straight-faced glare.

"What was it you wanted me for, sir?"

"Oh, yes, Sergeant, I digress. I've had a very, very angry General Davison here. Your new friend has been saying you are leaving her out."

Ashley sneers at Conners. "As ordered, sir."

"Well, now I am giving you permission to tell her what you know."

"Are you sure, sir?"

"I wouldn't say it if I didn't mean it, Sergeant!" Shirlow shouts, and the phone goes instantly dead.

Ashley looks at the screen and shakes his head. "What a fucking poncing prick!"

"What did he want?"

Mimicking Shirlow's posh accent, Ashley guffaws. "It seems your boss is not just angry he's very, very angry with me."

"And that's why he called?" she presses to find the truth.

"He said to get you some tissues."

Conners doesn't understand the humour and stares disdainfully. "What does that mean, Jimmy?"

"It means I have to tell you what I know."

The thought of eventually finding out what is going on brings a smile of accomplishment to her face as he points at the cargo ship, and she turns to look.

"That ship we've just got off is called the Dimitri Rossakovich which coincidently is the name of the arms dealer." He looks for the phone box on Hill Street and points. "And the call to St Petersburg was made from there."

She stares her increasing annoyance as he walks off laughing. "How are we meant to work together if I don't know what is happening?"

"You know the same as me, and that's piss all," he adds, understanding their situation. "The men with any idea are in London and don't trust a nobody like me to let me in on their little secrets."

Conners looks perturbed. "What did he say about the Wessex?"

"He was so pleased he is going to get back in touch when he can be arsed."

"Maybe he needs to look into it further."

"If there's one thing I have learnt since joining MI5, it's when I'm being lied to, and that's always. It would be nice to hear the truth for once, but even then, I wouldn't believe it."

"Surely that's the world of intelligence we live in?"

"He knows more than he's letting on.

"Now, who needs the tissues?" she said with a laugh that didn't perturb him.

"My days of giving a shit are well over. All I need now is a few beers."

"Don't you always?" she scoffs as they get into the car and drive off.

***

Shirlow sits at his desk in Thames House, pouring the dregs from a bottle of Dalmore into a recently drained glass. There's a knock on the door, and he looks at his clock, wondering who is disturbing him so late at night. "Come in!" he shouts, and the door opens for Caine to enter and see his inebriated demeanour.

"Everything alright, sir?"

"No, it bloody well isn't, Colonel. Get a glass and open a fresh bottle."

Caine moves to the drinks cabinet to pick up a glass and a new bottle to open. "Refill, sir?"

"Does my glass look full?" Shirlow condescends, and Caine instantly tops up his glass and his own. "It seems this Sergeant Ashley isn't as dumb as you thought, Colonel."

"I didn't say he was dumb, sir."

"Not the impression you gave, or I wouldn't have selected him," Shirlow adds as he takes a lingering sip of his whisky. "He knows about our presence on Kintyre."

"How come, sir? That's of the highest security."

Shirlow drains his glass and beckons Caine for a refill. "An RNLI volunteer saw something being winched off the Dimitri Rossakovich last night."

"That doesn't point to a military presence."

"He mentioned Kintyre Oil."

"Still not proof."

"No, but if news of SOKSAS got out, it would make the Micks think we don't trust the peace process."

"We don't."

Shirlow grins, amused. "I must inform the PM that our little secret may have been discovered. He's going to be well pissed."

"Probably give him the excuse he needs to close it all down, sir."

"Yes. I never thought about it that way," Shirlow said, then paused. "Maybe I won't tell him and will leave that to my successor when I'm gone, but it may be better to come from my lips than anyone else's," he adds on reflection.

"You mean the Yanks?" Caine adds, distraught at the thought. "What do you want me to do?"

"Explain to the sergeant the complexities of such intelligence being leaked."

"If he knows, surely the Yank will find out?"

"Then you'd better get the shuttle up and nip this in the bud at the earliest. The last thing I need is that pretentious prick Davison knowing any of our domestic policies."

***

CHAPTER 8

***

Enjoying a vodka and tonic in the sombre surroundings of the Argyle Arms Hotel in Campbeltown, Kilbride sits on his own in the corner and notices Ashley and Conners enter. Not wanting to be recognised, he shuffles further into his seat, out of sight as they move to the bar to be greeted by the landlord.

Always the first to get the round in, Ashley turns to Conners with a sardonic smile. "What would you like to drink, darling?"

Conners grimaces at being called darling, then grins to feign courtesy. "White wine, please, baby."

"Are you sure you don't want the triple whisky with red bull you normally have?" Ashley said, aware he had hit a nerve as he turned back to the landlord. "A large glass of white wine for my beautiful wife here and a bottle of Newcastle Brown Ale for me, please."

"Sorry, sir," the landlord said politely. "We don't sell Newcastle Brown Ale here."

Offended, Ashley looks around in disbelief. "You know I've drunk dog as far away as Brunei, and I can't get it in the country it is manufactured."

"Dog?" Conners questioned, but Ashley did not intend to explain that the word was used with polite pride in his local brew that would resonate with most in his hometown. "Quit your whinging, Jimmy, and order something else."

"Not many people drink Ale up here, sir, so there's no reason to keep it," the landlord explains, but it doesn't ease Ashley's woes.

"What else do you have?"

"All the taps are on the bar, sir."

Ashley looks along the counter as he takes in the draughts on offer. "What about bottles?"

The landlord stands aside to reveal small fridges behind with numerous differing drinks.

"I'll take an Erdinger Dunkel," Ashley said, and the landlord set about getting the drinks together.

"Erdinger what?" Conners questions making Ashley smile.

"Dunkel. You can get German beer, and not the best this country offers," he moans.

"You were quick to choose it, so it can't be too bad."

"A nice substitute when the dog doesn't want to go for a walk," Ashley said as he caught sight of Kilbride. "I don't believe it."

Aware he has been seen, Kilbride feigns drunkenness as he moves over. "I thought that was you, you Geordie bastard!" he shouts, catching Conners' attention.

Pleased to see his old commander, Ashley speaks with genuine admiration as they shake hands.

"Your drinks, sir," the landlord said as he placed them on the bar. "Do you want one, Roger?"

Kilbride blusters as he annoyingly slaps the counter to carry on the pretence of inebriation. "I'll have a very, very, very large V and T."

Ashley grins awkwardly perturbed by his friend's animation. "Put them down to my room, please."

"Do you have a room, sir?" the landlord questions.

"One has been booked under the name of James Ashley."

"What brings you up here?" Kilbride mumbles as his stare shifts lecherously to Conners. "And who's the bonny lass?"

"That's Julie," Ashley introduces dispassionately, but Conners interjects with amusement that she knows will aggravate her enforced husband. "That's Julie, his beloved wife."

"You've got to be kidding me? I thought you'd never marry again after Louise kicked you out."

Conners turns her interest onto Ashley, who looks away, unhappy his personal information is being divulged.

"I always thought the sarge was gay until Louise came onto the scene, but then I think he paid her to act as his wife," he said with a raucous laugh. "But she didn't last long anyway," he adds, making Conners laugh. "You see, even she has concerns."

Disliking his friend's drunk persona, Ashley glares at Kilbride but keeps his composure. "We are here on holiday."

"You've come here on holiday? I always thought you were soft in the head, James, but Jesus."

The landlord places Kilbride's vodka and tonic on the counter, and he scoops it up to swallow in one before slamming the glass annoyingly back onto the bar.

"Soft in the head and gay?" Conners reiterates. "You must be an old friend of Jimmy's."

"Jimmy?" Kilbride questioned, amused. "I seem to remember you hated being called Jimmy?"

Conners grins mischievously. "All the more reason to call him by it, don't you think?"

Kilbride laughs raucously at Ashley's touchiness as he picks up his and Conners' drinks, and they move to a table, followed by the major.

"It doesn't bother me these days," Ashley mumbles unsuccessfully as Kilbride laughs at his reasoning. "Scotland's a beautiful country, so we decided to tour it," he adds to change the subject.

"I can't believe you took time off to come to this shit hole. It's either raining, or you're being bitten to death by midges."

Puzzled by Kilbride's dismissive attitude, Conners enquires about his Scottish nationality, which genuinely has a patriotic fervour that he wants to remain secret.

"Only by birth," Kilbride answers with exaggerated animation. "My heart lies on a beach in the Caribbean next to a barrel of rum."

"My idea of a holiday isn't getting pissed then sleeping it off on the beach," Ashley criticises, making Conners snigger at his increasing irritability.

"Told you he was gay," Kilbride adds as he grins at Conners.

"Aren't you going to introduce us properly, Jimmy?" Conners said, making Kilbride laugh vigorously.

"I can't get over your lass calling you Jimmy. Considering how pissy you used to get about it, I would have thought you'd have that written in a pre-nuptial."

"He still does," Conners said with the broadest of smiles. "Don't let him think it doesn't."

"This pissed idiot was a friend of mine, Roger Kilbride."

Kilbride lifts Conners' hand to kiss gently. "Nice to meet you, Julie."

Uninterested in the answer, Ashley asks. "So, what are you doing here, Roger?"

"Classified, Jimmy. You know the score."

Displeased, his old comrade would revert to the slang version of the name he had never stopped hating, Ashley snaps. "It's James!"

"Classified?" Conners interrupts, intrigued. "Are you in the military or something like it?"

"That, darling, is also classified," Kilbride said, bigging himself up.

"You don't seem the sort who can keep a secret," Conners said, cutting into Kilbride's self-important manner.

"Hey, if you don't like it, you can always fuck off back to America!" Kilbride shouts, and Ashley grabs his arm harshly.

"That's enough of that."

"I thought you were up for a joke," Conners condescendingly adds to Kilbride's aggravation. "Obviously, I was wrong."

"You're right, Jimmy, err, James. I just hate fucking Yanks."

"I can't blame you for that, but if you're rude to her again, I'll put you on your arse, rank or not."

"That could be interesting," Kilbride said as they squared up, but Conners pulled Ashley aside to decrease the tension.

"Calm down, girls. If I couldn't take name-calling, I wouldn't travel the world as an American, would I?"

Ashley and Conners sit, but Kilbride remains standing as he carries on his pretence of inebriation and swings from side to side as he takes hold of the table to steady himself.

"Do you live around here?" Conners adds, attempting to break the testosterone-fuelled tension she can see in Ashley's eyes.

"No way, darling. I'm here for the job."

"What job is that?" Conners asked but instantly realised she had little chance of finding the truth as Ashley and Kilbride glared at her.

"Some questions shouldn't be asked, Julie. You should know that."

"Why should I know that, Jimmy?"

"Let's not get into another domestic," Kilbride adds to lighten the situation. "If I tell you, I would have to kill you," he said, gaining a stern look from Conners, who replied with venom.

"That would also be interesting."

Kilbride laughs at the imposed threat. "Surely you know James was in the job?" He mumbles but instantly regrets mentioning it.

Conners turns to Ashley, feigning interest. "And what job is that, Jimmy?"

"You don't think he got that limp because he has a stone in his shoe, do you?"

Ashley interrupts, wanting to take the onus off himself, "Never mind that shit!"

"Stupid as shit!" Kilbride blusters with a childish laugh, but Conners believes his swearing is aimed at her. "You have to be as stupid as shit to join, but only find out when it's too late."

"That's enough of that, Roger," Ashley pressed, understanding the joke, but Kilbride carried on without a breath.

"I was his boss in those days."

Unable to determine the discussion, Conners shakes her head vigorously as her eyes shift to Ashley for an explanation, he has no intention of giving.

"Fuck this!" Kilbride shouts, moving off and knocking into the table to spill their drinks over it as Ashley and Conners vault to their feet to avoid getting wet.

Concerned by the unusual behaviour of his old friend, Ashley moves to the window to look out. "What the hell has got into him? I've never seen him act like a fucking arse."

"And the gentleman dies," she said with a wry, mischievous grin as he turned his bewilderment onto her. "Two minutes ago, you were stopping that ass from swearing. Now you are acting worse than him."

"I was playing the part of a loving partner. When there isn't an audience, I can return to type."

"My ass. You were acting all chivalric."

Ashley smiles, then moves to the window to see Kilbride stumbling across the car park and into his Land Rover to drive off. "He never used to be such an inconsiderate arse."

Wanting to know more about Kilbride to gain intelligence on her enforced partner, Conners inquires. "He said he's here for the job?"

Ashley realises Kilbride's identity is hardly top secret but still grins his unease at revealing it. "He's SAS," he answers as she thinks over the major's words which bring a smile to her face.

"Stupid as shit. I get it. I take it you were Special Forces too?" she questions, but he has no intention of revealing anything of his past.

"Come on, Jimmy; you can tell your wife. They can't make me testify against you."

"If you need to know, we were in the Royal Regiment of Fusiliers together. Just the regular army."

"And he was your commanding officer?"

Frustratingly tired of being interrogated, Ashley answers and quickly changes the subject. "I want to know why I haven't been informed of him being here."

"Don't you mean we, Jimmy?" she gripes, genuinely annoyed. "You keep saying I, which is singular, and as you can see, there are two of us."

"Whether any British forces are deployed, it has nothing to do with a meddlesome American intelligence operative of the CIA," he said as she stared, attempting to figure out the man she had been forcibly paired with.

"I'm not with the CIA. You don't seem interested in a joint assignment. I get the feeling your heart's not in it, Jimmy."

"How do you come to that conclusion?" he snaps with sarcasm that has an underlying mistrust of being profiled.

"I'm an analyst paid by the United States government to read the mannerisms of people like you."

"People like me? You couldn't read me?"

Still playing to type, she keeps up the pretence of her cover. "No matter what your ass of a friend said, I don't think you have ever married. You've been in the service too long to get mixed up in the disjointed world of love," she adds, making him shake his head and laugh. "Which is what resulted in your injuries. How many places has the British Army been at war over the last years? You're too young for the Falklands. Iraq. Ireland could be a winner, but my guess would be Afghanistan. You haven't been in the Special Forces game too long; you still have the bubble wrap on," she says, making him laugh at the analogy. "I believe you were a Fusilier but went into the lofty world of the Special Forces for the excitement and adventure."

He shuffles as the truth hits home and takes a sizeable savouring mouthful of his Erdinger to calm.

"Your naivety to your superiors shows me you're new to the cloak and dagger game. You've worked with these people but under different circumstances. Now they are calling the shots, and you don't like it."

"I couldn't give a shit," he said honestly. "People like Kilbride and Shirlow have always called the shots. I wouldn't want to be an officer."

"Really?" she said, unconvinced. "I'd say me being a colonel boils your piss."

"What about you?" he growled, to her amusement.

"You can attempt to read me, Jimmy, but you will find nothing. I'm not a field operative. I have nothing to hide."

"But you're here on this sham of a mission which should be more important to those in command. Don't you think?"

"Very astute, Jimmy."

"Yeah, I'm full of astuteness."

"But I believe you're talking about yourself. I work behind a desk."

"Then we have something in common."

"I was selected to take on the role of your wife, that's all."

"Yeah, I can just see them walking past your desk in Langley's typing section and picking you from all the other ladies in the office. How lovely," he said as he took a large mouthful of his Erdinger.

"That's nearer to the truth than you would like."

"A marriage of inconvenience."

"So, what now?" she questioned, determined to discover what was on the Englishman's mind.

"Now I need to find out why I wasn't informed of Major Kilbride's presence."

"We, Jimmy, it's we," she said, but he ignored her ramblings as his mind mulled over the events of the past days.

"Him being here has nothing to do with us, but I believe something is off."

"Other than your self-aggrandising attitude, what could it be?"

"I'd like to know that," he adds with calm.

Wanting her role to be reaffirmed, she reiterates. "When you say I'd like to know, surely you mean we'd like to know?"

He takes his phone out and dials as he walks off.

"Who are you ringing now?"

"Jack Caine. He won't withhold information from me."

"Another old Fusilier?"

"He's why I'm here."

"And I thought all this was for Queen and country."

***

Drinking a large glass of 1969 Feuerheerd single harvest port, Caine sits in his London flat in Westminster relaxing when his phone rings, and he looks at the screen disillusioned as he takes a sip to savour the taste. "James. What can I do for you?"

"I've just bumped into Roger Kilbride," Ashley said, and there was a pause, then Caine spoke dismissively.

"Forget about him. What he's doing doesn't concern you or your American wife."

"As he's just left the misses and me, that may be hard."

Annoyed with the SAS major, Caine downs his port and refills his glass. "He's still in the job, James."

"I gathered that, but why wasn't I informed of the possibility of coming across the regiment?"

"Maybe you should have, but that intelligence was and still is, irrelevant to your mission and of the highest secrecy. What you have found has nothing to do with the SAS presence on the Mull."

"How do you know that?" Ashley questions confident in a connection.

"You know the score, James. There are some things you don't enquire about, and this is certainly the highest of the don't ask scenario. Enlighten me again," Caine adds as he takes another savouring sip.

"How do you know he's up there?"

"He was in our hotel rat arsed and acting like an arse."

Annoyed to the point of getting Kilbride court-martialled for his lack of professionalism, Caine sits back, rubbing his forehead. "Listen,

James, I can confirm what we have talked about isn't connected, but I can't explain over the phone. You are where you're meant to be, so hang tight, and I will see you in the morning."

"You're coming here?" Ashley questioned, dismayed, as the call was curtailed, and he turned to Conners, whose face grimaced, stunned.

"Why would he come here?" she said, agitatedly walking away.

"He said Major Kilbride being here is irrelevant to our mission and that the Dimitri Rossakovich and SAS presence aren't connected."

"But you don't agree?" she questions to see if her British counterpart thinks like her.

"How do you feel about doing some investigations of our own?" he adds to her puzzlement.

"Isn't that why we are here?"

"Is it?" he snaps, and she shrugs her shoulders and mimics the movement of a marionette. "First, we must find out who was flying that helicopter."

"We?" she said, exasperated, then added to irritate. "Nice to be invited to the party at last, but how do you intend to do that?"

"My ID will get us anywhere."

"You love the power your creds give you, Jimmy. So where do we start?" she said confidently, and he grinned knowingly.

"Shirlow said to forget about Kintyre Oil," he answers. "If ever there was a cover for a SAS OP, that would be it, so that's where we should start."

"Do you think someone in the military picked up the missiles?"

"There's one way to find out," Ashley adds confidently.

"Surely your old comrade wouldn't keep that from you?"

Ashley takes a holstered Walther P22 from his bag and clips it onto his waistband. "He wouldn't tell me his name if I didn't already know it, but that puzzles me more."

"Do you think you will need that?"

"I don't go into dodgy situations without one."

"And this is a dodgy situation?" she questioned, hoping he would answer truthfully.

"Experience tells me anything to do with the regiment is dodgy."

She opens her jacket to show a holstered Colt Mustang. "I also never leave home without one."

"That must have been a comfort sitting at your desk in Langley," he said ironically, but she didn't attempt to explain why she was armed as he headed for the door.

"What about your drink?" she shouts, and he stops to look back, disheartened at his half-drunk glass.

"German beer and semi-automatic pistols aren't good bedfellows. Herr Erdinger will have to wait until I get back.

Conners looks at her wine and smiles her agreement as she follows him out.

***

Kintyre Oil sits on a bluff at the end of a long winding single-track lane surrounded by twelve feet high anti-climb fences with motion detectors attached and razor wire and a security hut at the main gate with two security men inside looking out with the intent to harm anyone who dares approach. Designed to look like a builder's yard, you can't see what is happening behind the scenes as numerous well-placed containers prevent anyone from viewing its internal structure.

***

Illuminated by the Fiesta's headlights, Ashley drives with Conners in the passenger seat. They can see dim lights in the distance and carry on until the road ends with a barbed wire fence and a large sign for Kintyre Oil that states no trespassing with the risk of prosecution.

"How did you know it would be here?" she said, impressed.

"This is the only place it could be," he answers with tactical understanding. "Word of caution. Keep your mouth shut. They won't like a Yank on their base if this is the regiment."

He takes out his pain medication and drops two with a large mouthful of whisky from his hip flask.

"I thought alcohol and semi-automatics didn't go well together?" she questions with angst in her tone.

"I said Erdinger," he explained with mischievousness. "Whisky is the fuel of life."

"You're a fucking idiot, Jimmy. If you ever have to draw your gun pissed, my first bullet is going in you before you mistake me for the enemy in your blurred vision."

Playing the part of a minimum-waged employee, a guard exits the security hut as Ashley winds the window down. "You aren't fucking allowed here!" he shouts in a threatening tone that most would quiver on hearing, but Ashley speaks with an understanding of his predicament.

"What is this place?"

Showing no patience for idle chit-chat, the guard points. "Read the fucking sign and piss off!"

"Surely you shouldn't be speaking to a member of the public in that derisory tone," Conners condescends to Ashley's indignation.

"Listen, idiot," the guard said as he stuck his menacing head into the car window to be faced with Ashley's ID.

"Major Kilbride asked me over."

"Who the fuck's Major Kilbride?" the guard feigns, and Ashley laughs at the pretence. "Nothing was said to me."

"The state he was in when he left the pub, he probably forgot."

Having witnessed Kilbride's sober arrival, the guard looks bemused.

"What's your business here?

"How long have you been in the regiment?" Ashley said on recognising the type, but the guard played down the question to his irritation.

"Yeah, the fucking regiment?" he shouts, making the guard attentive to him.

"What has that got to do with anything?"

"When you have served as long as me, then I will tell you about my business. Now open the fucking gates!"

"You were in the regiment?" the guard said timidly, and Ashley nodded with self-effacing arrogance. "Hold on," he adds, then moves to the security hut to enter.

"So, you were SAS?" Conners questions making Ashley laugh.

"I only said it for his benefit."

"You loved that, Jimmy," she said as he turned his angry attention onto her.

"I told you to keep your mouth shut?"

"The authority that ID gives you," she said, mimicking his voice.

"When you have served as long as me, I will tell you about my business. What a dick! Now open the fucking gates," she adds with a laugh to his irritation.

The guard exits the security hut, followed by a more menacing-looking man who has anger in his eyes at being disturbed.

"What's your business here?" the second guard questions as Ashley laughs in recognition.

"Nothing to do with you, shit for brains."

The second guard stares his anger and then smiles his recognition.

"Sergeant James Ashley. What the fuck are you doing here?"

Ashley shows his ID. "Business."

"Fuck me. I never saw that coming."

"I didn't have much choice," Ashley said with a grin that quickly waned on noticing Conners' interest.

"Oh, yeah. Heard you walk with a mince these days."

"You get a bullet in the leg and see if you don't limp," Ashley said with self-pitying pain that is a constant.

"I said mince," the second guard said to Ashley's irritation. "But whatever."

"It was a promotion," Ashley pipes in, but the second guard's face shows he is having none of it. "Now I get to shit on all you low lives." The second guard laughs, turning his attention to Conners. "Who the fuck is this? The lad says she's a fucking Yank."

"CIA," Conners said with pride to Ashley's increasing irritation.

"It must be a fucking full moon!" the second guard shouts as he opens the gate. "Are you here long?"

"I hope not."

"Stay for a drink. I'm off soon."

Ashley calls out because he doesn't want to risk bumping into Kilbride.

"Sorry, mate, but I must be away soon."

"Fuck you then, you boring bastard. Welcome to SOKSAS."

"SOKSAS?" Conners questions. "What the fuck's that?"

The second guard looks at Ashley as if he should know the Special Forces site. "Special Operations Kintyre, Special Air Service."

"Never heard of it," Ashley adds, making it a joke as he waves through the open window as they drive through the gate.

"Another man who knows you, Jimmy."

"I thought you weren't CIA?"

"I'm not," she said with a broad smile.

"Then why say it?"

"To annoy you. I thought an American on their base. What would they hate the most, and the CIA came to mind as I know you have a personal appreciation of the agency?"

"I wish you'd kept your mouth shut."

"And miss all the fun from yours and their expressions. I couldn't do that," she said, looking around the decrepit site. "This place looks ancient. Surely you'd have known about this while in the regiment?" Ashley shakes his head, unsure how to answer. "I wasn't privy to every secret, and I feel this is well above my pay grade." He looks at her, and she grins, unconvinced as if he is withholding information from her again. "You got sent where they wanted and wouldn't be informed of what others are up to in case you were taken prisoner. You see, if you don't know, you can't tell."

"I understand the concept, Jimmy; I'm not a total dummy."

"Yeah, we can leave that discussion for when we've got more time." He looks around. "This place looks as though it was mothballed years ago."

"Do you know what it would have been used for?"

"No," he adds genuinely. "But if I had to guess, as the ploy had been used in many different places worldwide, it's a camp for a rapid response force."

"Rapid response force?" she questions as her mind doesn't confirm what her eyes see. "What for?"

"Northern Ireland would be my calculated guess."

"Doesn't make sense with all the bases you had in the province."

"Nothing makes sense when it comes to military thinking."

"Bit stupid making out Kilbride invited you," Conners adds to change the subject from what she sees as misdirection. "They could phone through to him."

"The state he was in. He'll be slumped over, slavering on his bunk," he explains as he turns his anger onto her. "The stupidity came from you."

"Really, Jimmy?" she argues, determined.

"Now they know you're a Yank; they will put extra suspicion onto our visit."

"You do know we are allies?" Conners explains calmly. "And our countries aren't at war."

"We've been at war since 1775 when you betrayed us and sided with the French."

"I think you will find we rebelled against tyranny and our allies; the French came to our aid."

"Bull-shit! You didn't want anyone meddling in your affairs, and that's all you've done as a nation since. Leaders of the free world, my arse."

"You know, Jimmy," she adds to offend. "I never knew you were so emotional. Next time I will stay quiet just for you."

"Can I have that in writing?"

Three Westland Wessex's sit outside a hangar that is only visible from the seaward side with a mechanic carrying out routine maintenance on one of them, and they pull over, alight and walk toward him.

"Keep your mouth shut this time," Ashley whispers, then smiles at the mechanic. "I need to see the flight log for one of your helicopters!" he shouts, and the mechanic looks bemused at the sight of strangers on the base and goes to question the order as Ashley flashes his ID, which belays his query.

"Which one?"

"Which bird went up last night?"

Vexed to have to stop the work he desperately wants to finish so he can get off for a few beers, the mechanic moves off, and they follow him into the hangar as Ashley keeps the area under fearful surveillance. They move to a table for the mechanic to pick up two log books, then look around in bewilderment.

"It's not here, but twenty-one went out last night." He hands the log books to Ashley, who glances them over and throws their uselessness onto the table.

"You say the log book for twenty-one isn't here?" Conners questions, and Ashley grins at her, considering how long she has remained quiet. "What's twenty-one?"

The mechanic points at a Wessex outside, with the number twenty-one, just visible, painted on the side.

"And it went up last night?" Ashley questioned, and the mechanic turned his uncertainty onto him.

"Lieutenant Thomas should know."

"Who's that?" Ashley adds, and the mechanic answers with what he sees as the obvious.

"The pilot."

"Where will we find him?" Conners enquires, and the mechanic points at the Wessex, where you can just about make out the figure of a man moving about.

"He's in the cockpit," the mechanic mutters as he heads off. "Tell him to put the log book back where it belongs."

Ashley and Conners move to twenty-one as Thomas alights with a clipboard, and Ashley flashes his ID.

"We're looking for information on a flight made out of here last night," Ashley said, but Thomas was curious about the harsh questioning and spoke grudgingly as his mistrusting stare shifted between the strangers.

"Mine was the only one up last night."

"We need to know what route you took."

"I was just writing the report."

"Shouldn't that have already been done?" Conners said, adding an air of legitimacy to their questioning, but her accent made Thomas uneasy. "What's going on?"

"Just answer the fucking question!" Ashley demands of the shaken pilot.

"Around here, things aren't done the same as at the squadron. I also had another flight today, so I incorporated the two together."

Kilbride steps soberly from the side of the hangar but keeps to the shadows to not be seen as he watches Ashley and Conners conversing with Thomas.

"I need a look at that report," Ashley said, reaching out, but Thomas didn't hand it over. "Do we have a problem, Lieutenant?"

"I can't show you anything without permission from the base commander."

Seeing his words as a hindrance, he could well do without and showing extreme disrespect for the serving officer with an exemplary record of service, Ashley snatches the clipboard and pushes him back as Conners moves to look over his shoulder, and he points to something of interest, and she nods her understanding.

"Is there a problem, sir?" Thomas questions, concerned.

"Routine flight to Ireland?" Ashley queries as he reads. "What do you mean by routine?"

"As in planned," Thomas rebuffs to Ashley's disdain.

"We need more than that," Conners presses, but Thomas remains defiant.

"If you get permission from the base commander, I will tell you what you want to know."

"Listen, Lieutenant," Ashley said, his tone more menaced. "So as not to carry on the bad way we started. I take it you like the tranquillity of life here," he adds, and Thomas shuffles uneasily. "I mean, you could be doing flights in and around Afghanistan or one of the many shitty places of the world that British forces are in if that suits you better or even to the extreme, I could see you demoted or dismissed from the service for not helping in what is a matter of national security."

Thomas doesn't take kindly to the threat, which shows on his weary face.

"I could go through other channels to get the information, but I would make sure your name is at the top of every page stating your interference," Ashley said, then turned to Conners. "What's his name again?" he said, and she answered straight-faced as they turned back on the nervous pilot who understood the threat.

"Last night's flight was the third I have made in nine days."

"It says you landed?" Ashley questions.

Thomas explains hesitantly. "Each time we drop into the same coordinates," he said, and Ashley took in their significance as he glanced over the report. "The only thing I can tell you about the drop-off is a windmill on the hill just north of the barn."

"Windmill?" Ashley questioned, unsure why such an inconsequential thing would be mentioned.

"Look, I've been in the game long enough not to question my orders."

"Did you drop anything off?" Conners interrupts.

Thomas doesn't like the line of questioning, especially from an American who hadn't shown any form of ID, but Ashley aggressively insists he answers. "In Ireland. No."

"Did you pick anything up?" she says, but he doesn't care enough to give his tormentors a truthful answer.

"I don't see anything about the Dimitri Rossakovich," Ashley said, startling Thomas, who had been ordered to omit all information about his rendezvous with the cargo ship.

"Dimitri Rossakovich?" Thomas mumbles unconvincingly. "What's that?"

"The cargo ship you visited!"

Visibly shaken, Thomas shuffles uneasily, but his actions give Ashley the required answer.

"Don't worry," Ashley confirms. "You did right in not recording it. Did you pick up the cargo?" he adds sternly as Thomas' unnerved glare shifts between his teasers in the belief that he is being tested. "Don't make me ask again," he adds, his tone darker.

"I knew nothing of the pickup until we were in the air."

Ashley looks around, hoping the missiles will be waiting to be picked up but can't make out anything in the chaos. "Can you show me the cargo?"

"I dropped it off earlier today as part of an exercise flight."

"Whereabouts?" Conners questions add to Thomas' curiosity.

"I flew blind."

"How can you fly blind?" Conners interjects to the flight lieutenant's unease.

"It was meant to go to Glasgow and not until tomorrow," Ashley interrupts, attempting to bluff the pilot, but this bemuses Thomas as his sceptical eyes shift rapidly between them.

"But there were two men waiting to pick it up."

"Sounds like a cock up to me," Conners adds, feigning irritation, but Thomas feels guiltless and shrugs his shoulders, not caring.

"The major conversed with the men. It seemed well planned and above board."

Ashley hands Thomas the clipboard and explains with confidence.

"Leave the last bit off the report as well."

"I was ordered not to put it in, sir."

"Are you sure you have no idea where you dropped the cargo off?" Conners insists, and Thomas shakes his head, annoyed that the foreigner is still questioning his integrity. "But surely you have a sense of direction?"

"Is this a test?" Thomas said, turning to his fellow countryman. "Why would you think that?"

"It's just after all I have done, this is the first time, I have been interrogated about a mission, never mind by an American."

"Just ignore her," Ashley said to Conners' disbelief. "We need to know because there has been a major ball's up, and if we find out where it went, we can prevent an investigation and save you the career breaker of being called to give witness."

Thomas thinks over his options. "If I had to guess, I would say somewhere in Ayrshire."

Ashley shakes Thomas' hand. "Thanks for your help, Lieutenant."

Thomas smiles, relieved to get away, then heads toward the hangar.

"Not a word about this!" Ashley shouts, but Thomas ignores him as he enters the hangar and disappears out of sight. "Let's get the hell out of here," he impresses. "This place reeks of corruption."

They go to their car and stop to look at each other over the roof.

"I don't believe what I've just heard," he said to her, nodding in agreement.

"It doesn't surprise me. I've met many gung-ho soldiers in my day, and this friend of yours fits the description of one."

Annoyed at the slur to any member of the regiment he served with pride, Ashley snaps. "We're not talking about the Marine Corps. Major Kilbride's a bloody good soldier. I've been in the shit with him many times, and he never let me or any of the other men down."

"He's obviously changed since you served."

"What do you mean by that?" he snipes.

"These days, he's corrupt and dealing in the arms trade."

"Don't mix him up with the drunk you've just met," he defends, not liking their conversation. "We all have a breaking point. Everyone's entitled to a beer."

"You're trying to convince yourself of his innocence and condone your alcohol intake," Conners said ironically. "He was the one who ordered that fly flyboy into doing his abetting, or maybe the lieutenant is in on it as well."

"He doesn't know what is happening and wouldn't want to. That's why they pick these pilots for 658 squadron. They follow orders, no questions asked."

"He may be a clever bastard."

Ashley looks to see Thomas place his report on the table and keeps his stare when he realises he hasn't looked back and is showing them no interest. "He gave away too much information freely. He'll have thought what he was doing was normal, and being confronted about it put him on the back foot. 'Ask no questions, and you'll be told no lies' is an unwritten motto of Special Forces."

"What about the missiles? Do you believe they were dropped off in Scotland?" Conners questioned, unconvinced. "Surely a good pilot would have an inclination of the flight path they are taking?"

"I'd have thought so, but we can leave that to the generals. Come on, let's get the fuck out of here," Ashley adds, and they get into their car and drive off.

Kilbride steps out slightly, and Thomas notices him standing in the shadows and moves to confront him.

"Major," Thomas said, pointing at Ashley's car heading for the gates. "They were looking for you. They had some queries about the cargo we picked up."

"I'm sorry I missed them," Kilbride feigned. "What did you tell them?" Thomas hesitates but, saying he has been asked a direct question, decides it is in his best interest to answer. "They wanted to know why the containers were transferred and said they were meant to go to Glasgow."

"Of course, he wouldn't have been informed about that. I'll call him and set the record straight," Kilbride explains as he produces his phone and moves off. "James Ashley knows about the shipment," he said. "We should stop now it is all out." He listens to the ranting voice on the other side, switches the phone off and smiles with mischievous achievement.

***

CHAPTER 9

***

Conners enters their room in the Argyll Arms Hotel and close the door as Ashley places his phone on the bedside cabinet.
"Who was that, Jimmy?"
"Caine."
"He can't be missing you," she said sarcastically. "You're never off the phone with him."
"As ordered."
"What did he have to say?"
Ashley remains quiet for a few seconds to make out that he has information, but this irritates the American. "He said you're to receive the Congressional Medal of Honor, and the President will decorate you himself."
"Another one," she said, amused but more interested in how their mission was going. "Why don't you go direct to General Shirlow instead of going through the colonel?"
"And break the chain of command?" He laughed. "I'm just a small cog in the world of intelligence who does as ordered," he said, his eyes fixed vacantly on the wall.
"What's wrong, Jimmy?"
"He didn't want to know what I had to say. I don't think we were meant to find out about this SOKSAS. He wants us to stay put until he comes up tomorrow."
Conners doesn't understand why Caine's presence would be required. "I don't get that one. So, I'll have two clowns to deal with," she said as she entered the bathroom to shower.

***

The Argyll Arms Hotel has only two car park lights out of six working, casting ominous shadows over the cars that sit the night out as the most responsible drunks sensibly walk home. The quiet of the night is broken by the sound of two silenced bullets followed by breaking glass, leaving the area in total darkness. A Range Rover drives in, without lights and parks in the corner to sit for several moments until the engine switches off and Bright and Westwood alight and make their way to the back door. Bright knocks as Westwood draws his silenced Glock 17, and due to the early morning hours, the landlord calls out, angered by the interruption to his time off but Bright impatiently bangs harder on the door.

"Police! Open up, Mr Logan, we haven't got all night!"

Having heard his name, the landlord opens several bolts and then looks out. "It's two in the morning," he whinges as he fastens his robe to keep out the cold. "Couldn't this wait?" he questions as Westwood points his Glock into his face making him lift his hands submissively. Bright pushes the petrified landlord aside and then steps inside. "Are there any other people here?"

"My wife and daughter and some guests," the landlord answers with tears rolling down his terrified face, but this adds to the thrill Bright gets with his power over others.

"Do as I say, and no harm will come to your family. I'm looking for James Ashley and an American woman."

"Room six," the landlord blurts out, hoping his help will protect his family. "They're in room six."

"Alright, you can go," Bright said, and the landlord nervously backed off then turned, drawing his Sig Sauer P320; he smashed him on the back of his head to knock him bleeding and unconscious to the floor. "You heard the man," he commands of his colleague. "Room six."

They enter the bar area where the optics take Westwood's attention, and he rounds the counter to pour himself a whisky to down in one. "What the fuck are you doing?" Bright questions as Westwood pours another.

"Getting a fucking drink. Murder's thirsty work. Do you want one?

"No, I fucking don't. Let's get this shit over with, then we can have a drink back at the hotel, but first, I am looking forward to putting a hole in the arses head."

Westwood downs the whisky, then pours another.

"You've got a fucking problem."

Curious about where her husband is, the landlady exits from a side door and stops in shoat of a stranger helping himself to her stock.

"Who the bloody hell are you?" she shouts, and Westwood, in a knee-jerk reaction, brings up his Glock to bear and shoots her in the head and she falls to the floor with a heavy thud as Bright turns, shocked by the change into violence that was against their standing orders.

"We don't want some stupid cow waking our friends up," Westwood explains as he downs the whisky, and Bright heads off, leaving him to pour another.

***

Startled, Ashley comes around to sit on the side of his bed as his subconsciously trained mind tunes into the sound of a discharged bullet that haunts his dreams, but this time, he feels the sound is real enough to investigate. He looks at Conners lying in her bed, fast asleep aware he wouldn't get back to sleep unless he had checked out the possible threat. He takes his cocked Walther from under his pillow and pulls the hammer back as he moves to the door to open slightly and look out onto the empty landing. He hears Bright and Westwood's whispered voices emanating from downstairs, and not recognising them, he closes the door softly and gets himself ready as he makes his way to Conners to nudge her several times until she stirs.

"What are you doing, Jimmy?" she snarls grudgingly as she comes around. "You'd better not be on a booty call?"

Ashley laughs as he lifts his Walther to his lips, and she sits disconcerted by the sight of his weapon in play as the creaking corridor gives away Bright and Westwood's approach. She draws her Colt to aim at the door as she struggles to put her clothes on.

Believing their approach had gone unnoticed, Bright and Westwood stop outside room six and raise their guns offensively as Westwood kicks the door in and charges forward into a hail of bullets that knock him back against the landing wall and then onto the floor dead. Bright fires aimlessly through the open door as Ashley and Conners return fire, with bullets ricocheting and smashing into the walls and furniture around them. Under sustained fire, Bright takes cover behind the wall and Conners, aware the plaster structure is no match for her 9mm bullets, puts one through the plasterwork to hit him in the shoulder and catapult him back against the adjacent wall as he drops his Sig Sauer and screams in agony. Grabbing his bleeding shoulder, Bright races off with several more bullets smashing through the wall in pursuit. Cautiously, Ashley makes his way to the door, then looks to see the passage empty apart from the crumpled body of Westwood, and he picks up his Glock and Bright's Sig Sauer to throw well out of reach, then makes his way guardedly along the passage.

***

Bright stumbles out of the hotel and runs toward the Range Rover, which he struggles to open, then lifts an MP5 out to cock and bring to bear. As Ashley exits the rear door, he comes under sustained fire, forcing him to the ground as the bullets smash into the wall and doorway. Outgunned, Ashley moves his Walther to his side but keeps it ready for action as Bright moves over to tower in confidence. He has the upper hand.

"We meet again, Sergeant."

Ashley looks up through the light from the open door behind, but his bemused face shows he has no recollection of the threatening man who finds amusement in his vagueness.

"You don't remember me?"

"Can't say I do."

"It's not a wonder," Bright said with a sneering laugh. "You were as pissed as a twat and cocky to boot."

"Sounds like me, but maybe you should tell me when we met so we can both laugh."

Bright goes to speak, but Conners comes around the door, and with one tap from her Colt, the threat to Ashley's life is taken as the assassin drops to the ground with blood exiting a hole in his forehead.

"You could have waited a couple more seconds!" he shouts to her disbelief.

"What? For him to kill you?"

He rolls over to show he had his would-be assassin covered with his Walther. "He was just about to tell me who he was."

Unsure how she was meant to have that information, she stares her dissatisfaction. "You don't need to thank me, Jimmy."

He stands holstering his Walther. "We need to get out of here. We don't have time to explain ourselves to the local coppers!" He re-enters the hotel, leaving Conners unhappy with his attitude to her saving his life; she takes a defensive posture waiting for him to exit with their cases.

A siren sounds with the approach of a lone police car, which hastens their exit, and they get into the Fiesta and drive with hesitant calmness onto the main road for a short distance as the police car races passed on the opposite side of the road with its sirens blaring and lights flashing.

Relieved, Ashley looks through the rear-view mirror to witness the police car turning into the hotel's car park. "We just made it."

Conners looks back, equally pleased. "Who do you think wants us dead?" she questioned, determined to get an answer, and he laughed at the thought of all the people he has come up against who could target him for death.

"Have you got any enemies because I've got plenty?" he said, breaking the car into a skidding halt to her frustration as the seat belt cuts into her neck again. He slaps the steering wheel several times and bursts into fits of laughter. "I know who they were!"

"Who?"

"Stan and Ollie," he answers to her bewilderment. "The two who came to kill us," he adds, and her attention is quickly overtaken with interest. "They were the goons sent to pick me up for the meeting with you and General Patton."

"And you forgot?" she adds, disheartened at his inability to recollect an event that had only happened.

"I was looking through hazy drink-fuelled eyes and didn't recognise them," he explains to her increasing bewilderment. "I was pissed!"

"Brilliant! Now I can think of two people who could want us dead," she calls out, and he turns expectant of an explanation. "Shirlow and Caine."

"I can't vouch for Shirlow, but I have known Jack Caine a long time," he argues. "I trust him with my life and have on numerous occasions."

"Who knew we were here, Jimmy?" she bites, unwavering. "Who told us to wait at the hotel until he arrives?"

He ponders all that had happened. "I see your point, but it doesn't make sense. What have we discovered could make us a target for assassination?"

She smiles, satisfied. "Something we weren't supposed to."

Impatient to find out what his colleague thinks, he grins his irritability. "The SAS presence. Major Kilbride. Kintyre Oil. The Westland Wessex's. The Dimitri Rossakovich. They all tie together somehow."

"They're all secrets in their own right," he confirms with understanding as his mind races over everything that had occurred.

"All far too important for us mere mortals to know about," she adds.

"But if we weren't supposed to find any of this, why send us in the first place?"

"Exactly," he answers. "If that ship hadn't been called into port, we wouldn't have found anything."

"And that points the finger at the people who sent us here, which includes your friend," she adds confidently, distressing his thought process.

"Why would they send us if there was even the remotest chance of us finding anything out?"

"You nailed it with the ship being called into port. My calculated guess would be that wasn't meant to happen."

"I'll never believe Jack would betray me," he argues decisively. "So, where does that leave us? Who can we trust?"

"The only person I trust is General Davison," she said sincerely, but he laughed, adding animated sarcastic slaps to his knee.

"I trust him less than General Shirlow."

"That's not fair, Jimmy. You don't know the man, yet you sit there in judgement of him."

"I've seen enough to know I don't want to," he argues. "He's brash, obnoxious, big-mouthed and a fucking Yank to boot."

"I resent that," she defends patriotically. "You've taken a rash judgement of a man you only met for minutes."

"And that was enough," he snaps. "He's everything I hate about you Americans."

"That's not fair, Jimmy."

"So, you keep saying, but what's fair, for fucks sake? How can I trust anyone?"

"I hope that doesn't include me?" she questions, and he laughs loud enough to aggravate her code of honour.

"Up until two days ago, I didn't know who the fuck you were. Trust has to be earned, my want to be American friend."

"Yes, it does, Sergeant," she criticises with a derogatory tone on his rank. "But that works both ways."

"Surely you didn't know General Davison before being selected for this shit?" he presses, and she grins weakly with no intention of answering.

"Unless it was he who passed you when you were typing, and your eyes caught each other in the fluorescent lighting. The only thing we have in common is that they sent men to kill us both. The only people we can rely on is ourselves."

"I disagree, but I will play along with you for now. So, you have something in mind?"

Not having thought that far ahead, he turns to stare into the darkness of the surrounding area. "When I looked at the flight plans for the Wessex," he answers, unsure but confident. "I noted the coordinates where it landed. The same ones every three days, meaning if it all goes to plan, it will return tomorrow night."

"He could have walked for miles."

"They were on the ground less than ten minutes," he said, exciting her at the thought.

"And if they landed in the dark, they must have a close point of contact."

"We should go to Ireland and find out what is happening, but we must go in as virgins. No guns, no phones, no ID. Give me your mobile."

She passes over her phone, and he snaps it in half, then produces his own to carry out the same act.

"We could have just taken out the sim cards."

"The phones have their own serial numbers that can be tracked, so destroy the sim cards and smash them up more."

She sets about taking out the sim cards to snap them in half. "How will we get to Ireland?

"Ferry."

"Where will we get that?"

"Cairnryan," he answered confidently, having used that route while undercover in the province. He restarts the car. "Come on; we've got a long drive ahead of us."

"What about our guns? We can't just smash them?"

"We'll leave them locked up in the car when we park up, then pick them up on our return."

"And the broken phones?"

"They're going to the bottom of the Irish Sea."

***

CHAPTER 10

***

Having travelled straight back from Glasgow to arrive thirty minutes prior, Gardiner sits at the bar of the Argyll Arms Hotel, exhausted and in desperate need of the whisky he is holding. Caine enters, looking around to see the superintendent, giving the impression of not wanting to be disturbed. "Superintendent Gardiner?" he calls out, but the police officer doesn't take his tired eyes off his glass as he moves to show his ID, which Gardiner glances over unimpressed as they shake hands.

"What can I do for you, Colonel?"

"I'm looking for James Ashley," Caine said as Gardiner downs the whisky and poured another.

"He's gone. Your man and the American left me two dead."

Caine looks around, unable to see any signs of violence.

"There's a dead man outside your man's room and one in the car park at the rear," Gardiner explains, shocking Caine, who keeps his thoughts to himself. "And the landlady is in the kitchen with a bullet in her head."

"That's three," Caine queries making Gardiner grimace.

"I believe the landlady was murdered by one of the men who the landlord said broke in last night."

"So, you think this was a robbery gone wrong?"

Almost choking on his whisky, Gardiner laughs. "For the smallest of seconds. Then I remembered your people are involved, and the penny dropped."

"This is the real world, Superintendent, not Hollywood."

"Kintyre isn't the real world. We don't get three murders in a lifetime, never mind on the same night."

"May I take a look at the bodies?"

"Please yourself, but don't touch anything. I'm waiting for forensics, but they have to come from Glasgow."

Caine walks off but turns on, realising Gardiner hadn't moved. "Aren't you coming?"

Disinterested, Gardiner downs the whisky and then refills his glass. "I'll wait here. Their sight makes me want to drink."

***

Caine moves along the landing and stops in shocked recognition of Westwood. He looks around to confirm he is alone, then searches the body for his ID, which he places into his pocket along with the dead man's wallet and phone. Gardiner's voice can be heard explaining the scene to a forensic officer, and he stands to straighten himself out and moves off slightly as they exit the stairwell. The forensic officer places his case on the floor and leans to check the corpse.

Gardiner looks at Caine's concerned expression but grins weakly to play down the incident. "What do you think, Colonel?"

"Looks like a robbery. Luckily my people were here to thwart it."

"You say that, but my policeman's mind tells me, where have they gone if they weren't part of the robbery and foiled it? Why aren't they here explaining their actions and receiving the rewards they would duly deserve?"

Aware there is another body in the car park, Caine mumbles and moves off. "That I would like to know myself, Superintendent."

***

Bright's body lies covered by a sheet, with a police officer standing a short distance off, keeping guard. Caine exits the hotel and walks over to flash his ID, and the police officer nods and then moves off a short distance. Expecting to see a recognisable face, he pulls the sheet back and sighs in confirmation as he takes several breaths, then searches Bright for his ID, wallet and phone to pocket before throwing the sheet back over and walking off.

Gardiner exits the hotel as Caine nears his car. "Hold on, Colonel!" he shouts. "I need to speak to your people!"

"Don't we both," Caine replies ironically, but Gardiner only has his agenda in mind.

"If I don't hear from them, I must swear out an arrest warrant."

"You need to hold back on that, Superintendent."

"The law ties my hands, Colonel."

"It's essential I find out what's going on first. I must cite National Security matters."

Gardiner stares his disbelief that the nervousness of the time overrules the world of law and argues impotently. "My superiors won't allow this to pass unanswered."

"Neither will mine," Caine said as he shook the veteran police officer's hand. "You'll get a full report as soon as it is written." He gets into his car and drives off as he produces his phone to dial but gets an engaged tone. "What the hell are you doing, James?" he mutters as he puts the phone down.

***

The European Highlander P and O ferry moves through the choppy waters of the Irish Sea toward Larne on the Northern Irish mainland. Looking aimlessly toward the coastline in the distance, Ashley and Conners stand on the deck as the cold wind makes them uncomfortable with their surroundings. They take the broken parts from their phones to drop into the unforgiving water below.

"What do you intend to do when we land?" she questions, but he has only one thing in mind.

"I still have the cash Shirlow gave me, so we can book into a hotel and be fresh for tomorrow night."

Feigning vulnerability and tiredness, she mumbles. "I could do with a bed and a good night's sleep."

"After a few beers, that is," he smiles.

"Of course," she said, disillusioned by his constant hunt for alcohol.

"I take it you haven't had to suffer in the field?" he gripes to her grinning embarrassment.

"Only during basic training. I've told you I ride a desk."

"Sounds very comfortable," he said jealously. "But some of us have had to suffer if the job is to be done."

"You don't look like you've suffered in years, Jimmy," she adds, making him snipe back to shame.

"So how did you get to the lofty heights of colonel sitting at that desk in Langley? Hopefully not for services to your commanding general."

"I'll choose to ignore that, Jimmy," she said, moving off. "I'm off to the ladies."

"I'll be in in a minute for a beer if you want to set them up," he adds, and not caring if he had upset the American, he leans onto the rail to look at the waves crashing against the ship and reverts into the tranquillity the sound carries.

Keeping an eye on Ashley to confirm he hasn't followed, Conners stops at the door, takes out a phone, and dials. "We have a problem, sir," she said as she stepped into the ferry's interior warmth.

***

Looking toward the Dimitri Rossakovich, Caine stands in isolation until a Suburban SUV pulls over and stops at his side, but he doesn't instantly show an interest until he sees the two occupants. Aware he is under surveillance, he paces off to look toward Davaar island and takes out Bright and Westwood's phones to throw into the water with the realisation he is being pushed into a situation with no escape and has no other option but take his phone out and has one last glance at the SUV as he turns away to dial. "Get me, General Davison," he said as he unclipped his Remington R51 to make drawing easier. "Colonel Caine."

***

Davison's office in the US Embassy in Grosvenor Square overlooks Roosevelt's memorial. He sits at his desk speaking on the phone when his intercom beeps. "Hold on a second, Major." He presses the intercom button and Watkins' delicate voice comes over the speaker.

"Colonel Caine's on line two, sir."

Already aware of the call, Davison smiles broadly as he presses for line two. "Colonel, what can I do for you?"

"We have a problem, General," Caine mutters to Davison's glee.

"Don't tell me your operative has gone missing?" Davison questioned arrogantly, and Caine's glance shifted toward the SUV with the realisation they must be CIA. "Why aren't you calling General Shirlow? Surely he should be your first port of call."

Belittled, Caine carries on. "That's hard to answer, General."

"Has this anything to do with the two men that tried to kill your man last night?"

Aware he is being played, Caine grins deflated. "You're well informed, General."

"My operators keep me informed." Davison condescends. "Where do you stand on such a policy?"

Embittered by the words he is about to say, Caine grins and takes a restless breath. "You have the advantage over me, General."

Davison makes himself comfortable at having one-up on his British counterparts. "Let's get to the crux of your call. What do you want from me?"

"I don't know who I can trust, General."

"What about General Shirlow?" Davison adds, but Caine is aware he is being baited. "You are standing on Campbeltown Quay looking toward the cargo ship that bears the name of the Russian arms dealer you forgot to tell me about, are you not?"

With confirmation that the men are CIA, Caine glances over, feigning disinterest.

"I'm going to give you the benefit of my doubt," Davison said. "There's a well-built American vehicle parked to your side. Get into the rear, and it will bring you back to London. You've got five minutes."

He closes the call and presses to reconnect the first caller. "I've given him five minutes, then leave without him, Major," he said, placing the phone down.

A CIA man alights the Suburban and then opens the rear door as Caine glances between him and the Dimitri Rossakovich as he walks over, drawing his Remington to surrender as he gets into the rear.

***

CHAPTER 11

***

Ashley and Conners make their way through the busy ferry terminal in Larne as armed police officers, mistrusting everything, scrutinise everyone who passes, unnerving Conners as if they are waiting for them.

"I see by the armed officers that all is not well on the Emerald Isle?" she mumbles, amused, but he doesn't see their presence as good.

"Hatred and religion will always make sure of that, but armed Police on the streets of the UK aren't unusual these days," he explains with disquiet as they exit onto the street.

***

Davison sits behind his desk when the door opens, and Caine enters uncomfortably unnerved in the belief he had given in too easily.

"Colonel Caine," he blusters. "Please take a seat."

Bemused to hear Davison's true voice, Caine expects his host to stand and shake his hand, but the American remains seated, staring his mistrust of him.

"You're wondering what's going on?"

"You could say that, General."

"Then I will start at the beginning," Davison explains with an air of superiority. "We had intelligence on a Russian general selling arms to our many enemies and buying others to be used in the future, so we followed him when he left Russia for Switzerland. At first, he looked like he was on vacation until a familiar face appeared." Looking for any signs his visitor knows who he is talking about, he keeps his stare on Caine but doesn't receive any inclination of such. "General Shirlow."

The news that his friend is being accused of dealing in the illegal world of arms dealing shocks the normally unmoved Caine, who believes the intelligence is wrong.

"You don't believe me?"

"General Shirlow wouldn't betray the office he worked so hard to achieve," Caine defends, and Davison laughs patronisingly.

"There's nothing wrong with loyalty, as long as you've picked the right side, but we recorded him negotiating to buy two Russian S40e missiles," Davison adds, but Caine doesn't understand the significance.

"Even the loyalist among us are subject to the thrills of treason, Colonel, but I must say he's an enigma to me."

"Not General Shirlow, sir," Caine interrupts, determined that Davison or his intelligence is wrong. "It must have been a British intelligence mission, General. Since the Russians invaded Chechnya in 1994, then Georgia in 2008 and Crimea last year, we've been monitoring them closely."

"And when does Shirlow get off his ass to carry out such things?"

Caine is unsure how to answer and blurts out his words without thinking. "It's been known, General."

Davison gives Caine a disappointed look. "We know there are others involved. Mainly a Major Kilbride who is in command of a rapid reaction force based on the Mull of Kintyre in case the troubles in Ireland flare up again."

As the complexity of the unravelling conspiracy hits home, Caine's face twists in shock, but his only concern is that Ashley's stupidity has given up the SAS presence. "I don't know of such a unit," he said, playing down the most secret of operations, but Davison interrupted with glee. "Special Operations Kintyre, Special Air Service, which is abbreviated to SOKSAS, or if you prefer, Kintyre Oil."

Caine writhes in angst that such knowledge is known to a foreign intelligence agency. "That information is of the utmost secrecy, General. If the Irish were to find out, it could flare up the troubles in the province."

Davison prides himself on cooperating with the British intelligence community over many years and would never betray a trust. "You needn't worry. That information won't leave this room."

"I'm sure the PM will be pleased."

"He'll never know, I know," Davison said with an upbeat grin. "I'm not in this for praise. That's not the way I roll. I want those missiles and don't care who I take out to get them."

Caine shuffles uneasily. "I don't get it, sir. What would General Shirlow have to gain by this? He would lose everything he had worked so hard for."

"The oldest reason known to man," Davison explains. "Greed."

Caine cannot believe Shirlow would betray his country and everything he believes in. "He's far from poor, sir. He comes from aristocratic stock and is very affluent in his own right."

"That just adds to my reasoning."

"Who's he selling to?"

"We believe Irish terrorists."

Caine laughs uncomfortably. "That's even harder to believe."

"We don't know if it is Republicans or Loyalists?"

"I don't see him dealing with any terrorists, but the Irish, for fucks sake."

"My opinion of the general is he would sell his mother to the devil if it would help keep up his standard of life," Davison explains. "He's used many people to do his bidding; most probably don't know they've been pawns, like yourself and no doubt Major Kilbride and the assassins sent to kill your man." He stares curiously, but Caine remains motionless to the intended slur.

"Major Kilbride is SAS. So were the two men who tried to kill James and Colonel Conners."

"How do you know this?"

"I knew them. Phil Bright and Davy Westwood," Caine explains as he takes their IDs and wallets out to place on Davison's desk.

"What's this?"

"Proof, you might say, General."

Davison picks up one of the IDs and opens it to see Bright's photo, confirming that MI5 employs them. "What about Sergeant Ashley?" he questions, and Caine nods. "Not just a Fusilier?" he adds with a condescendingly knowing laugh. "So, he could be part of the SAS connection you have inferred to?"

"You can't think James Ashley could be part of this, General?" Caine said stupefied.

"Since he was thrust upon my OP by Shirlow," Davison said, then paused and smiled brightly. "I think I'll withhold my judgement until I get to know him better."

"I was his commanding officer, but I don't think he knew Bright or Westwood," Caine explains. "I recruited him into MI5 after." He pauses, not wanting to say anything about his friend that may incriminate him. "Where do you come into this, General? You said you had a tip-off about a Russian general selling arms to General Shirlow. Why didn't you pass that intelligence to MI5?"

"The same reason why I wasn't informed of the Dimitri Rossakovich," Davison said cynically.

"How did you get the tip-off?" Caine presses, but Davison has no intention of informing him.

"After MI6 informed MI5, Shirlow was obliged to inform the CIA due to the threat to the President's life, but unknown to them, we already knew of the plot and were looking into it. Knowing Shirlow's involvement, we approached him hoping he would lead us to the missiles."

"But he didn't," Caine adds, hoping to prove his commander's innocence.

"He hasn't moved from London. We have monitored him for weeks, but he hasn't spoken to anyone suspicious on the phone," Davison adds, downhearted that the intelligence received hadn't panned out. "Anyone we would be interested in that is."

"He's been in the game a long time. Probably has an idea he's under surveillance."

"We are the nasties in this game, so if he does have that inclination, he knows we will be gunning for him, and he knows our reputation and that we won't stop until we get him."

"Do you believe the missiles bought by the IRA are to be used to kill the President?" Caine questioned, unable to believe they would have such a capability.

"That's where the intelligence has taken us."

"The IRA wouldn't be stupid enough to assassinate the President. Too many Americans still believe in the Irish cause," Caine explains naively.

"Not all Americans would be sad to see their President dead," Davison explains with an awkward sense of the truth.

"But that would surely turn them against it."

"Since 9/11, many Americans look upon terrorism differently."

"Shit on your own doorstep would change most sympathisers' minds," Caine interrupts with a grin, but Davison believes the jibe was aimed at all Americans and stared his contempt.

"I believe so."

"But if you're talking about your militia types, I can't see them having any connection with the IRA."

"You keep saying IRA, Colonel. Do you know something I should be made aware of as there are many terrorist organisations still active on the Irish mainland?"

Caine smiles with confidence in the American's attempt to unnerve him. "If you mean about this, then no."

"Then why keep mentioning them?" Davison presses.

"They were my enemy for many years," Caine explains melancholically. "When I think of terrorism, they were the people who wanted to kill me, and I wanted to kill them."

Conscious of the troubles, Davison smiles unconcerned. "What about a planned accident to make the British Government look bad?" he adds, and Caine can see the global repercussions of an Anglo-American incident on British soil.

"That would work. So how are you going to stop this?"

"I'm going to find the missiles," Davison said confidently, and Caine smiled with hope.

"What about James and Colonel Conners?"

"They've gone off the grid."

"Don't you know where they are?" Caine questions, aware Davison knows more than he is letting on, but the American shakes his head convincingly. "What about General Shirlow?"

"At this moment, he's in his office wondering what has happened to his players."

"What about me?" Caine adds impatient to be a part of the action.

"You're out of the game," Davison blusters. "Best for you to stay here until it is over."

"I take it you don't trust me?"

"It's easy to say I trust anyone, but there is no way I am placing my operator's life on the line any more than necessary to achieve a successful outcome."

Feeling the room closing, Caine moves to the window to gaze at Roosevelt's monument below.

"We've got all mod cons to make your stay comfortable," Davison adds, unable to answer the question.

"I'd rather be out there helping James, General."

"He has all the help he needs for now," Davison said, and Caine turned curiously to receive a wry grin and wink in reply.

***

Northwest of Carncastle, just off Ballygoose road, the windmill overlooked Eallach farm and had been used as a vantage point for the Republican cause to spy on the British throughout the troubles.

Looking around lost, Ashley drives through the heavy rain and notices the windmill, confirming that he is in the right place. He pulls onto the grass verge and alights, followed by Conners, and they make their way cautiously along, conscious they may be under surveillance. Aware their approach is unorthodox to their situation, they move up a dirt track that leads to the barn, and Ashley stops outside to look around, amused at how he would never start a reconnaissance mission, but the time in hand had prevented any form of planning.

The barn is split into two levels, with numerous missing panels that allow the cold bracing wind to enter and is empty apart from some old rusted farm machinery and old milk churns in the corner with hay and straw strewn over the floor. They enter the darkness uneasily until

Ashley produces his key ring, with a little torch attached, and shines it enough to lighten the area.

"Are you sure we are in the right place?" she enquires above the level any operative would find unnerving on a recce.

"Keep it down. You're not in your office now," he replies in an exaggerated whisper as he moves to the door, but she keeps her stare insistent on an answer. "No, but this is the only place near the landing point, and Lieutenant Thomas mentioned the windmill."

They make their way up some rickety ladders to the higher level to settle and make themselves as comfortable as their surroundings will allow. Unimpressed by the dismal situation she finds herself in, Conners mutters with the apprehensive concern that they aren't where they need to be.

"What are you bitching about now?" he shouts higher than the volume he would want, which adds to her wretchedness as she argues with what she has in mind.

"You were the only one who saw the LZs coordinates. I think we are in the wrong place."

"We aren't!" Ashley grumbles confidently. "You saw the windmill."

"There could be hundreds of them around here."

"But there isn't," Ashley argues. "I checked Google Earth while in the hotel, and this was the only one near the coordinates, and this is the only barn they could meet in."

"They could meet in the middle of a field or, for that, the windmill itself."

"The distance to the windmill, being on the top of a steep hill, wouldn't give him the time on the ground to get up there and back, and they wouldn't be stupid to meet out in the open where they could be observed. Hence the barn."

"I'm not sure," she said, but he added confidently.

"We'll soon find out. Anyway, you looked at the same report as me, so if you didn't pick up on the relevant information, blame yourself and your training."

"Piss off, Jimmy," she shouts with venom as he takes his hip flask out and downs a mouthful of whisky. "Do you have to keep doing that?" she gripes, but his answer comes in another mouthful. "It would be nice to work with you when you're not pissed or high on pain meds," she adds, and even though her words cut deep into his professionalism, he keeps up his argumentative persona.

"You deal with life your way, and I will deal with mine the way I want."

"That's not dealing with it," she adds, but he can't see any other way. "That's riding the devil and one day, it will kill you."

The barn is lit up by a car's headlights approaching the farm track, and they cover themselves in hay and settle down.

"This conversation isn't over, Jimmy," she whispers, dogged, but his eyes show it is to him.

The car stops outside, followed by a door slamming and the mutterings of faint Irish voices as the barn doors open, and a rusted Vauxhall Insignia drives in and stops, followed by McInley, who closes the door as Flynn and Robbie alight.

"Robbie, the fucking light!" Flynn commands angrily, which instantly stands him out as the leader, and Robbie lights a lamp to brighten the area into many shadows and darkened corners. "That bastard will be here soon."

Robbie takes a Lee Enfield rifle out of the car boot, glances into the rain, then exits and closes the door behind them as he moves into the bushes to settle for a cold, damp wait. Flynn sits on an old milk churn and lights a cigarette to blow smoke rings into the air.

"Have you got one for me, Niall?" McInley mooches expectantly, but Flynn has no intention of sharing.

"Smoke your fucking own!"

"I ain't got any."

"Tough shit, dummy," Flynn adds, indifferent to his colleague's plight as the sound of a helicopter landing brings him to his feet in anticipation.

"Come on, Niall, I'm gagging for a smoke," McInley pleads as Flynn takes a heavy draw and then discards the cigarette across the floor for him to rush after and pick up.

Flynn shakes his head, disgusted. "You're a fucking low life." He draws his Webley. "Are you ready?"

McInley takes several draws and then drops the cigarette as he moves into the shadows to be grabbed around the mouth as a Sig Sauer P230 is pointed into his face to understand the threat instantly. He looks back nervously in recognition of Soames standing behind him.

There's a loud bang on the creaking door, and Flynn opens it to see Kilbride standing in the rain.

"Aren't you going to invite me in. It's rather inclement out here," Kilbride said with jest, and Flynn stood aside to allow him to enter the doorway.

Ashley's face turns red with rage as he witnesses the man he had trusted with his life cavorting with the people, peace process or not, he will always see as his enemy. He taps Conners on the shoulder and mouths the words. "Fucking Bastard," to her nodding agreement.

Kilbride shakes his head to throw rainwater all over a disgruntled Flynn, who, although annoyed, doesn't flinch. "Is it ever bright in this god-forsaken shit hole of a place?"

"Don't take the lord's name in vain, you English bastard."

"I'm a Scottish bastard, not English, you Irish bastard."

"Maybe it will wash some of the shit off you," Flynn said to Kilbride's amusement. "And when you Brits leave, and there is a United Ireland, the sun will never cease to shine.

"Good job, you're used to the rain then," Kilbride snipes and McInley sniggers giving away his position, but Soames grabs him tighter to not have his given away. "I take it that's your man hiding in the corner," he said without looking. "And the other idiot outside in the bushes. I take it you don't trust me, Mr Flynn?" he adds, but Flynn does not intend answering. "Well, why don't we leave the friendly banter aside for a while," he says cynically. "We've got more problems than two idiots playing hide and seek in the dark. I'm afraid I have bad news for you on the missiles."

"Oh, yeah?" Flynn interrupts expectantly through gritted teeth.

"We've been betrayed."

Flynn lifts his Webley to point into Kilbride's face.

"You've missed what I said, so let me enlighten you again so as not to be misunderstood," Kilbride adds calmly. "We have been betrayed."

Flynn pulls the Webley's hammer back.

"That isn't required."

"I'll be the judge of that."

"We have the missile, but the Russians have held back the guidance system."

Flynn bites his lip in disbelief as he grips his revolver tighter.

"They want another million."

Flynn laughs. "Pounds, Euros or Dollars?" His face straightens as the information hits. "You're telling me the Russians, who I have already paid one million Pounds, want another million?"

"I'm just the messenger."

"Are you?" Flynn adds with an ever-increasing mistrusting stare. "I think this extra million is a nest egg for your retirement. I'm not sure the missile is worth it."

"That depends on what you want it for."

Being the only one who knows his true intentions, Flynn shuffles uneasily. "That's none of your fucking business."

"And that's the way I like it," Kilbride said. "Kill me, and you'll lose all your money and the missile."

Flynn debates his best course of action, then lowers the revolver and paces off. "For all I know, I may already have lost it and may have to take my shot while I have you in my sights."

"It's on the mainland waiting."

"I will be on the mainland soon to pick it up."

"Not a problem as long as you bring the other million."

"I think you're taking me for a fool, but I will tell you this so you know where I stand. Another million will still be worth it, but if you're trying to fuck me, you will die painfully." He drops the hammer of his Webley and places it back into his belt. "Now, get the fuck out of here before I change my target."

"It's always nice to see you," Kilbride said as he moved off.

McInley exits the darkened corner but keeps glancing nervously to where he knows Soames is listening to the intelligence unfolding. "We should kill that prick," he feigns a hardness to impress the unimpressionable MI6 man.

Flynn fights the urge to chase Kilbride down and kill him. "He's safe for now."

"Some fucker's getting greedy," McInley adds to what Flynn angrily believes is obvious.

"Every fucker's greedy!"

Robbie enters as the helicopter lifting off echoes through the barn as it flies into the distance. "Why don't we kill him?"

"We will," Flynn said with glee. "After we get the missile." He walks to the car and opens the door. "It's far too important to jeopardise its delivery at this late hour."

"How are we going to get the extra money?" McInley questioned naively. "We struggled to make the first million."

Unaware of the roadblock in front of their plan, Robbie interrupts in shock. "Extra million? What the hell's going on?"

"Shut the fuck up!" Flynn shouts, turning to his loyal men. "I'm trying to think."

"How can we get a second million?" Robbie questions. "We cleaned ourselves out getting the first."

"I know where and have enough to last a long campaign," Flynn said as his face broke into a smile. "Sean will back us."

McInley glances into the corner, where he knows Soames is listening but doesn't want to introduce the clandestine man, aware that if he wants to show himself, he will.

"You think so?" Robbie questions. "I think he's going the way of the old guard and giving in."

McInley shakes his head to exaggerate his disagreement. "Sean will always help the cause."

"He will front me the money," Flynn explains confidently.

"He never struck me as a man who would go against the ruling army council," Robbie carries on, but Flynn won't have none of it, to McInley's relief.

"He's helped me numerous times without the army council's approval. He'll do anything for a United Ireland. It will be a loan until we can repay him with the money from the Morrison twins' robbery."

"I'd forgotten about that," Robbie said. "How's it going?"

"Our man reckons we will walk away with multi-millions of Pounds, Dollars, gold, silver, diamonds," Flynn answered. "Millions to fund our fight against the bloody British until I achieve the goal of a United Ireland." His ranting over, he gets into the rear of the car and closes the door as Robbie gets into the driver's seat, and McInley opens the barn door for the vehicle to reverse out.

Unable to make Soames out, McInley nods his subservience into the shadowy corner and then exits, closing the door behind, followed several seconds later by a car door slamming and driving off.

Ashley and Conners stand rubbing themselves down of the hay and straightening themselves out.

"What the hell's going on?" he said, but she was just as bewildered and didn't know how to answer. "We need to find this Sean before he fronts them the money."

"Do you know how many Irishmen have the name Sean?" she adds, dismayed to his nodding confirmation.

He takes a mouthful from his hip flask, but she decides not to continue the conversation she had threatened. "We can't go to Thames House and look up Sean of the IRA," he said with sarcasm she understands. "But he must be known to them."

They descend the ladders and move for the door.

"What about the Morrison twins?" she questions. "Who are they?"

"The only Morrison twins I know are the eccentric billionaires who head the Morrison Corporation," he answers. "They own, or have shares in, almost everything of significance."

"I know who you mean," she interjects. "They retired from business life and moved to their island off Bermuda."

"You don't hear from them these days, but they were notoriously ruthless in whatever they did," he explains with knowing. "There's more to this than we are being led to believe."

"How do you come to that conclusion, Jimmy?"

"Do you know who that was in there?" he questions.

"Kilbride?"

"No. The angry Irishman giving the orders?"

"How could I know that, Jimmy?"

Ashley grins with overconfidence. "Niall Flynn. A top IRA commander of old who is still a wanted man even after the ceasefire. He's dangerous and more than capable of bringing down the peace process. If we knew more about the missiles, I would have put a bullet in his head and ended it now."

"A bullet with no weapon," she teases, and he looks around for anything that could be used as a weapon. "You could have thrown a hay ball at him."

He stares his contempt as he exits, followed by her.

Conscious that if he is seen, his cover will be blown; Soames exits the darkness with his Sig Sauer strategically placed and moves to the door to see the danger moving off. He grins with accomplishment as he makes his way out of the rear, having been enthused by the intelligence of the Morrison robbery.

***

Ashley and Conners go to their car and look at each other over the top.

"At least we know who's buying."

"Do we? He could be a front for the real IRA."

"But they aren't active anymore," she said naively.

"The IRA has fractured into many branches. The official IRA say they aren't in the fight but have never stopped their terroristic ways, and Flynn will carry on the fight no matter what happens in the political arena. He'll not be doing this under their banner but some other fucking anti-British republican movement."

"An Irish republican terrorist cell getting help from a serving British Army officer," she debates, bemused. "That doesn't make sense."

"Especially considering who it was, but it wouldn't be the first time," he said as his mind raced over past events he had witnessed while on active service. "Corruption comes in many different forms and guises."

"Treason?" she adds, and he grimaces as their situation hits home. "I think you'll find what your friend is doing with this Irishman is treason."

Ashley's mind races back to his time in the regiment during the troubles. "I once had Flynn in my sights while on an OP in Armagh. Even then, we needed permission to engage, and when I requested ending the bastard's life, it was declined."

"Rules of engagement?" she mumbled, bemused by the hindrance of any army's ability to carry out total war.

"Why would a decorated British special forces officer, who had put his arse on the line for Queen and Country on numerous occasions, be dealing with a killer like Flynn?" he questions with what he can't answer himself.

"Money!" she shouts, then calms. "But he isn't my worry. We need to determine what's going on. We have two missiles. One is for an IRA splinter cell, but the other is an enigma. Obviously, the Irish will want theirs for a British target, so the other must be for the President."

"I agree to the first but who would want to assassinate your President?"

"You're shitting me, Jimmy?" she questioned with an awkward laugh. "Just about everyone who isn't American."

"Don't rule out your own people," he adds, straightening her face with understanding. "People don't look at the Presidents of the day as our fathers and grandfathers looked at Franklin Roosevelt.

"That's too near to the truth to be funny."

Believing he is out of his comfort zone with no one he can truly rely on, he speaks, having never taken the lead role of commander on an OP even though he had the rank and experience to do so. "What now then, Colonel? We've found the puppet but don't know who the master is pulling the strings."

"There's only one thing to do."

"And what's that?" he questioned, isolated and disillusioned. "We are stuck in the middle of nowhere with nowhere to go. Who do we inform?"

Conners' face straightens into a mischievous grin of knowing. "General Davison."

"Bull-shit! Why would I tell that arse anything?"

"Why not?"

"Why not Caine or Shirlow?"

"For one, he didn't send men to kill us," she argues, annoyed by the insult.

"Do we know that for sure?"

"It was you who recognised the assassins as MI5."

"They could have been guns for hire. How come you think Caine or Shirlow sent them?"

"It could have been both," she adds, but he would never believe his friend would betray him. "You can do what you want, Jimmy, but I intend to report to General Davison with or without you."

Ashley is reluctantly aware he has no one he can truly trust other than Conners, who, if she goes, will make him more vulnerable to another attempt at assassination. "We are in this together," he argues, making her laugh.

"Now we, are we? What happened to I?" she adds with a mischievous grin. "What are we going to do? We don't have any authority to change the outcome," she adds, putting the onus on the word 'we' each time.

"I see your point, but only because there's no other option open to us."

"So now it's us?"

"Quit your bile!" he snipes. "But if the shit hits the fan, it will be all down to you."

"I accept full responsibility," she adds confidently, but he still doesn't see it as their best option. "That's what comes with rank."

"How do you intend to approach the general?"

"There's a helicopter waiting for us at Belfast airport."

With the realisation he had been played, Ashley turned agitated to find out how long he had been the patsy.

"General Davison sent it just in case we needed it," she said, amused by the Englishman's mannerisms.

"I get the feeling I'm being pulled from both ends and not in an enjoyable way," he said, but his attempt at humour dismayed her at the thought of his sexual connotation and she shook her head as he restarted the engine and drove off.

***

CHAPTER 12

***

Having been transported to the US Embassy in London, Ashley and Conners sit in Davison's office, waiting for him to appear. Showing the boredom, the isolation is taking on him; he looks around until his eyes fixed on her. "I don't believe this!" he shouts, irritated by her nonplussed relaxed demeanour. "We race down here only to sit on our arses for hours waiting."

"The general's a busy man, Jimmy," she explains to his ever-increasing frustration.

"We haven't even been offered a fucking cup of coffee."

"Shut up, Jimmy. Everything that comes out of your mouth is a whinge."

"And everything that comes out of yours is a bitch," he snipes to her amusement at getting a rise out of him.

Davison enters, and Conners stands attentively, but Ashley remains seated and pulls his right foot onto his knee, disrespecting the important man who waves for Conners to relax. "Sorry to keep you."

"I don't know about the colonel," Ashley gripes. "But I don't like sitting around with my finger up my arse."

Aware Ashley's words were aimed at him; Davison turns his gaze onto him but ignores the disrespect. "Good one, Jimmy."

"That's James, Captain," Ashley said scathingly, downgrading the general's rank, adding to Davison's entertainment.

Only having heard his name in its slang form from his operator, Davison turns to Conners. "Not Jimmy or the Limey or the whinging Brit?"

"What is it with you, Yanks? You don't seem able to get a name right."

"And for the record, Sergeant," Davison adds, deadly serious. "I'm neither a general nor a captain." As Ashley's eyes turn, he sits back in his comfortable chair, determined to discover what he means. "Around here, they call me director."

"Director?" Ashley questions, shocked. "I take it of the CIA?" He looks between Conners and Davison, who shakes his head unwilling to give away more information.

"Excuse Jimmy, Director. He doesn't know what respect means, having been part of an armed rabble for a long time."

"An armed rabble you wish you had under arms," Ashley quips to Davison's nodding amusement.

"Yeah?" Conners argues, and Ashley nods his patronising answer, which forces Davison to interrupt and end the petty squabble that leaves them staring contemptuously at each other.

"What did you find out?"

"We went to the barn as said, Director," Conners answers subserviently, which amuses Ashley.

"You've been in touch with him all this time?"

"Of course," Davison answers promptly. "My operators keep me informed."

"Operators?" Ashley said, confused by the terminology.

"Because they operate under my instruction."

Ashley laughs at the self-aggrandising thought. "Even after we got rid of our phones?"

"I prefer it that way, and what would be the point of being a director if not to direct?"

Ashley turns to Conners. "I take it you're not a desk jockey?"

Conners still doesn't want to give away too much information about herself and condescends her answer. "Like you, Jimmy, I follow orders."

"I wouldn't be surprised if you're not a woman?" Ashley questions with mirth. "Are you even a colonel?" he adds, uncaring of the answer, but she ignores him and turns to Davison.

"We overheard three Irishmen and Kilbride discussing one of the missiles."

"That's interesting."

"The main terrorist is Niall Flynn. Jimmy says he's a top IRA commander still wanted by the British."

"IRA?" Davison mutters, alerted by the mention of the Republican movement again. "I was under the illusion they had laid down their arms since the Good Friday agreement, and their members had been given an amnesty."

Ashley answers quickly to represent the honour of the uniform he wore for many years. "Not Flynn. He's fanatical and won't stop until he gets his goal of a United Ireland."

"One man's terrorist is another man's freedom fighter," Davison said, then laughed as if giving away a part of his soul. "At least some idiot quoted that as any man who fights against the United States is a terrorist in my eyes."

"Sounds like your war of independence in reverse," Ashley criticises as he takes his hip flask out and turns to Conners for a reaction.

"I know the colonel has looked over your excessive drinking, but I have no intention of doing so, so put that away in my presence," Davison orders and Ashley, using exaggerated animation, opens the hip flask to take a large drink without another word then carries on as if he hadn't been chastised.

"And your country's foreign policy to date."

Believing he should explain his outburst, Davison turns his ire on Ashley, but Conners beats him to the punchline.

"So, you keep saying, Jimmy, but you don't know what you are talking about."

"As the general, err, the director said, it's only terrorism if it's against you, Yanks. Two hundred years in the shadows, then you are attacked, and suddenly, it's your forte. If you didn't have an enemy, you would cease to exist. First, there was us, then the Mexicans, the Germans, the Japanese."

"Alright, Jimmy," Conners snipes, but he carries on without taking a breath.

"The Koreans, the Vietnamese, the Cubans."

"Alright, Jimmy!"

"Iranians, Iraqis, Afghans. Did I miss anyone? Surely a five-year-old in some third-world country is playing with a catapult with a drone bearing down on him?"

"I don't think I like this joker," Davison snipes, but Ashley is determined to be heard.

"You're not meant to like me, Director! You're meant to direct the likes of me."

"A man of conscience," Davison adds condescendingly. "How did you get your role at MI5?"

"I'm the cannon fodder sent to pull the ruling classes, like yourself, out of the shit."

Amused at the thought of ever being a member of the ruling classes, Davison had worked his way up from nothing and grins, humoured that he likes the Englishman.

"Oh, and let's not forget the most important of all. Native Americans and African Americans. All men are born equal, my arse."

"Alright, James! We get your point." Davison shouts, aware they are going off script, but Conners sees the opportunity to end the petty bickering.

"Kilbride informed Flynn that the Russians have withheld the guidance system and want another million Pounds for it."

Davison ponders his knowledge of Russia since the fall of the Iron Curtain. "Interesting but unlikely. The average arms dealer wouldn't disparage his name by bickering over trivialities like money. Respect and reputation are what open doors in the world."

"They intend to gain the funds from either a man named Sean or the Morrison twins," Conners interjects, and the mention of the philanthropist British twins catches Davison's attention.

"Sean could be anyone, but the Morrison twins can only be the billionaire British philanthropists who have worked closely with the American and British governments. What could all this have to do with them?"

"I doubt they have Irish Republican sympathies," Ashley interjects, and Conners continues.

"They intend to rob them and have a man on the inside for such an intent."

"That opens doors that will need further looking into," Davison said calmly before looking between his operators. "If it's going to fund future terrorist activity," he adds hastily.

"This is on top of the original million," Ashley adds with the obvious.

"The Russians were paid five hundred thousand Pounds for both missiles," Davison explains. "Which is way cheaper than their true value."

"So, Flynn could be right," Conners said, looking at Ashley for confirmation. "Kilbride is creaming off the top."

"Kilbride and Flynn only discussed one missile," Ashley adds. "The other's a mystery."

Believing he knows the second missile's destination, Davison grins confidently.

"Do you know who the buyer is?" Ashley said as his glance shifted to Conners. "Don't tell me she knows."

Conners looks to Davison for his approval, and he nods back.

"General Shirlow," she said, and Ashley laughed in disbelief.

"By the way, the men who tried to kill you in Scotland were ex-SAS," Davison adds as he turns to Ashley. "Phil Bright and Davy Westwood. Did you know them?"

Knowing he is mistrusted, Ashley shakes his head after pondering their names. "I didn't know everyone in the regiment. Maybe Colonel Caine will know them."

"He does," Davison answered, heightening Ashley's curiosity.

"Where does he fit into this?"

"As far as I have been led to believe, he doesn't."

"Shit!" Ashley shouts as it dawns on him. "He'll be in Kintyre."

"He's downstairs enjoying our hospitality," Davison interrupts to Ashley's bewilderment. "We brought him from Kintyre. In from the cold, you might say."

"So, he's safe?" Ashley questioned, to Davison's amusement.

"He doesn't think so. He'd rather be in a firefight with the Taliban than here as our guest."

"When you say, guest. Do you mean prisoner?" Ashley adds with sarcastic intent, and Davison shakes his head in vigorous denial. Feeling the claustrophobia of being a prisoner, he moved to the window to look at the freedom it beholds.

"The thing is, Director, Flynn doesn't have the extra million to pay for the missile."

"That's not good for him. If we could trust MI5 or MI6, we could ask them," Davison adds solemnly as he eyes his operators. "You'll have to leave that with me."

"That I am pleased to do," Ashley said as he moves for the door.

"What now, Director?" Conners interjects, but Ashley interrupts, not giving him a chance to answer.

"Can I see Jack?"

Davison looked at Conners, who believed it to be a good idea and nodded. "I don't see why not. I will see you get an escort."

"So, the mistrust comes all the way down to me?" Ashley confirms, but Davison carries on with a laugh.

"In this building, I get escorted. Oh, and I will see you get a cup of coffee, and I understand you will want sugar."

As it dawns on him that he is under surveillance, Ashley stares at Davison but doesn't rise to his words.

***

CHAPTER 13

***

Reading an old copy of Janes defence weekly, Caine sits on a sofa and looks up as Ashley enters. "James, you old bastard. So, they've put you in this prison too?" He stands, and they shake hands with genuine affection for their friendship.

"Surely, you aren't under duress, Colonel?"

"I volunteered!" Caine said with an awkward grin. "Mind you, I don't think I had much choice. Have you heard anything from General Shirlow?"

"No, but I wouldn't expect to."

"The Yanks believe he paid the Russians for the missiles, and Kilbride is his go-between."

"The Irish paid, he negotiated," Ashley adds to Caine's amusement that he knows.

"Two missiles in their murdering hands. I don't believe it."

"They're only getting one," Ashley explains, catching Caine's increasing attention. "The Yanks aren't sure who the second is for."

"He's probably sold it to fucking Al Qaeda."

Finding humour in the irony, Ashley and Caine laugh in unison.

"They bought two missiles for half a million Pounds and have sold one to the Irish for two million."

"Two million?" Caine interjects, shocked at such an amount.

"The Russians want another million."

"Hold on. Who's buying and who's selling?" Caine interrupts, insistent on an immediate answer. "If the Russians have already been paid half a million, how come they want more?"

"For the guidance system," Ashley explains to Caine's disbelief. "They believe Shirlow has pocketed the money."

"That's some fucking coal."

"What?"

"Nothing," Caine adds to play down his words.

"The Yanks believe one is to be used on their President."

"They've put two and two together and come up with seven. I can't believe General Shirlow and Major Kilbride have anything to do with this."

"All evidence to the contrary," Ashley said as he moved to Caine and whispered. "Be aware, Colonel, we are under surveillance."

Caine looks at the camera in the corner that has them zoomed in.

"They trust no one."

Ashley follows his stare, takes his hip flask out to take a large mouthful of the whisky, and then lifts it in salute. "You can't blame them for that, but the sooner I get out of here, the better." He hands the hip flask to Caine, who gazes at it in remembrance before taking a mouthful and handing it back.

"You like the cheapest whisky, James," Caine said, and Ashley grinned unmoved. "I take it you have plans?"

"I'm getting the earliest train back to Newcastle."

"What about your role at MI5?"

"What role?" Ashley said solemnly. "I don't know why I allowed you to persuade me into this shit."

***

Staring at a monitor, Conners and Davison stand in Davison's office, listening to Ashley and Caine talking.

"Do you trust him?" he enquires as he turns his full attention onto her, and she answers without hesitation.

"I do, Director." Aware that Davison knows about Ashley's excessive alcohol and pain medication, she debates her words to come. "He's all spit and bile, but I believe that's a front to hide his true feelings," she adds, but the director's face shows he needs to hear more. "He knows all the protagonists in this story and maybe able to put the pieces together for us that we don't know."

"That makes him more vulnerable in my mind. Also, he could be one of them."

"I don't believe so, Director."

Davison debates all he has witnessed. "What about his drinking?" he said, ashen-faced, and she turned to him. "And he seems to be taking copious amounts of pain medication that don't seem to work."

"Those two aside, Director, I believe he'll be a good asset on our side in this fight."

"Then I will withhold my judgement," he adds, but she sees that the consequences will all be on her if the Englishman messes up. "Inform them of Shirlow and Kilbride. See if you get a rise out of them." Conners nods and then exits, and Davison turns back onto the monitor.

***

Ashley and Caine sit on the sofa with their backs to the camera as they whisper of better days when the door opens, and Conners enters.

"Hide, here comes agent one of the CIA," Ashley said with a laugh, and Caine added to the misplaced humour she misses.

"What a lovely organisation it is."

"Cut the crap, Jimmy!" she shouts seriously. "There's business at hand."

"Well, get on with it and leave us alone," Caine adds to Ashley's amusement.

"I wish I could, but Jimmy's part of this."

"Am I fuck!" Ashley calls out, shocked. "I'm not with the CIA."

"That's obvious by your shitty attitude."

Ashley looks at Caine, who laughs. "What's wrong with having a shitty attitude?"

"You're a cantankerous fucker, Jimmy, and for the record," she carries on determined to Caine's amusement. "As I have told you, I'm not with the CIA, but the director would still like your help."

"Who's this we then?" Ashley said, disbelieving as he took his hip flask out to take a mouthful, and Conners looked at the camera, aware that Davison's condescending eyes were fixed on her. "CIA, NSA, FBI, ABC, 123," he adds immaturely. "The mighty Central Intelligence Agency wants the help of a broken-down British infantryman?" he questions. "Well, it can fuck off because I'm going home as soon as you release me from this prison. I don't want to miss Newcastle playing at St James' on Saturday."

Caine wants out of his imposed incarceration but doesn't want to be left out in the cold. "What about me? In a past life, I was also a broken-down British infantryman," he interjects, but she ignores him.

"Shirlow and Kilbride have disappeared," she said as her eyes shifted between them, hoping to gain evidence they were already aware of. "Do either of you have any ideas?"

Ashley and Caine look at each other with confirmation that they are mistrusted.

"They'll have known you were onto them," Caine answers. "They didn't get to where they are by being fools," he adds as her attention turns to Ashley.

"I told the director, you know Kilbride."

"Director?" Caine said, and Ashley shook his head for him not to continue his inquiry.

"I know him well," Ashley answers. "Couldn't say I ever liked him, though," he adds, but she knows he isn't speaking the truth.

"Can you stop the constant misdirection?" Conners shouts. "Director

Davison wants to know where they may have gone?"

Wanting to distance himself from the traitors, Ashley interjects his innocence, hoping that release will come soon. "How could we know? We've been here for ages and still haven't had that coffee I was promised."

Conners' mistrusting eyes shift between Ashley and Caine. "Are you prepared to help us find your friends?"

"Am I fuck," Ashley shouts, but Caine isn't sure.

"Then you're no good to us and will be here until we can close this all down."

"You can't hold me," Ashley protests impotently. "I'm going home."

"Of course you are, Jimmy," Conners said as she moved off. "I look forward to reading about your escape."

"And how long will that be?" Ashley questioned, concerned, as all he intended to do was get to his bedsit in London and pack to get home to Newcastle.

"How long's a piece of string, Jimmy? You've done nothing to instil us with trust," Conners said, even though she was aware Ashley's help had got them this far, and she turned to exit, but Caine shouted, stopping her.

"Didn't you have them under surveillance?"

"Not Kilbride. He was new to the game and disappeared before we could put anything in place."

"What about General Shirlow?"

"We lost him at Heathrow," Conners mutters, embarrassed even though she had nothing to do with the surveillance on him.

"Did he get on a plane?"

Her embarrassment escalating, Conners answers. "We are looking into it, but we can't exactly ask your security services or the BAA where he went."

Caine turns to Ashley. "Can you remember what Kilbride used to brag about?" he questions, but having never had a conversation with his major about anything other than military matters, Ashley shakes his head, bewildered. "His family home in Scotland," he adds as if reminding Ashley of something he must have forgotten, which makes him laugh.

"Of course, I'd forgotten how often I visited for tiffin and cucumber sandwiches."

Ignoring Ashley's humour, Caine carries on. "From what I can remember, it's in the middle of nowhere."

"The flight lieutenant said he dropped the cargo off in Scotland, and two men picked it up."

"No doubt Bright and Westwood!" Caine said to Ashley's interest. "If I remember rightly, it's somewhere in Strathclyde, east of Ayr."

"How do you know about Stan and Ollie?" Ashley questions.

"I saw their bodies when I went to meet you."

Ashley's interest turns on Conners, who doesn't understand, and he turns on Caine. "They were the goons you sent to pick me up."

Caine tetchily explains that he is being accused of coercion in the attempt at Ashley and Conners' lives. "General Shirlow sent them. I only knew them from my days with the regiment."

"Have either of you been to Kilbride's home?" Conners presses as she looks for answers, but all they can do is shake their heads in unified denial. "Didn't you get the coordinates off the helicopter's report, Jimmy?" she snipes as he turns his ire on her.

"Yeah, as if I knew what to look for."

"A good operator would have read everything on that report," Conners snipes, and Caine laughs at Ashley's irritation.

"Operator, my arse. I remember your neck almost breaking to look over my shoulder."

"And I seem to remember you turning your back on me," Conners argues, but he was having none of it.

"You're a woman! You had enough time to read it all, so how didn't you note them down?"

"It shouldn't take long to find out now that we have an idea," Caine interrupts to break up the petty bickering. "Just a few phone calls and we will have it."

"No phone calls," Conners instructs with determination to be heard. "We don't want anyone finding out what we are planning."

***

A UH60 Black Hawk of the United States Air Force sits at RAF Northolt, Ruislip, Greater London, with its rotors turning as Ashley, Conners, and Caine run across the tarmac and climb on board to put on their headphones as it takes off and flies into the distance. They sit next to a crewman and prepare for their noisy trip in the comfort-free flying bucket, which travels flat out at 180mph.

"We need more firepower," Ashley said, looking around. "If Kilbride's there, he'll be ready for every eventuality."

"This bird is well-armed," the crewman said, handing them all M4 carbines, which Ashley and Caine rapidly set up for action.

"Kilbride's no mug," Ashley adds soberly, which isn't lost on Conners, who turns her constantly irritated ire onto him.

"Do you want us to drop you off, Jimmy?"

"Yeah, Newcastle's on the way. Drop me off at HMS Calliope on the quayside, and I will make my way from there."

"As if that's going to happen."

"Fucking Yanks!" Ashley shouts. "Always going in shit first. You see it on the telly. The LAPD gets a call that someone's taking a piss in the street."

"Alright, Jimmy," Conners interrupts, tired of his whinging.

"Next minute, he's surrounded by SWAT, forty cars with lights and sirens blaring, two helicopters above and a B52 circling with its bomb bay doors open."

"Alright, Jimmy. We gung-ho Americans get your point, but it's a lot better than the Metropolitan Police turning up on a bicycle," she said, making Caine laugh, but her face stayed emotionless as Ashley contributed with a snigger.

"I wish I could argue but don't forget Kilbride is a major in the finest fighting force this world has ever produced. He shouldn't be taken lightly."

"The US Marine Corps?" Conners said for Ashley and Caine to shout their derision in unison, and she laughed, having got a rise out of them. "Oorah! There's a support helicopter following."

"So why didn't we wait?"

Showing Ashley's sarcasm had hurt her sensibilities, Conners answers straight-faced. "Director Davison was worried in case Kilbride was urinating and thought we'd better get there fast before the B52s bomb the shit out of his home."

"You wouldn't have thought that at the embassy when we were sitting with our fingers up our arses," Ashley adds to the American's disdain.

"I wouldn't worry anyway; they'd probably hit Glasgow."

"You may have had your fingers up your asses, Jimmy, but Director Davison was working hard at finding where these missiles are."

"But in the end, it was down to us mere foot soldiers of the British Army to pull you out of the shit," Ashley said as he and Caine laughed at her touchiness.

***

Six miles east of Auchinleck, Strathclyde, Kilbride's cottage sits in a remote part of the Scottish countryside that suits his life while away from the regiment. A brand-new Range Rover and Kilbride's trusted 1968 Land Rover sit parked on the driveway leading for miles to the A76 that cuts through the county's middle. Sipping whisky and enjoying the tranquillity of their isolation, Kilbride and Shirlow sit in the lounge talking about the good old days when they hear a car approaching. Kilbride picks up an MP5 and moves to the window. "Put that down, Major!" Shirlow commands his over-anxious colleague. "It's only Flynn."

Nervously aware of what had transpired with him and the mad Irishman, Kilbride, turns shocked. "What's he doing here, General?"

"I invited him."

Kilbride places the MP5 on the sideboard but keeps it within reach. "What for? I don't want him knowing where I live."

"I wouldn't worry about the Fenian bastard having that knowledge. He won't retain it for long," Shirlow said with intent. "Plus, with all the money you are in line to receive, you won't be living here much longer."

Kilbride looks around his family home and hideaway from the twenty-first century with sadness at the thought of leaving. "But we can't trust him."

Shirlow grins disbelieving. "More than he can trust us, but things had to be brought forward if we want to succeed."

Wanting to get things over with, Kilbride enquires. "When do we get paid, sir?"

Shirlow moves to the window as a Ford Mondeo drives up and stops. "When we get to Geneva." He pauses in traumatised thought. "All those years for Queen and country! What a fucking idiot when I could have been as corrupt as this country's leaders." He laughs. "When that missile hits number ten, we'll at least be rid of the bastards."

Not having been made privy to the intended target of the Irish missile, Kilbride questions it in shock, and Shirlow laughs with accomplishment the Scotsman can't see as a positive.

"Hopefully when Cobra is meeting, but that's for reasons of a personal nature."

Kilbride's mind haunts him with his service to the colours. "All my mates killed by the IRA. I've sold them all out."

"I haven't put much thought into it. Especially as their target will be the corrupt government that sent your mates to be killed."

***

Flynn and Robbie alight the Mondeo to gaze upon the cottage and the surrounding area's quaintness as if they had been removed from the real world.

"Let's go and see what these Brit bastards have to say."

"I don't trust them, Niall," Robbie adds nervously about what they are walking into.

"Keep it that way. They are still our enemy."

"Should I take my gun?" Robbie questions, making Flynn turn angrily onto him.

"You'd be a fucking idiot if you didn't!"

Robbie opens the boot and takes out his Beretta as Flynn reaches into his belt to confirm the presence of his Webley.

The cottage door opens, and Shirlow exits, waving an exaggerated welcome to the visitors he usually wouldn't have any time for. "Good to meet you at last, Mr Flynn," he blustered, ever the diplomat who would shake the hand of the devil if it would get him what he wants, and he reaches for his enemy's hand, but Flynn has no intention of carrying out what his late father would see as treason against the cause. Having only spoken to each other over the telephone, Flynn recognises Shirlow's condescending voice. "If it isn't my favourite Englishman," he said, but apathetic to the slur, Shirlow lowered his hand.

"Hopefully, when I get to know you a little better, I will be able to call you my favourite Irishman."

Amused by their hatred of each other, Flynn smiles with menace as Shirlow stands aside to allow them to enter.

***

Flynn and Robbie enter the lounge, followed by Shirlow, to find Kilbride standing at the window, glancing at the MP5 as he takes hold of his holstered Glock.

"I believe you know each other," Shirlow introduces, but he notices Flynn staring his hatred of Kilbride. "You look troubled, Mr Flynn."

"I'm struggling to come up with the extra money," Flynn explains tentatively. "I've set a plan in motion, but you'll have to give me more time."

"What extra money?" Shirlow questions bemused, and Flynn's glance shifts rapidly between him and Kilbride.

"The extra million for the Russians," Flynn explains, but Shirlow's expression looks for confirmation of his words.

"For the guidance system," Kilbride interrupts, looking at a betrayed Shirlow, hoping he will go along with his ploy.

"Will they give me more time?" Flynn enquires as Shirlow moves to the window and draws his Browning Hi-Power. "I will get the money. I

mean, the fucking missile's useless without the guidance system."
Aware it could only have been Kilbride who had put that notion in the Irishman's head, Shirlow shoots his colleague in the chest to knock him to the floor, writhing in pain. "What were you thinking, Major?" he mumbles with extreme calm as Robbie fumbles to draw his Beretta to point. "You've been misinformed, Mr Flynn," he adds as he disarms Kilbride of his Glock.

Flynn draws his Webley slowly and pulls back the hammer to point at Shirlow as he moves to the sideboard, places Kilbride's gun on top, and then holsters his own.

"The Russians aren't after any more money," Shirlow explains to Flynn's bewilderment as the Englishman lifts his hands submissively to show he is no longer a threat. "The missile and the guidance system are waiting for you."

Angered at being deceived, Flynn lashes out at the furniture, but Shirlow remains calm as he turns his stare onto Kilbride.

"He lied to you, but for my life, I don't know why?"

"He could have fucked my plan up."

"You can lower your revolver now, Mr Flynn. I assure you it isn't required."

As his mistrust takes a tighter hold, Flynn reluctantly lowers the hammer and places his Webley at his side but keeps it tightly clenched in his hand. "So, the Russians don't want any more money?" he questioned with exasperated relief.

"I am pleased to say they don't," Shirlow confirms.

Unable to understand the intended deceit, Flynn moves to Kilbride and kicks him in the stomach, making him scream in pain. "You fucking bastard!" He signals Robbie to holster his Beretta as he walks to the window. "What's up?"

"I can hear something," Robbie said as a helicopter could be heard nearing. "It's a fucking chopper!"

"Don't worry about it," Shirlow explains to calm the already tense situation. "It will be the police helicopter passing over."

"It's military!"

"Are you sure?" Shirlow questioned as he moved to the window to search the sky.

"He's seen enough of them to know the difference," Flynn interjects. Aware there aren't any military bases nearby, Shirlow looks out as a Black Hawk comes into view. "It's American. No doubt a present from that bastard Davison."

"Who the fuck's Davison?" Flynn demands as he lifts the Webley offensively and pulls back the hammer.

"He's my problem but don't allow their presence to change your plan," Shirlow explains as he produces car keys to throw at Flynn to catch. "The Range Rover outside has the missile inside. Get yourselves out of here."

***

The Black Hawk flies over the cottage and hovers a short distance off as a crewman opens the side door for Ashley to look out. "There are three motors down there!"

"Can you see anyone?" Conners shouts, and Ashley's eyes fix on Shirlow exiting the cottage without concealing his identity to stand in the open.

"It's fucking Shirlow."

"Get us onto the ground!" Conners orders and the Black Hawk moves sideways to an adjacent field where Ashley, Conners and Caine are quickly out, carrying their M4s, to take up offensive positions with views of the cottage. Conners turns to the crewman, who sits in the doorway with an M134 GAU-17 Gatling gun pointing and gives hand signals for them to get back up to cover their approach. The crewman nods his understanding, and the helicopter rises slowly to take up its protective position.

***

Shirlow opens the boot of the Range Rover and pulls out an AT4 84mm portable shoulder launch missile and takes aim at the Black Hawk and fires for the rocket to fly through the air and hit the tail rotor, which instantly sends the twenty-two million Dollar machine into a spin, with the concussion of the explosion so violent it throws Conners to the ground as Ashley and Caine dive for cover further off as it comes to earth with a belly-flopping bang and explodes into a giant ball of flames to set the surrounding area on fire and coldly take the lives of the four crew. Conners scurries across the ground as Ashley dives next to her in panic for her safety, and she rolls over, distressed at the Black Hawk engulfed in flames with black smoke billowing.

"Are you alright?" Ashley said, and she nodded her reply. "Well then, get off your fucking arse!" he shouts as he stands. "We still have a fucking job to do."

Flynn and Robbie exit the cottage as Shirlow throws the missile casing aside and laughs hysterically.

Uncaring of the lives taken, Shirlow shouts with a broad smile of accomplishment. "They're on foot now. Get out of here as fast as you can before they regroup."

Robbie gets into the Mondeo as Flynn gets into the Range Rover, and they drive off, leaving the general looking around casually as he enters the cottage.

As the Mondeo and the Range Rover race down the driveway, Caine steps from the foliage and opens fire with his M4 for its 5.56mm bullets to smash into the Mondeo's thin shell that, forces it off the road and into a tree to catch fire. He lowers the M4 but brings it back to eye as the Range Rover passes, and he puts his last three rounds through the rear window when the magazine clicks empty, and throws it aside to draw his Remington and carries on firing until the car is out of range. He walks to the Mondeo and watches the body inside burning with no intention of helping as Ashley and Conners walk over and take in the heat.

"Was that Shirlow?" Conners enquires, but neither Caine nor Ashley has an opinion as they look at the Range Rover heading into the distance.

"I assume he'd be in the Range Rover," Ashley explains to a dismayed and frantic Conners as her head shifts around.

"So, he got away?"

"Looks that way," Caine said as he followed her stare to the cottage.

"Who do you think was in this?" Ashley enquires pointing at the Mondeo, and Caine answers, unhappy with the thought of taking his friend's life.

"I get the feeling it was Kilbride."

Saddened that his old colleague may be dead, Ashley takes his hip flask out and takes a large mouthful. "Until the driver's identified, we go off they both got away," he interjects to Caine's amusement at him barking out command decisions he isn't known for.

Conners cocks her Colt and heads toward the cottage with Ashley, but Caine stays staring curiously in the direction the Range Rover travels.

***

With an air of supreme accomplishment that all was going to plan, Shirlow stands on a hill overlooking the cottage and burning helicopter and smiles delightedly at a job well done as he moves off with a long walk to freedom ahead of him.

***

Ashley and Conners enter the cottage into Kilbride's private life and into the lounge to find the man lying in a pool of blood, but neither goes to his aid.

"Kilbride," Ashley said, initially shocked as he bore down on his ex-colleague.

"That's all the treacherous bastard deserved," Conners said, believing him dead, but he groaned in pain.

"He's still alive," Ashley adds, stopping Caine in the doorway as he draws his Remington to keep him covered.

Kilbride smiles through the pain. "Nice to see some friendly faces."

"Hardly, you treacherous bastard!" Ashley sneers, uncaring of his old friend, who groans and then laughs his discomfort. "I hope that fucking hurts."

"You've got it wrong, James. I'm one of the good guys," Kilbride pleads, making Ashley laugh, but Conners remains straight-faced and emotionless. "Who do you think informed the Yanks of the missiles?" he adds to Conners' instant interest. "I told them of a plot to kill the President."

"Bull-shit!" Ashley shouts, but Conners moves him aside.

"Let him talk, Jimmy."

"I had to stop the missiles."

"Why would you stop your payday?" Conners asked, unconvinced, and Kilbride shuffled uncomfortably, unsure whether to answer.

"Shirlow knew I'd been a bad boy."

"Don't believe the fucker!" Ashley shouts, but Conners angrily calls his name to quieten him.

"He found out I had sold military equipment to pay off a gambling debt and blackmailed me, and I've been doing his bidding ever since. At first, it was just a bigger set-up than the one I had but more lucrative."

"So, you were making money?" Ashley snarls, but Kilbride believes himself guiltless as his eyes fix on Caine entering.

"Then he changed the goalposts and brought in the IRA, which I couldn't stand for."

"General Shirlow is heading up an arms ring?" Caine implied, directing his question at the major whose attention fixes on him.

"If it isn't my old friend, Colonel Jack Caine," Kilbride mumbles as he attempts to get comfortable. "All I know is he bought arms from a Russian general."

"General Leonid Klamenkovich," Conners understood with knowing.

"I don't know names," Kilbride said, playing down the intensity of his involvement, but Conners needs to hear more.

"What about the missiles?"

"Up until the missiles, it had only been small arms."

"To the fucking Irish!" Ashley screams, gaining Kilbride's full attention. "And who the fuck else?"

"I wouldn't deal with the Provos, James. They've killed far too many of my mates, your mates, for me to stoop so low."

"I remember them all, and I hope you do, and I hope they haunt your every waking moment, you piece of shit."

"How could I forget?" Kilbride said solemnly, but Ashley was far from finished.

"Then answer me this. Who the fuck is Niall Flynn if not a Provo of the lowest form?"

Kilbride can't comprehend how Ashley could connect Flynn to him and attempts to deflect the accusation that links them. "I was being blackmailed, James."

"You've pissed on their graves, you fucking bastard."

"We sold to third parties in Africa, Iraq and the like."

"No doubt Islamic state, so that they can kill our soldiers."

"And the Russians?" Conners adds to Kilbride's unease as he looks around, pleading in the hope of sympathy.

"Shirlow had me by the short and curlies. I had the choice of money or being dropped in the shit, which would have seen the end of my career, and me sent to Colchester for a long time."

"And you took the easy option and sold out?"

"Too fucking right! Shit stinks; money doesn't."

"Hold your petty squabbling!" Conners interrupts angrily as she stares at Ashley as her intelligence thinking mind takes over.

"Why inform on what was going on?" Caine questioned, but Kilbride didn't know what he was referring to.

"Just answer the fucking question!" Ashley gripes. "Why inform on illegal activity that you are up to your balls in?"

Kilbride thinks over the question. "I thought if the Yanks heard of a threat to their President, they would be able to stop Shirlow. I couldn't go to MI5 or MI6, so I phoned St Petersburg garrison hoping the CIA would be listening."

"But it was MI6, and they informed MI5," Conners explains, shocking Kilbride. "The CIA only got brought in because Shirlow was obliged to inform them."

"I didn't know that, but at least my plan worked in the end."

Amused, Ashley interrupts. "You could have dropped yourself right in the shit."

Kilbride lifts his blood-covered hands in an attempt at mirth, but Conners interrupts showing where her interest lies.

"What about the plot to assassinate the President?"

"I made it up," Kilbride answers, but his words deflate Conners, who instantly doesn't believe him. "When I heard, through Shirlow, that MI6 had approached him about an arms sale in this country, I upped the intelligence, telephoned St Petersburg again, and used the only name I was aware of, Dimitri Rossakovich. I knew it was the name of the cargo ship as they'd used it before, and I hoped it would be intercepted and the missiles seized."

"Why didn't you inform Jimmy or me when you met us in the Argyll Arms?" Conners questioned, hoping to calm the situation, but Kilbride turned deadly serious.

"Do you think I'm a fucking idiot? I didn't know why you were there. Shirlow used many ex-SAS men, and James could have been one of them. I left enough clues that even he could follow," he adds, and Ashley smiles unperturbed but slightly amused at the slur. "I couldn't give you all the answers. You had to look like you'd done some of the groundwork yourselves, which wouldn't bring the shit onto me."

Annoyed that his old comrade had betrayed his country, Caine shouts his disbelief, but Kilbride continues calmly.

"We aren't a club that gets together on a Tuesday night to play dominoes, for fucks sake."

"Do you know what the target is?" Conners interjects, annoyed that the critical issue is constantly being taken over by trivialities, and Kilbride toys with the answer he wants to hold to himself until his proper interrogation begins.

"I've only just found out myself."

"Come on then!" Conners adds impatiently.

As the pain increases, Kilbride knows he is in a greater position to demand something and speaks with determination. "I need medical attention before I say anything more."

"You'll get that after we get the information," Ashley reasons, but Kilbride believes he has the upper hand and confidently grumbles that belief.

"You'll die where you lie unless you fucking answer the question," Ashley adds acrimoniously.

"Who put the bullet in you?" Conners asks clinically, and Kilbride grins, believing his answer will help his defence.

"Shirlow."

"He sussed you out for being a treacherous turncoat," Ashley said laughing. "I wonder how many times you've flipped sides to suit yourself?

"Fuck you, Jimmy! I want it on your honour that I will get the attention after I tell you."

"It doesn't work like that," Ashley adds with reason.

"Then you'll have nothing, and I know that's not what your paymasters require."

"I don't have the power of life and death over others, but the colonel here does," Ashley said, looking at Caine, who nodded his reassurance. Caine knows that the intelligence must come first and mutters with all the compassion he can muster. "I will see you are looked after, Roger. Just tell us what you know."

Kilbride stares directly into Caine's eyes as he speaks. "Ten Downing Street."

Conners turns to Ashley, believing he would be just as shocked, but he doesn't stir to words that should disturb him.

"Could the missile hit Downing Street?" Caine enquires, panicked, but Kilbride shrugs his shoulders, unaware of its capabilities.

"Within fifty miles, it could hit a pin," Conners explains calculated. "It powers itself into space, and then by using satellite technology, it comes down with devastating accuracy."

"So, it would be no good at shooting down Air Force One?" Caine adds, but Conners carries on solemnly.

"Stationary or fast moving. Ground or in the air, it's deadly."

Uninterested with the capabilities of the terror weapon, Ashley questions. "When is it set to be fired?"

In the hope of stalling intelligence and gaining medical treatment, he desperately requires Kilbride to answer. "That I don't know."

"Do you know where it is to be fired from?"

Kilbride's glance shifts around with arrogance. "I need reassurances, Colonel."

"You'll get medical attention when the follow-up chopper arrives," Caine mediates. "Your boss shot down your only means of help."

Feigning he has relevant information, Kilbride's smile annoys Ashley, who bends over to look directly into his eyes as he produces his hip flask to take a mouthful of whisky which Kilbride can smell.

"Would you like a drink, Major?" Ashley said, and Kilbride smiled, pleased, but he put the lid back on. "Well, you can fuck off, traitor," he adds, then viciously punches him in his wound to make him scream as Conners, unhappy at his treatment, goes to his aid.

"What are you doing, Jimmy?"

"If you don't like it, go take a breath of air."

Conners goes to intercede, but Caine takes her arm and gives a vigorous shake of his head to impress on her not to interfere.

"You know me of old," Ashley said, determined to intimidate. "You were about to say?"

Kilbride takes several breaths to recompose himself. "I wasn't privy to the ins and outs of the set-up."

Conners pulls away from Caine's hold to give him a sneering look as her stare fixes on Kilbride. "What about Shirlow?"

"Didn't you get him?"

"We stopped one of the cars, but the other got away," Ashley explains, and Kilbride laughs at their incompetence.

"The Range Rover is Shirlow's and had a missile inside."

"You said a missile?" Conners questioned, disheartened. "What about the other?"

Ashley grabs Kilbride harshly by the throat, making it hard for him to breathe. "Who else was here?"

"Flynn and one of his goons."

Feeling the need to report to Davison, Conners interrupts. "Do you have a telephone, Major?"

"I haven't even got running water," Kilbride groans as Conners takes her phone out and looks at the screen to see no signal. "So, the bastard got away?" he adds, annoyed that all he had done was for nothing.

"We don't know," Ashley answers, pushing Kilbride aggressively back. "Only one man was visible in the car Jack shot up."

Unable to comprehend what is happening, Kilbride looks at Caine. "Well done, Colonel."

"What about the guidance system?" Conners interjects.

Bemused about how she could know of such a thing, Kilbride turns his angry stare onto the American.

"We were in the barn at Eallach," Ashley answers with glee, and Kilbride shuffles awkwardly, humiliated.

"So, you're cleverer than I thought," Kilbride said with a scathing laugh. "I made it up to scupper the plan. That's why General Shirlow shot me."

"You can't blame him for that," Ashley said with humour that Kilbride doesn't like. "I haven't believed a word you've said, and I want to shoot you myself."

"Do you know where he would be heading?" Conners interject, and Kilbride pauses without answering.

"The treatment you require depends on your cooperation," Caine interjects.

"I was to meet him at the Banque Genève in Switzerland for my share."

"When?" Conners shouts, eager for an answer.

"Next Tuesday," Kilbride feigns, hoping this will give him time.

"Are you sure it's next Tuesday?" Caine presses, but Conners is unperturbed by the paper trail and needs an immediate answer.

"We need to stop that missile and find the second one," she said, only caring to find out which one she believes is destined to assassinate her President. She moves to the window on hearing the sound of a helicopter approaching. "Here's our ride."

"What about him?" Caine enquires.

"You and Jimmy can lift him to the chopper," Conners interjects scornfully as she exits. "I have no intention of helping the bastard."

"I need attention now!" Kilbride whinges, but his cries for help fall on deaf ears as they prepare for evacuation.

"You relieved yourself of that right when you betrayed your country," Ashley said purposefully, but Caine interrupted to calm the situation. "You'll get it on the chopper."

Ashley drags Kilbride to his feet and throws him over his shoulders, making him scream in agony. "Quit your whinging!" he shouts as they exit. "If I had my way, I'd leave you in that room to die."

Caine gathers the Glock and MP5 and then follows.

The Black Hawk comes over to land thirty feet to the side of the burning helicopter. Conners exits the cottage and runs over as Ashley, still carrying Kilbride, follows with Caine behind, but nobody shows the injured man the care and compassion he should receive as he cries in pain. The door to the Black Hawk opens, and two armed Marines alight, looking to Conners for orders as they take up offensive positions and patrol outwards. Conners gets onto the helicopter, Ashley and Caine load Kilbride into the fuselage, and she orders the pilot to lift off with the return destination already in mind.

***

Davison, Lawrence and a small crew of medics wait as the Black Hawk comes out of the night sky to land at RAF Northolt. The doors open, and Ashley, Conners and Caine alight, leaving Kilbride bandaged but stable as a medic climbs on board and sets about helping him.

"This is Admiral Lawrence," Davison introduces, and they all nod their recognition.

"He's Shirlow's second in command and obvious successor."

"Congratulations on your promotion, sir," Caine said as he shook Lawrence's hand with genuine friendship.

Lawrence had served through all the officer ratings within the navy until command and then naval intelligence, where he was assigned to MI6, then MI5, where he had remained for the past eleven years. He grins with the accomplishment of achieving what he had always hankered for. "I would have preferred it under better circumstances," he feigns with narcissistic modesty. "But I will take it any way it comes."

"Well, you knew you had the job, sir," Caine adds. "It's just the timetable that has been sped up."

Uninterested in the happy reunion of the MI5 cohorts, Conners moves to Davison. "We know what the target is, Director," she said, and his attention turned directly onto her. "Ten Downing Street."

Lawrence's eyes shift around in panicked disbelief until focusing on Caine, who nods his confirmation. "Just how accurate is this missile?" he adds, and after the information given by Conners to her bemusement, Caine answers with self-promotion in mind.

"It's an experimental missile, sir, but it's believed to be top-notch and accurate."

"It's almost unstoppable after being fired," Conners adds confidently. Having studied detailed intelligence on the missile, Davison explains with knowledge. "It's more than capable of flattening Downing Street and the surrounding area of government offices."

"How do you know about it?" Lawrence questions, and Davison looks around, embarrassed.

"The technology was stolen from the United States government."

"I see," Lawrence mutters with condescending amusement at the director's unease. "I know the PM won't move a cabinet meeting because of the threat of terrorism."

"He doesn't have a choice?" Conners interjects, but Davison waves his hand for her to calm down.

"He won't allow terrorism to dictate his day."

"Then he's a fool!" Conners snipes, making Ashley laugh.

"He needs to take the threat seriously, sir," Caine adds reassuringly, but

Lawrence isn't convinced.

"General Shirlow didn't inform anyone of what's going on, including the PM and myself."

"I was on the understanding the PM and Home Secretary were fully aware of the threat," Caine explains. "He told me it had been discussed in Cobra meetings."

"To my knowledge, nothing about this was ever brought up with Cobra," Lawrence explains, unnerved. "And I was present at several of those meetings and read the minutes of the ones I didn't attend. Do we know where the missile is to be fired from?"

"It could be anywhere within a fifty-mile radius," Conners answers.

"That's a hell of a lot of square miles. We'll never find it."

"We still need to look," Davison interrupts.

"What about General Shirlow? Surely he would know?"

"We don't know if he's dead or alive, sir," Caine explains, but Lawrence is aware there is no intelligence to confirm or deny what had happened. "He may be with the missiles."

"Kilbride said there was a missile in his Range Rover, but we don't know if he or the Irish terrorist was driving," Caine explains. "The second one is an enigma."

"So, all the intelligence we have to go on could be false?" Lawrence questions, and Davison interjects determined.

"We need to find out if Shirlow is alive. He's the only one we know who has the intelligence required on both missiles."

"Kilbride said they were to meet at the Banque Genève in Switzerland next Tuesday," Ashley said, but Lawrence stared his contempt and stepped back aware his rank didn't allow him input in a discussion of the top table.

"Then, if he's still alive, we should give him a hearty welcome," Davison said, and Lawrence nodded as he turned his determined stare onto Caine. "Our old friend should have a welcoming committee waiting for him in Switzerland. Just in case he shows up."

Showing she is more panicked by the intelligence than her British counterparts, Conners interrupts. "We need him alive."

"That goes without saying," Lawrence said, but he didn't sound convincing. "He may have the information on Flynn we require."

"I hope I'm a part of that," Ashley interjects. "I'd love another go at that Irish bastard, but I intend to have my Walther with me this time."

"Straw just won't do, will it, Jimmy?" Conners said, but Davison ignored her as he turned, amused by Ashley's enthusiasm to see the task through.

"Haven't you had enough, Sergeant?" he enquires, and Ashley shakes his head vigorously. "You wanted to be dropped off not so long ago."

"Not until he becomes a hero," Conners adds to his irritation.

"If it's alright with the admiral, I would like Colonel Conners to go along," Davison said, looking to Lawrence for confirmation.

"I don't see a problem in her seeing this to its conclusion," Lawrence adds. "So, Major Kilbride made up the attempt on the President to get you interested in our domestic problems. I can't say I agree with his course of action, but you need to confirm or decry it. Until then, we'll go off the threat is credible and would appreciate any assistance the CIA can offer."

"Count on it, Admiral," Davison said confidently, nodding at Conners.

"Maybe Colonel Conners will become a heroine," Ashley snipes to her amusement.

"Too late, Jimmy."

"What about me?" Caine interrupts. "I'd like to be a hero too."

Curious about why he would want to remain involved, Lawrence looks at Caine, debating his best course of action. "I don't see why not, Colonel, as you've been in it from the start."

They all walk off, but Caine lags, saddened at his old friend being lifted out of the helicopter and onto a stretcher by two medics.

"Good luck, Roger," Caine said, and Kilbride nodded, then grinned, defeated.

***

Surrounded by 6,000 acres of ancient woodland, Cuckoo Brook lies thirty miles from central London within Epping Forest. Flynn drives the Range Rover up a dirt path into a small clearing surrounded by trees and pulls over to conceal his presence. Alert to his surroundings and any threat to his intentions, he looks around suspiciously as he alights and rounds the vehicle to open the boot and pull out the container which conceals the missile and its launcher. Having read the instruction manual the night prior, he opens the container and takes out a tripod to open and fix solidly into the ground with anchors to hold it in place. He takes out the two-foot-long warhead and fastens it firmly to the top of the three-foot rocket booster, then places the rocket onto the launcher and elevates it to an angle of eighty degrees. He connects a specially designed raspberry pie computer to the side of the tripod and sets about putting in the pre-selected coordinates he has written on a piece of paper, then looks at his watch with the realisation he has a little time and sets himself up with a cigarette as he sits on the tailgate to smoke.

A short distance off, concealed by the bushes, Soames watches with his Labrador dog, Meg, sitting at heel. The MI6 man steps out of cover and walks the dog. He moves up the dirt path, sets her free, and watches her run towards Flynn, who sees her nearing and discards his cigarette as he jumps from the tailgate with her sniffing his legs. "Hello, my beauty," Flynn said, stroking Meg as she jumped around. Aware that where there is a dog, there is an owner, he takes hold of his Webley, ready to draw, as he pulls back the hammer.

"There you are, Meg," Soames said in his English accent as he walked up behind. "I spend all my time looking for her." He puts her leader on as he looks at the missile. "What the hell is that?"

"Nothing for you to worry about," Flynn said, drawing his Webley and turning calmly with it outstretched but stopped in recognition of his IRA colleague. "What the hell, Sean."

"Hello, Niall," Soames said pleasantly, and Flynn, not feeling any threat, passively lowered the revolver to his side.

"I didn't realise you intended to be here."

"Well, I had nothing better to do."

"So, what are you doing here?"

"I've come to see you."

Flynn mumbles, bemused. "Well, you don't need to worry, as the plan's well underway."

Soames moves off, looking into the distance. "That's good to hear."

"What's with your accent, Sean?" Flynn enquires, perplexed, and Soames answers menacingly.

"There's a thing, Niall. No matter how much I despise the British government and how much the union needs to fall, I couldn't allow you or your likes to be the ones to kill them."

"What's going on, Sean?" Flynn said, unable to believe he was being betrayed, and Soames calmly lifted an X26 Taser to put 50,000 volts through the Irishman to catapult him back against the Range Rover and then onto the ground, where several more blasts made sure he was no longer a threat.

"That's for us to do, fucking Fenian idiot," Soames said with glee, then set about searching the body for the Range Rover keys and disarmed him of the Webley and pulled the wires off the body before dragging him next to the missile. Well aware the Webley had been used on numerous occasions against British military personnel and the Irish people during his terroristic ways over the years, he places the revolver onto the stunned man's chest, then takes out a parcel of C4, connected to a detonator and puts it on the side of the missiles booster rocket before making his way to the Range Rover. "Come, girl," he shouts as he opens the door and gets in, followed by Meg, and they drive off down the dirt track and onto the road at the bottom to stop. He takes out a small remote to flick the safety to danger. Uncaring if anyone is near the missile, he presses the button for an almighty explosion to rip through the hill and buffet the Range Rover with a violent concussion. Amazed by the size of the blast, he alights with Meg running around his legs and looks up at the devastation of the burning trees, then walks nonchalantly off down the track as if nothing had happened.

**

Ashley, Conners and Caine walk along a corridor within the US Embassy in London, followed by a Marine who makes the Englishmen feel untrusted and uneasy.

"What do you think he wants to see us about?" Ashley enquires, but Conners doesn't know what is happening and answers off the cuff.

"Details of our travel to Geneva, no doubt."

"I hope after we've finished, they'll leave us to have an all-expenses paid holiday," Ashley adds naively, making Caine laugh.

"You're definitely not a field operative, James."

"We are still trying to work out what Jimmy is," Conners said, adding to Caine's humour.

They stop at Davison's office door, and Conners knocks until the director calls his permission for them to enter and they move inside to find him behind his desk with Lawrence on a side chair, both drinking whisky.

"Take a seat," Davison said in an over-welcoming tone, which unnerved Ashley and Caine as they sat. "We've got good news, but I believe Admiral Lawrence should be the one to brief you on it."

"Thank you, Director," Lawrence said conceitedly. "I'm pleased to tell you that Niall Flynn is dead."

"One less IRA bastard is good news in my world," Caine said in coldness, but Conners is interested in what she believes is the only question that needs to be answered.

"What about the missiles?"

"We believe it killed him, but we found very little of his body."

"So, there was only one missile?" Conners adds concerned.

"Going off the blast radius, we believe so," Lawrence answered to everyone's dismay.

"What about Shirlow, err, General Shirlow?"

"Don't worry about his rank, Sergeant," Lawrence explains. "He lost that privilege with his treachery. His empty Range Rover was found about half a mile away."

"Half a mile away?" Caine said. "Flynn must have had help."

"That we don't know," Lawrence carries on. "But it's imperative we find him and make him tell us where the second missile is before it falls into the wrong hands."

"You mean like the IRA?" Ashley criticises to Lawrence's discomfort at the intended insult.

Apprehensive that all the intelligence could be wrong and that it is intended for an assassination attempt on his President, Davison interrupts. "It may already have."

"All the more reason to find him and the missile."

"That, Admiral, goes without saying," Davison adds, irritating Lawrence with his belittling tone. "I won't rest until it is found."

"What about the Russian general who sold the missile?" Conners interrupts. "Maybe he will know what the intended target is?"

"Klamenkovich and his organisation are known to the intelligence community," Davison explains. "And the Russians have been informed and have promised to act on it."

"They'll probably promote him," Ashley said, making Davison laugh.

"All I'm interested in is getting the second missile so it can't be used in terrorism," Lawrence said. "Oh, and capturing my predecessor, of course."

"You're all on a flight to Geneva tomorrow," Davison added. "You're booked into the Hotel Royale across the street from the Banque Genève."

"The car Colonel Caine shot up in Scotland carried only one occupant, who we now know was a Robert Donovan," Lawrence explains. "A known associate of Flynn's who went by the name of Robbie."

"And can we be sure that Flynn was the person who was killed in the missile explosion?" Ashley enquired with hope.

"We are still waiting for the DNA evidence, but every bit of intelligence points at it being him."

"Until then, we go off the premise that Shirlow is alive," Davison interrupts.

"Do you think he will turn up, Director?" Conners asked as her eyes fixed on her superior, who smiled confidently back.

"He has no reason not to," Davison explained. "He believes Kilbride is dead, and intelligence has him as the only man he was working with. Unless anyone here has anything to say." His eyes shift around as an uneasy calm comes over the highly trained operators who observe each other's mannerisms for clues of treachery until Ashley speaks to break the tension.

"How long do we have in Geneva, sir?"

"As long as it takes, Sergeant," Lawrence answers.

"Who's paying?" Ashley adds, and Davison's immediate answer makes him smile broadly.

"This time, the tabs on Uncle Sam, Sergeant."

"Good," Ashley said with the broadest of grins. "If it were British expenses, we'd have to share a Burger King."

Unhappy at his subordinate's derogatory attitude toward the Intelligence community he serves, Lawrence snarls. "That's enough of that, Sergeant!"

"I bet you wish you could argue with him, sir," Caine adds with a mischievous grin that makes Lawrence rearrange his posture at the uncomfortable truth.

***

CHAPTER 14

***

Staring apprehensively out of the window, Conners stands in room 403 of the Hotel Royale, Geneva, as Ashley and Caine lounge around, uninterested in the task. "There's a good view from here," she said, but neither Englishmen moved to confirm her words until she shouted, and they reluctantly stood to take in the view.

"It's beautiful," Ashley said sarcastically. "I thought when I agreed to come, I would be out and about not stuck in a fucking hotel room."

"You weren't bothered when the two of you were soaking up room service and the mini bar earlier," Conners disapproves, but neither Ashley nor Caine feel the need to defend themselves.

"Surely it's pointless watching the bank until Tuesday?" Ashley adds impatiently. "We may as well forget about it and visit the Jet d'Eau."

"I'd rather stay here," Caine said to Ashley's amused agreement.

"Do you think he'll stick to what Kilbride said if he thinks he is dead?" Conners questions.

"Firstly, what makes you think what Kilbride said was true?" Caine adds. "He could have made it up to get medical treatment."

With compassion wasted on Ashley and Caine, Conners interjects. "He knew he'd get that."

"Did he?" Caine adds. "In my world, he'd have got a bullet in the head if he hadn't told us what was happening."

"We could be here on a fool's errand," Ashley said, annoying Conners with his pessimism.

"We're not barbarians," Conners argues, concerned. "Look, until we find out if Shirlow's alive, we must go on."

"So, what are we going to do?" Ashley muttered, disillusioned. "Watch the bank's doors until Tuesday?"

"Something like that. First, though, we should eat," Conners said, turning to Ashley. "Who fancies a Burger King?" She laughs as he grins unamused.

Caine looks at his watch. "You two go. I'll stay here and keep my eyes on the bank."

"That's nice of you, but you haven't done much watching since you got here," Conners explains, curious to his attitude. "You've been in your room most of the time, no doubt having a power nap."

Caine gets the joke but doesn't rise to its intended conclusion. "When you get back, I will go for something a damn sight better than a cheeseburger."

Pleased with the thought of refreshments, Ashley moves for the door.

"Let's go before he changes his mind. Who's paying?"

"Why?" Conners questions

"Because if it's on Uncle Sam, it won't be a cheeseburger."

***

Ashley and Conners exit the grand portico of the Hotel Royale and look upon the Banque Genève's magnificent neo-classical façade. As he steps off, she pulls him back into the doorway, then points at the bank for his eyes to follow and see Shirlow exiting.

"Confirmation," he said, but she didn't like what she witnessed as her eyes switched up and down the street. "He's waiting for someone."

Shirlow's glance shifts between his watch and all around as he walks off.

"We need to follow him," Conners adds, moving off, but Ashley takes her arm and holds her back.

"We don't want to spook him. He'll be used to looking for a tail."

Shirlow moves slowly, looking into shop windows, then glances at his watch as he surreptitiously uses his training to see if he is being followed. Suddenly his phone rings, and he answers and listens before lowering it to his side and carrying on at speed. Keeping pace, but at a safe, reassuring distance, Ashley and Conners follow on the opposite side of the street until Shirlow enters an apartment block. They stop to make sure he isn't coming back out, then cross the street and enter a hallway to see the lift going up and stopping.

"Third floor," he said with the obvious, and they entered the stairwell and ran up the stairs, drawing their respective side arms as they went, but she left the limping Englishman behind as he pushed himself with pained stamina to keep up.

They stop at the door to the third-floor landing, and Ashley opens it cautiously and looks into its emptiness as the sound of a door closing informs them of which direction to follow. They make their way cautiously along, then stop outside a door and stand either side as they look at each other with air of accomplishment until she reaches to bang on the woodwork.

"It's open," Shirlow shouts, and Ashley goes to enter, but Conners grabs his arm, untrusting of her surroundings, which seems way too easy for them, but he carries on, and she reluctantly follows with her gun drawn offensively.

Unthreatened, Shirlow sits in a chair with his back to them and his phone on a table to his side. "What happened?" he said as the chair swivelled slowly to reveal his Browning in hand, and after a few seconds of taking in the scene, he laughed in awkward betrayal.

Keeping the traitor covered, Ashley draws his Walther and moves to one side as Conners moves to the other.

"Come quietly," Ashley ordered to Shirlow's amusement.

"You know there's no such a thing in this line of business."

"Not who you expected?" Conners said.

"Now you mention it, Colonel, no," Shirlow answers, resentful of the unexpected situation he finds himself in as his eyes shift mistrustingly between his captors. "If it isn't Angel Bait and our very own Sergeant James Ashley, ex-Fusilier and SAS trooper, and might I add, cannon fodder to Queen and country."

Ashley understands the slur, but he is more interested in the description given to Conners, and she explains it with no enthusiasm to the joke.

"It's the code name given to me by your friends at MI5."

Shirlow laughs at her unease. "She was picked for her resemblance to your ex-wife, Sergeant."

Ashley stares at Conners but can't see any resemblance apart from her blonde hair. "Not the code name I'd have given her."

Even though he hadn't named her, Shirlow carried on defensively. "I think it was very perspective. An unsuspecting beautiful angel," he adds as he smiles complimentary at her before turning sourer. "Used as bait."

"Like yourself, Jimmy. They mistakenly took me for someone else," Conners explains confidently, which Shirlow confirms as his face changes to a stubborn grin. "Drop the gun. There's no way out for you."

"There never is for the betrayed?" Shirlow said with knowing, but his words don't sit well with Ashley and Conners, who don't like the downplaying of his treason to impact sympathy on his behalf.

"How do you get that?" Ashley inputs aggressively.

"You wouldn't have found me without help," Shirlow adds, disgruntled. "Few people know of this place, and until you walked through that door, I believed I could trust them all."

Ashley looks at Conners. "All sounds more than two?"

Shirlow's mind raced over the potentials and smiled gently. "But who would betray me?" he adds, looking between the people threatening him for any signs of them knowing. "Well, I know, but that doesn't concern either of you at this time, but to make life harder for you, the list of my enemies is endless."

"Surely the list you're thinking about includes friends, not enemies?" Ashley said, and Shirlow smiled reservedly.

"Sadly, Sergeant, you may be right for once."

"Drop the gun," Conners orders, increasing her tone aggressively as she takes a tighter aim. "The time for debate and repercussions are for later."

"Why would I do that?" Shirlow adds, confident that he has the upper hand. "You haven't got the balls to kill me, Colonel."

"Not in the physical sense," Conners replies humorously. "But if you don't drop your gun, you'll soon find out what I am capable of. You've got to the count of five."

"One! Two! Three! Four! Five! Fire!" Shirlow shouts rapidly. "They say you don't hear the shot that kills you, but as I am still alive and not bleeding, I can only assume you didn't pull the trigger."

"Your money will be confiscated. You won't get a penny."

Shirlow laughs. "How are you going to confiscate what has already gone?"

"You're going to jail."

"I don't know about that, Colonel," Shirlow said with a sizeable confident smile. "You haven't heard my plea bargain yet."

"You've got nothing to plead with," Ashley growled, and Shirlow leaned back into his chair, making himself comfortable.

"You'll be surprised, Sergeant. You're forgetting the second missile." With confirmation that it exists, Conners looks at Ashley, who keeps his stare on Shirlow.

"I'm sure its intended targets would want me to have one," Shirlow said as he turned his ire onto Conners, aware she was the beginning of his bargaining chip. "You wouldn't want such a sophisticated weapon pointing at Air Force One as it comes into land, would you?"

"Kilbride made that up."

"Did he?" Shirlow condescends to Conners' mistrust.

"The President's visit is on hold until we find the missile."

"Really?" Shirlow interrupts. "But if you'd read the literature on the missile, you would know it can be programmed to remain dormant for a very long time."

Ashley didn't believe a word, but Conners had already been briefed on its capabilities. "Bull-shit! I don't think it even exists."

"Well put, Sergeant. I take it you went to Eton for your oh-so-eloquent

English tuition?"

"Fuck you, traitor!" Ashley snarls, but Conners wants to hear as much as she can about the threat to her President.

"Can you shut up for a fucking minute, Jimmy! We need to know what he has to say."

"You should listen to her, Sergeant!" Shirlow said. "Unlike you, I believe she is the genuine article."

Showing intent to fire, Ashley stretches his arm to aim. "Your words don't hurt. I've been insulted by the best, and you certainly ain't that."

"Put that away before you do something your American puppet master doesn't want you to do," Shirlow condescends, and Ashley grimaces at the thought of working for the Americans.

"Lower your gun, Jimmy," Conners reasons as she lowers her own.

"Listen to the lady," Shirlow said with hilarity. "The missile is already prepped, and you won't get within ten yards of it, but I won't spoil your fun. I will let that be a surprise."

"Electronic sensors?" Conners questioned to Shirlow's admiration.

"Top marks, Colonel. I had to be here, so it seemed a good idea to add them just in case I was betrayed," Shirlow said, then grinned despondently. "Seems to be a lot of that going around lately."

"But the President isn't coming anymore," Conners interrupts. "So, how could you shoot him down?"

"Why would I want to assassinate the leader of the free world?" Shirlow said with a condescending laugh. "You know you can tell the missile to do what you want." He looks at Conners. "Shame you Americans handed the technology to the bad guys."

Aggravated by the affront, Conners snarls. "It was hardly handed over!"

"No, I suppose not," Shirlow adds with his renowned smugness. "Outsmarted by a Russian." He tuts aloud. "You should be ashamed."

"The fault doesn't lie at my doorstep."

"I suppose not, but it lies on the top table within your organisation." Ashley turns his confirmed glare onto Conners that she is CIA, but aware of his attention, she doesn't return the look.

"Do you see me on the top table?" Conners questions with an awkward grin.

"It's a remarkable piece of kit," Shirlow blusters. "You can tell it when to take off, what to do if tampered with, what to fire at if tampered with before a certain date. Oh, it's wonderful, and as it is originally an American design, you could ask that idiot Davison if what I have said is true. Maybe I should give you five to call him. Well, five minutes, not seconds; that would be unfair on my behalf."

Caine exits the stairwell into the corridor, and on hearing Ashley's distinctive Geordie accent, he draws his Remington as he moves toward the sound to stop outside the door to listen as he looks around for any threat.

Considering they have Shirlow with his hands in the till, Ashley cannot understand his posturing and questions his sanity. "Why would you set up a missile to kill innocent people?"

"Who is innocent, and who is guilty," Shirlow answers indifferently. "It's not for me to Judge."

"Yet here you condescend," Conners criticises, but Shirlow's narcissistic demeanour isn't dented. "Judge and executioner."

Shirlow grins arrogantly. "You could say it's my get-out-of-jail card." He glances toward his phone.

"I take it, it's capable of being fired by cell," Conners adds, and Shirlow smiles, not needing to answer.

"You won't make it," Ashley grumbles confidently, and Shirlow laughs. "You need to get yourself an IQ, Sergeant, if you think I am stupid enough to fire the missile and lose my bargaining chip."

"You've betrayed your country, and I'm going to put a bullet in your fucking treacherous head," Ashley said with patriotic anger, but Conners was concerned by his constant bickering.

"Money before country," Shirlow adds hard-hearted. "One day, you will wake up to that concept, Sergeant. Maybe when you have worked closely with the petty corrupt people who wield the power of life or death over others, you will come to the same conclusion."

"My military career has always been doing the bidding of arseholes like you."

"Touché, Sergeant" Shirlow mumbles with a bow. "So, you do understand?"

"Yet you sit there all arrogant with that power over the innocent," Conners interrupts, but Shirlow has an egotistical belief he isn't one of those and defends his actions.

"I mean people like the PM and the Home Secretary," Shirlow argues intensely. "And that dried out cowboy Davison."

"So, you decided to betray your country for profit and side with the IRA?" Ashley condemns catching the general's ire which he believes is a slur on his honour.

"I have no sympathies for the United Ireland cronies. It was purely business," Shirlow adds pretentiously. "The government betray us daily, and we allow it. I have no intention of working for a corrupt establishment anymore. This is all for the good of the union."

"Bull-shit!" Ashley gripes. "How can killing innocents be good for a country?"

"Who said innocents would die?"

"He's after the same target as Flynn," Conners deduces. "But he wants the glory to himself."

"I'm giving nothing more away," Shirlow adds. "The rest comes at a price, so you had better get on the phone and get me that plea bargain. Then I will tell your bosses all they need to know."

Ashley and Conners look at each other unsure whether to trust the traitor.

"You could say I am reborn."

"How righteous," Conners patronises. "If what you say is true, you're no better than the bureaucrats giving the orders."

"I would rather be classed by history as a traitor than an ignorant fool."

"And there's me thinking one of the worst crimes is treason," Ashley interrupts. "Next to rape and murder, of course, and there's only one way for a traitor to die, and that's at the end of a rope."

Conners' concern heightens, and she beckons Ashley to calm down.

"That won't happen. I have far too much to plead with," Shirlow said assertively as he turned the Browning on itself and reached it to Conners. "Now get on the fucking phone and get me that bargaining chip!"

As Conners reaches for the Browning, the door crashes open, and Caine bursts through with his Remington pointing offensively and sees the weapon in Shirlow's hand and instinctively taps two rounds into his chest to knock him back into the chair as a third hits him in his forehead to make sure he isn't a threat. Conners and Ashley turn in disbelief as Caine grins, believing he has saved at least one of their lives.

"What the fuck!" Conners shouts, shocked and dismayed at the senseless killing and Caine's glare shifts between them in bewilderment at her attitude.

"He was going to shoot you," Caine argues as Conners paces off angrily before turning that anger onto him.

"He was giving in! Now we're up shit creek without a paddle."

"He had a gun."

"He was going to tell us where the missile was as a plea bargain."

Conners said calming.

Caine lowers his Remington. "I saw the threat and acted on it."

Ashley stares in shock at the blood trickling down Shirlow's forehead without sympathy and takes his hip flask out to drain its contents. "You came in like fucking Rambo," he said with awkward amusement, but even though Caine finds his words funny, he remains emotionally chastised.

"He said the missile has motion sensors, and if someone gets inadvertently near, it will fire."

"Did he give you a target?" Caine questions to redeem himself.

"He didn't have the time, but because of his anger of the British government, it must have something to do with them," Conners explains. "Jimmy thinks it could be the same target Flynn failed in hitting."

"Ten Downing Street? Why have two missiles for the same target?" Caine reasons.

"In case the Irish missed the first time," Conners said, taking her phone out and dialling as her angry stare shifted between Ashley and Caine, who both looked nonplussed by the loss of the intelligence she desperately needed.

Ashley shakes Caine's hand. "How did you know we were here?"

"Hunger got the better of me, and I saw you enter here in bewilderment and followed you. Finding the apartment took me a little time, but I could hear you bellow."

Conners waits until Davison answers. "Director, we have an unforeseeable problem." She turns her glare onto Caine. "The colonel saw fit to end Shirlow's life." Davison's angry voice can be heard ranting, and her face reddens in failure as she switched the phone off. "What a fucking ball's up." Her glare shifts rapidly between Ashley and Caine. "Special Forces, my ass," she adds, making Ashley laugh. "Just confirms why you need to hide behind a rock somewhere instead of having to do some intelligent thinking."

Ashley goes to complain, but Caine is unconcerned by the insult. "She's right, James. Maybe it's time we retired from the world of backstabbing and bitchery."

"That's easy for you to say. You undoubtedly have a pension plan to allow you to live the good life when work ends. All I've got is my army one, which equates to three shillings a week."

Unsure of the monetary denomination, Conners grins her understanding of the ordinary soldier's lot as she exits, leaving the two ex-special forces men staring uncaring at Shirlow's body.

***

CHAPTER 15

***

Watched by a mistrusting Marine, Conners, Ashley and Caine sit uncomfortably in an office in the US Embassy on Sulgeneckstrasse 19 in Bern, Switzerland.

"Because of your actions," Conners snipes her embarrassed irritation. "I'm a prisoner in my own embassy."

The door opens, and a Marine enters carrying a tray with cups of coffee to place on a table in front as he turns to Ashley. "Director Davison said to tell you there's plenty of sugar, and your cookies are on their way."

"They're biscuits, not fucking cookies!" Ashley argues, then grins awkwardly as Conners nods her appreciation of the Marine as he exits. He reaches for a cup of coffee. "What now? Where would Shirlow hide the missile?"

"I could only hazard a guess," Caine said. "But it must be on the flight path Air Force One was to take."

"He wouldn't have known what that was in advance," Conners interrupts. "Plus, we now know that was just a faint."

"Do we? We know the missile has a long range?" Caine reasons to Conners' panic on remembering.

"I don't think the President is the target," Ashley explains, but this adds to Conners' irritation as she believes he is guessing without the intelligence to back up his words. "Shirlow said that to help his plea bargain. I still believe it is Downing Street, the Houses of Parliament, or some other government building in London. It could be Thames House so he can get back at MI5 or Vauxhall to get at MI6."

"I have an idea, but it's a shot in the dark," Caine calls out, then pauses in thought. "I have a feeling I know where he stashed it." Watched by the alert Marine, he moves to the window. "Kilbride used his country cottage; what about Shirlow?"

"Does he have one?" Conners questions excitedly at their first sign of a breakthrough, and Caine places his hand onto his forehead as his mind races over past conversations with his ex-boss.

"I think it's called Hutton Hall, Hutton Grange, or something similar. I think it's somewhere in Kent."

"Sounds like the first place to look," Ashley said with the obvious. "Have you been there?"

Caine laughs. "Since when have I been in Shirlow's social circle? He talked about it as where he intended to retire to."

Ashley takes a sip of his coffee but finds it too strong and looks for sugar.

"Leave that, Jimmy, you haven't got the time," Conners said, and he took another sip for no other reason than annoying her. "You know, Jimmy, you're a massive pain in the ass."

"What's got us in a hurry now?"

"Kent," Conners explains. "That could have been on the President's flight path into London."

"Weren't you listening," Ashley said sarcastically. "That was just a faint."

"That's a risk I'm not willing to take."

"No!" Ashley interrupts. "Like everything from your organisation, you keep changing the plot to suit yourself. How could Shirlow know about the flight path?"

"He was in a position of command within British intelligence. He could have been made privy to things about the President."

"Surely he wouldn't be informed of his security measures?" Caine interjects, but Conners is nervously unaware if that is the truth.

"Maybe he has allies in America who want to assassinate the President?" Caine adds, and Conners moves for the door as the Marine moves to intercept.

"Relax. I will take it from here," she reassures, and the Marine backs off as Ashley stands ready to follow, but Caine remains seated.

"Aren't you coming, Jack?"

"This is a Yank problem, James, and with Shirlow dead, my part is over."

"And miss the plaudits," Ashley interjects, attempting to beckon his friend to stand. "You can't miss the best bit." He laughs at Conners. "There may be medals."

"You'll find it isn't an American problem, Colonel, but as always, we seem to be taking the lead," Conners said, and her words annoyed Caine but he didn't let it show.

"If his target is the same as Flynn's, we need to stop him," Ashley adds. hoping it will enthuse his friend to remain involved, and Caine reluctantly stands to follow them out.

***

A Black Hawk sits on the tarmac at RAF Northolt with its rotors turning, and a Hummer pulls up alongside for Conners, Ashley and Caine to alight and get on board for it to take off and fly into the distance.

***

Reading through some recently delivered intelligence briefs, Davison sits at his desk within the US Embassy in London when his attention is taken by the words unfolding in front of him and he presses the intercom. "Watkins!" he calls out, and his aide's gentle voice is decidedly calmer than his. "Something's wrong. Get in here!" Expecting the worst, Watkins enters offensively but quickly calms at Davison's frustrated stare. "Get me the list of calls made to Shirlow's apartment in Geneva and his cell?"
Seeing no impending threat, Watkins exits slowly as the director screams for him to hurry up.

***

The Black Hawk races over the Kent countryside and the medieval village of Hutton Grange to hover, causing so much chaos that the villagers exit their cottages to see what is disturbing their peace. A crewman opens the side door for Conners and Caine to survey the area.
"Shirlow said it has three chimneys," Caine explains as they look around.
"It must be on the outskirts!" Conners shout over the noise, but Caine's eyes pick up the silhouette of the chimneys sitting atop a quaint cottage set in several acres of its own land further off.
"There it is!" Caine shouts with a point. "About half a click north!"
They all move to whatever vantage point they can get in the cramped fuselage and look out to see if anything is visible as the Black Hawk moves sideways to hover over the cottage at one hundred feet.
"We need to be on the ground!" Ashley shouts to Conners' nodding agreement.

***

Going through the intelligence briefs, Davison sits at his desk when his face changes to a broad smile as he lifts a phone transcript to take in further details. He presses the intercom for Watkins to answer subserviently. "Get me, Colonel Conners, ASAP."

***

The Black Hawk lands in an adjacent field to Shirlow's cottage, and Conners, Ashley and Caine alight, and it lifts and moves off a short distance to hover.
"Take it easy," Conners orders as if in command. "Watch out for the sensors."

"Good job, you're here," Ashley said sarcastically. "We'd never have thought of that."

"Don't be too cocky, Jimmy, and keep your feeble mind on the job at hand."

Keeping their eyes on the foliage surrounding their approach to the cottage, they move hesitantly across the beautifully tended lawn.

"Got one," Ashley said as he motioned to the inanimate vigilant guard's position to his right, and Conners nodded with appreciation that she now knew what she was looking for.

"They're all over," Conners said, noticing several further off. "The bastard knew what he was doing." She looks for Caine, who is moving stealthily along the opposite side of the lawn. "Can you see any, Colonel?" she shouts but he doesn't answer.

Caine notices a sensor in front and looks at Conners and Ashley, who aren't paying him any attention as they stealthily scan the surrounding area without hesitation and move within its detecting range. The missile's engine starts giving away its well-concealed position. Seeing the immediacy of the threat and without thought for her own safety, Conners runs toward the missile with Ashley screaming for her to stop. She draws her gun but quickly realises that isn't a good idea and drops it as she carries on to dive feet first at the tripod to change the weapons flight path so as the missile launches, it skims across the ground, setting the foliage on fire before hitting a tree to explode in a massive concussion enthused fireball that smashes into their bodies and forces the Black Hawk to gain height in the pilot's kneejerk evasive manoeuvre to save it from being destroyed. As Ashley and Caine are thrown across the ground, the tree falls to cover Conners in branches, and she instinctively turns into a tight ball to protect herself as it catches fire to burn with fuel-covered intensity. Ashley stands frantically looking for his American colleague, and seeing her in distress and struggling to escape her burning imprisonment, he runs over to drag her unceremoniously onto the lawn where she can catch her breath. Caine stands, recomposing himself and looking around in accomplishment of a job well done as he casually moves to Conners as she stands, wiping herself down.

"What the fuck!" Ashley screams as she smiles, relieved to have survived the horrifying thought of being burnt to death.

"It worked, didn't it?" Conners explains with apprehension.

"Only just," Caine said, grinning, relieved to lighten the tenseness.

"What were you thinking?" Ashley questions to straighten Conners' amused face.

"I knew if I aimed it for a tree, it wouldn't have the time to arm itself," Conners explains, but Ashley can't understand her reasoning.

"That was still a large explosion and could have hit any of the cottages around here."

Not having given that outcome a thought, Conners grins discomfited. "I banked on it being just fuel."

"You'll get the Congressional Medal of Honor for this," Ashley adds, using Davison's terrible Southern American accent, which amuses Caine. "That had to hurt."

Ignoring their concern, Conners looks at the tree engulfed in flames with smoke billowing and sighs, relieved. "I'd better report to the director." She takes her phone out and moves off.

Ashley looks at Caine and laughs. "She keeps saying she isn't CIA, but the way she went in to save the President's life, she must be Secret Service."

"Just a patriot, Jimmy," Conners said, looking at her phone. "Surely you'd do the same for your Prime Minister?" she adds, and Ashley laughs, leaving Caine to answer categorically.

"Fuck no!"

"What about the Queen?" Conners asked in the belief there would be two positive replies.

Ashley grins. "That's a different question."

"But the same fucking answer!" Caine interrupts, deadly serious, as Ashley looks unsure. "You've got to be shitting me, James. You'd take a bullet for an over-privileged lady who doesn't know you exist?"

"I swore allegiance to her and the crown."

"So did I, but what you've said sounds like what a Nazi would say to rationalise genocide. I was acting under orders."

Ashley doesn't know how to answer such a cutting remark and stares his contempt. Having paid no attention to their petty bickering, Conners sees she has no signal, and Ashley produces his phone to look over.

"Mine neither, but there must be one in the cottage."

"Just inside the hallway," Caine directs with a laugh. "I'd love to witness you saving the Queen by taking a bullet for her, James."

"Yeah, maybe the next time I go for tea at a Buckingham Palace Garden party."

Conners makes her way towards the cottage, then up the garden path to the front door to find it locked and with a swift kick, she smashes it in, then enters through the hallway to pick up the phone from a small table, then dials and waits until Davison answers pleased to hear her voice.

"Colonel, where are you?" he said with haste. "I've been trying to contact you."

"Shirlow's cottage, Director," she explained calmly, despite her heightened adrenalin. "We've neutralised the second missile but have destroyed a part of Kent in the process," she adds with an uncomfortable laugh that isn't reciprocated.

"Excellent work. Are you alone?" Davison presses, and she looks past the broken door to witness Ashley and Caine beckoning the Black Hawk to land.

"Jimmy and Jack are outside," she explained, bemused. "Why have you been trying to contact me, sir?"

"One of them is playing for the other side," Davison said, increasing Conners' curiosity, and she walked to the door to look toward them with a deep pang of sadness. "Several calls were made to Shirlow in the hours before you confronted him, and one was made moments before, so I had it triangulated, and it came from within a mile radius. Any ideas?"

"None, Director."

"Think, Colonel," Davison adds impatiently. "There must be something that makes you suspicious of one of them."

Conners' mind races over past events as she reaches for her Colt but remembers she had dropped it as she ran toward the missile. "Shit, Director, I'm unarmed! Can you get in touch with the pilot?"

Davison presses the intercom button. "Watkins put me through to BH73. What do you have in mind?"

"I need the crew to cover me when I confront them."

"Do what you have to do, Colonel. Good luck."

Conners puts the phone down and exits as the Black Hawk lands on an adjacent field. She looks around cautiously for her Colt but can't see it, then turns her stare onto the Black Hawk pilot and stops at the bottom of the garden path to stare at Ashley moving over.

"Everything alright?" Ashley enquired on noticing her anxiousness, but she looked distracted as her eyes fixed on the helicopter. "What's wrong?"

Feigning injury, she answers. "I don't feel too good."

Caine walks over and stops with his back to the Black Hawk. "It's not a wonder," he said, concerned. "What did your director have to say?"

The Black Hawk's pilot gives Conners a reassuring nod of understanding as Caine reiterates his question, but her eyes remain on the helicopter as her mind goes over what she has to say. The Black Hawk's rotors slowed as the engine cut out followed several moments later as the pilot and a crewman alight, unknown to Ashley and Caine. "Christ, Colonel," Caine insists, determined for an answer. "What did he have to say?"

Conners' curious stare shifts between Ashley and Caine as her mind goes over the time they'd spent in the hotel and attempts to work out who the traitor could be. "He said one of you was playing for the other side and working for Shirlow," she said, making Ashley and Caine laugh.

"How do you come to that conclusion?" Ashley questions, but she ignores the intensity of his directness.

"The more I think about it, the more it seems right. We've been lucky with the things we've found. The Dimitri Rossakovich. Major Kilbride's cottage. The Banque Genève. Here."

"Kilbride said he left many breadcrumbs," Caine explains, making light of their awkward situation.

"I didn't think we were that lucky," Ashley explains, awkwardly looking to the others for confirmation.

"You wouldn't?" Conners shouts. "This was your first outing, but the colonel here is different."

"How so?" Caine questions with light-hearted defensiveness. "I've got nothing to hide."

"Not now Kilbride's spilling the beans."

"Beans?" Caine said confidently. "What beans does he have to spill?"

"Come on, Julie," Ashley presses, uncomfortable that his friend was being accused of betraying them and was being questioned in such a way. "What the hell is going on?"

"I shot Shirlow before he shot you," Caine defends. "Why would I do that if I was in cahoots with him? It would have been easier to shoot the two of you and put your deaths onto him," he adds with reason.

"He has a point," Ashley adds, but Conners doesn't take a breath as she continues.

"Then the director would have known it was you and hunted you down. No, the easier option for you was to kill your cohort before he could inform on you."

"That doesn't make sense, but Jack's words do," Ashley interjects to Conners' irritation.

"Keep out of it, Jimmy, or I may think you're in on it too!"

"Fuck you!" Ashley shouts, annoyed at being suspected of treachery.

"It all makes sense," Conners adds as her mind races through past events. "You said you didn't know about this place, yet you have just told me where the phone was."

Seeing reasoning in her words, Ashley turns his mortified stare onto Caine, who explains confidently without a moment's thought.

"Most houses have their phones in the hallway."

"I don't even have a house phone now I have a cell," Conners explains with conviction as she looks to Ashley for confirmation.

"You've got it wrong," Caine argues, but Conners is confident in her accusation that she has the right man.

"I don't think I have. Kilbride is at this moment telling the director all he knows about your cartel."

"Cartel?" Caine said, both shocked and amused at such. "Well, that's good because he won't be able to say anything derogatory about me."

Unnerved by Conners and Caine's tense staring, Ashley shouts in the hope of breaking the deadlock. "What the fuck's going on?"

"He worked for Shirlow," Conners said with a confident nod toward the irritated colonel, who defends himself with menace, but Ashley can see she believes it and, having gained trust for her, convinces him.

"What the fuck, Jack!"

"What the fuck, Jimmy!" Caine screams back. "So, you're going to take the word of this fucking Yank over me?"

"I never said that, but what she says has an element of the truth. Maybe if you explain how it isn't true?"

Not feeling the need to justify his reasoning, Caine draws his Remington to point at Conners. "Shut the fuck up, arse wipe!" he shouts at Ashley. "This bitch is only here because I handpicked her."

With devastated reality, Ashley's stare shifts to the Remington, confirming that the accusation he hadn't taken seriously is accurate.

"Angel Bait," Conners said with a laugh.

"Yeah? Guess who's the angel and who's the bait?" Caine said belittlingly, but neither Ashley nor Conners were perturbed.

"We heard this from your boss," Ashley said. "But I still don't get it."

"They thought you were a broken-down infantryman with nowhere to go,"

Conners explains to Caine's pleasure and Ashley's nodding agreement. "And with the help of the director, they thought I wasn't a field agent. They gave me the code name as a form of sarcastic satire lost on me."

"They say sarcasm is the lowest form of wit," Ashley said straight-faced and to Conners' bewilderment, considering most of what comes out of his mouth is the height of sarcasm.

"You're the joke, Jimmy!" Caine snarls. "You weren't meant to find anything out. You're a fucking useless agent."

"But we did, didn't we?" Conners interrupts to Ashley's smiling amusement. "Did you notice, Jimmy? I said we. That means the both of us foiled his retirement."

"Sheer fluke," Caine whimpers. "You had so much help you didn't need to be here."

"I may be fucking useless agent, Jack, but luckily for me, she isn't."

Seeing Caine threatening Ashley and Conners, the pilot and crewman walk up behind.

"Drop the gun!" the pilot shouts as he draws his Colt side arm but the ex-special forces commander turns and puts a bullet into his arm, forcing him to drop his gun to the ground.

"I could easily kill you all, so let's have no more heroics," Caine demeans.

The crewman lifts his hands submissively as Caine moves aside to keep them all in sight, then fires above the rotors as a warning to the co-pilot and second crewman, who raise their hands to show they are unarmed.

"What the fuck are you doing, Jack? I thought we were friends," Ashley questions making Caine laugh.

"When it comes to money, you don't have friends. That pension you whinged about," Caine explains with melancholic truth. "Well, mine's also piss poor and probably worth four shillings a week."

"Still better than mine," Ashley interrupts and Conners calls his name, angered by his frivolity in the tense situation. "What made me stand out from the pack?" he asks desperately.

"You were in the right place at the right time, and your constant whinging about your fucking desk made you the ideal patsy."

"At least it wasn't anything that would hurt my feelings," Ashley adds, sardonically unperturbed.

"All those years of service to be screwed over at the end. I wasn't going to be a victim."

"No, you just got together with your corrupt friends and committed treason," Ashley moans, but Caine is nonplussed by the slur.

"I played them all into your hands, and you were unaware of it."

"Including yourself," Conners interrupts, making Caine shuffle, unnerved as the truth of his situation dawns on him. "You're not as clever as you think," she continues, and Caine turns his condescending stare onto her. "Director Davison sussed you out."

"Sitting with several million Pounds in the bank and having you rid me of some of the men who would want a share, I don't think so."

"Some of them," Conners said observantly. "So, there's more in this cartel."

"There's no fucking cartel!" Caine shouts angrily. "I'm a lot cleverer than you think!"

"You're not that clever, Jack. They know where the money is and will be able to get it out of the Banque Genève."

Caine laughs. "Shirlow transferred it out; then I transferred it several times as I played him into your hands."

"And you killed him to conceal your treachery?" Conners questions and Caine grins with menaced achievement.

"He was about to betray me. I could hear him conspiring to save himself. He would have given you everything, so he was the fucking traitor."

"You thought you were going home in that helicopter," Ashley interrupts. "You're not that clever, but your actions have grounded it by injuring the pilot."

Believing he would just kidnap the crew of the Black Hawk, Caine glances at the pilot, but this takes away his attention long enough for Ashley to draw his Walther offensively, but he pre-empts his move and grabs Conners by the neck and pulls her around to face the threat.

"You lose, Jimmy," he growls as he prods the Remington into her temple.

"What now," Conners teases. "You've got nowhere to go but the morgue."

"The money gives me numerous places to go," Caine answers arrogantly. "Most with the sun blazing high above my head."

"You misunderstand me," Conners adds with calm. "You're going to have to kill me to escape; then Jimmy will put a bullet in your head. Ain't that right, Jimmy."

"You'd better believe it."

Aware he has been outmanoeuvred, Caine keeps up the pretence of being in control. "He hasn't got the balls. He's a fucking pussy."

"In fact, Jimmy," Conners carries on unmoved. "I'd rather be shot by a friend than this idiot, so if you don't mind, put that bullet through me as long as it kills this bastard."

Caine laughs, pulling her in tighter. "You know, Jimmy. This is above your pay grade, and no matter what you think of me or what you assume has happened, it has all been for the good of the union."

"What fucking union?" Ashley questions and Caine explains what he hopes his ex-friend will understand.

"This country. The government must fall to be reborn into the empire's strength to take on the Russians."

"But you're working with them."

"And your plan didn't work," Conners scoffs to Caine's irritation. "It failed with the death of the Irishman who you got to pay for doing your bidding."

Caine grins with a sense of accomplishment. "He was never going to get the chance to fire that missile. I would never be able to live with myself if I allowed the IRA to get the glory. We intended to carry out the operation ourselves, and if the colonel hadn't carried out her heroics, that missile would have done just that."

"So, the union lives another day?" Ashley adds sarcastically. "You know, Jack, you called me a joke, but I'm just a simple foot soldier, so you'll need to explain in greater detail if you want me to understand," he adds, but as Caine goes to speak, he carries on. "On second thoughts, don't bother. I don't give a flying fuck."

"Don't talk, Jimmy," Conners said calmly. "Shoot the bastard."

Caine grabs Conners tighter and backs off, with Ashley following. "Stay where you are, Jimmy, or I will be forced to shoot you."

"Take him out!" Conners screams, but Ashley keeps his cool. "Come on, Jimmy, do it for the Queen."

Ashley doesn't feel confident enough to take the shot, and Caine, knowing the man of old, can see it in his eyes and grins menacingly. "You were a dick the day I met you, Jimmy, and you'll still be one the day you die."

Ashley stops walking as the insult hits home, and Caine carries on dragging the reluctant Conners, who has no choice but to do as told. "Jack, I don't believe a word of it. We are old friends and will always stay as such. I don't think you'll hurt the colonel."

Caine laughs, attempting to increase his speed backwards but has to look around to confirm that the aircrew isn't a problem.

"I know I'm a dick and don't need you to remind me of such," Ashley carries on, not feeling sympathetic to himself but stating what he believes to be a fact. "But mostly, that has been for putting up with self-righteous, pompous pricks like yourself and the other cronies all these years." He readjusts his firing stance. "But I must say, Jack, you were right about me being a useless field agent."

"Get over yourself, Jimmy," Caine interrupts as Ashley puts a bullet into his shoulder to catapult him backwards across the ground pulling Conners over with him before two more rounds enter his chest, killing him before he hits the ground.

"But I'm a fucking great shot."

"That was some shooting, Jimmy," Conners said, impressed, as he walked over and helped her stand.

"Just lucky."

"I hope not. You aimed, didn't you?"

Ashley's face straightens roguishly. "I couldn't; I had my eyes shut."

They laugh in unison as Conners moves to help the pilot.

Ashley looks at Caine with confirmation that the holes in his chest have ended their friendship and his treachery. "I earned those fucking crossed rifles, you piece of shit." He takes out his pain medication and hip flask to swallow two tablets with a mouthful of the whisky as he limps off with Conners staring her concern.

***

CHAPTER 16

***

Situated on Bank Street in the centre of the Northern Irish capital, Kelly's Cellars is a popular haunt for locals and tourists who love the best Irish hospitality. Reading the Belfast Telegraph, Soames sits in the corner drinking a pint of cold Guinness feigning paying no attention to his surroundings but keeps glancing tentatively around for any signs of his many enemies.

McInley enters and moves straight to the bar to get himself a pint of Guinness and takes a large mouthful of delight as he turns his back to the counter to see Soames. "Sean," he said nervously about encountering the IRA man, aware of his reputation as he moved over. "What brings you around here?"

Soames keeps his eyes on his newspaper as he speaks with a broad Northern Irish accent. "To see you, of course, Mr McInley. Please, sit down."

Nervous as to why a top-ranking IRA commander would want to see him, McInley reluctantly sits with his back to the wall to keep the bar area under surveillance.

"You don't need to worry," Soames explains with calm. "Nobody knows me around here."

McInley takes a nervous sip of the black gold but spills some awkwardly down his chin to wipe away embarrassed in the hope he hadn't been seen. "What do you want me for?" he said in a heightened tone that entertained Soames, who grinned with intent to harm.

"Now, who's become a brave little soldier since we last met?"

"Things are different now, Sean," McInley whispers as his confidence increases. "I'm not a member anymore. You have nothing on me."

"You've got it wrong, Mr McInley. I want to talk about our mutual friend, Niall Flynn."

McInley looks around, panicked at the mention of his old IRA commander. "He's dead," he whispers.

"I heard," Soames said, amused. "He was good for the cause but outlived his usefulness."

McInley takes hold of his Guinness and stands, intending to take a different table. "Then we have nothing to talk about!" He moves off, but Soames slams his fist on the table, catching everyone's attention in the bar and the panic-stricken Irishman freezes to the spot.

"Sit down, you fucking idiot!" Soames shouts then calms. "I thought you liked money?"

His nerves at breaking point, McInley sits and takes a mouthful of Guinness as he looks around. "Keep it down, Sean," he mumbles. "I don't want anyone made aware of my past affiliations."

"Once IRA, always IRA," Soames said, smiling menacingly. "After all that posturing, you're not as tough as you are making out." He produces an envelope and hands it over for McInley to swiftly pocket. "There's two grand in there and another eight if you have what I want."

Having had rough times since his IRA paymaster was killed, McInley's eyes widen at the amount and he gives a relaxed grin at the thought of getting off the dole and moving to the Republic of Ireland to live in peace where he is unknown. "What does the IRA want with the likes of me?"

"It's not the IRA," Soames explains. "They are long defunct, apart from the odd dreamer like Flynn who wanted to return to the dark days. This is for me." He places car keys on the table. "You can drive."

McInley picks up the keys, then stands as he downs his Guinness and moves for the exit without looking back. Leaving his pint aside, Soames calmly folds his newspaper and stands to exit onto the street to find McInley looking timidly around.

"Which car, Sean?"

"The white Audi."

McInley opens the car doors remotely and then gets into the driver's side but curious to him, Soames gets into the rear. "So, you need a chauffeur?" he laughed. "I'll take ten grand to drive you around."

"I'm aware of your penchant for apery, Mr McInley, but that's your last barb," Soames said with a calmness that McInley knows can't be taken lightly.

"Where are we going?"

"Just drive."

McInley starts the engine, and they drive off down the main road.

"What do you want to know?" he said impatiently.

"Let's start with the Morrison's robbery."

Unnerved, McInley looks at Soames through the rear-view mirror. "How could you know about that?"

"Flynn and I discussed it before he was killed, but I didn't get all the information required."

McInley laughs awkwardly as his mind prevents him from having a reasonable thought. "I thought you knew everything, Sean?"

Soames draws his Sig Sauer but keeps it out of sight. "Don't be a clever shit," he grumbles. "You know I don't have a sense of humour."
Having forgotten the threat, McInley apologises with a deep gulp of dread. "Sorry, Sean, I didn't mean to offend. The plan to rob the twins, you say? I didn't get to know everything, but it involved a lot of money, jewels and gold."
Soames' tone turns more menacing. "You've got to earn that two grand, Mr McInley. It isn't a handout."
"Flynn wasn't a man to let anyone know his business."
"I thought you were one of his lieutenants?"
"That meant he trusted me less," McInley adds awkwardly.
Feeling he is getting nowhere, Soames screws a silencer onto the Sig Sauer.
"He had a man on the inside. I can't remember his name, but Flynn kept the information in a safe box in the barn. It may still be there."
"Then why don't we start at Eallach," Soames said with imitated happiness. "That's nice and remote."
"If that's where you want to go," McInley said as he turned the car in the road to head in the opposite direction.
"And you haven't been there since his demise?"
"I haven't been near the place since his murder," McInley blusters, believing that was his best course of action.
"Murder? I heard he was killed in an accident," Soames feigns as if it hadn't crossed his mind to such an eventuality.
"He was killed by the fucking Brits," McInley rants with hatred. "They were after him for years."
"If that's so, why haven't they taken you out? After all, you were a member of his breakaway troop."
"I didn't want anyone knowing I was with him, so I've kept a low profile."
"You mean other members of the IRA?"
McInley looks nervously through the rear-view mirror. "I'd be dead if they knew. You aren't gonna tell them, are you?"
"It serves both our purposes them not knowing," Soames explains to McInley's relief.
"Flynn wanted to take the war against the British in his name and was after money to keep up the fight."
"He came to me for an extra million on top of what he had already paid."
"Yeah, but he didn't need it," McInley explains, unaware Soames

knows what had transpired. "The Brits were playing him."

Soames grins roguishly. "Weren't they just. Look, if the information is still in the barn, you're in for a good payday."

McInley grins broadly at the thought. "I saw where Flynn hid all his shit. He didn't know I had seen, but I was born a nosey bastard."

"That could have cost you your life," Soames explains, but McInley was already aware of the threat.

"Maybe then, but today, it will save it and give me enough money to get away from here."

"I take it things have been lean of late?"

"All I've got in my pocket is fluff," McInley laughed, but his face straightens on witnessing Soames' irritation.

      Eallach's remoteness guarantees anonymity to those aware of its existence, and arriving in the brightness of day doesn't perturb Soames as much as it should as the Audi drives up and stops outside the barn. McInley alights, looking around nervously as he moves toward the door. Confident he isn't under surveillance; Soames follows as he places the Sig Sauer into his jacket and enters the barn's emptiness to find McInley lifting a hatch and disappearing underneath into a void. He moves closer as the Irishman comes up, holding an envelope to place on the floor as he ducks back down.

A loud shriek of excitement is followed by McInley coming up holding a wad of money. "There must be twenty grand here."

"Then you've scored again," Soames mutters to McInley's disbelief. "If that envelope has what I want, you're welcome to keep it all."

McInley climbs out and hands the envelope to Soames as he moves off, counting the money with the eagerness to get the extra eight thousand promised. "Is that what you need, Sean?"

Soames opens the envelope to read its contents. "It certainly is." He draws the Sig Sauer and shoots the Irishman in the back of his head for him to drop to the floor with the wad of money bouncing aside. "What would make you think I would do business with an Irish bastard like you?" he growls as he picks up the wad, then searches the body for the envelope containing the two-grand and pockets them both. "You're right, Mr McInley, this has been a nice little earner." Using his feet, he pushes the corpse into the void, then replaces the hatch and exits as he produces his phone and dials. "It's on, Captain. Set things in motion on your side, and I will see you soon." He switches the phone off, gets into the Audi, and drives off with the largest smiles at the riches to come.

***

CHAPTER 17

***

Having succeeded at halting the attempts to destroy Downing Street and the British Government and possibly the assassination of the President of the United States, Davison had been tasked with setting up an Anglo-American Anti-Terrorism Intelligence Unit to incorporate agents from both sides of the Atlantic. First to be chosen had been Ashley and Conners, along with numerous other American operatives taken from several intelligence agencies, and Vice Admiral Lawrence, being made his second in command, had chosen from the ranks of the United Kingdom's intelligence agencies and police forces.

***

Reading an old copy of Vogue magazine and enjoying the tranquillity of the sunny afternoon, Conners sits in the main terminal of LF Wade international airport, Bermuda, when Chaucer walks over to sit next to her. Even though the terminal is busy, she is uncomfortable with his closeness and places the magazine down and walks off, but he stands to follow.

"Excuse me," he said. "Rupert Chaucer."

"Wrong person," she said as she carried on, but he grabbed her arm with an awkward laugh and forced her to pull away from his creepy hold.

"That's my name," he adds as she looks him up and down.

"Then you have me at a disadvantage."

"You're right. I know everything about you," he adds condescendingly, but her words to come cut him down in awkwardness.

"I doubt that very much, Rupprecht!" she snarls, unnerving him as he gives a condescending sneer.

"That's Rupert! I am head of agency activity here on the island." He gets out his ID and flashes it, to her dismay.

"I'm working here," she mutters, moving off, hoping his idiocy hadn't been noticed, but he follows. "Look," she adds impatiently. "I'm waiting for."

"Jerome Adler," he interrupts confidently. "I wouldn't worry about him. He's getting held up in customs."

"That's not a good idea!" she said irritably. "He's well known on the island and wouldn't normally get pulled aside."

Chaucer pulls a small parcel out and hands it over for her to rapidly place in her bag.

"What's that?"

"A state-of-the-art listening device!" he mutters boastfully to her increasing annoyance. "There's also an eyes-only message from London."

Unable to comprehend such reasoning, as it breaks the chain of command structure she is used to working under, she repeats her query expecting an immediate answer.

"Put it in the room the twins use most, then I can listen to them conversing as they relax."

Flabbergasted by his idiocy, she questions his true intent and authority, which he believes will allow him to gather inside information on the stocks and shares of the business world, but he has no intention of answering honestly.

"Then we can gather primary intelligence on them," he feigns, but she isn't fooled.

"It isn't in my brief to put the twins under surveillance that way."

"I'm giving you your brief!" he snipes, then calms. "Also, if you need any help, you can request assistance," he adds off the cuff. "Then I will be able to send some."

"I can't see why I would need any help," she said, but his eyes informed her the conversation wasn't up for consideration, and she was being ordered to carry out his demand. "The twins get the mansion scanned for monitoring devices all the time," she continues. "It will be found, then questions will need to be answered," she reasons, but he is unhappy with her inability to understand his mandate.

"I'll be able to delay such an action occurring," he adds confidently.

"Do you want me to make it an order!" he shouts, and she looks around to ensure he hasn't been overheard. "I will have a boat sitting off the island monitoring what is happening, so just say the word, and my men will come to your rescue. I mean, we don't want a lady being left on her own." he condescends, but Conners doesn't take kindly to the demeaning, sexist comment.

"What makes you think I'm alone, and for that, what makes you think I would need to be rescued?"

Not privy to such intelligence, he questions in desperation to know what is being withheld from him, considering his position in the agency. "Who else is with you?"

"That's need to know, Robert."

"It's Rupert, and I don't like your attitude toward your superior!"

"Superior?" she argues but quickly calms. "I'm on an OP, and you mince over and interfere, which will cause me a great deal of shit, and you don't like my attitude?"

Uneasy at being spoken down to by a subordinate, which all women are in his misogynist world, he shuffles his inexperience. "We are on the same side, you know."

Conners laughs. "If you think that, you're as stupid as you look. Now if you don't mind, Rudolf," she snipes, putting the onus on the name. "I have someone to meet." She walks off, then stops to look back. "And because you've held him up, he'll be a bigger pain in the ass than he normally is."

Chaucer looks at his watch, uncaring of her complaint. "You'd better get on with it then. Oh, and don't forget to holler if you need assistance."

"I can't see that happening, Royston!" she shouts, and even though he is irked, he grins, walks off, and turns back to see she hasn't moved.

In his egotistical world, Jerome Adler is the most important of men and is infuriated at being held up by a public sector employee. Carrying his hand luggage, he exits the arrivals lounge, followed by an apologetic customs officer who races to keep up with the pace. "I'm not taking this, you bloody idiot!" he shouts, playing to all the inquisitive eyes in the terminal, which turn interested onto the conceited man. "Don't you know who I am?"

"Of course, Mr Adler," the customs officer answered self-effacingly. "I can only apologise for the officer; he's new to the job."

Adler turns his indignation onto the customs officer and shouts so everyone understands his pomposity. "I want your names, and I want them now!"

"But, sir," the customs officer pleads, but Adler is only interested in himself.

"I am a most distinguished resident of this Island."

"Yes, sir, I'm aware of that."

"I'm not sure you are, as you wouldn't have dared draw me aside and embarrass me if you knew the consequences," Adler grumbles in an unsympathetic threatening tone. "I intend to take this up with your superiors." He takes out a notebook and pen. "Name?"

"Senior Customs Officer David Culkin."

Adler growls with menace as he writes in his note book. "And the other idiot?"

Having never met the fictitious customs officer before, the customs officer has to improvise his answer. "Customs Officer Dean Laing."

"You should start thinking about your jobs," Adler growls menaced, as the government official attempts to explain, but he has no concern for their livelihood as he arrogantly pushes him aside and moves off with Conners attempting to keep up.

"Mr Adler, sir!" she shouts, and the irate man drops his hand luggage as he carries on for her to pick it up and follow.

"I will have someone's balls for that!"

In a contrived attempt to show she is concerned, Conners enquires. "What happened, sir?"

Annoyed at the thought of being questioned by a servant, Adler stops and turns his contempt onto her. "None of your bloody business, and know your place! Where the bloody hell's that helicopter?"

"It's waiting for you on the tarmac, sir."

"Then don't waste my time," he shouts as he continues. "I have things to do even if you haven't!"

Isolated, Conners looks at Chaucer, who grins his mocking indifference.

"I am waiting!" Adler screams.

"Sorry, sir!" Conners shouts. "I'm coming!"

Distracted, the customs officer watches Adler racing off, followed by Conners as Chaucer moves up behind to take him by surprise.

"I see my man done well?"

"I wish you'd informed me who you wanted to be searched. Mr Adler is a big fish on the island and will make it awkward for my staff and me until he gets his way. You know he's the nephew of the Morrison twins?"

"I know exactly who he is," Chaucer answered with pompous self-indulgence.

"He wanted the name of your man."

"But you don't know it," Chaucer said with a laugh that made the customs officer more uncomfortable.

"I had to make one up to appease him. Now he'll report a member of my staff who doesn't exist."

"His status doesn't warrant any favours in the law."

"That's because he has no pull over you or your staff!" the customs officer adds timidly. "When he reports to my staff, I assume as I helped you, you will be able to help me?"

"I don't think so. All this is on the hush-hush, you might say."

Aware he's on his own, the customs officer attempts another way of deflecting the incident blame onto others. "I take it he's been up to no good?" he questions, but Chaucer walks off smugly.

"That doesn't concern you!"

The customs officer takes a nervous breath and whispers. "Now, because of you, it bloody does."

***

A Bell Relentless helicopter, with the Morrison Corporation logo and name proudly painted on the side, stands with its rotors turning as it awaits to fly the short flight to Mill Island. Adler exits the executive reception across the tarmac as Conners attempts to follow, feigning fearfulness for the benefit of the Morrison's obnoxious nephew, who believes he has the executive power over those under their employ. He gets to the helicopter, and the pilot opens the door for him to climb into its luxurious rear. Conners nears, and the pilot takes the bag off her.

"I take it he's giving you a bad time again?" the pilot whispers, and she smiles her thanks as Adler bangs impatiently on the window and bellows, but his words can't be heard over the noise of the rotors. "Get in the front," he adds, turning coyly to say what he had wanted for a long time. "Hey, maybe we can go for a drink in the staff lounge later?"

"I appreciate the offer, but don't think I'll have the time."

"Make the time. It will be fun."

Even though she is interested in the handsome pilot, Conners doesn't want romance to complicate her mission. "Hey, you just fly them in and out of the island. I'll have to wipe his ass later," she explains calmly, and he looks bemused but doesn't question her reasoning. "Well, you don't want him having to do it himself, do you?" she adds, making the polite rebuffed pilot giggle awkwardly, but this is witnessed by Adler, who snarls as they get into the front.

"What's so funny?"

"Nothing, Mr Adler," the subservient pilot said as he carried out his start-up procedure.

"Then stop messing about and get me to Mill Island."

"Of course, Mr Adler," the pilot adds to his lameness as they take off. Conners' stare shifts curiously from the pilot to Adler, who turns his browbeating stare onto her.

"Keep your eyes forward," he commands, and she turns away chastised. "And keep your mind on the job at hand."

Conners grins her discomfort, then takes the parcel out and looks at the pilot, who is paying her no attention, as she removes the message to read.

***

CHAPTER 18

***

Bathed in the warm waters of the Atlantic gulf stream, Mill Island takes its name from the 17th Century flour mill that had been out of commission for over eighty years. Sitting eight miles off the coast of Bermuda, the 1,900-acre island had passed through many owners and had at one time been a sugar cane plantation that had become derelict until being transformed into the private home of the Morrison twins, who had paid three million US Dollars in 1997 to make into their home when they retired from the world of business in 2006.

***

Enjoying the midday sunshine without a care in the world, Ashley relaxes with his feet on the dashboard of a golf cart outside the security office. Feeling his pain increase, he takes out his pain medication and hip flask to drop two tablets and washes them down with a swig of whisky when the island's head of security, Hazen Knox, exits the purpose-built building.

"Don't let the twins see you do that, James," Knox said, and Ashley grinned uncaring of being found out as he placed the hip flask and pain medication into his pocket. "Choppers en route."

Ashley straightens himself out. "The eagle's about to land," he said, laughing as he started the golf cart's electric engine. "I'd better be off then. We don't want the little shit having to wait too long."

"One second late, and he'll have your balls."

"Too late. He had them as a main course the last time he was here."

"You won't need to worry about that soon!" Knox starts, and Ashley grins broadly as he interrupts.

"Don't forget, Hazen; I need to be on that chopper when it returns to the main island after Adler spits his dummy out and decides to leave."

Knox laughs. "He may fly to Newcastle with you."

"But he'll be in first class while I'll be in the cargo hold with the cases."

"I'd be surprised if they allowed you on the same plane."

"He will be private, and mine scheduled economy, but you can't take away my pleasure at going home," Ashley adds with a smile. "This here's my last job before a well-earned rest."

Knox laughs bemused. "You've only been here two months, and I think you're missing the fact that this is paradise."

"Paradise to me is watching Newcastle United play at St James Park.

This is for people with money, not lowlifes like myself, who work to make a living. This is just hot weather work for mere mortals."

"When you start working for that living, maybe you'll be able to count yourself amongst the put upon."

Ashley drives toward the landing pad, situated eight hundred metres north of the mansion, as the helicopter comes into land and stops just shy of the pad. Adler alights, followed by Conners, but the unlikable man jumps straight onto the golf cart and, not giving her a second thought, barks his command to get him to the mansion. Expecting to give his American friend a lift, Ashley looks at her when Adler repeats the irritated order that shows he hadn't mellowed since his last visit, and he grins as he drives off with her staring in bewilderment at her ride passing without her on board.

"I take it I'm walking?" she shouts as she lifts Adler's hand luggage out of the helicopter and starts on the short walk to the mansion with the pilot calling for her to think about their night out, but she ignores him and carries on.

***

Ashley stops the golf cart outside the main doors to the twenty-bed, ten-bath, purpose-built mansion that the Morrison twins had designed to suit their retirement, and Adler alights straight inside without a word of thanks. With desperation to show the ill-mannered man the way of the world, Ashley clenches his fists, then flexes them out as he turns the golf cart to face Conners and laughs at her discomfiture as she nears. "Come on!" he shouts to her irritation. "The eagle needs his bag, pronto."

"Thanks for waiting, Jimmy."

"Nothing to do with me. Mr Cantankerous ordered me to go, and far be it for me to ignore the exalted one's demands," he said, taking his hip flask out to take a much-needed sip of whisky after dealing with the man he despises.

"Come on, Jimmy!" she shouts, despaired at his blatancy as he takes a second sip. "I wish you'd stop doing that." Hot and flustered, she attempts to give the luggage to him, but he doesn't show any interest in taking it. "Ever the gentleman, Jimmy."

"I dare not take it for being accused of being a right-wing misogynist Nazi who doesn't understand the fairer sexes' quest for dominance of mankind."

"And calling me the fairer sex will certainly endear you to the cause." Aware she is as equal to him in every way, if not better, he laughs at pulling the feminist card out now and again to get a rise out of her. "I notice you don't worry about being called a misandrist," he adds, but she doesn't believe in disparaging anyone's ability on the platform of sex and laughs at his candour.

"Two big words in as many sentences, Jimmy. You'd need a rest if you weren't always sitting on your ass. I take it you're ready for your leave?"

"We've been here for months, and nothing has happened. I can't see me coming back."

"I don't think you've been needed, but your side has found the body of a man called McInley. He was one of Flynn's compatriots."

"I remember him!" he snaps to show he hasn't forgotten. "He was in the barn in Northern Ireland."

"They found his body in a void under the floor with a bullet in his head. There was a safe next to him."

"Empty, no doubt?" he questions, and she nods her answer.

"You see, Jimmy, your talents haven't been wasted on that golf cart."

"Surely the barn was under surveillance?"

"He was killed after it was pulled."

"How could the killer have known that?"

"It could be a coincidence," she adds, even though she doesn't believe such.

"I don't believe in them. So, who pulled it?" he said, genuinely interested, but the intelligence hadn't been deemed relevant to the eyes-only report. "Where did you get the info from? I thought we were on radio silence."

"I was approached at LF Wade by a man who introduced himself as Rupert Chaucer. Have you heard of him?" she questioned, but he shook his head. "He said he's the head of the agency in Bermuda."

"Sounds suspect to me."

"It would to me," she explains. "But I got a good look at his creds."

"Why would the director inform someone about what's going on?"

"He wouldn't," she said with knowing. "You know what he's like? He doesn't pass all the relevant intelligence to us. He says it just complicates things."

"The killing of McInley must be connected. Maybe I shouldn't go on leave," he adds, considering their situation.

"I'd keep to the script," she adds, concerned. "If you stay, Flynn's inside man could turn suspicious, but I'd prefer it if you stayed in Bermuda if needed."

Touched by her confidence in him, he smiles as she takes the package out to throw into the air several times.

"What's that?" he asked curiously as he attempts to focus on it.

"It's a listening device."

"You're shitting me?"

"Chaucer wants it placed where the Morrison's sit the most."

"That's way off script. Hazen will find it in a heartbeat."

"I agree, but it came as an order, and the director isn't here to countermand it."

"So, we don't know if this is what the director would want?"

Stephens, the twins' conceited valet, exits the mansion and seeing his staff fraternising, heads with angst toward them.

"Shh, here's dick head," Ashley adds loud enough for the Scotsman to hear and not needing to look at whom he is referring to, Conners moves off.

"Hold on there, Conners!" Stephens shouts, but she ignores him and carries on. "I will be speaking to you later about this! Now what's going on here?" he adds impotently as he turns to Ashley, who has no intention of explaining and shrugs his shoulders which irritates the majordomo more. "How many times have I told you not to speak to that maid in the front of the mansion?"

Feigning contemplation, Ashley looks at the sky and places his right index finger over his mouth to tap his lips several times.

"Well?" Stephens adds impatiently.

"I'm trying to work out which question to answer first," Ashley said with the comic timing of the sarcastic expert he is.

Constantly irritated by the handyman he believes is below him, Stephens cries his bewilderment.

"You wanted to know what's going on, then you asked how many times you have told me not to speak to the maid in front of the mansion," Ashley adds, amused. "I didn't know which to answer first, so I was thinking about it. I didn't want to upset you any more than you already are by giving you the wrong answer."

"Don't be clever, Ashley."

"I dare not without permission."

"It's not becoming a member of this prestigious staff to act in this derisory way."

Ashley holds in the urge to laugh. "Do accept my humblest apologies, Mr Stephens. It was never my intention to be clever. Far from it." He drives off waving. "It won't happen again!"

Even though he knows he is wasting his time, Stephens shouts out. "It had better not, Ashley or I will report you to the sirs!"

"Just don't ask me two questions at once!" Ashley adds. "You know I'm just a handyman without the ability to think independently."

"I hope when you're away, you decide to stay away, you bloody fool," Stephens mumbles as he moves off.

***

Conners enters the reception to find Adler impatiently pacing. "Would you like a drink, sir?" she enquires politely, and he turns his indignant glare onto her, believing that the task should already have been carried out.

"Cognac! Large!" he demands.

She moves to the drink's cabinet, places two pieces of ice into a glass, then covers them with Remi Martin Louis XIII Cognac and hands it to the ingrate to receive no acknowledgement of thanks. "I will inform the sirs of your presence, sir."

He takes a sizeable savouring sip of the cognac, then scoops the ice out to discard onto the sideboard for her to pick up and place into a new glass before wiping the area clean then, leaving the obnoxious man to his tentative thoughts, she exits into the hallway to find the philanthropist twins, Charles and Gordon Morrison listening amused by their nephew's whimpering.

"Sirs, Mr A," she starts, but Charles mischievously places his index finger over his mouth to stop her.

"So, we see Conners," Charles whispers. "Doesn't he sound agitated?" Unable to see any difference in the obnoxious man's behaviour, she grins but doesn't answer.

"He must be after more money," Gordon adds with an equally broad smile of mischievousness, but Charles interjects with the thought of torturing his arrogant nephew.

"Let's go have some fun, Gordon."

Believing it to be a harmless bit of ribbing, Gordon adds excitedly. "Yes, lets."

"Would you like some drinks, sirs?" Conners enquires delicately of the two elderly gentlemen, who smile their delight at her well-meaning enquiry.

"A Southern comfort for me and a diet Pepsi for Gordon," Charles answers.

"Ice, sirs?"

"Of course," Gordon adds. "Only alcoholics want their drinks neat he adds, amusing her with Adler's antics moments prior.

"Stop being soft, Gordon," Charles grumbles. "And a Valium for our nephew and no ice for me," he said, gaining his brother's irritation. Aware that after the twins have finished their fun, Adler will be harder to deal with, Conners grins perturbed at the thought as she knows he will be her problem. Charles and Gordon enter the reception, amused to see the angry stare of their financially seeking nephew.

"Look, Gordon, it's our beautiful nephew, Jerome," Charles said with sarcastic intent that Adler doesn't take kindly to. "He's come from London to see how we are."

"Very nice of him," Gordon said, playing to the humour.

Conners moves to the drinks cabinet, pouring the twins their respective drinks.

"What can we do for you this lovely morning, Jerome?" Gordon adds, and Adler's eyes switch between the twins for a reaction to his unexpected visit.

"I thought I may stay a couple of days, uncles."

Gordon smiles with genuine pleasure. "You're always welcome, Jerome. You know that," he said as Adler sheepishly downs his cognac and looked to Conners, expecting a refill.

"I told you of my multi-million-Pound deal?"

"And speak of business," Charles gripes to his brother's disdain. "We informed you we're not interested in your shady venture?"

"We don't deal in the unforgiving world of business now. We have people to deal with that for us," Gordon explains politely, but Charles snipes his exhaustion of the subject he thought he had left behind on the day of his retirement.

"You need to speak to our people, but you already have, or you wouldn't be here."

"So, you keep in touch with the autocrats who run your empire," Adler snarls with knowing. "And they keep you informed."

"It doesn't matter how much money you believe is involved, Jerome," Gordon explains, hoping he will understand their company's stringent policy at some point. "We don't and never have dealt with third parties."

"Not interested in making money?" Adler said testily. "I find that hard to believe." He moves to the drinks cabinet and knocks Conners aside as he frustratingly refills his glass. "All you have to do is go to the vault and get what I need."

Not a man to toy with, Charles growls his increasing anger so his nephew will understand his irritation. "Don't be bloody clever,

Jerome!"

"Calm down, Charles," Gordon mediates, but his brother turns his full ire onto their nephew.

"Why the bloody hell should I? Anyway, nephew, why are you involved in this? That's not your role in the company."

Conners hands the twins their drinks, then nods and exits as fast as her obligations allow.

In the hope he can at least sway Gordon, the more composed of his uncles, into his way of thinking, Adler carries on with a pitiful show of self-sorrow. "I know you believe I am just a lowly accountant."

"We don't think that," Gordon explains, but Charles interrupts angrily and then looks at his brother, who wants him to calm and keep his blood pressure down.

"We started as bloody accountants! You're learning the business from the bottom up as we did. Just because our little sister is your grandmother does not give you the right to an easy ride. We had to do without on many occasions."

Wanting his nephew's visit to be peaceful, which the two elderly men desire, Gordon adds. "You need to have patience, Jerome. Learn your trade first and foremost; then you may go into that business side."

"I haven't asked for an easy ride," Adler continues ignorantly as he sips his cognac with only his interest at heart. "I just want a chance to prove myself and be taken seriously. Don't you think I am clever enough?"

Gordon feels compassion for his nephew's position but knows his brother is co and explains with guilt. "Nobody is questioning your academic skills."

"Well, this time, I have proven you wrong!" Adler arrogantly harangues as Gordon attempts to calm the irrational situation.

"You have nothing to prove to us."

"This deal is worth tens of millions of Dollars."

"You're missing the point, Jerome. We have obligations to the British and American Governments," Charles explains most simply. "The technologies you are looking for aren't for third-party countries."

"We owe the British and American Governments total loyalty," Gordon reasons, but Adler snipes as tears of frustrated impotence well in his eyes.

"You owe them nothing!"

"Bull-shit, Jerome!" Charles shouts his patience at breaking point. "We owe them everything."

In the hope his brother will calm down, Gordon stares at Charles until he glances over, then looks away embarrassed.

"You molly coddle the fool, Gordon."

"You think I'm a fool and want me to look like an idiot in the business world?"

"If you look a fool, it's your own making," Charles continues. "This Egyptian you want to deal with." He adds curiously. "How did you find out he was after buying our technology?"

Adler speaks to the twins' amusement. "They need the technologies to keep up with the Israelis."

"And why would we allow that to happen? We are Jewish."

"Your acting Anti-Semitic without understanding your heritage, Jerome," Charles adds, disgruntled. "The Americans would be furious if we sold technologies to the enemies of Israel."

Adler downs his cognac and then moves to the drinks cabinet to pour another. "I shook on the deal," he adds pitifully, but he isn't ready for Charles' scathing criticism.

"Then you've learnt another valuable lesson about the world of business. Never shake on a deal unless you can personally deliver on it."

Adler's eyes shift impatiently between his uncles as he whimpers impotently. "So, you're not prepared to back me and want to make me look an incompetent fool?"

"I believe I have answered that," Charles said, uncaring.

Adler's naïve attempt at gaining sympathy is wasted on the hardened octogenarians. "My apparent incompetence will reflect on your reputations."

Needing to laugh, Charles calms with reason. "I think not."

Adler downs the cognac and then snarls his ever-increasing angst. "I suppose I'd better get back to my desk and vegetate! I will inform Grant you aren't prepared to back me."

"Grant?" Charles calls out angrily. "What has this to do with him?"

Aware his uncles won't be happy, Adler cares for nothing in his self-aggrandising world other than himself. "He assisted me in the negotiations with Faisel."

Charles' face reddens as his blood pressure rises. "He had no right! He's a company lawyer, not a go-between. I will bloody well see to him." He turns to his brother, who is waving his arms for calm. "I want to know why we didn't know of his involvement?" he questions, but Adler doesn't care for the repercussions that will likely be pressed onto his surreptitious business partner.

"He acted at my bequest," Adler explains as if his involvement meant it was for the good.

"You don't have the authority to give out assignments!" Charles adds, but Gordon is curious and adds calmly to defend his naive nephew. "Are you sure it wasn't Grant or this Egyptian who approached you, Jerome?"

"I don't bloody believe it!" Adler snarls. "More embarrassment!"

"What about this Egyptian?" Charles presses, but Adler is unwilling to answer what he believes is a slight on his business acumen. "It's important that we find out the truth. Did he approach either of you?" he presses but taking it as an insult, Adler exits into the hallway then heads straight out of the mansion, almost knocking into Conners, who had positioned herself by the door to eavesdrop on their conversation. Conners recomposes herself, then enters the reception to find Charles, smiling with agonistic belief in himself and Gordon looking timidly uncomfortable by the confrontation he so readily avoids.

"Has the bloody idiot gone?" Charles enquires, and she answers coyly, amused.

"I believe he has, sir."

"Good riddance to him!" Charles shouts, but Gordon is unhappy with his brother's lack of compassion. "How does he know what we have in our vault?" he says, catching Conners' attention, but neither of the twins notice her interest. "It will be that bloody Grant!" he shouts angrily. "Next time I see him, I will sack him."

"I agree," Gordon explains with consideration. "But don't you think you were a little hard on Jerome?"

"I should have kicked his money-grabbing arse out of here years ago," Charles shouts but instantly calms on noticing Conners looking uncomfortable. "Excuse my foul language, Conners, but business is hard. We had to climb a very steep ladder to get to the top. It wasn't handed to us on a silver platter."

Unhappy with the memory of the unscrupulous things that conspired on their way to success, Gordon mumbles uncomfortably as he turns from Conners' stare. "I remember, brother, I was there. We had to do some terrible things."

Aware Conners is in the room, Charles calls to his brother, and they turn onto her as Gordon gently holds her hands.

"Would you please bring him back? He did say he was staying for a couple of days."

"Let the idiot go! We can do without the miserable sod spoiling our relaxation," Charles shouts hard-heartedly, but Gordon is having none of it.

"We have plenty of time to relax and not enough for family."

"He's attempting to undermine my corporation," Charles carries on angrily as Conners' glance shifts between the twins, unsure what she should do.

"Please, bring him back," Gordon adds, and she smiles and then exits with little haste on her hunt for a man; she couldn't bring herself to have empathy for.

***

Travelling as fast as its lithium batteries will carry it, a golf cart nears the helipad with Stephens driving and the embittered Adler sitting at his side. Believing he has a good relationship with his silent passenger because of his high standing within the twins' household, Stephens enquires about Adler's well-being, but he is unhappy at being addressed by a servant and snarls his irritation. Stephens stops at the helipad, and Adler alights like a petulant child and walks off with no word of thanks.

"Start her up!" Adler demands that the pilot, without a word of complaint, carry out the task without explanation.

***

Ashley drives his golf cart up and stops outside the security office as Knox exits to greet him as he takes a mouthful of whisky from his hip flask.

"Is that you finished, James?"

The elation of escaping the drudgery of being a lackey to people like Adler, Ashley answers with pleasure. "Too right." He takes another mouthful of whisky.

"Now you can get pissed in your own time," Knox adds to Ashley's amusement but ignores the comment as if it hadn't happened.

"Firstly, I'm going to have a swim to cool down. Then I'm," he adds, but Knox interrupts as the helipad takes his eye with the helicopter lifting off.

"What time's the chopper leaving?"

"Depends on the eagle," Ashley said then bursts out singing to the Clash's classic song. "Will he stay, or will he go?"

Knox points for Ashley to turn and look. "I think he's going without you."

"What the fuck," Ashley shouts as the helicopter flies over, and he sees Stephens driving up on his golf cart smiling with distorted delight.

"What's going on, Stephens?" he complains, but this irritates the man with the high-standing ego.

"That's Mr Stephens to the likes of you."

Ashley's horrified stare stays on the helicopter heading into the distance. "I was supposed to be on that."

"You did say you were going for a swim, James," Knox said with a smile that turned into a laugh which Ashley found amusing.

"I wish you weren't, but, well, it looks like you are stuck here," Stephens said, instantly dropping Ashley's mood.

"When is it due back?" Ashley apprehensively enquires about Stephens' indifference.

"That I don't know. Mr Adler may decide to return, but that has nothing to do with the likes of you."

"Brilliant!" Ashley shouts, making Knox laugh uproariously.

"I don't know why you want to return to the UK, and its bloody awful weather?"

Well aware of why he is leaving, Ashley turns on Stephens. "The likes of me would like to know why the eagle has gone this time?" he questions, but Stephens believes he should know his place,

"That's Mr Adler and no business of a bloody handyman."

"I prefer multi-skilled maintenance technician or general dog's body."

"Or lazy guttersnipe," Knox adds to Ashley's nodding agreement.

"He'll have fallen out with the twins," he adds, then mimics a baby's dummy coming out of his mouth. "You know what a huffy shit he is."

"That's also none of your business, Knox," Stephens interjects.

"They probably won't give him this week's fifty K pocket money," Ashley adds.

"That's enough of that. If either of the sirs hears you talking like this, you will lose your cushy jobs."

"They'd agree," Ashley said with humour that doesn't sit well with the self-important Stephens. "I have plenty of time now."

Ashley alights the golf cart but stumbles as he throws the keys for Knox to catch.

"Have you been drinking?" Stephens questions and Ashley looks at Knox's amusement as he answers with a vigorous shake of his head.

"I was just going to carry out such an act."

"I take it you aren't going for that swim, Ashley?" Stephens adds in a poor attempt at humour that doesn't receive any attention.

Ashley looks at Knox and grins as he walks off. "Surely you should be Mr Knox, and I should be Mr Ashley."

"I can't see that happening," Knox said.

Stephens goes to drive off. "Now get back to work."

Ashley laughs. "I don't know what you're going to do, Mr Knox, but this lazy shite's on holiday and has a bottle of whisky waiting for him in his room."

***

The twins stand in their lavishly furnished reception, looking at the helicopter heading toward the mainland as Conners moves over to hand them their drinks and Charles downs his in one.

"Don't worry about Mr Adler; he'll be back, sirs," she said, concerned for Gordon's good nature.

Charles moves to the drinks cabinet and pours himself a Southern Comfort, then lifts it in salute. "We could have done with these earlier to pour over the little shits head to cool him off," he said with meaning, but Gordon didn't like the humour as he turned to Conners to take a loving hold of her hand.

"It's a good job you are here. You are the highlight of my retirement," Gordon said to Charles' amusement.

"Gordon Morrison! That's enough of that."

Conners' smile shows the friendship she has for the calmer twin. "It's a pleasure to be here, sir."

"If I was five years younger, I would be after courting you," Gordon said adoringly, but the angrier twin laughed, giving an embarrassed shake of his head.

"Try Fifty, you old sod."

Gordon hands his untouched Pepsi to Conners, "Could you take our drinks into the lounge, please? We'll be along in a minute."

Conners smiles as she takes Charles' glass and then exits.

***

Conners crosses the hallway into the lounge, places the drinks on the table, and then closes the door to ensure she won't be easily disturbed. She produces the parcel and opens it to reveal the listening device to place into the interior of a lampshade situated on a side table. "For whoever is listening," she whispered. "You're on."

***

A boat designed to look like friends fishing in the Atlantic sits two miles off Mill Island with an agency operator seated on the rear with his rod in the water, and inside, two operators sit with a large amount of electronic equipment around as they listen to Conners' voice resonating out of a speaker.

"Tell Rupprecht he's a dick," she calls out with a laugh.

"Who's Rupprecht?" the first operator said as he switched on the recording device attached to the listening device and then picked up the phone to be connected to the man whose name was alien to him. "Sir, we have ears," he adds, then listens to Chaucer's demanding voice before replacing the receiver. "I get the feeling that's Rupprecht."

***

The helicopter comes out of the brightness and skirts the tarmac of LF Wade to travel the short distance and stop just shy of the executive reception. Not giving the rotors time to slow, Adler alights at speed and produces his phone as he enters the terminal.

***

Enjoying the fruits his one thousand Dollars had paid for, Grant lies on the super king bed within his large home as he messes about with a scantily clad woman. Not the nicest person to have to deal with, he carries the same arrogance Adler purveys but doesn't have the means to carry out the bravado being a salaried employee of the Morrison Corporation and not the playboy millionaire he desires to be which had landed him the debt of a compulsive gambler that a good business transaction would clear him of. Sitting on the bedside table, his phone rings, and having expected the call, he moves onto the side of the bed to answer as the high-priced lady massages his neck and shoulders. "Grant here!"

Adler moves through the executive reception. "Mr Adler here," he said, expectant of instant obedience.

"Mr Adler. Can you hold for a second?" Grant said as he stood and moved from the prostitute's touch to the drinks cabinet to pour himself a whisky as he knew Adler would shuffle in anger as he awaited him to speak. "How's everything going in the octagon?" he said, but his reference to his favourite sport fell on deaf ears of the ignorant man listening.

"I told you the old bastards wouldn't go for it!" Adler shouts, and Grant downs his whisky and then pours another.

"And they know how much money is at stake?"

"What's money to them?" Adler groans. "They weren't happy about your involvement."

Grant lowers the phone to his chest, cringes as he downs the whisky, and then lifts it back to his ear. "What brought me into the conversation?"

Even though he is aware Grant had specified not to be identified,

Adler adds without apology. "I thought it would help them rethink the deal if they know your experience was on board."

Angered but not wanting Adler to be aware of his misgivings, Grant holds his thoughts. "Where are you now?"

"I'm on the main island," Adler answers to instantly increase Grant's anger as he had blatantly changed their plan at the first sign of trouble. "What are you doing there? You have to get back to Mill Island and talk them around."

"They won't listen," Adler whimpers, his defeatist nature. "We can't get this deal off the ground without their say-so."

"Grow up, Jerome!" Grant growls, annoying Adler at being talked down to by a man he classes as an employee. Aware of Adler's penchant for petty-mindedness and inability to work under pressure, he adds, not wanting to be the one to confront the twins. "Go back to Mill Island and work on Gordon. He's the soft underbelly and will break first, but you have to let them know how good a deal it is and that there is money to be made."

Believing he is better than others, Adler doesn't want to carry on with what he classes as begging for scraps from his uncle's table. "That won't work."

"It won't if you do nothing!" Grant shouts. "Look, I will fly to Bermuda tomorrow and meet you."

Adler has no intention of returning to see his condescending uncles alone and smiles at the thought of an ally to accompany him. "That's a good idea. I will await your arrival."

Even though he disagrees with Adler's submissiveness, Grant interjects, aware that nothing will change his stubborn, immature mind. "If you feel that is for the best, don't worry. This deal will go ahead, and I will see you tomorrow afternoon." He switches his phone off and moves to the bed to sit as the woman sidles behind to kiss his neck.

Having listened to the private conversation, the prostitute enquires, unaware of the danger her words place her in. "Why didn't you tell him you're in Bermuda?"

Even though he had used the same high-class prostitute numerous times, he didn't like her eavesdropping on his business. "Never give away your true intentions," he snarls. "I'm not going to tell that dick any more than I need to." He dials his phone and moves off slightly as he nervously awaits an answer. "It's me," he said to hear an Irish accent question the reason for the call. "Look. Mr Adler has got nowhere with the twins, so we have to go to plan B," he adds, and the call is instantly curtailed for him to place the phone down. He looks the prostitute up and down lecherously. "Anyway, where was I?" He takes her aggressively around the neck. "Your prying is going to cost you, dear."

***

Adler exits the executive reception onto the tarmac, and the unsuspecting pilot straightens himself out at his approach.

"Mr Adler, I was just off to have a bite to eat."

"Have your food, but you're not to return to Mill Island tonight." Aware of Adler's petulance, the pilot is placed into a situation he doesn't want to find himself in. "But, sir, I have been requested to return," he explains, dreading not doing as Charles had requested, but Adler interrupts furiously.

"I'm giving the fucking orders here! You will wait until tomorrow when you will fly Mr Grant and me back, or you will have me to deal with. Have I made myself clear?"

Bemused about why he is being ordered to wait, the pilot instantly shows the arrogant man subservience. "Yes, sir, but where will I stay?" Only caring about his own predicament, Adler snarls back. "That's not my problem! I want you here first thing, ready and waiting." He heads off, leaving the pilot disgusted by his degrading treatment.

***

CHAPTER 19

***

Looking for his last payday to help in his quest to retire, Raymond Reynolds is a British Army veteran with over twenty-five years serving the colours at regiment level, Special Forces and military intelligence. After being forced out of the military, he used the skills gained to become a soldier of fortune, which he had carried out for the past five years and earned him a solid reputation as a man who gets the job done, no matter how nasty or distasteful that may be. A beautiful sunny day finds him standing at the edge of the pool in a rented villa situated just outside Hamilton, Bermuda, as the men he had personally hand-picked to carry out the mission ahead lie on sun loungers as they catch the heat of the early afternoon and enjoy their time to relax. His telephone rings, catching the attention of the men, and he moves inside to answer and then listen before disconnecting the call. He picks up a cigar to light with a broad smile. "It's time you found out why you're here!" he shouts, and the dogs of war enter as he makes his way to a DVD player to put a disc in.

With very little in the form of a future, Coby Duggan had joined the American Army at the age of seventeen to get away from the poverty of his birth in New Orleans and remained within the ranks, including several years with Delta Force, before leaving to chase the almighty Dollar and join the unscrupulous world of the mercenary. Showing his enthusiasm for the fight, he shouts his interest, but Reynolds ignores his inflated attitude.

Mick Miller had served twenty years with the Australian Special Air Service, then a brief non-eventful experience with his country's Secret Intelligence Service. Disillusioned with his minor role, he missed the daily slog of the infantry. However, being too old to re-enlist, he chose the same road as most disillusioned fighting men and entered the world of the private military to carry on his lust for action. "Great Porn!" he shouts with several claps of his enthusiastic hands. "This will give you a bigger hard-on than a pair of tits!" Reynolds shouts, catching all their attention.

"That's got to be money!" Duggan shouts, and Miller adds to the humour that most find funny except the German Holzmann.

"It could be a cock fest for the Kraut."

Having recently left the ranks of Kommando Spezialkrafte of the German Army, Klaus Holzmann doesn't understand the ill-discipline of the men in the room and calls out with menace to their hilarity as he debates whether to re-enlist or carry on with the charade, he finds himself a part of. "Fuck you!" he shouts with meaning. Showing when business needs to be discussed, he hasn't a humorous bone in his body, Reynolds shouts angrily. "Shut the fuck up and listen! This is serious shit and will make you all rich men! You've all been hand-picked to carry out a task where professionalism is required, so start acting as such."

The television comes to life, and news footage begins with the newsreader's self-important smile. "Today, two of the richest men in the world. The seventy-year-old twins, Charles and Gordon Morrison, have retired from business." The screen shows footage of the twins' business careers up to their retirement onto Mill Island, with little interest from all watching. "The Morrison Corporation," the newsreader carries on. "Which was set up over fifty years ago and have an estimated value of five hundred billion Pounds and will still trade, but the twins are to retire to the island they bought off the coast of Bermuda. Now with business being a thing of the past, all they have to look forward to is sun, sand and plenty of relaxation. Good luck the both of them."

Reynolds pauses the DVD as he looks around at the disinterested faces. "Were you fucking listening?" he shouts, and the room goes deathly quiet.

"When's the exciting bit?" Holzmann questions, gaining a laugh from several of them, but he hadn't meant it as a joke and looked bewildered by the unintentional humour.

"Weren't you fucking watching?"

"I was and still don't know what's going on," Duggan interjects. Unable to understand the men's mentality, Reynolds shouts angrily but instantly calms. "The job is the biggest robbery of all time."

Duggan stands feigning protest. "Robbery? I'm a soldier, not a criminal!" he shouts, but Reynolds isn't in the mood for the prima donna antics of any professional soldier and speaks with the menace all in the room are aware of.

"You're a soldier of fortune without a fucking war and a fucking empty bank account to boot, so stop your shit!"

Richard, Richie, Johnston, a man born in Wales, had served all over the world with the Royal Marines and SBS but was dishonourably discharged for conduct unbecoming a member of her majesty's armed forces. The reason for the discharge had been classified so as not to cause alarm. Still, he was mistakenly accused of killing civilians in Afghanistan, and to his eternal disgrace, that had led him into the unforgiving arms of the mercenary. Having taken an interest in the monetary value of the film, he interrupts. "So, you intend to rob the Morrison's? Why would you need us?"

"Surely they'll be well guarded?" Duggan interjects to Reynolds' deepening contempt.

"I thought you wanted a war, soldier boy?"

"Like Duggan said," Miller interrupts. "Won't they be guarded?"

Reynolds restarts the DVD. "Just shut the fuck up and watch."

***

With a towel wrapped tightly around his waist, Ashley stands in his en-suite bathroom, looking at himself in the mirror and grins at how haggard he looks. He opens his pain medication, pops two into his mouth, then turns the tap on to take a mouthful of water and swallow. He moves into the living area to find Conners sitting on a chair, waiting for him to finish his shower. "If it isn't my favourite maid. Could you turn the bed down, please?" he said to her, smiling amusement.

"As if that's going to happen."

"Come on. You do the old farts' beds every day."

Having taken a liking to the two elderly gentlemen, she defends the relationship she has with them. "They're not old farts, Jimmy."

"Aren't they!" he interrupts in disbelief. "Surely you read the brief on them?"

"I don't think they're as bad as portrayed."

"You're kidding me? One wants to fuck you, and the other wants to kill you," he adds to her staring disagreement.

"We're wasting our time here."

"There are worse places to be assigned," he adds with reasoning. "We could be back in that barn in Ireland, or I could be up to my balls in piss and shit in a cave somewhere in Afghanistan, or you could be taking the minutes of a meeting at Langley," he adds with hilarity.

"I suppose so, but at least in that barn, I only had your pissy attitude to contend with."

"We all have to deal with the dicks. You're too far up your own arse and don't like your role as a maid."

"I don't mean the twins. It's the eagle I don't like. He's a real ass and for reasons only known to them, they always get me to deal with him," she said bitterly. "I'd like to put a bullet in his fucking head."

Feeling he had outstayed paradise, Ashley added with hope. "Maybe the director will call it a day soon."

"I can't see that happening with the listening device being brought into play."

"Yeah, I don't get that one," he adds to her equal bemusement. "Ours is to do as ordered. Well, now I'm officially off duty. Why don't we drink some wine and relax?"

"Wine?" she calls out shocked. "Get a bottle of single malt, and I will join you."

Mimicking Shirlow, Ashley makes his way to a cabinet and pulls out a bottle of whisky. "I've only got this eighteen-year-old Dalmore," he said, and she laughed comically.

"I don't mind slumming it," she said, and he gave her a curious stare as to the use of her words as he lifted a bottle to show a cheap blended supermarket whisky.

"Well, you'll have to because I've only got this shit." He fills two glasses and hands one to Conners, who grins at the volume as he lifts his in salute. "To the end of this hell assignment."

Conners takes a sip and is instantly discouraged by the taste. "That's great coming from someone whose ass hardly comes off that golf cart."

"We all have our parts to play," he said laughing. "No matter how small that is."

"This is awful, Jimmy," she bemuses. "Can't you ever get the good stuff?"

"Its only purpose is to take over my mind, and I prefer doing that on the cheap. Whisky's whisky to me, so next time, bring your own. When I get to Bermuda, I'll find out the director's intentions when he gets there," he adds, but she is more inclined to stay on the island paradise. "Don't bother the man. I will stay until he pulls me."

***

Reynolds switches the DVD off and looks around the money-hungry mercenaries who don't understand the significance of what they have just watched.

"That was the shittest film I've ever seen!" Duggan shouts for the majority of the mercenaries to laugh.

"But I would imagine the most lucrative," Reynolds said straight-faced. "As you should have seen, the mansion is full of art and riches."

Not seeing anything to make him believe there was money to be made, Richie shakes his head and calls out. "Where did you get the film from?"

Tired and frustrated by the constant interruptions, Reynolds shouts angrily. "Shut the fuck up!"

Amused by the rebuke, Richie smiles. "Sorry, boss. Just a bit of light-hearted banter to help get through the day. Please, carry on."

"I'll get to the fucking point," Reynolds instructs with what he knows will be the intense part of their gathering. "Your wages for this operation will be five hundred thousand Dollars per head."

The room lightens at the thought of such riches, but Richie is perplexed by the amount on offer.

"Is that five hundred thousand US Dollars, and you did say each?"

"And all we have to do is rob the place of its treasures," Reynolds continues.

"Surely the art will be traceable?" Richie adds perceptively, but Reynolds explains in greater detail.

"The intelligence is most of it is already stolen. Old masters and the like."

"They couldn't have them on display."

"They aren't," Reynolds adds. "They have a vault but we'll only take the valuable stuff. Everything else has been earmarked for removal for others."

Showing his mistrust of a mission that pays so much for minimal effort, Holzmann adds. "We must have a man on the inside."

"What about guards?" Duggan interrupts to the German's irritation at not receiving an answer.

"Three, security."

"Armed?"

Reynolds shouts angrily. "Tell me, when was the last fucking time you went anywhere without a weapon?"

"Sounds suspect to me," Daniau interrupts, adding to Reynolds' increasing irritation.

Claude Daniau served his country with distinction from boy to man. A long-established member of Commandement des Forces d'operations speciales du Canada, he is a true patriot and only left the service to gain the money needed to set himself up in the reclusive life in the wilds of Ontario which he desperately pines for and believes where he will be able to live out his life as a good French Canadian. "I agree with Duggan," he adds on moralistic grounds and his value toward human life. "I am a soldier, not a robber."

"Tell me an easier way of making five hundred thousand Dollars, and

I'll listen?" Reynolds questions, but the proud French Canadian doesn't know how to reply to such directness.

"Don't listen to my shit," Duggan adds, laughing. "I'm well up for this."

"Good," Reynolds adds. "And you, Claude?"

Daniau gives the mission more thought and then stands, straightening himself out. "I must decline. I'm a soldier, not a common criminal."

Attempting to hide his disappointment, Reynolds adds. "I'm sure you will understand if I ask you to wait outside."

Believing he can be trusted and doesn't need to be dismissed, Daniau interjects. "I'm a man of honour who takes pride in my father's values."

Reynolds goes to Daniau's side to help him to the door and enter the pool area. "No doubt, but what I have to say must remain for the ears of those involved. Hopefully, a war of honour will come along, and we can work together again," Reynolds said sarcastically, and Daniau nodded his misunderstanding and then moved off. "Anyone else want to leave?"

Showing enthusiasm, missing earlier when the call of monetary reward was mentioned, Miller calls out. "Count me in."

Impatiently dismayed with the need to get on, Reynolds' eyes shift menacingly around the room. "Well?"

No matter what the morals of what is expected, all in the room show they have no intention of walking away from such a windfall, but Richie enquires with what is on all their mistrusting minds.

"Where is the money coming from? Who's bankrolling this?"

"That's no concern of yours," Reynolds answers as he closes the door. "All you need to know is it's coming."

"What about Claude's share?" Richie adds to receive rapturous applause. "Surely it should be shared between those who stayed?" he carries on, but Reynolds can only reason a reply without the say of the man pulling the strings.

"That decision isn't for me to take."

"Whose then?" Miller interrupts, looking around for the backing of the others. "Who makes that decision?"

"That's no concern of yours, but be reassured, I will put it to him personally," Reynolds explains. "Now, back to the fucking plan. We do have a man on the inside."

"That's good to know," Holzmann said, but Duggan still mistrusts outside involvement.

"Is he the source of our information?"

"He'll be after a cut of the takings?" Miller interrupts.

"He will," Reynolds said. "But he's not one of us, so the only cut he will be getting will be to his throat."

"Good," Holzmann interrupts callously.

"I wouldn't be too happy, Kraut," Daniels said. "That may be your payment too."

Annoyed at the constant interference, Reynolds shouts out. "Will you shut the fuck up and let me get on with this!"

"Is it him who's bank rolling this?" Holzmann adds. "Places like this ain't free, so somebody must have come up with the money."

Duggan draws his knife and lifts it into the air, and laughs. "What's his cut?"

"He wants the art and valuables," Reynolds explains as Duggan feigns the knife crossing his throat. Aware of who controls the mission, he doesn't want his men being overheard by Soames, who he knows doesn't have a sense of humour and could be listening and would kill them all without compunction. "Don't be fucking idiots! All the works of art are well known, so unless you know an unscrupulous art dealer, they are no good to us." He pauses, taking in the scene. "We're being well paid to rob the mansion. Well, fucking paid!" he adds in mind that their payment is far too large for the menial task at hand. "No more fucking questions!"

"Who's our sponsor?" Duggan persists with what he doesn't want to know to gain a rise out of the angry Reynolds, who snipes back bitterly. "You're being paid not to fucking ask!"

"Shit," Richie said. "It could be a set-up."

"Who would want to set you up?"

"I've been in many situations where people would want me dead."

"Yeah, like here!" Holzmann shouts to Richie's irritation.

"It's not a fucking set-up!" Reynolds shouts. "If you're unhappy, you can go out the same fucking door as Claude."

Geoffrey Daniels, a former major in the Coldstream Guards, was once trusted to guard the British Royal family and doesn't suffer fools gladly and carries a dislike of any one of the Germanic Heritage stemming from the stories his great grandfather had told him about his mistreatment as a POW in World War 2. He had only served eight years under the colours until his court martial for being drunk and disorderly while on duty and had been sentenced to eighteen months in Colchester and to be dishonourably discharged from the service. Like most soldiers, he struggled to make a living as a civilian until a close friend showed him the money he could earn as a mercenary, and he hadn't looked back after twelve years of serving in many conflicts around the world. "Yeah, why don't you fuck off, you Hun bastard," he interjects. "We'll dole out your share like Claude's."

"You'd like that, wouldn't you," Holzmann aggressively argues.

"You bet I fucking would. If there are only three guards, you're not needed."

"Neither are you!" Holzmann shouts as they vault to their feet and scuffle across the floor with punches thrown.

"Sit the fuck down, idiots!" Reynolds shouts, but they continue and he draws his Glock 19 and puts two shots into the floor to separate them in panic. "If you're not fucking interested in what I have to say, you can fuck off with Claude!"

Holzmann and Daniels separate but glare their petty bickering isn't over and will be taken up later.

Reynolds walks to a drawer, opens it to take out an envelope, and throws it onto a table. "That's a plan of the mansion and island. Study it, and don't leave out any detail."

"When do we go?" Richie enquires calmly.

Reynolds produces a wad of cash to throw onto the table. "First thing tomorrow. There's a grand there. After you get yourselves well versed with the plan, get yourselves into Hamilton and have some food and a few beers," he said, and the room livens at the thought of food and drink. "But don't get pissed! I need you working on all cylinders tomorrow." He points his Glock between Daniels and Holzmann. "And if I hear you two have carried on your spat, you'll have me to contend with."

All the mercenaries exit, and Daniau enters through the open doors. "Just a second, Claude," Reynolds said, moving to the sideboard and writing a few lines on paper. "When we're gone, our sponsor will come and pay you your expenses in person."

Daniau looks the paper over with mistrust on having it handed to him. "You may get some other work when he's here," Reynolds adds, and Daniau smiles and then exits more easily. He produces his phone and dials. "All is going to plan, but the Canadian frog doesn't want anything to do with it," he said, listening to Soames' voice on the other end and adding. "He's waiting for you to pay him what's owed."

***

Charles and Gordon stand in the lounge, and Charles replaces the phone receiver and turns to his calmer brother.

"Still no answer?"

"I've tried his mobile and his house phone."

"Maybe he's in a meeting."

"Don't be naïve, Gordon. He'll have ordered his staff not to answer. The obnoxious little bastard that he is."

"I will send him an e-mail," Gordon adds, moving for his phone.

"Leave it!" Charles shouts annoyed. "I could do without listening to his petty snivelling excuse.

"What about Jerome?"

Charles turns his contemptuous stare onto his brother but doesn't answer as he walks off.

***

Amused at the frantic actions of the billionaires, the two operators sit on their boat, listening to the radio speaker relaying their every word.

"This Grant's avoiding them," the first operator said with a laugh, and his colleague nodded his agreement.

"Can't blame him? If I'd gone behind the backs of the Morrison's, I'd be shitting my pants. What I know of Charles, he's a bastard."

"They reckon Gordon isn't too bad," the first operator adds to his colleague's amusement.

"But he ain't the dominant twin."

"I'd better keep Rupprecht abreast of what's going on," the first operator said, picking up the phone. "We don't want him throwing his handbag at us."

***

CHAPTER 20

***

Powering through the calm waters of the Atlantic, a small rigid raider assault craft, propelled by two 140bhp outboard motors, comes up onto Ridley beach on the north-western side of Mill Island, and the mercenaries jump into the surf as Holzmann stays on board to hand small backpacks to each of them.

"Take the boat to the marina," Reynolds orders. "Then go to the mansion to help with the goods."

"I remember the fucking plan!" Holzmann barks. "I'm not a fucking retard like Daniels!" he adds as the former guardsman screams back his irritation.

"For fucks sake, leave your petty bickering for after this shit!" Reynolds reasons as he pushes the boat into the surf for it to reverse out.

As Holzmann turns the boat, he sees Knox driving toward them on a golf cart and points for Reynolds to look.

"We've got company," Reynolds said, gaining all the mercenaries' attention. "Leave him to me."

The golf cart skids to a halt, and Knox jumps off. "Bring that boat back!" he shouts as he walks into the surf. "This is a private island!" Reynolds reaches into his backpack and draws his Glock to point at the unsuspecting security guard, who steps back, terrified by the threat.

"Are you alone?" he demands, and Knox replies with a nervous nod as he is shot in the chest to knock him into the surf, where two more bullets finish the job as the waves lap over his lifeless body and crash him unceremoniously onto the beach.

To get what he wants without argument, Reynolds opens the backpack and produces a Heckler and Koch MP7 machine pistol. "You know what to do!" he shouts as they arm themselves and put their backpacks on. "Increase the pace in case those shots were heard."

***

Having worked for the Morrison family for over five years, Douglas Henderson had never seen the need to be on edge as nothing life-threatening had ever happened on the island. Flicking a coin into the air and catching it in his boredom, he relaxes in the security office as he awaits Knox to relieve him of his night shift.

Carrying his MP7, Daniels enters, and Henderson almost falls off his seat as he stands in horrified shock. "Are you alone?" he demands, and the security officer nods nervously, unaware the aggressor has no intention of taking prisoners, and his body is sprayed with an excessive number of bullets that tear him apart as he falls to the floor dead.

***

Reynolds and Duggan enter the mansion through the hallway to the bottom of the grand marble staircase, envious of the wealth on show. Stewart exits a side room with two chefs and a maid, all having surrendered under the threat of death.

Reynolds grabs the maid by the hair and points his Glock hard into her face. "Scream." he menaced, and she looked at him, unaware of his meaning. "Scream, you fucking bitch!" he growls with intimidation as he takes a twisting hold of her hair, and she screams in mortified pain until her throat croaks, forcing her to catch her breath.

Charles and Gordon exit their rooms upstairs to stare over the balustrade into the hallway in bewilderment at the armed man abusing their maid.

"What the bloody hell is going on?" Charles shouts, unhappy at the unnecessary treatment of a staff member. "Leave that girl alone."

"Join us, Mr and Mr Morrison!" Reynolds calls with mirth, but Charles demands to know what is going on, and he fires several bullets into the ceiling above the landing to echo all around the mansion and force Gordon to duck in fright, but Charles stays steadfast as the plaster falls around them. "I won't ask again."

Gordon straightens himself out and takes his brother's arm, but the headstrong man remains motionless to the threat and must be tugged several times to escape his lame stare. Gordon walks downstairs, and after several tense seconds, his reluctant brother follows as he keeps his angry stare on the aggressor, who still has a bullying hold of his employee.

"Take your hands off her!" Charles blusters impotently to his brother's angst.

"Charles! We don't need a dead hero."

"Listen to your brother," Reynolds menaced, and Charles moved to demonstrate but Gordon pulled him back.

"Stay calm, Charles," Gordon whispers. "We need to find out what's going on."

"Nice to meet you, gentlemen," Reynolds said with the sarcastic pleasure of an evil man, but Charles didn't see any sincerity and spoke determinedly.

"Now you can let go of her. She isn't a threat to you."

Reynolds turns lecherously on the maid and grins with intent as he pushes her aggressively aside.

"You have my attention!" Charles growls. "What can I do for you?"

Daniels enters through the main doors, and Reynolds turns to see him.

"Have you done it?"

"There was only one in the security hut."

"That's two dead," Reynolds said nonchalantly to Charles' and Gordon's shock.

"What the bloody hell's going on? Who's dead?"

"What about the others?" Daniels questioned, and Reynolds answered, ignoring Charles' desperate query.

"Don't worry about them. Find our man. He said he would be in the comms room and destroy all the equipment."

Richie heads off, leaving Charles shifting uncomfortably as he awaits the answer to his question.

"Take everyone into the lounge," Reynolds orders. "Duggan, we are missing three people, a security guard, a maid and a handyman. Bring them here."

In an over-exuberant show of threat that no one in the room misses, Duggan cocks his MP7 then nods as he heads off, aware his brief isn't to take any prisoners.

"What do you hope to gain from this?" Charles demands but is knocked aside as Stewart aggressively pushes the chefs and maid into the lounge to be used as pawns against the twin moguls.

Reynolds steps aside and bows arrogantly. "After you, gentlemen."

Gordon enters the lounge, but Charles stays conceitedly still and forces his body erect with the intent not to be intimidated.

"You don't frighten me," Charles said, determined. "I demand to know what you want from us?"

Reynolds lifts his Glock to point into Charles' face. "At this moment, you in that fucking room."

"I'm not afraid to die," Charles postures angering Reynolds, who takes a tight hold of his shirt and pushes him through the lounge door to crash onto the floor with his brother coming to his aid.

"That's brave of you but don't forget there are two of you, and I only need one, so killing you won't be such a miss."

Upset at his brother's disposition, considering the severe health problems he had gained in later life, Gordon pleads with Charles in the hope that the violence will end.

"Keep him quiet, or I'm going to kill him," Reynolds threatens as Gordon helps his brother stand, and they shuffle to a chair where the frail old man drops into its comfort.

"There was no need for that."

"Just a lesson in what will happen if you don't play my little game. Have you learnt anything yet, Mr Morrison?" Reynolds menaces as he turns onto Charles, and Gordon answers, but this isn't good enough as he lifts his Glock to point. "I want to hear it from the mighty Charles Morrison himself," he demands, and after several fraught seconds, Charles reluctantly nods. "I want to hear those fucking words, Charlie."

"Yes!" Charles mumbles defeated.

"Louder!" Reynolds shouts, and Charles repeats his reply with his tone increasing until he shouts back at the top of his voice demeaned. "If he doesn't do as he is told. Kill him!"

Duggan laughs with psychotic excitement about carrying out his boss's bidding.

"I'm not afraid to die," Charles blusters his impotence which angers Gordon.

"So, you have said," Reynolds adds with meaning as he holsters the Glock, "But there are many ways to die. The majority most unpleasant."

***

Chaucer lies fast asleep in bed next to the male escort that had cost him five hundred Bermudian Dollars for the night when his phone rings, bringing him around, and he answers as he sits on the side of the bed. "Chaucer here. Hold on," he said, then covered the mouthpiece into his bare chest and nudged the escort until he woke. "Harry. This is business," he adds, and the naked man gets out of bed and enters the bathroom as he watches lecherously. He lifts the phone to his ear to be reconnected to the first operator on the surveillance boat. "Why have you disturbed me?" he sighs, disinterested.

"Sir, the Morrison twins are being held by armed men."

Hardly taking in the situation, Chaucer mumbles and then laughs. "Armed men, you say?"

"We've heard shots then voices but cannot make out what is being said. What do you want us to do?"

Chaucer doesn't take the information with the seriousness it deserves, as the disruption to his morning only perturbs him. "Nothing. It's not in my brief to intervene. Anyway, we have people on the island in case of such an eventuality, and as they haven't reported anything, we can assume nothing is happening."

"Sir," the first operator said, then paused as he looked at his colleague.

"I have reason to believe their lives are in danger."

"Nonsense!" Chaucer dismisses. "Just sit tight until I order you to do something."

Unable to agree, the first operator switches on a digital recording device to record the phone call and then enquires to lay the decision onto his obnoxious superior. "So, you want us to do nothing even though we believe they are under threat, sir?"

"That's correct. You've just overheard the television or radio!" Chaucer bellows. "Now, don't bother me again!" He puts the phone down and lies back, provocatively uncovered. "You can come out now!" he calls, and the bathroom door opens for Harry to exit. "Come," he letches. "I believe I still have you for another hour or so."

***

Even though the surveillance boat sits only two miles offshore, the operators know they are helpless without the say-so of the island's agency head.

"He thinks it's the television or radio," the first operator said awkwardly as he put the phone down.

"Well, it's all gone quiet now."

The first operator taps his finger on the digital recording device and switches it off. "If shit happens, Rupprecht will get dropped in it, not us. From now on, we will record everything. No matter how insignificant it may seem, I believe we will need it as a defence.

***

Fully clothed and asleep on the settee, Ashley comes around slowly as he feels the effects of the excessive alcohol, he had drunk last night. He stands to rub his tired, unshaven face and looks at Conners, lying fast asleep in the bed and shaking his head. "Equal rights, my arse," he said as he stretched out his aching body, then picked up his pain medication to take two and swallowed with the dregs of the whisky bottle as he headed into the bathroom to look in the mirror at his tired, haggard reflection staring back. He goes to turn the tap on when the sound of a crashing door takes his attention, and he instinctively steps behind the door out of sight, then looks through the crack to see Duggan staring at Conners with his MP7, pointing threateningly at her.

"Well, well, pretty lady," Duggan creeps as he moves to take a closer look. Even though she is fully covered, his perverted mind is already playing games with him, and he kicks the bed several times until she comes around to see her would-be assassin smiling with depraved

181

delight. "I wish I had the time to partake, but sadly, I don't."

Only having her underwear on, Conners gets out of the bed slowly and stands with Duggan grinning lecherously at what he believes is her vulnerability.

"I don't know what the captain would do, but I think I need to partake in a little of you," Duggan stalked as he moved with debauched intent to rape. Still, she sees the immediate threat and without taking the time to check out the scene properly, Ashley races out of the bathroom to grab the MP7 as several bullets are discharged into the ceiling. He twists the gun in Duggan's fingers, making him cringe in pain, then punches him in the face knocking him sideways against the wall. Believing he is up against a handyman, Duggan opens fire, forcing Conners onto the floor as the nine-millimetre bullets smash into the wall, but as the machine pistol nears Ashley, he takes hold of it and then elbows his attacker in the face to force him onto the floor and leave the machine pistol in his hands. Panicked at being disarmed, Duggan goes for his Glock as two bullets smash into his chest to neutralise the threat.

"Looks like the robbery is in process," Ashley said, looking at the MP7. "They're certainly well-armed."

Conners gets dressed as fast as she can as Ashley searches through the backpack to relieve Duggan of ammunition to place on the bed along with the Glock.

"What the hell did I have to drink last night?" he said, rubbing his aching head.

"As always, too much," she said with mirth he doesn't find humour in. "Single malt and I don't mix."

"Single malt, my ass. Oh, and just in case you've forgotten, we made love four times before you passed out," she said, and he turned in shock at his grinning colleague. "As if you could."

"What?" he adds, disorientated by the statements he doesn't understand.

"As if I would," she adds to his dismay.

"Nice to hear, but to less serious things. I've had a skin full, and the bastards decide to turn up."

"Looks that way. Hopefully, Rupprecht heard, and reinforcements are on their way."

They turn their stares onto the bed to see the ordnance at their disposal.

"An MP7 and a Glock 19 with a spare mag for each. If we are going to war, I hope he's on his own," he said, making her laugh.

"As if that would ever be the case."

***

CHAPTER 21

***

Reynolds makes his way along the large lounge wall banging on the plasterwork. He looks under several paintings with a broad smile of arrogance as he keeps glancing at the twins to see if they have an unnerved interest in what he is doing. "Am I hot or cold?" he said humorously.

"What are you looking for?" Gordon questions, intrigued, and Reynolds turns his stare directly onto the old man as he answers with a mischievous, knowing grin.

"The vault, of course, Mr Morrison."

"What vault?" Charles shouts, feigning surprise, and Reynolds laughs as he continues his search with sarcastic delight.

"So, this is a robbery?" Charles condemns. "You've killed two innocent people who were no threat to you for monetary gain?"

"Look at you are sitting there and saying for monetary gain as if it means nothing when you have a shit load of it yourself and don't share the spoils with people who serve and wipe your pristine arses daily."

"I resent that," Gordon complains to Reynolds' appreciation.

"We didn't always have money," Charles interrupts. "And we give millions to our favourite charities and good causes yearly."

"Well, I'm my favourite charity, and I can't wait to receive my donation," Reynolds said. "That's unless it's already in the post?" he adds with mirth.

"We never give to scum, and you certainly aren't a good cause!" Charles snarls to Reynolds' increasing amusement.

"Today you do, Charlie, my old son, today you do."

"You'll never find it," Gordon calls out to his brother's irritation. "And we won't tell you, and none of my staff know."

With great flamboyance, Stephens enters, followed by Richie, and all in the room see he isn't in distress. "That's where I come in."

Charles' shocked stare shifts between his brother and Stephens. "How could you betray us, Stephens? We are family."

"There you go with that Stephens shite."

"But that's your name," Gordon reasons.

"Is that right, Morrison?" Stephens said to Charles' facial damnation. "I bet you don't know my first name."

Charles looks at Gordon for an inclination but doesn't receive a reply.

"I'm just a fucking number like the other idiots you employ."

"When have we mistreated you so badly as to deserve this?" Charles carries on, but Reynolds puts a bullet in the marble floor wanting the petty bickering to cease.

"Daniels, go help Duggan. He's been away too long," Reynolds orders, and Daniels heads off at pace. "Mr Morrison's," he adds as an ironic introduction that is discourteously too late. "You know, Mr Stephens, Mr Stephens, you know your users."

Charles stands to confront, but Reynolds fires a round into the floor in front to stop him in terror.

"Sit down, you old bastard, before I knock you on your arse again."

"He won't be able to help you," Charles said confidently. "He doesn't know where the vault is."

"That's where you're wrong, Morrison," Stephens scolds with glee. He walks to the wall panelling and presses a concealed button for a flap to open, revealing a numbered keypad as everyone watches in shock. "I put a camera in here. I even saw the code."

"We change it all the time!" Charles calls out petulantly.

"Unless you changed it this morning, we'll be alright."

"But you've worked for us for years," Gordon said melancholically as the Scotsman snapped back.

"You said it! Worked! Used! Taken advantage of! No matter how you word it, I was here to do your bidding."

Defeated and aware he can't do anything, Charles stares at Reynolds' Glock. "Just take what you came for and leave us alone."

"I intend to," Reynolds said, then added with venom. "Now sit the fuck down!"

Charles sits and shuffles uncomfortably as he watches Stephens press a number into the keyboard, then step back as a door in the wall opens slowly to reveal the secret vault.

"Da, da, da, da, da, da, dah!" Stephens sings with sarcastic pleasure, which echoes as he enters the vault.

"Miller, keep an eye on them," Reynolds said as he entered the vault. "Any problems, kill them!" he shouts back, and Miller cocks his MP7 and turns onto his prospective targets with pleasure.

Measuring ten metres by six with numbered compartments and glass displays holding multiple treasures on one side and a line of display cabinets on the other, the vault is dimly lit with the coolest air-conditioned temperatures to keep the oldest of relics cool and protected.

Reynolds and Stephens gaze in awe as Stephens walks off, pointing as he talks.

"Legal documents, gold, diamonds, cash." He stops at a cabinet with old photo albums on display and laughs. "Look at this shit!" he shouts, knocking it disrespectfully onto the floor, but Reynolds is disinterested as he opens the compartments.

"I want out of here ASAP, so get a move on," Reynolds said as he moved to the legal documents to rummage through the drawers.

***

Ashley and Conners make their way across the open ground and stop at a vantage point that gives them a good view of the mansion.

"Can you see anything?" she asked as his offensive thinking mind shifted in all directions.

"Not a thing. You?"

Having seen Richie standing at a window with his MP7 visible, Conners points. "Looks like they are being held in the lounge."

Ashley's eyes fix on the highly effective weapon with dread. "We need to find out how many of them are and where they are situated."

***

Daniels enters the lounge looking disappointed, and Reynolds turns to him.

"Where's Duggan?"

"He's dead," Daniels answered, and Reynolds dragged him into the corner out of earshot of the others. "I found his body in the staff quarters," he continues. "He's been shot, and his weapons are missing."

Unable to comprehend the possibility of losing his men, Reynolds shouts out angrily. "Jock! Get your fucking arse out here!"

Expecting the worst, Stephens exits the vault with haste.

"Maybe you can enlighten me?" Reynolds said with calm. "Who else is on this island?"

The Scotsman takes in all the people in the room. "You killed Knox and Henderson."

"They were your friends!" Gordon interjects.

"Bastards don't have friends!" Charles adds, but Stephens ignores the insult.

"That's not true," Reynolds interjects. "I expect out of all the people who labour to your every whim, one of them will like you. It's against the law of averages for that not to be true."

Stephens shouts angrily. "When it comes to money, I have no friends!"

He calms. "Other than money itself and certainly not fuck pigs like you two. This is for a United Ireland."

"United Ireland!" Charles shouts, dismayed at such. "What has this got to do with a United Ireland?"

"But you're Scottish," Gordon questions.

"I was born in Ireland and taken to Scotland at five, but my heart has always been in the land of my birth where many of my family still live."

"There should be three others," Reynolds said, ignoring their conversation as he thought over the information on their plan.

"The people missing are Victor, but he's on leave and Ashley and Conners."

"Why wasn't I informed about this, Victor?"

"I was unaware he was gone until last night."

"You should have informed me!" Reynolds screams. "What about the other two?"

"Conners is a maid and Ashley, well, he's the general dog's body."

"And should we worry about either of them?" Reynolds questions and Stephens laughs, but his humour isn't reciprocated in the mercenary's washed-out eyes.

"I can't see why. Conners is the butch of the two."

"I'll tell you fucking why," Reynolds carries on. "Someone has killed one of my men and taken his weapons which wouldn't be easy for a professional, never mind a maid or a general dog's body."

"I can't see it being either of them," Stephens excuses.

"Are you sure about that?"

"Well, no, but," Stephens flusters until Reynolds interrupts. "Danny, find out who's responsible! Stew, check the rest of the mansion and make sure we are alone."

Uncaring of which, Daniels questions. "Dead or alive, boss?"

"Fucking dead!" Reynolds screams, and Stewart and Daniels exit.

Brian Stewart had served twelve years in the Parachute Regiment of the British Army, but in his later years, he preferred solitude and not the bull-shit of regular army soldiering where every newly passed out first lieutenant from Sandhurst requires a salute even though his military experience out does theirs. Being a man of few words, he lets his soldiering do the talking and decided to retire from the colours and take up the odd mercenary job to keep up his high standard of living.

Reynolds turns his ire back onto the Scotsman, aware his timetable has been speeded up. "Stop pissing about and get on with it."

"That's a thing," Stephens mutters melancholically, frightened he isn't doing what was expected of him. "I'm struggling to open one of the drawers which have extra security on it," he adds, as this was a recently introduced measure that he hadn't come up against.

"Extra security in a vault that nobody knows about?" Reynolds said, turning with menace onto Charles, who laughed.

"Finding it hard, Judas?"

Wanting his brother to quieten, Gordon calls out. "Charles! You need to remain calm to keep the calm."

"So, you have a perfect security system," Reynolds said, composed. "I expected that, but I've got my eyes on those photo albums." He scrutinises the sentimentally placed items, but Charles doesn't want the robbers to see how much they mean to him and has to suffer in uncomfortable silence. "Maybe your staff will know how to open the security boxes." He exits the vault and draws his Glock to point around the frightened faces.

"Hardly," Charles answers, decidedly calmer. "They didn't even know the vault was there."

"Which chef is your favourite?" Reynolds menaces as he looks out of the vault toward the staff, and Gordon answers bemusedly.

"I don't understand."

"I'll rephrase the question as I know you will have to answer this one for yourself. Who is your best chef?"

"I couldn't choose," Gordon muses with pride. "They are both the greatest at their art."

"Then I will choose for you," Reynolds said, putting a bullet into the nearest chef's chest, knocking him across the floor as the maid screamed in terror, and Gordon vaulted to his feet to go to his aid only to find him dead.

"What are you doing?" Gordon cries out. "That was bloody unnecessary!"

With the sadistic pleasure he holds in abundance, Reynolds turns the Glock to point between each person. "I would ask who is your best maid, but as there's only one here." He takes aim at the maid. "Maybe we will wait until the other gets here then, you can choose for me."

"You bastard!" Charles shouts with venom that would usually see him obeyed.

"You can prevent another death by telling me how to get into the extra security?"

"You can kill us all!" Charles carries on to his brother's increasing disdain. "But I'm telling you nothing."

"That's brave coming from a man at the end of his life," Gordon reasons, but his brother snaps his resentment. "I begrudge another life being taken in this farce!" he shouts. "This stops here." He turns to Reynolds. "I will show you how to open it."

Reynolds looks at Stephens. "See that he opens them all."

Feeling the pressure of being unable to fulfil his role, Stephens follows Gordon into the vault.

Reynolds turns to Richie. "Get the body out of here. It's spoiling the ambience of this over-indulgent setting."

With no care, Richie drags the chef's body across the immaculately clean marble floor out into the hallway to leave a thick blood smear which Reynolds notices and turns to the maid to speak with a charm that is wasted on all in the room for her to clear up the mess.

Unsure what to do, the maid looks at Gordon for the permission she doesn't require, and he nods, aware of the consequences if she doesn't. "I have no cleaning supplies," she explains nervously and showing no charm, Reynolds rips a 15th Century tapestry off the wall and throws it to the floor.

"Just do your best."

***

Ashley and Conners make their way closer to the mansion but stop some distance off to survey the area for threats.

"What now, Colonel?" he questioned, and she looked toward Bermuda, disillusioned at not seeing any helicopters nearing.

"Hopefully, the cavalry will be on its way."

"I don't think so," he said with understanding. "We're ten minutes from the main island, so if they were coming, they'd have been here by now."

"Great!" she said, betrayed as her mind raced back to Chaucer's reasoning for a listening device.

"There has to be many more of them, and at this moment, they'll be in the vault stripping it of its wealth."

"They'll only get into the vault if one of the twins lets them in," she said, but he explained with dread.

"They're not common criminals. Robbers don't carry MP7s and Glocks. They're mercs."

"I thought that myself," she said. "They won't hesitate to kill, and if they use the staff as a bargaining chip, Gordon will open the vault at the first threat of violence toward them."

"That will have already happened."

"We need to find out what numbers we are up against," she said, looking around to see if she could count on any more. "Well, they didn't land by chopper, so it must have been by boat."

"The marina!" they said in unison.

"There's one way to find out. Let's go take a look."

Keeping as low profile as possible, they head toward the marina without threat. Once in sight, they take cover in the undergrowth to look upon Holzmann tying up the rigid raider, then nonchalantly walk toward the mansion.

"I only see one," he said, but she looked closer at the marina for confirmation.

"There will be more. We need to prioritise," she adds. "We need to get the Morrison's to safety."

"And the rest of the staff," he adds. "Well, except that arse Stephens, then we can deal with the marina."

"Sounds good to me, but we don't know how many men they have."

"Going off, there's only one rigid raider, I would hazard a guess at between six and ten, and as we've already killed one and there's one there, there must be between four and eight in the mansion."

She laughs, bewildered. "Your math is brilliant."

"It's maths. Not your bastardised version of the English language."

"I had no idea you were so well-read," she blusters mockingly as he shakes his head. "Look, if Chaucer hasn't heard what's happening, maybe we can get a message out." She pauses in thought. "We need to get to the comms room! Sorry," she adds, putting on a snotty sarcastic English accent. "The communications chamber."

"That would be the first to go," he said, then sniped with something that had bothered him since arriving on the island. "If we were allowed our fucking mobiles, we could have called for help."

"But we weren't," she argues, distressed at something he had whinged about on several occasions. "The twins don't allow their staff to carry cells for security reasons."

"We could have still had them," he said to her disagreement.

"The director deemed the chance of us being found with one and chased off the island too great a risk considering how long it had taken to get employed in the first place. So, as we don't have cells."

"Mobiles!" Ashley shouts, but she ignores his whinge.

"We don't have the opportunity to make that call. So, what now?"

"Now we take back the island," he adds calmly, making her laugh at his bravado, but he doesn't see what had caused such amusement. "You don't think we can do it?

"We don't know how many men there are. There may be fifty."

"Between six and ten," he said confidently, and she grinned, amused. "But that doesn't worry me."

"It should, as all we have is a machine pistol and a sidearm with about forty rounds of ammo."

"Do you have something planned for this afternoon?" he snipes to her amusement.

"Alright, Rambo, calm down."

"A manicure perhaps!"

"Shut the fuck up, Jimmy. Anyway, somebody has to babysit you, or you'll go in all gung ho."

Ashley laughs. "That's fucking rich coming from a Yank. However, you say it, I don't care as long as you watch my arse."

"That's a better option than watching your face."

He looks her up and down, feigning lecherousness. "I had a feeling you were checking me out," he jokes to her irritation.

"In your dreams, Jimmy. In your dreams."

"If you've finished ogling me, we'd better get on with it," he mutters with humour as he moves off, followed by a distraught-looking Conners.

***

His impatience at breaking point, the first operator taps his fingers on the desk, which irritates his colleague.

"Will you fucking stop that?"

The first operator picks up the phone and dials. "I'm going to call this Rupprecht and tell him what's going on. Something has to be done." He switches the digital recording device on. "We can't just sit here and listen."

"Do you think that's a good idea?" the second operator said nervously, aware of the outcome of the first call.

"If it isn't, at least we'll be covered, and that arse can take the fall instead of us."

***

Harry sits on the bed in Chaucer's bedroom as the shower runs in the background. Chaucer's phone rings and Harry stands to answer it but pauses, debating if it is the right thing to do. "Rupert, do you want me to get that?" he calls out, and with a towel that hardly fits around his waist, Chaucer exits the en-suite.

"No. Leave it."

"What if it is business?"

"Then I lose the deal. Come and join me!"

Harry moves toward the en-suite. "You want your money's worth today, Rupert."

***

The two operators look at each other as the sound of muffled voices coming directly from Mill Island via the radio speaker.

"No answer," the first operator said as he replaced the receiver and switched off the digital recording device.

"Forget it. He's not interested anyway."

"That shot wasn't from a TV or a radio," the first operator argues.

"We are under orders just to listen and record their conversation."

"What about the people in there?"

"Who gives a shit?" the second operator said uncaringly as the first operator picked up the phone and dials. "Who are you calling now?"

"Hopefully, someone who gives a shit," the first operator said, dispirited, as he switched the digital recording device on.

***

Ashley and Conners lie in the undergrowth, looking toward the mansion.

"I've just realised," she said. "They aren't concealing their identities."

"I'm aware of that. Mercenaries don't take prisoners," he said with the experience of many theatres of war as he takes his hip flask out and takes a sip of whisky. "They must be holding everyone captive until they empty the vault."

"Didn't you have enough of that shit last night?" she questions, concerned.

"Never!" he answers vibrantly as she shakes her head. "The hair of the dog will put me right."

"No, I suppose you never could. You keep topping yourself up like the functioning alcoholic you are," she adds, making him grin weakly at what was meant to be meaningful criticism and help him carry on the task at hand.

Ignoring her, he takes another mouthful of whisky then places it into his pocket. "We have to get in and save them."

"Did you bring your cape?" she said. "And by the way, there's no such thing as the hair of the dog. It's just the after-effects of being pissed," she laughs and he lifts the MP7 to cock mockingly.

"No, but I have the Kryptonite."

"But do you have enough?"

"No, but no doubt every man I kill will give me more."

***

CHAPTER 22

***

The agency's Gulfstream travels across the Atlantic toward the director's planned rendezvous with his operators in Bermuda. Davison relaxes in the comfort of its luxurious setting as he sips a glass of Jack Daniels. Watkins approaches determined and questions his intent but his subordinate's delicate expression tells him all is not well.

"We have problems at Mill Island, Director. London has received reports from a surveillance ship sitting off the island."

Bemused, Davison interrupts. "Hold on, did you say surveillance ship?"

"Shots have been heard," Watkins explains, and Davison interrupts with greater zeal.

"Forget the shots. Who ordered the surveillance ship?"

"That I don't know, Director."

"Lawrence?" Davison bellows. "That bastard can't get used to the fact I run this Anglo-American shit. If his country put in the finances we do, maybe he would be in command. Come to think of it, how come it's called Anglo-American? Surely it should be American Anglo."

"They both sound ridiculous, Director," Watkins explains to Davison's amusement.

"But then we aren't here to sound good. I mean, A.A.A.T.I.U, sounds like I need a hanky before I sneeze."

"Wasn't the admiral the only one to oppose you, Director?"

"All the Brits blackballed me," Davison said amusedly. "I wouldn't be surprised if some of my American colleagues did the same, but the President had the final word and me and him go way back."

"Nothing like a bit of nepotism to keep you on top," Watkins said to Davison's added amusement. "What about the operators on the boat? They've gone over the head of their superior, who isn't prepared to do anything and isn't even in communication."

"No doubt one of Lawrence's stooges. Do we have a name for this ass?"

"Rupert Chaucer, Director."

"Never heard of him," Davison said. "He's one of the admirals." He presses the intercom on his desk. "Captain, how long before we land?" The pilot's voice echoes over the intercom. "An hour, Director. Forty minutes at a push."

"Make it so," Davison said, letting go of the intercom. "That's my

Captain Picard."

"Outstanding, Director," Watkins creeps, aware Davison doesn't like yes men. "I will go engage myself in some other duties."

Davison laughs. "Good one, Watkins. Make one of those a refill of my Jack Daniels and the other this Chaucer on the tarmac in Bermuda."

***

Reynolds enters the vault as Gordon opens the secure box to find a single envelope.

"I don't believe it!" Stephens calls out, angered. "What the fuck is this shit?"

"You need to promise me the safety of my staff," Gordon pleads, unaware he had just lost his last bargaining chip. "I've done what you asked."

Reynolds isn't in the mood to negotiate as he walks over to take the envelope. "Important classified military information, do not remove," he reads off the sleeve. His face brightens as he opens it to see two data discs inside before placing them into his pocket without being noticed.

"They're no good to you," Gordon explains, but Reynolds pushes him back toward the lounge. "Can I get your assurance that my staff will be safe now that you have what you want?" he reiterates, but Reynolds ignores him as he walks over and looks into another box. "Diamonds!"

"They must be worth a fucking fortune," Stephens said as he lifted a handful to drop through his fingers.

"Enough for us to never work again," Reynolds adds as he turns to Gordon. "Why hoard so much wealth? Why not have it all in a bank?"

Gordon's irate stare shifts between Stephens and Reynolds, who stare curiously to hear the answer. "Because you can't trust anyone these days. You never know who wants to steal it from you."

"You never could," Reynolds said ironically, and Gordon shuffled uncomfortably in the presence of the obnoxious men.

Gordon adds, defeated. "Now, can I be excused?"

"Oh yes, Mr Morrison. Please, you're excused!" Reynolds snarls with disdain as he stands aside to allow him to pass. "Thank you for your assistance." He exits the vault and gives Charles a patronising wink of triumph that annoys the old man.

"So, this is for money?" Charles questioned with the obvious. "Just a bloody robbery?"

"No, Mr Morrison, this is for power, and as you know, money is power, so yes, I suppose you could say it's for the money."

"There's no power in running for the rest of your life," Gordon said, but his words amuse Reynolds.

"What makes you think we are going to be running?"

"We can identify you," Gordon adds to his brother's ever-increasing irritability.

"Don't be naïve," Charles said as his eyes fixed on Reynolds for confirmation. "He has no intention of leaving us alive," he adds for Reynolds to grin roguishly back.

Shocked his staff had been brought into the terror, Gordon interjects. "But these people have nothing to do with our wealth."

"They can identify us, which would harm my future freedom."

"I can't believe you would kill these people for money."

"I've killed for a lot less, but hopefully, this will be the last time. I intend to retire peacefully to a nice big house in the country. I may even buy this place when it comes on the market."

"Well, I hope for your sake no bastard will want to spoil that for you."

***

Looking out of the window of the agency jet, Davison sits impatiently as Watkins approaches through the fuselage to place another glass of Jack Daniels in front of him.

"Director, we'll be landing in ten minutes."

"And the chopper?"

"On the tarmac."

"And Chaucer?"

"Also, on the tarmac."

"As efficient as ever," Davison said with an appreciative nod.

"Thank you, Director," Watkins said modestly, and Davison smiled mischievously.

"I was talking about myself, but if you need the praise. Well done to yourself."

Amused, Watkins moves off. "How silly of me to covet appreciation for all I do."

***

Ashley and Conners lie among the foliage debating their best course of action. He believes they should rush in and kill all the bad guys, but her level-headed mind thinks they should plan everything out in greater detail.

He notices Daniels heading toward them. "Looks like we are going to have a visitor," he said, pointing as her eyes shifted all around.

"Got him."

"He's looking for us."

"No," she said, taking the MP7 off him and handing over the Glock. "I'm looking for him."

"I take it you want the big gun?"

"Why not?" she adds confidently. "He's mine."

"I take it your sit back and see how it fans out approach has changed?"

"It has to. They are obviously on the hunt for us now."

"He may be on a nice walk," he jests, but she keeps her determined stare on the man approaching.

"Everything about his mannerisms tells me we are his quarry."

Daniels passes casually, and Conners vaults to her feet, pointing the MP7 at the veteran soldier, who looks back, amused by the comedic value of her stance as she demands him to drop the gun. "You must be the bloody maid?" he said, believing he had the upper hand as he attempted to lift his MP7, and she put two bullets into his chest, killing him as he fell to the ground.

"I take it we're taking prisoners?" he complains, bewildering her.

"How do you get that, Jimmy?"

"You gave him time to surrender. You can't give men like these any chances."

She moves to Daniels' body, picks up his MP7 to throw for Ashley to catch, and then takes the Glock. "Now we have the same you can stop your whinging."

In disbelief, she still doesn't get his sarcastic humour after all their time together; he shakes his head. "Has he got any spare mags?"

She pulls two magazines out of the backpack to hand over. "You know, Jimmy, killing has never come easy to me, so giving someone a chance to surrender helps me sleep at night."

"I've never enjoyed it myself, but there are times when you ain't got a choice and use all your aggression to make sure your enemy isn't a threat," he said, then contemplated their situation. "I don't know why I got myself roped into this Anti-Terrorist shit. I left the SAS to escape the killing and hiding in bushes, but that's all I've done since meeting you."

"You got selected because you're the best man for the job," she said complimentary, and he laughed with hilarity.

"Now, who's talking bollocks?"

"The director wouldn't have selected you for this important assignment if he didn't think you were his man."

"Well, this man doesn't feel he's the best for the job. Not these days anyway."

"Now who's talking bollocks?" she said. "Since our last mission, he believes we are joined at the hip and are a good team."

"Now I know you're joking," he said with a deep concerted sigh that showed he had nowhere to go. "Well, now that we've started," he begins, but she interrupts enthusiastically.

"We need to finish it, but first, you must stop feeling sorry for yourself."

Not feeling the part, he smiles awkwardly, then moves off with her following to settle defensively within the foliage with good views of the mansion as he looks around with a deep hint of Deja vu.

"What now, Colonel?"

"I love how the rank thing comes out when the shit hits the fan, Jimmy," she said. "But if I must be recognised as being in command, I believe we should get to the mansion and sort this out."

"As easy as that?"

"As easy as that," she repeats, determined. "How many do you think there are?"

"Well, as I explained before, using mathematics."

"Alright, Jimmy, forget I asked," she interjects, and he laughs, adding in a bad John Wayne accent.

"All I know is they are two less. Well then, let's go and kick some butt." He goes to move off but drops back down. "Movement."

They instantly change their offensive postures to defensive as he witnesses Reynolds exiting the mansion carrying a box to place on the rear of the golf cart and Stewart following, taking another box to place alongside. Ashley stares at Reynolds in recognition but can't remember where he knows him from and decides to keep that to himself until he can confirm his initial thought. Having made his way from the marina, Holzmann gets into the golf cart and drives off, without a word as Reynolds and Stewart head back inside.

"Looks like they are taking the goods to the boat. That means there aren't as many as we thought," he explains the obvious, which she questions.

"So, your math was just a guess?" she jests. "How professional of you."

"My constantly changing analytical mind works out the intelligence as it comes in, but I did say between six and ten if you remember."

"Oh yeah?" she snipes.

"Think about it. They need more space in the boat for the goods on their return journey."

Sarcastically impressed, she adds. "Maybe that is why the director kept you around."

He taps his temple. "Intelligent thinking on the hoof. The sign of a good soldier."

"I believe you, Jimmy," she adds with a smile. "But millions wouldn't."

"My arse. You know I'm right. Come on, let's get this shit over with," he said, determined, as he made his way toward the mansion,

Aware something is troubling about her British colleague, she stands and follows as they keep the terrain under observation. On reaching the mansion, they look around, unnerved by its calmness and using hand signals; he shows her he will go through the window above and for her to check out the rear, and she nods her understanding and then heads off. He climbs a drain pipe onto a single-story roof and over the sloping tiles, but he slips to his knees, causing a loud bang which stops him dead in the hope he hadn't been heard, but Stewart exits the mansion to see him standing vulnerably in the open and points his MP7 with a wide grin of accomplishment.

"Alright, the game's over!" Stewart shouts, and Ashley's eyes shift to the window as he debates whether he can make it. "Drop the gun, boy."

Given that he is older than the man threatening him, Ashley grins, amused, then runs the short distance to crash through the window with bullets smashing all around as he lands on the bedroom floor with the shattered glass covering him.

Reynolds exits the mansion as Stewart runs past. "What the fuck's going on?"

"The handyman's upstairs!" Stewart shouts as he carries on.

"Kill him!" Reynolds calls out. "Kill the bastard, now!"

Stewart and Reynolds enter the mansion and go through the hallway to stop at the bottom of the stairs.

Cautiously aware of the threat, Stewart hesitantly moves forward to Reynolds' irritation. "He's armed!"

"So are you!" Reynolds screams. "Pretend you're a professional soldier, and go get the bastard!"

Bemused by the animated commotion, Richie exits the lounge but keeps one eye on those inside. "What's going on?"

"The handyman's upstairs. Kill the bastard, now," Reynolds reiterates, and Richie follows Stewart up the stairs, two steps at a time as if racing each other.

Amazed he isn't seriously injured, Ashley gets to his feet and leans dazed against the wall to recompose himself, as his would-be killer approaches, then stumbles across the floor to take up a defensive position at the back of the door. He can hear them conspiring but can't make out a word they are saying.

Offensively ready for action, Richie and Stewart make their way along the landing. Richie signals to his cohort that he is going through an adjoining room, and Stewart nods his understanding as he enters an adjacent bedroom. Ashley stands rigidly still as Richie exits the adjoining door and points his MP7 into his neck, taking him by surprise.

"Drop the gun, sucker," Richie said arrogantly, to Ashley's embarrassment at being taken so easily, and he dropped the machine pistol to the floor. "And the handgun," he adds, and Ashley draws the Glock to throw aside, then lifts his hands in submission. "Alright, Stew, it's clear."

Smiling with admiration, Stewart enters straight over to Ashley and questions with concern. "That had to hurt?"

Richie nods his agreement, but Ashley doesn't answer.

"I'll take it from here," Stewart said, and Richie moved off.

"Don't fuck about, Stew. Do as Reynolds has said."

The mention of Reynolds' name catches Ashley's attention, allowing him to put a name to the face he had just witnessed, and he turns swiftly on Richie but goes unnoticed as the mercenary exits onto the landing.

"The way you went through that window," Stewart carries on. "You must be ex-military,"

Having gained entry through one of the rear bedroom windows, Conners enters the adjoining room and looks through the gap in the door to see Ashley covered by Stewart.

Ashley smiles, his discomfort at being taken prisoner so easily. "Yeah, but a long time ago."

"What Regiment?"

"Paras!" Ashley answers on recognising the type.

"Were you shit!" Stewart shouts as he beckons Ashley to lower his arms. "I was with Two Para for twelve years and know a Para when I see one. You're just a fucking hat."

Conners bursts through the door to cover Stewart with her MP7, but this bemuses the highly experienced mercenary.

"You must be the fucking maid?"

"Just the maid," Conners replies in jest. "I haven't done any fucking since I got here."

Ashley sniggers to Conners' irritation as she calls out with menace for Stewart to drop his gun, but he believes he has the upper hand.

"You drop yours, or pretty boy's gonna get it."

"By the way, you are right about the Paras," Ashley said melancholically. "I was in the Royal Regiment of Fusiliers."

"I knew you were a fucking hat. I used to fight arseholes like you on the weekend around Aldershot."

"I heard that about you Paras."

"You cheeky fucking bastard!" Stewart shouts and taking advantage of his touchiness, Ashley elbows him in the stomach then punches him in the face knocking him back against the wall, but he quickly recomposes himself and brings his MP7 to bear as Conners riddles him with bullets that hammer him to the floor dead.

"Nice shooting," Ashley said, amused by the ammunition used. "I take it we've got an endless supply of ordnance that we can carry on until the mags empty?"

"SAS!" Conners snarls with hilarity. "The way you were caught, I'd be surprised if you were a boy scout," she ridicules to his amusement.

Ashley picks up his MP7 and Glock as Conners looks out onto the landing to see Richie at the top of the stairs lighting a cigarette, unperturbed by the firing he believes had ended Ashley's life.

"Come on, Stew!" Richie shouts. "We've got a fucking job to finish!"

Conners lifts her machine pistol to eye and moves offensively onto the landing to take Richie by surprise as his MP7 points impassively at the floor. "Drop your gun and move over here slowly," she demands.

Still, he believes he is better than a woman, even though she has him covered and laughs as he lifts his machine pistol she puts two shots into his chest to knock him backwards as he opens up to blast the floor with automatic fire, then she taps off twice more to drop her would-be killer to his knees as he slumps down the stairs to stop in the middle in a crumpled heap.

"Well, at least you'll sleep tonight," Ashley said to her irritation.

"No one wants to surrender."

Having heard the shots, Reynolds exits the lounge in shock of Richie's lifeless body and opens fire aimlessly onto the landing above, forcing Ashley and Conners back into the bedroom out of range.

Miller exits the lounge and moves up behind. "What the fuck's going on, boss?"

"Take care of the Morrison's as planned," Reynolds orders. "And I'll take the next load to the boat. Then get rid of the fucking maid and the handyman."

Miller looks around, bewildered as to where they are, and Reynolds looks to the landing to see Conners tentatively looking over the balustrade.

"They're fucking upstairs!" Reynolds shouts as he opens on full-automatic forcing her into cover as the bullets ricochet. "Kill the Scotsman first," he whispers. "And fast. The boat can't wait forever."

Miller enters the lounge as Reynolds exits outside.

Ashley and Conners stand against the back wall until the firing ceases. They look at each other, then Conners grins and looks tentatively over the balustrade to see nothing moving. The sound of a golf cart catches their attention, and Ashley moves to the window to see Reynolds driving into the distance.

"One's getting away."

"Stop him!" she screams as she walks down the stairs.

Reynolds drives the golf cart at its flat-out speed of ten miles per hour as the sound of glass smashing is followed by bullets thudding into the ground around, and one hits him in the leg to knock him onto the grass as the golf cart rolls a short distance as it catches fire. He crawls then rolls onto his back to open fire toward the upstairs window, but his MP7 clicks empty after three rounds, throws it aside, then stands awkwardly as he draws his Glock to fire several shots, then limp off as fast as his injured leg will carry him.

Ashley pulls his spent MP7 from the window and turns to Conners to see her gone. He moves to the balustrade to see her crouching over Richie's body, relieving him of magazines from his backpack and moves down the stairs to be handed a magazine, and he nods his appreciation as he drops an empty one to reload and cock.

With lust to carry out his commander's order, Miller points his MP7 at all gathered in the lounge as he waits for Stephens to exit the vault carrying another box.

"Time to get rid of the witnesses," Charles said, shocked at the atrocity to come. "That means you, Stephens," he adds to the Scotsman's amusement.

"I don't think so!" Stephens said with calm, as he still believes the robbery is to fund the fight for a united Ireland, and he looks to Miller for confirmation of the smiling murderer, and he drops the box for money to go all over as he is shot twice in the chest and falls to the floor dead.

The maid screams in panic, and Miller turns the MP7 onto his intended targets as Ashley and Conners crash through the door and turns offensively but his body is shattered with bullets as he falls to the floor, no longer a threat.

"Conners! What the bloody hell's going on?" Charles shouts frantically as he squirms to get out of his chair, but they don't have the time to explain and move off at speed.

They exit the mansion toward the marina to see Reynolds limping and fire the odd shot in his direction.

Reynolds hears then sees them nearing and unsuccessfully attempts to up his pace and turns to fire several rounds as he carries on as fast as he can. "Klaus! Klaus!" he shouts at Holzmann, who is sitting on the side of the rigid raider and turns on hearing his name to see the Englishman waving with Ashley and Conners closing on him fast. Unbecoming of a man well paid to ply his trade, the German starts the engines, as avarice overcomes with the sight of the many boxes of valuable goods that now won't need to be shared with so many, and shoots the rope tethering the rigid raider to the marina and the boat rears up in the water then moves off with uncontrolled speed. Conners stops to take aim and puts several rounds into the grass around Reynolds, forcing him to the ground as Ashley carries on firing at the rigid raider, but his bullets are no threat and fall well short. Reynolds rolls onto his front to see his only means of escape moving off and shouts in frustrated panic of the German's cowardice as he fires at him, speeding into the distance, then turns onto his back to find Ashley and Conners have him covered from separate directions. Conscious he couldn't kill them both, he throws the Glock aside and lifts his hands, defeated.

**

CHAPTER 23

***

Davison looks toward the terminal building at LF Wade as the agency jet powers down and an AW101 Merlin of the British Royal Navy powers up with its rotors turning. Believing he's an important man on the island, Chaucer exits the terminal as Davison looks him up and down.

"I have special clearance."

"I'm not here about that, sir. I work for the agency on the island," Chaucer arrogantly explains as Davison turns his attention onto him.

"Is that so? Then have you heard of a Rupert Chaucer?"

Chaucer answers with an awkwardly nervous laugh. "That's me."

"That's director, and why don't you get your ass over here fast?" Davison shouts with confirmation, and unsure of the irritation caused, Chaucer makes his way sedately over. "Why didn't you send back up for my people when you knew they were distressed?"

With no means of answering truthfully, Chaucer looks open-mouthed, and Davison punches him in the face, then grabs him harshly around the scruff of the neck.

"You slimy piece of shit!" Davison shouts, tightening his grip, making it hard for the Englishman to breathe. "I hope for your sake your actions haven't cost my people their lives."

In a vain attempt to redeem himself, Chaucer interrupts even though he is unsure if he is speaking the truth. "They're still alive, sir."

"They'd better be."

"I was acting under orders," Chaucer mumbles, and Davison tightens his grip until he can't breathe, then pushes him aside to gasp for air.

"I don't give a fuck what Lawrence told you; you shouldn't have left my people without backup."

Chaucer stares at the director, he had never met, in bewilderment at his treatment.

"I wouldn't worry about the admiral. He's been trying to destroy my unit since it was set up."

"I know nothing about that, sir."

Davison calms and rounds on the nervous-looking Chaucer, who backs off, rubbing his pained neck. "When you report to him."

"I don't report to Admiral Lawrence, sir?" Chaucer argues to Davison's irritation.

"It's director, you fucking idiot!" Davison snarls. "Next time you speak to him, tell him from me he's a lousy Limey bastard."

"He won't take too kindly to that, sir, err, Director."

"Well, then, the kick in the balls he's due won't go down too well either," Davison adds as he moves off, pushing Chaucer aside. "Now get out of my face before I do you serious harm, you fucking worm."

Holding his bleeding nose, Chaucer walks off dismissed, unsure how to relay the director's words to the man giving him the orders.

"If I were you, I'd be on the first plane back to London!" Davison shouts. "My people won't be as nice as me."

Having only recently been promoted to command of operations in Bermuda by Lawrence, Chaucer is unaware if what Davison had said is an order or a warning, but he carries on as fast as he can with the intent of escaping the inevitable wrath to come.

***

Conners keeps Reynolds in her sights as Ashley moves over to look down on his old colleague.

"If it isn't my old mate, Sergeant James Ashley," Reynolds said, showing no liking in his tone to Conners' amusement.

"I knew I recognised your face but couldn't put it together until one of your goons mentioned your name," Ashley said, pointing at the mercenary. "This here is Sergeant Raymond Reynolds."

"Captain!" Reynolds interrupts, angered at the downgrading of his self-appreciating rank. "That's Captain Reynolds!"

"Captain?" Ashley questioned, humoured as he sat on the grass, rubbed his aching leg, and took a sip from his hip flask. "When were you promoted to such lofty heights?"

Even though he believes it isn't required, Reynolds explains. "I was awarded the rank."

"Really?" Ashley interrupts sarcastically. "Who by?" he adds, but Reynolds does not intend to answer. "Sounds like self-promotion to me. From now on, I want to be a general." He turns to Conners, who instantly understands the sarcasm irritating Reynolds.

"Surely, Field Marshal?"

"Hold on, hold on. I feel a promotion coming on. How about Commander in Chief of the world," Ashley carries on as Reynolds shuffles his discomfort.

"The Universe, at least," Conners adds.

"Alright, I get the joke."

"What joke?" Ashley said with a wink at Conners. "How about a promotion?"

"No thanks. I'm happy living in the real world," Conners answers serenely.

Reynolds is desperate to change the subject off his conceited values. "So, what brings the SAS here?"

"I'm not SAS," Ashley explains to Reynolds' bewilderment.

"Then who do you work for?"

"Charlie and Gordon," Ashley answers flippantly as Reynolds' stare shifts between his captors in disbelief. "You're the fucking handyman?" he said then, looked at Conners, who grinned back. "And for a maid, you certainly know how to handle a gun."

"I'm just as nifty with a vacuum," Conners said straight-faced.

"No doubt an Amazonian Guard," Reynolds jests to Conners' bewilderment

"Gadaffi's female guard," Ashley explains. "The Revolutionary Nuns."

"Hardly," Conners said, disturbed by the thought. "Although I do like the thought of being an Amazonian Warrior, only not one of that raping bastard's bodyguards."

"Well, you ain't no maid," Reynolds grumbles at being bested by a woman. "That's for sure."

"Get him up, and we'll take him back to the mansion."

"Looks like your booty got away without you," Ashley said, amused. "I take it your man's in for a good windfall."

Reynolds sneers with the knowledge that the men he had selected were expendable.

"Where's the boat heading?" Ashley adds, but Reynolds has no intention of giving away information that may be required during the prosecution process and grins his mistrust.

"What does that matter to you? Surely, you've done your job in saving the megalomaniac's lives? You can go home and enjoy the rest of your existence."

"Your man left you in the shit, so why protect him?" Ashley questions and Reynolds stares directly at him as he answers.

"If you need to ask, you'll never understand."

"Honour among thieves," Conners interjects. "Does that exist?"

"Honour among the fighting man!" Reynolds adds with superiority as Ashley shakes his head in disbelief at combining the two.

"That will have to do for now; I'll search him first," Ashley said, only to receive a laugh.

"Don't you trust me, James?"

Ashley hands his MP7 to Conners then, helps Reynolds stand, and then searches him to find the envelope with the data discs inside. He reads off the cover, which catches his attention enough to hand to Conners. "That's why I don't trust you," he said as he searched and took his phone.

Conners lifts the data discs as Reynolds glances over. "What's this?"

"Just some snide DVDs I picked up in Bermuda."

"And you brought them on an OP?" Conners adds, and Reynolds shrugs his shoulders nonchalantly.

"You thought that one through," Ashley said humoured. "They're data discs." Aware he would never be believed, Reynolds stares at Ashley. "I've been fucking ripped off. Hand them over, and I'll take them back," he said, but Ashley could see he was hiding the fact they were important to him and laughed.

Ashley takes Reynolds around the shoulders and helps the murmuring man to limp off. "I hope you're not in too much pain, Captain. Or have you been promoted in the past minute to major?"

"I don't find humour in your words, James. If you'd stayed in the military, you might have become an officer too."

Ashley laughs, distraught at the thought. "Who the fuck would want to be an officer?" He looks at Conners, who is irritated by what she knows is meant to condemn her and the officer class as she follows. "Anyway, you left the regiment before me, and were a sergeant, so God knows who promoted you."

"Maybe it was God that done the honour," Conners jests.

***

Conners enters the lounge, followed by Ashley and Reynolds, to find all in the room still tied. Reynolds limps to a chair and flops into its comfort to get off his painful leg.

Gordon's concern turns to Conners, whom he sees as a vulnerable woman needing his protection. "Where have you been, Conners? We could hear gunfire."

"He was worried," Charles said with a loud echoing tut as Conners went around the room, untying everyone.

"There's nothing wrong with having compassion for your fellow human beings," Gordon argues. "You should try it someday, Charles."

"Alright, Gordon, but we could do without your sermonising. Don't forget I know you of old," Charles said to his brother's disquiet.

To break up the unwanted squabble, Conners enquires about everyone's health.

"As can be expected," Charles answered, but Gordon added his concern

"We'll have to inform the authorities of what has occurred."

"They already know, sir," Conners explains to Charles' bemusement as he moves to Reynolds, who looks up arrogantly.

"So, you captured the robber giving the orders?"

"He's a mercenary, sir," Conners adds to Gordon's shock.

"Where are the rest of my staff?" Charles questions, but Reynolds shows no empathy for the loss of life and laughs his indifference.

"Haven't they served you your tea?" Reynolds sneers and Charles can see he is bleeding from the leg and kicks him hard enough in his injury to make him scream in pain; then attempt to stand to retaliate, but Ashley knocks him into his chair as he screams with venom. "You wouldn't fucking do that if you didn't have your stooges here to protect you."

Showing his renowned determination, Charles speaks with a menacing calm. "You're right. I always get people to do my dirty work for me. That's what comes of being so bloody rich." He bends closer to Reynolds and whispers. "You see, you're going to prison, and while there, some of my associates will visit you. These associates I am talking about aren't the sort you want visiting; they tend to leave you, how can I say this nicely, dead or at the very least severely mauled."

"You don't frighten me, you old bastard."

"That's because he doesn't need to," Ashley interjects with a smirking grin. "Weren't you listening? He gets others to do that."

"We can assume all the people missing are dead, sir," Conners interjects to Gordon's shocked earnestness.

"We knew he had no intention of letting anyone live," Gordon explains with sadness as he smiles at Conners. "Call me naïve, but I don't think you are a maid!"

"No, sir, but that will become apparent later."

"They're spooks! Can't you smell the shit?" Reynolds shouts with spite as he turns on Ashley. "And to think when you were in the service, you hated them as much as myself."

"Do you know this man, Ashley?" Gordon enquires, concerned, as Charles adds a second question for him.

"You were in the service?"

"Yes, to both," Ashley answers, and Conners interrupts to calm the situation.

"As I said, sirs, all will become apparent later."

"Spooks!" Charles carries on. "That's a spy, isn't it?"

Reynolds sneers. "They're sneaky bastards!"

"They are intelligence officers, Charles," Gordon explains, looking to Conners for confirmation. "And as Conners has said, all will become apparent later."

Ashley and Conners back into a corner out of earshot.

"You see. Little spooks have their little secrets," Reynolds sermonises, angering Ashley with his constant whinging.

"Shut the fuck up, General!" Ashley shouts, but this invigorates Reynolds, who feigns crying.

"General?" Gordon shouts in shock, and Ashley explains the joke, then kicks Reynolds to scream in pain.

Reynolds' phone rings and Ashley takes it out to look at the screen. "Soames," he mutters as he glances at Reynolds, who turns away, conscious he shouldn't have put the name onto his phone's sim card.

"Answer it," Conners said, but Ashley was unsure whether to until she nodded her insistence, and he pressed the answer button and puts it to his ear but didn't speak to her bewilderment.

***

With his phone to his ear, Soames stands on the jetty of the villa in Hamilton as he looks out over the water. "How's it going, Captain?" he questions, expecting an instant answer, but when it doesn't come, he throws the phone into the water and then takes another out to dial. "I want full payment within the hour." He switches the phone off with the understanding of his plan's failure.

***

Ashley lowers the phone and then looks at Conners to see her annoyance.

"I take it you got all the information required?" she growls, but he turns on Reynolds, who is paying him no attention.

"It's all in a name. Isn't that right, your Royal Highness?"

Understanding the connotations, Reynolds grins awkwardly but offers no reply.

Seeing an MP7 on the floor, Charles picks it up and walks to Reynolds to point at the unthreatened man. "You killed those good people, you bastard."

Conners goes to intervene, but Ashley holds her back.

"Like Stephens!" Reynolds said with calculated menace, and Charles pushed the barrel hard into his chest.

"He was a piece of shit, like you!"

Not taking the threat seriously, Reynolds laughs. "Who are you to say who's a piece of shit and who isn't? Sitting here in your fucking ivory tower, you know fuck all about the real world."

Charles pushes the MP7 into Reynolds' face, but the mercenary remains calm under threat.

"You ain't got the balls."

Charles pulls the trigger of the un-cocked weapon, and nothing happens as Reynolds dives back in fright.

"What the fuck, you piece of shit," Reynolds screams.

Charles looks the gun over in bewilderment as to why it hadn't fired as Conners breaks from Ashley's hold and pulls him aside.

"He may have the information we require, sir."

"You may as well shoot as you ain't getting any info from me."

Sick of listening to the mercenary's self-aggrandising, Ashley punches him in the face, knocking him back into the chair.

"You can't do that; I know my rights," Reynolds argues, and Ashley punches him with such ferocity that he is knocked out cold.

"For the likes of you, we don't play by those rules."

"I'll take the gun, sir," Conners said, but Charles kept a tight hold until she reasoned with him, and he reluctantly relinquished it into her hands as he sat.

The sound of a helicopter approaching catches everyone's attention, and Conners moves to the window. "Sounds like the cavalry."

"I don't hear a bugle," Ashley adds with mirth lost on the twins.

"Better late than never." He hands Charles his MP7 back but makes sure it's still on safety. "Keep hold of that in case he comes around but don't kill him. We need him alive."

Charles looks at Reynolds with menace and smiles delightedly as Ashley and Conners exit.

***

Unaware of what had happened to all his players, Soames stands next to the pool when the sound of an approaching boat catches his attention. He moves to the jetty to see Holzmann at the controls of the rigid raider and waits patiently as the German brings it alongside and throws him a rope to tie it off. "Where are the others?" he questions, but Holzmann is unsure what had happened and draws his Glock to point.

"Who are you?"

Soames remains calm as he stares down the barrel of the gun. "I'm your boss, Klaus," he said, bemusing the German. "I set this up."

"Really," Holzmann adds sceptically. "So, you're the man who bankrolled this? The decision maker?"

"That's me."

"You're the man who will pay me my due?"

"That's correct."

"Five hundred thousand Dollars?"

"Every cent. So, what happened?"

"We got bumped," Holzmann answers nonchalantly as he holsters his gun.

"Bumped?" Soames said as he looked into the rigid raider. "Who by?"

Holzmann laughs. "No idea. I only just got away with my life." He looks at Soames to see what reaction he will get to his words to come. "But that means more for me and you, does it not?"

All the goods on the boat mean little to Soames as his interest is only for the data discs. "Did Reynolds give you anything for me?"

Holzmann believes everything in the rigid raider was given by Reynolds and looks back to point.

"Where is the captain?"

"He was getting chased as I came under fire."

"You left him behind?"

Unaware he had just brought forward the timetable for his fate, Holzmann grins uneasily. "I had no choice. They would have got me too."

"You did right," Soames reasons. "Come up to the villa, and I will pour you a drink to a successful outcome for us, and then I will get you your money."

"Surely there should be more for us?" Holzmann adds with avarice as he jumps onto the jetty and follows Soames toward the mansion.

"We'll only know when we calculate its value and share it equally."

***

CHAPTER 24

***

Ashley and Conners exit the mansion as the Merlin lands on the lawn in front.

"Did you get the bug in place?" he enquires, and she nods. "Then how did it take these so long to arrive?"

Aware he's right, her glare shifts to the helicopter as Davison, Watkins and several operators alight. "That's why. They've come all the way from London," she said in light hearted disbelief that made Ashley laugh.

"Check the area out," Davison commands the operators to fan out as he looks around at the wealth on show. "Paradise stolen," he mumbles to himself.

"What was that, Director?" Conners questions, but Davison doesn't intend to explain his dislike of the Morrisons due to his knowledge of their unscrupulous business dealings.

"One of the Mercs is in the mansion," Ashley informs for Watkins and an operator to head toward it.

"Good to see you, Director," Conners said subserviently to Ashley's amusement.

Still carrying the MP7, Charles exits the mansion, and Watkins quickly disarms him. "I have one of the robbers inside!" he calls out as if he had captured Reynolds himself.

"I don't know about you, Jimmy," Conners said. "But I don't see General Reynolds as the mastermind."

"General Reynolds?" Davison questions, to Ashley's amazement.

"I'll explain later, Director," Conners adds, but Davison doesn't like the feeling of being out in the cold, which shows on his intelligence-hungry face.

"He was a clever soldier!" Ashley explains with a hint of admiration that is lost on the Americans. "If he hadn't gone into the SAS, he could have been an officer, but he lived life too dangerous even for Special Forces."

"Crazier than the SAS?" Davison questioned to Ashley's understanding.

"That's why they discharged him. He always seemed to have something missing."

"You know, Jimmy," Conners interposes. "I've come up against your mates twice of late, and I don't think I've met one who hasn't had something missing, including yourself."

Aware he is unable to argue the point, Ashley interjects. "You can't be the best in the world and go through the shit we have without being burnt somehow."

"That touched a nerve," Conners said in the amused belief she had got a rise out of the Englishman, but he is deadly serious.

"Call me what the fuck you want, but never slag off the regiment or the British Army to me."

"If only you felt the same loyalty to us, James," Davison said with a piercing stare, making Ashley grin, disinterested.

"But I hardly know you, Director," Ashley said. He moves off several paces, keeping his back to the Americans and takes a mouthful of whisky from his hip flask, but Davison ignores the obviousness of his attempt to conceal.

Charles moves to Davison, whom he can see through his years of business dealings, must be in command. "I think your brevity is lost in this moment, Ashley. People have lost their lives here."

"I actually took some of them," Ashley snipes to Charles' astonishment, and Davison quickly intervenes diplomatically.

"And people have had theirs saved, Mr Morrison."

"And you are?"

Davison reaches for the philanthropist's hand to shake. "Director Harold Davison."

"Director of what?" Charles presses, but Davison has no intention of explaining. "If you're not prepared to answer that, what is your business here?"

"I'm here to oversee the developments of," Davison begins, then changes the subject. "Your company is in discussions with a man known as the Egyptian for him to buy military technology from you?"

"It certainly isn't!" Charles argues, angered that a business outsider could know of such. "Our idiot nephew has been trying to get us to have business dealings with what I can only describe loosely as an Egyptian gentleman."

"And you have no intention of dealing with him?"

"We don't deal with businessmen who go under the title of the Egyptian. If I were ever suspicious of anything, it would be that."

"Then, can you tell me why your nephew is meeting with this man known to deal with terrorists?"

"Terrorists?" Charles said shocked. "We know nothing about terrorism. Jerome was after dealing, but we forbade it, and he can't do any business without mine or my brother's permission."

"What about other members of the Morrison Corporation?"

"Not without my permission!"

"Is that so? Then why is this Egyptian clearing customs at LF Wade as we speak?"

Exasperated by the news of the intended betrayal, Charles can only explain what he believes is true. "That's news to me, but surely you should explain why you are allowing such a man to enter Bermuda?"

"He isn't travelling under the name of friend to the terrorist, Mr Morrison!" Davison barks. "He's a legitimate businessman, but we've had him under surveillance for some time."

"He's wasting his time as Jerome doesn't have the authority to deal with him."

Unseen to all, Gordon exits the mansion and moves up behind.

"He isn't a man to take no for an answer," Davison carries on with the intent to shock. "If he thinks he's here to deal and can't, no matter the reason, there will be trouble."

"Is that what all this was about?" Gordon shouts, and they all turn in unison to him.

"No, Mr Morrison," Davison answers calmly. "We had Intelligence that an IRA splinter group were looking for funds."

"And who are you?" Gordon demands, and Charles answers on the American's behalf. "Director of what?"

Charles turns his stare on Davison as he remembers his initial question hadn't been answered. "That's what I would like to know."

"That's for another day."

Gordon looks lovingly at Conners. "There seems to be a lot of that going around," he said, making her smile uneasy.

"Your wealth made you the ideal target," Davison explains, and Charles calls out angrily.

"You said IRA, but Stephens was Scottish?"

Davison turns to Conners. "Who's Stephens?"

"The inside man, Director. He's among the dead."

Discouraged at being unable to interrogate him for intelligence, Davison looks at Conners, who nods in confirmation.

"The treacherous bastard was killed by his own side," Charles adds, uncaring of his death. "That's all he deserved."

"Did they get away with any valuables?" Davison questions, unnerving the twins.

"How could we know that at this time? We will need to do a thorough inventory," Gordon explains. "I think they were stopped before they could get away with anything."

"What about documentation?" Davison questions, heightening Gordon's interest as he looks to his brother, who shakes his head, unable to answer, as he moves off.

"What do you mean, Director?" Charles explains reluctantly. "Until we have a thorough check, we won't know if anything is missing, but I believe you have something in mind, so please enlighten me as to what you believe that is?"

"Something that could be used against you or your company," Davison explains tentatively, but Charles keeps his angry stare on him to find out more. "Any secret information to do with your business or dealings with America or the United Kingdom?"

Aware he is being furtively interrogated, Charles answers with calm. "We don't keep business information here, never mind that of the secret type, as it's all under lock and key at our head office in London." Davison sees Gordon has gone. "Where's your brother?"

Unaware he is missing, Charles quickly looks around and heads toward the mansion. "He'll be inside doing his I care for people act."

"I take it he's the nice twin?" Davison said with a broad grin after waiting for Charles to enter the mansion.

"You don't believe him, Director?" Conners queries and Davison looks to ensure no one can over hear him.

"If you knew what I know about the Morrison family, you wouldn't believe him either. It's rumoured they keep detailed plans of military technology here within their vault, which is against the expectations of both the US and UK governments."

"Is that why we are here? Nothing to do with a robbery?"

Davison explains. "Many roads seem to have led us here."

"Do you think the robbery was a dodge to get the technology?" Conners questions.

"I don't know what it started out to be," Davison answers. "But at some point, it got hijacked and ended up as such, leaving us with a major headache. Many governments want to get their hands on the technologies, and I know both the CIA and MI6 would be pissed if those details were left in this unsecure place."

"So, do you think we staged the robbery?" Ashley questions and Davison looks as if he'd never considered such an outcome.

"I have no intelligence to back that up, but if I knew they were holding secret information here, I would have endeavoured to retrieve it myself."

Conners takes the data discs out. "These may have been what they were looking for, Director," she said, handing them over. "Jimmy found them on Reynolds."

Davison looks the envelope over. "Important classified military information, do not remove. Keep this to yourselves." He places the envelope into his pocket. "I don't want the Morrison's to know we have this as they may have to answer as to its contents later. We also need to find out what is on them." He produces a photograph of Grant to hand to Conners, who looks without recognition, then gives it to Ashley.

"Never seen him before."

"He works for the Morrison Corporation, and we believe he was the one who sold the specifications for the S40e missiles to the Russians."

"If you know who he is," Ashley said. "Why not arrest him?"

"If only it were that simple," Davison said, taking the photo off Ashley and handing Conners another. "Do you recognise either of those two?" Conners scrutinises the photograph showing Soames and McInley outside the barn at Eallach. "That's McInley, the IRA man found dead, but I don't recognise the other." She hands the photograph to Ashley.

"Is this a test?" Ashley said as he turned to Davison, who remained straight-faced. "That's Mile End Soames."

"What?"

"Milton Soames."

Already aware of the answer and with confirmation, Ashley wouldn't withhold information from him; Davison smiles. "And he is?"

"A major pain in the arse even though he's a colonel," Ashley said, keeping his eyes on Davison. "Another test?" he adds, and Davison grins but doesn't answer. "It was said he was Shirlow's liaison with MI6 I but couldn't confirm that."

"How come I haven't heard of him?" Conners questioned agitatedly.

"There's no reason why you should. He's a deep cover agent with no past, so when all the shit went down with Shirlow, he was on an assignment, which didn't warrant discussions in polite circles," Davison interjects. "No connection to the arms deals could be put on him. He was clean. Squeaky clean, you might say."

"That makes him more suspect," Conners said to Davison's agreement. "He commanded the surveillance of Eallach but pulled it days before this photo was taken."

"He's MI6, so how could he be in charge of surveillance on British soil?" Ashley asked, but Davison was unwilling to answer. "He also knew Caine."

"They are questions for another day, but just in case it is relevant, you need to know that a large cache of weapons and explosives was also found under the barn floor at Eallach."

"Flynn really wanted the troubles to return," Ashley said.

"I don't think he was the only one, as Soames had to know what was being stored there."

"He could have reported such to his superiors."

"My intelligence says he didn't but may have done this like you said so that the British can get back the information on their technologies."

"Surely they would inform you of their intentions as it involves both countries?" Conners adds.

"You'd think so, but it wouldn't be the first time one country left the other in the cold of their intentions."

"How did you get the photo?" Conners questions, and Davison winks and smiles back.

"He hasn't the authority to pull my surveillance."

"Why were you keeping an eye on the barn, Director," Conners asked, but he was not inclined to answer.

"Does Admiral Lawrence know about that?" Ashley adds, and Davison grins.

"I told him about the same as I tell you two."

"No, then," Ashley said.

"Why did you have it under surveillance, Director?" Conners repeats, and Davison's grin turns mischievous. "I'd like to know."

"That's for another day, and when I say another day, I mean never."

"Since seeing that photo, I now believe Soames does have a part in this."

"What brings you to that conclusion?" Davison questions, and aware it was a mistake to answer, Ashley hands Reynolds' phone over. "He telephoned."

"Did you answer it?"

Ashley looks at Conners, then nods insecurely, aware it was the wrong decision. "Maybe we can track his phone?"

"That cell is long gone. He's got a James Bond complex. Believes in all this espionage shit."

"And you don't?" Ashley jokes.

"It's just a job, James. Nothing more, nothing less."

"It's your life, Director," Conners interrupts with the pride she has in her boss, and Davison smiles broadly.

"Saving the world pays the mortgage," Davison jokes, then turns deadly serious. "We need to find out what this Jerome Adler knows. I'll send that ass from Bermuda to check him out.

***

CHAPTER 25

***

Chaucer pulls his Mercedes S500 up outside Adler's five-million-Dollar mansion, and as if invited to a grand dinner party, he alights to ring the bell, which after several seconds, the door opens as he flashes his ID. "I've come to see Mr Adler."

"I will see if he will see you, sir," the butler said subserviently, and as Chaucer went to speak, the door was closed on him.

Impatiently rebuked, Chaucer shuffles uncomfortably until the door opens and the butler stands aside.

"Mr Adler will see you now, sir. Please follow me."

Chaucer enters a large, ornately decorated marble-tiled hallway with a grand stairway and enters the drawing room.

"Would you like a drink, sir?"

Chaucer debates the question, and even though he could do with a stiff gin and tonic because he's on duty and a stickler for the rules, he decides against it.

Bombastically full of life, Adler enters. "Go on, Rupert, take a drink on this beautiful day."

"I'm on official duty, Jerome."

"There's no official duty between members of the Victoria club," Adler said as he turned to the butler. "I don't want to be disturbed again," he said, and the butler nods then exited. "I thought you worked for," he adds as Chaucer shows his ID for him to read. "Anti what was that?"

"I need to ask you some questions about your uncles, Jerome."

A knock sounds, and the butler enters, to Adler's annoyance. "I'm sorry, Mr Adler, but you have another official visitor."

Angered, Adler calls out. "I don't have the inclination to see anyone else!"

"I think you'll want to see me." Soames menaced as he enters arrogantly and flashes his ID, which Chaucer checks while showing his own. "I'll take it from here."

With his belief in himself, Chaucer's glance shifts uncomfortably around. "On whose authority?"

"Mine, of course, old fruit," Soames belittles, but Chaucer questions his authority and he draws his Sig Sauer and shoots him twice in the chest, knocking him onto the floor in a crumpled heap with Adler screaming, and he turns the gun onto him then the butler, who lifts his hands in shocked surrender as he is shot in the head to end his life in blood splattering violence that terrifies Adler as the gun is turned back onto him. "I've come for my money."

"Money?" Adler said in terror. "What money?"

"Five hundred thousand Dollars for each of my men and one million Dollars for my part. That makes a total of five million Dollars. Payable immediately."

"Five million Dollars?" Adler questioned nervously, shocked. "For what?"

"For the robbery of your uncles, of course, but because of the inconvenience, I am changing the Dollars to Pounds."

Understanding the reasoning, Adler takes several breaths and confidently lowers his hands. "It's Grant you need to see," he said, believing that the threatening man was just another employee and becoming decidedly calmer as he moved to the drinks cabinet to pour himself a cognac. "He set it all up. I don't know what he was after."

"I do," Soames said with menace as he took the silencer off to place into his pocket. "So, you have nothing to do with the payment I require?"

"No, you, err," Adler mumbles, then takes a mouthful of the cognac. "Grant will pay you in full if you have what he wants."

"And where will I find this Grant at this minute?"

Even though he knows the robbery was a failure, Adler picks up a pen and paper to scribble a few lines, tears the top sheet off, and hands it for Soames to look over. "He's at this address."

Soames launches himself forward to grab Adler harshly around the neck, places the Sig Sauer into the weaker man's hand, lifts it to his temple, and pulls the trigger to slump to the floor dead with the gun falling in forensic correctness at his side. "Killing yourself after killing that agent and your servant, how disgraceful," he said with psychotic glee as he exited.

***

Grant sits in the lounge of his large house with Faisel Mohammed and two bodyguards in the corner, attentively looking on. "If you want our lucrative business arrangement to carry on, you will have to come up with the goods, Mr Grant," Faisel said menacingly to Grant's increasing nervousness. "I am under pressure from my superior to gain the knowledge of it all."

"As I have in the past, Mr Faisel, there will be no problems coming up with the required goods."

"Is that so? Well, when will you have the discs I require?" Faisel enquires, impatiently of the nervous-looking Grant, which isn't missed by the Egyptian constantly looking for intelligence to use against others. "I need all those technologies. Not one at a time as in the past, I want them all, and you know I am willing to pay for them."

"You'll get it soon," Grant explains, but Faisel can tell he is lying. "I am instructed not to telephone the seller but don't worry; he will get in touch when he has them."

"This man. Do you trust him?"

"Err, yes, of course I do," Grant mutters nervously. "I've worked with him before," he feigns.

"I'm unsure about the outside influence I don't control."

"Why have you heard something?" Grant adds with a cowardly laugh that doesn't impress.

Having listened to their conversation, Soames enters through the French doors and speaks with belief in his ability. "He should trust me as I am the best."

"Thank God," Grant said as the bodyguards went for their side arms, but Faisel lifted his hands for calm to deflate the situation.

Faisel walks to the drinks cabinet to pour himself a vodka. "I take it I am waiting for you?"

"You could say that."

"Do you have what I require?"

"Do you have the five million Pounds for myself and my men?" Soames answers confidently to Faisel's increasing impatience as he looks at Grant's nervousness.

"Pounds?" Faisel questioned, aware of the original denomination of Dollars being used.

"Yes, Pounds," Soames said confidently, and Faisel shuffled his unease at the increase in his expenditure.

"Do you have what I require?"

"I think we are having two conversations at once," Soames said with a laugh as the tension in the room, which could so easily turn to violence, got the better of Grant, who bellows without thought.

"He's bluffing you, Mr Faisel! The robbery was a flop. He lost all his men."

Faisel nods, and his bodyguards go for their side arms, but Soames beats them to the draw, and four taps later, they are bleeding all over the floor, no longer a threat.

"That was rather silly," Soames said, turning his Sig Sauer onto Faisel, who remained calm as he lifted a vodka to take a sip. "You hadn't considered what sort of a threat I am. Now let's see if you have the answer to my question. Do you have my five million Pounds?"

"Do you have what I require?" Faisel asked unphased.

Soames turns on Grant as his intelligence mind clicks into action. "How could you know the mission had failed?"

Grant's terrified stare shifts between the two antagonists waiting for an answer. "I got a call from Mr Adler," he said confidently. "He told me what had happened."

"And when were you going to tell me?" Faisel interrupts angrily as Soames laughs about what he would have done if the roles were reversed.

"He thought I would turn up, and you would get your goons to kill, then put the blame on me," Soames said with reason.

Faisel pauses in thought. "I see," he muttered. "Did you get what I require?"

"Do you have my money?" Soames insists as his glance shifts between Faisel and Grant.

"Don't look at me; I didn't bankroll this," Grant blusters in the hope his minor involvement will keep him from danger, but Soames' stare stops on Faisel's straight face then he turns his menaced stare onto him. "I am the middle man. The broker, you might say," he blusters with self-importance. "I had the inside information on the robbery and helped set it up."

"With the IRA man?" Soames said with knowing, making Grant shuffle uncomfortably and bewilder Faisel that the Irish Republican movement had anything to do with his business dealings.

"What about the Russians you approached?" Soames said, turning to see Faisel's reaction to his comment.

Uncomfortable with the intelligence they thought was between them, Grant and Faisel look at each other.

"What Russians?" Grant defends.

"Now it has failed. You are no good to anyone."

"I wouldn't say that," Grant said confidently as he stared at Soames. "I know you," he said as the MI6 man grinned amusedly. "You were with Stephens the day we discussed what was to be done, but you had an Irish accent," he adds, making Soames uncomfortable. "Let's see if I can remember your name." He pauses in thought as Faisel takes a greater interest. "That's it." He goes to speak, but Soames puts a bullet in his forehead and he falls to the floor dead as the smoking Sig Sauer is turned onto Faisel, who remains deadly calm.

"So, you have another identity?" Faisel said, uncaring.

"Do you have my fucking money?" Soames shouts, increasing the intensity of his question.

Unperturbed by the loss of life, Faisel shows his coolness under intimidation. "We are back to the first conversation you seem to be avoiding, so I will ask again. Do you have my goods?" he insists, and Soames answers soberly.

"I'm afraid he was right."

"Then that ends my part in this conversation."

"But not mine," Soames menaces. "I still want my pay."

"Why should I pay for something I haven't received?"

"I'll give you that reason. I know who you are," Soames adds in fluent Russian, but Faisel looks bemused as if he doesn't understand.

"Polkovnik Victor Sokolov. An agent of the Sluzba Vneshney Razvedki," he adds, then goes back to English. "The Russian foreign intelligence service. You worked for General Klamenkovich, who was a section head of the main intelligence directorate of the general staff of the armed forces of the Russian Federation, before his sad demise."

With arrogance adding to his confident demeanour, Faisel adds.

"Where did you get your information from?"

"This, Colonel, is all a front so Russia can obtain military technologies and make a Muslim nation take the blame for future acts of aggression against the West."

"You don't know what you are talking about!"

"Well, the Muslims have made themselves such an easy target these days," Soames carries on off-topic. "With the help of the Western Allies, that is, but it's all their fault, and I have no sympathy for them."

"Why would an Egyptian work for Russia?" Faisel interrupts. "I am a patriot and a proud Muslim."

"Of course, you are sitting there drinking what I can only assume isn't water. Quote something from the Quran for me."

Even though Soames wouldn't be able to corroborate anything written in the Islamic holy book, he was equally confident the man twitching in front of him wouldn't be able to as well. "You don't remember, but I met you in St Petersburg three years ago when I was there to see your ex-boss."

In the pretence that his persistence will take the pressure off him, Faisel carries on with his cover story. "I have never been to Russia."

"Considering you were born in Staraya near St Petersburg in 1975, I find that hard to believe."

Faisel shuffles unnerved that his cover story, only known to him and his SVR commander, is unwrapping through the words of a foreign intelligence operative.

"You're here because of me," Soames said confidently, but Sokolov didn't question his words as he wanted to hear more. "Who do you think informed General Klamenkovich of the military technologies and brought that arse in to act as a go-between. If the plan had gone as arranged, you would have your discs, and I would have all my money," he adds as Sokolov shuffles uncomfortably and looks at Grant. "His future was preordained when he agreed to do as I said."

"So, who are you?" Sokolov questions, but Soames does not intend to give him any information about himself.

"Your nom de guerre is safe with me, but now it comes at a price." Aware there is no way of carrying on his cover story, Sokolov keeps his deep, menacing stare on Soames. "I can get you the money, but I need those discs."

"We're past that now," Soames said as he pointed at Grant. "You were paying that joker ten million for the discs?"

Sokolov looks coy but doesn't flinch.

"Now, you can pay me direct, but as I said, I want Pounds, not Dollars."

"Can you get me the information I require?" Sokolov questioned, determined by his standing orders to be able to finish his mission.

"I can, but I need an assurance from you."

Sokolov takes his phone out and dials. "I need to get this sanctioned."

"Considering you are paying me direct instead of him, I can't see what the problem could be," Soames menaced as he moved to the window but kept the Russian in his peripheral vision. "You also need to ask how much your cover is worth to your superiors?"

Sokolov speaks over his phone in Russian, which Soames understands, then switches the phone off. "Get me the information, and I will pay you the ten million."

"That's Pounds Sterling, not Egyptian Pounds," Soames said, then laughed. "That would quarter the amount."

"I don't care who gets paid as long as I get the information required." Soames grins victoriously, then adds sardonically. "I would shake on the deal but your word is as worthless as mine. I'll be back in a couple of hours. Have my money waiting for me."

***

CHAPTER 26

***

Ashley and Conners watch Reynolds being loaded onto an Air Ambulance helicopter and flown to the mainland as Ashley waves with juvenile contempt.

"What goes through your simple mind, Jimmy!" she said, unsettled.

Davison stands further off, talking on his phone before moving over.

"What's up, Director?" Conners asked.

"Chaucer's been found dead," Davison explains, and Conners' shocked stare shifts to Ashley as he moves over. "Local police found the bodies."

"Bodies?" Conners questions.

"In the home of Jerome Adler. The police think Adler shot his butler, then Chaucer, before killing himself."

Conners shakes her head in disbelief. "The eagle didn't have it in him. His threats were always verbal and non-threatening."

"I agree," Ashley adds. "He was just an annoying pussy who needed a slap."

Davison looks up on hearing the sound of an approaching helicopter.

"Colonel Soames is on his way," he said as he headed toward the mansion, leaving Ashley and Conners in confusion. "See to him for me!"

Soames' Robinson R44 flies over and banks dramatically as it comes into land. Having flown himself, he alights and walks over like a guest.

"What's been going on here?" he says, showing his identification, but neither Ashley nor Conners pay it any attention.

"That's need to know?" Ashley answers as he stares directly into the colonel's eyes but gets no signs of recognition.

Soames believes his ID should command reverence. "Didn't you see what I flashed?"

"We've got them too," Conners said with smiling arrogance of getting a rise out of the MI6 man who looked non-plussed by the bluster. "Who are you?"

Just beating Ashley to the punchline, Conners answers determined. "That's also need to know."

Soames' glare shifts menacingly between them. "Who's in command, and before you say that's need to know, I need to know."

Davison exits the mansion, and even though he is aware of the man who could wreak havoc on his intelligence life, Soames is at first shocked to see him, then enquires with polite curiosity.

"Are you in charge here?"

Davison reverts to his clichéd American General disguise. "And you are?"

Soames shows his ID for Davison to peruse.

"A fellow spook. What can we do for you, cowboy?

Suspicious of Davison's acting ability, Soames keeps a straight face as he answers. "I'm working on something," he said as his glance shifted from Ashley and Conners to smile at the American. "It's need to know, but I need to look around."

Davison feigns interest. "That's not a problem but don't take or move anything. This is a crime scene."

"I know the score," Soames said arrogantly.

"Fill your boots, Colonel."

Amused, Soames grins as he makes his way toward the mansion.

Mystified by what he had witnessed, Ashley questions Davison's reasoning. "I wouldn't let that idiot anywhere near the scene."

"Don't worry about him," Davison said with glee as he watched Soames enter the mansion. "He knows who I am."

"He looked like he recognised you," Ashley said.

"Looked like you were playing each other off," Conners adds, looking at Ashley. "I thought you knew him, Jimmy?" she questions, and his positive reply makes her laugh. "You wouldn't have thought so. He ignored you."

"That's Mile End at his finest. He would have been a Hollywood A-lister if he hadn't become a spook. He has a great love for himself."

***

Soames enters the lounge to find Charles and Gordon drinking fine whisky, intending to drown out the day's cruelty.

Seeing their uninvited visitor, Charles stands to greet him. "Can I help you?" he questioned, but Soames moved off with no intention of answering, forcing the old man to move with haste to intercept. "Excuse me, but who are you?"

"Just someone doing his job, Mr Morrison," Soames said as he flashed his identification to settle Charles' angst. "Now, excuse me." He walks toward the vault and enters its mayhem.

***

Davison keeps his intense stare on the mansion as Ashley and Conners look at him, then each other, bemused by his interest.

"Is everything alright, Director?" Conners enquires anxiously, and he answers without diverting his stare.

"When he comes out, he'll want to return to Bermuda. Ask him for a ride, then follow him. He'll take you to Faisel, and when you get them together, arrest them both."

"I thought you had Faisel followed?"

Davison is aware Faisel had evaded the agency's attempt to follow, and even though he knows it's the British agents at fault, he refrains from answering. "I'll have a team on standby to back you up."

"Will that be required, Director?" Conners asked concerned.

"He thinks he's made a deal with Faisel, but he's in for a shock when the SVR intelligence man reneges on it and has him killed."

"SVR?" Ashley said, shocked that the Russian Foreign Intelligence Service was now part of the scene, but Davison continued ignoring what was meant to be a query.

"I want him alive and dealing with Faisel."

"Surely, you've got enough on him, Director?" Conners questions and Davison smiles.

"I want him with his fingers in the SVR till. I need as much evidence against him as possible if we are going to take it to MI6 to find out if they have any involvement in this. I don't want to give Admiral Lawrence another reason to go against me, and this will certainly upset his little game," Davison said as he handed Conners a signal receiver, tracking device and a phone. "Use these," he said to Ashley's bewilderment.

***

Soames rummages through the debris of the vault as he throws things aside with a clatter until he notices the open, secure box and moves to look inside and pick up an envelope. "Important classified military information, do not remove," he reads off the cover, opens it to gaze at two data discs inside, then quickly places them into his jacket and exits.

***

Ashley and Conners look towards Soames' helicopter when he passes at speed, ignoring their presence.

"Excuse me, sir," Conners shouts, but the MI6 man doesn't stop. "Can we hitch a lift to the mainland?"

"You can, but I'm not sure about your boyfriend!"

Conners laughs. "Why not?" she questioned while simultaneously glancing at Ashley.

"Just get the fuck in."

"That was a quick visit," Conners adds delicately, but the wily MI6 man has no intention of giving away intelligence.

"It's all action in the A team," Ashley commented, and Soames turned his ire onto him.

"If you need a lift, get in! If not, piss off and swim," Soames said as he moved to the R44 and got in, leaving Conners shaking her head at the laughing Ashley.

***

After ten minutes of silent flight, the helicopter lands at LF Wade and Soames switches the engine off and conscious of his passenger's true intent, he alights and heads off without a word leaving them behind.

"Your friend's a nice sociable type," Conners said to Ashley's amusement. "No doubt ex-SAS."

"He's like the rest of us," Ashley explains with delight. "He doesn't like Yanks."

"I'd say his problem was you, Jimmy."

Feigning a lack of haste, Ashley and Conners alight and follow Soames through the executive reception and out of the other side into the drop-off area, where the MI6 operative gets into a waiting Ford Taurus taxi which drives off at speed.

Totally out manoeuvred, Conners' head whips around frantically.

"Obviously, we aren't as well organised as our traitor friend." Having dropped the tracking device into Soames' jacket pocket, she takes the signal receiver out and switches it on. "He's on the move," she said seriously, making Ashley laugh in understanding what Davison had given her.

"Are you shitting me? Did you get that information from the trillion-Dollar satellite orbiting our heads because I've just seen him drive off and could have saved your country the money!"

"Alright, clever shit," Conners said, amused. "Why don't you track him from here?"

"Touchy," Ashley adds with hilarity as a Range Rover pulls up in front, and they get in and it drives off with him in the rear, fumbling to take out his pain medication.

Conners places the bleeping receiver onto the dashboard and then looks at the driver's youthfulness. "I take it you know this area?"

"Yes, ma'am," the driver answers politely.

"He's in a Green Ford Taurus taxi and can only be three minutes ahead."

"There he is, ma'am," the driver explains, noticing the taxi further off.

"Forget the ma'am shit. I'm Julie; he's Jimmy."

"James!" Ashley moans.

"Ignore him; he prefers Jimmy. Don't lose him," she adds impatiently, unaware of the young driver's skills. "The director will be well pissed if we don't catch him with his pants down."

"Pants down?" Ashley questioned sarcastically. "You're taken with him?"

Conners smiles, then adds with mischievous intent for the benefit of her British counterpart. "Well, he's the best-looking man I've seen in a long time." She turns to the driver. "Next to yourself, of course," she adds, and he blushes and smiles coyly at her sarcasm.

"So, I'm in third place?" Ashley said, but Conners shook her head.

"Don't tell me Davison is ahead of me?" he adds, and Conners grins but doesn't answer. "Well, hopefully, you'll have time to hump the colonel before we arrest him," he adds, making the driver snigger.

"Do I detect a hint of jealousy, Jimmy?"

"Of course. I've been chasing your tail since the day we met," Ashley said as he turned to look out of the window. "You're every man's wet dream."

"He's pulling over, Ma, err Julie," the driver said as the Range Rover passed Soames' taxi to stop thirty metres up the road.

They all look through the rear window as Soames alights, looking mistrustingly around before walking up the drive to knock on the door, which opens for a sizeable menacing man to glare out.

"What's your plan, Colonel?" Ashley asks to Conners' amusement.

"There's that colonel shit again. You do know we're the same rank in this thing?"

"It must be with you being American. I just assumed you would be in command."

Even though the driver is one of Davison's agents from America, he gets the joke and turns away to smile to avoid being noticed by Conners.

"Really, Jimmy?" Conners said, unconvinced.

"Well, Colonel, what do you have in mind?"

Unsure whether he is being serious or his usual cantankerous self, Conners shakes her head. "Let's wait a minute to see if anyone comes. If they don't, we'll go in and arrest him."

"Going off the door being answered," Ashley adds drolly. "They're already inside."

Conners turns to the driver. "Go around the back and make sure no one leaves," she orders, and he nods, then alights and moves off. "Now, let's go see who comes for tea."

"They're already there," Ashley snipes to her disdain.

"You know, Jimmy. Sometimes I wish you'd piss off and leave me to do my job!" she shouts, making him laugh as he alights, and she follows.

***

Soames enters the large lounge, followed by the bodyguard, to find Sokolov sitting with a second bodyguard standing behind, whom he can see already has his Makarov pistol drawn and is attempting to conceal it.

"Have you got my goods?" Sokolov calls out.

"Have you got my money?"

Sokolov nods at a briefcase on the table, but as Soames walks toward it, the first bodyguard lifts it away.

"So, it's like that?"

Sokolov turns decidedly darker. "Do you have my goods?"

Soames throws the envelope onto the table for the first bodyguard to pick up as he puts the briefcase down.

"One disc and what looks like a small tracking device."

"I was led to believe there would be two?" Sokolov questions, not taking in that Soames had placed into the envelope what Conners had put into his pocket and he smiles his answer. "But you wanted to see the money first? Well, let me tell you, you killed two of my men, and I didn't like that."

The second bodyguard lifts his Makarov, but Soames beats him to the draw, shoots him in the chest, then turns to the first bodyguard and, with supreme accuracy, puts a bullet in his head for them to crumple to the ground in unison.

With arrogant confidence, Soames moves over the bodyguards, and even though he can see they are dead, he puts two extra rounds into each. "You're still getting me mixed up with a fool, Victor. You forget I worked with General Klamenkovich for many years before his death. We had many a drunken session where he would tell me about SVR tactics, and I would tell him nothing but shit."

Sokolov stands readjusting his expensive hand-made suit. "The general was a traitor selling arms to the enemy." He moves to the envelope and picks it up to look inside to see the tracking device, which he throws aside.

"So, a traitor sells the secrets and a hero either buys or steals them? Sounds like double standards to me," Soames deduces, but Sokolov ignores the apparent slur.

"I'm happy with the one disc for now. You can take your money."

"That's nice of you," Soames said, moving to the briefcase.

Sokolov turns his back and draws his Izhevsk MP 446 Viking pistol, then turns fast to face the man he had been ordered to kill but who already had him covered with his Sig Sauer and the empty briefcase to his side.

Soames grins, angered. "I take it you forgot to put my money in?"

Sokolov lifts his hands compliantly as his gun swings harmlessly through his fingers. "Against my wishes," he pleads.

"Shame about Klamenkovich being dead, as he could have vouched for me."

"It was you who said he was dead?" Sokolov said to Soames' increasing interest. "I said he was a traitor."

"So where does this leave us?"

"My superiors won't deal with you."

"That's sad to hear, but it doesn't matter. You'd have soon discovered the discs have no data on them."

"What?" Sokolov shouts, betrayed.

"As I said, neither of us can be trusted," Soames adds as he aims.

***

Ashley and Conners arrive at the front door when a single shot rings out, and they draw their side arms, and Ashley kicks the door until it breaks in, and they enter to find Soames standing over Sokolov's body as he opens fire, forcing them into cover with bullets smashing too close for comfort around them. Still firing, Soames exits through the French doors and races over the garden as he drops a magazine and introduces another as the driver comes through the bottom gate, he puts several bullets into the young man's chest to take his life as he hits the grass with the murderer racing past. Ashley and Conners exit the mansion offensively to see the body of the driver and Soames disappearing out of the gate, and Ashley discharges several shots into its woodwork, missing his quarry, as he follows at speed onto the street where there is no sign of the highly experienced MI6 man. Attempting to hear a sound that would give away his prey, he pauses for several fraught seconds, but a garden mower's shrilling drone overwhelms and negates his actions.

She stands over the motionless driver as Ashley enters. "I take it he got away?" she said with certainty as the distraught-looking Ashley caught his breath.

"Check the tracker."

She looks at the signal receiver to see the tracking device in the house, then drops it angrily.

"Isn't your trillion Dollar satellite working?" he jokes, but she isn't in the mood for his sarcasm and turns her scathing stare onto him. "God knows where he went."

Angered at the driver's senseless killing, she snarls. "He now knows we're onto him."

"That makes him more dangerous," he adds with knowing as she takes her phone out and dials. "As if I didn't know, but who are you calling?"

She paces off speaking. "Sorry, Director, he got away." She looks at Ashley and winks. "Jimmy couldn't catch him. Too old and out of shape, I'm afraid." She listens to Davison's ranting disappointment. "There are three dead in the house; one is Faisel. Yes, Director. Straight away, Director," she adds, then listens to what is expected of her. "No, the tracking device is in the house."

"Three bags full, Director!" he shouts sarcastically, unaware Davison had overheard him as she switched the phone off. "What now, Colonel?"

"Fuck off with the colonel shit, Jimmy. We've been pulled," she explains with Davison's annoyed voice resonating in her ears.

"Pulled? Why?"

"Because you know Soames, you've made it personal."

"Bull-shit! I've known most of the players in this."

"And because you had to run twenty feet, the director believes you need a rest."

"Piss off!" he growls, aware it is too near the truth to be a joke.

"He wants us on his plane within the hour."

"I can live with that," he adds, hoping his holiday would soon start. "What about the scene?"

"That's for others to deal with," she explains as her eyes fix with sadness on the driver. "There's been enough killing for one day."

"You think so," he adds, determined. "I think there's at least one more needed."

"We've done our bit. Leave Soames to the witch hunters. They'll get the bastard now they know who they are looking for."

Ashley looks at the driver's innocence. "For the murder of that boy, I hope I'm the one to put a bullet in his head."

"I hope they take him alive and drop him in a shit-filled hole for the rest of his miserable life," she adds with reason. "Death will be too easy for him."

***

Soames moves to the security fence at LF Wade airport and looks toward Davison's agency jet as it gets refuelled and restocked. He can see an unarmed, lowly paid security guard standing at a gate further up, giving him some curious attention, and moves over to show his identification to be allowed through and smiles his false appreciation as he walks toward the Gulfstream.

***

Enjoying the comfort of the jet's luxury, Watkins sits at Davison's desk when Soames enters, looking around with a bright beaming smile of delight.

"Well, isn't this lovely?" Soames said as Watkins becomes aware of his presence but doesn't recognise the new number one man on the agency's most wanted list.

"You're not allowed in here," Watkins directs, standing to confront, but Soames flashes his ID as he passes to the cockpit to glare into its emptiness.

"I was told to meet General Davison here," Soames said, alerting Watkins using the military rank. "Do you have a time scale for his arrival?"

Watkins looks nervously at his watch. "Can I have another look at that ID?"

With no intent of reintroducing himself, Soames draws his Sig Sauer and shoots Watkins in the shoulder to knock him onto the floor, where he takes hold of its ache and groans as blood seeps through his fingers. "No, and keep the noise down," he said calmly. "I've had a major shitty day." He searches the injured man in amazement to find him unarmed. "You don't carry a weapon?"

"I'm not a field agent," Watkins explains as he moves to a chair to slump onto its comfort.

"The way you were easily taken, I can see why," Soames said with satire as he sat opposite.

The sound of a car approaching and then stopping, followed by doors slamming, catches Soames' attention, and he steps out of sight. "Here's your boss," he said, gesturing to Watkins with several flicks of his Sig Sauer. "No calling out, or the next bullet will ruin your day."

Davison enters with the pilot and co-pilot to see the ashen-faced Watkins sitting covered in blood, and the director goes instantly to his aid as Soames steps out, pointing his Sig Sauer to make sure everyone can see he's armed.

"Hello again, General."

Davison turns to see the newest nemeses on his hit list, and even though he knows exactly what is going on, he uses his American cliché to act shocked as he queries what is happening.

"Cut the crap and get this bucket into the air."

Davison turns to the pilot. "Do as he says, Captain."

The pilot and the co-pilot enter the cockpit as Soames frisks them for weapons.

"They're unarmed," Davison explains, and Soames grins his mistrust.

"And you?"

"I don't carry a gun these days. It ruins the line of my suit."

"Excuse me if I don't trust what you have to say," Soames said as he frisked Davison to find in amazement that he was telling the truth.

"I take it you have a destination in mind?"

"I'll keep that to myself until we get near," Soames adds smugly.

"Don't forget we need to put forward a flight plan."

Soames gives a sarcastic sneer. "I know this bird can go where ever you want, so get her up and point her at Blighty."

Davison presses the intercom. "Captain, get us underway." He turns to Soames. "We were already heading to England, so I take it that's to your liking?"

"Tell the pilot I require radio silence," Soames insists, and Davison goes to speak, but he carries on. "Inform him your life depends on it."

Davison lets go of the intercom. "He heard. What about Watkins?"

Soames looks at Watkins unconcerned. "I only winged him."

"He needs attention."

"Get your co-pilot to give him first aid."

Davison presses the intercom. "Send Young back with the first aid kit. Watkins needs a little help."

***

Watkins sits bandaged and uncomfortable as Soames sits opposite with his eyes fixed rigidly on Davison, who is aware of the attention his presence is bringing to the situation.

"There must be a reason for this?" Davison questions and Soames smiles reassuringly as if he were in a friend's presence.

"Of course, General, please excuse my bad manners. I was getting wrapped up in the comfort of your ride. I want fifteen million Pounds placed into my bank account before we land."

"And why would I do that?"

"Didn't I ask nicely enough?" Soames menaced. "Surely your life is worth such a measly sum?"

"So, we can add kidnapping and extortion to your rap sheet," Davison said straight-faced making Soames laugh.

"I don't think anything else will add haste to the warrant for my arrest, General."

"You keep calling me general," Davison said with a mischievous grin as he returned to his natural accent. "I've never spent a single day in the military," he adds, and Soames grins with knowing.

"Of course not, Director," Soames said, and Davison smiled with confirmation he knew all along. "I just thought you had split personalities and played along with it to avoid offending, but now I have the real you. We can go back to what I said. Surely your life is worth the sum I require?"

Davison laughs. "I wouldn't think so."

"How much for a Gulfstream these days?"

"Thankfully, the accounts aren't my problem, but please tell me. How do you come across such a sum?" Davison enquired curiously.

"That's how much you and your organisation have cost me today," Soames said, adding a large amount of value which bemuses Davison as he waits to hear more. "When you temporarily closed down my operation."

"Temporarily?" Davison said with an intelligence-finding grin. "With Shirlow and co? I had an inclination that you were part of it, but I didn't have the evidence to back my suspicions. I was still under the assumption you were working for MI6," he adds, but Soames has no inclination to answer such a blatant question.

"I've shown my hand too soon," Soames said with a wretched grin, but Davison's surly expression informs him he is wrong. "Or not. I had the feeling I was under surveillance."

"That was probably your own side since I had confirmation of your involvement," Davison carries on and Soames interrupts.

"Confirmation? You were guessing and fell lucky."

"After the surveillance of the barn was pulled, I set up my own and guess who showed up with a known IRA sympathiser then left alone," Davison said, and Soames shook his head slowly as his cover unravelled. "And you'd never guess who had the surveillance pulled?"

he adds sarcastically, and Soames grinned, humiliated at being played. "Then I wondered what MI6s involvement in a domestic matter run by MI5, and a few sources very close to me gave me the answer. You closed it down yourself. Now the only reason I could come up with as an explanation is that you were pulling the strings all along. Not Shirlow, Caine, Kilbride or MI6."

Soames laughs in recognition of his old cohort's but changes the past to the present. "I take it you planted the envelope for me to pick up." Davison smiles with an air of accomplishment but continues with what is important to him. "I would like confirmation it was you in command?"

"There were more gaffers than workers," Soames explains, amused. "Shirlow thought that it was him because he was the highest rank. Caine thought he was the cleverest and Kilbride. Well, that idiot was nothing."

"And you the most devious, no doubt," Davison interrupts to Soames' amusement.

"And don't forget the most dangerous."

"Just for my own mind. Were you aware of the arms cache at Eallach?" Soames, at first, looks shocked but grins as if he is fully aware.

"You either didn't know or care?"

"Why wouldn't I care?"

"Well, you sold them a missile to kill the PM and his cabinet, so no doubt you also sold them the rest?"

"That was nothing to do with me," Soames protests. "And when I found out about it, I stopped it. Who do you think destroyed the missile and the Irish idiot?"

"Is that so? So, you could still be undercover for MI6?" Davison said, making Soames grin.

"Go and ask them," Soames gripes determined. "Shirlow wanted the government attacked, not me," he explains, aware the rest of what he would say won't look good for him. "When I found out we bought the missiles for next to nothing."

"And sold them for a healthy profit."

"That's the arms trade, director; surely you know how it works?" Soames adds, making Davison grin. "I found out that the missiles were sold on the cheap as the Russians wanted to see if they were as good in the real world at the same time as getting rid of the British government."

"So, they never intended to assassinate the President?"

"If the Russians had thought it possible, I believe they would have tried, but the IRA attack was the best ploy for the British and wouldn't have worked as well against you, Yanks."

"And now you're going to collect after saving the free world?"

"Now we're back on the subject; I want the money transferred into this bank account," Soames said as he wrote a number onto a piece of paper and handed it to Davison. "When I have confirmation of its deposit, we can land, and you will never see me again."

Davison looks the paper over. "Is the money going to MI6 or you personally?" He questioned, but Soames had no intention of rising to it again. "I'll have to e-mail London for the go-ahead." He looks at Soames to see his reaction to his following words. "I'll get Admiral Lawrence to deal with it personally."

"Does it have to be him?" Soames moans. "I've never liked the jumped-up snobby bastard."

The fact that Soames is protesting the use of Lawrence intrigues Davison. "Other than myself, he's the only one with the authority to sign over such an amount."

"Then he will have to do."

Davison pulls his laptop in front and switches it on. "I will e-mail the bank account number before telephoning the admiral. We don't want the number being spoken over the airwaves."

"I suppose we don't."

"Well, I don't care, but you don't want everyone knowing where you've stashed your ill-gotten gains."

Soames laughs. "Ill-gotten? More like hard fought for, but you needn't worry. It won't be there long enough for anyone to take an interest in it, so why don't you stop pissing about and get on with it?"

Davison types the e-mail, with Soames looking over his shoulder and smiling in recognition of the number. "Pour me a Jack Daniels, Colonel. Being exploited has given me a hellish thirst."

Soames grins with menace but quickly calms. "I think I will join you. Exploiting has the same effect on me."

"I'm afraid it isn't Dalmore," Davison said to get a rise out of the MI6 man by mentioning Shirlow's favourite drink, but Soames showed no sign of recognition. "I prefer Jack Daniels."

"I don't mind, Jack, but what about your stooge?" Soames said making Davison laugh.

"Would you like one, Watkins?"

Too enthralled in his discomfort to care, Watkins mumbles through gritted teeth. "No, thank you, Director. I couldn't drink with the man who tried to kill me."

"Don't be like that," Davison said. "This is purely business. There was no malice intended. Isn't that right, Colonel?"

Soames turns to the drink's cabinet. "If I'd wanted you dead, you would be!" He sets about pouring two Jack Daniels, and Davison taps the computer keypad twice in rapid succession, making the armed man turn with mistrusting anger and point the Sig Sauer with the intent to harm. "What was that?"

"You wanted me to send it?" Davison explains, and Soames nods as he hands him his Jack Daniels and takes a large sip.

"You're a wealthy man if you don't need to share too much of it," Davison said to Soames' delight. "But I would spend it quickly if I was you," he adds, picking up the phone on his desk. "Put me through to Admiral Lawrence. It's urgent."

***

Looking around in bewilderment, Ashley and Conners stand on the tarmac of LF Wade International. Even though he couldn't recognise it, he enquired about the director's plane.

"It ain't here," she answers with the obvious as she takes her phone out and dials. "It's not like him to do something different from what he said."

***

Davison's phone rings, and he looks at the screen, switches it off and pushes it aside as Soames enquires to the caller. "It was Colonel Conners. She'll be wondering where her ride to England is," he explains light-heartedly. "She's an exceptionally clever operator and will put two and two together and soon have the wolves knocking on your door."

"If you want her to achieve that goal, you need to unshackle her from James Ashley," Soames said, bemusing Davison with words meant to demean. "But I must add I look forward to the chase, Director. Of late, life has become rather tedious, so the excitement will give me a world of good."

***

Conners switches her phone off. "Something's wrong, Jimmy. He switched his cell off mid-call."

"This smells of Mile End."

"The director can look after himself."

"So, can Soames."

Ashley's words concern Conners with the realisation that her director may have been kidnapped by a man known to be a stone-cold killer. "We need to find where his plane's heading."

"He's on his way to London," he said to her annoyance.

"I know that, Jimmy, but if Soames has anything to do with it, the destination may have changed." She hastily dials her phone and speaks when answered. "You need to track the director's plane." She listens to be informed that her request is against agency policy. "Just do it!" she screams, angered by the red tape that engulfs everything they do, then listens for several tense seconds before switching it off. "The director had fifteen million Pounds put into a numbered bank account in Switzerland."

"Looks like Mile End has him by the short and curlies."

"That will be the day, but it confirms he's on his plane. We need to get to England ASAP."

"Scheduled flying's no good," he insists. "It would take us an age. We need to charter a plane," he explains, and she smiles with understanding as she uses her phone to carry that out.

***

Soames relaxes in a comfortable leather recliner with a phone to his ear as if on a leisurely holiday flight. "And the full amount has been deposited," he said with the broadest of smiles. "Appreciate it." He puts the phone down and turns to a grinning Davison. "You know the landing strip north of Tod Hills in Northumberland?"

"I know it well."

"You should. You use it often enough. Put me down there."

Davison smiles knowingly. "I hope you have a good hiding place."

"Fifteen million Pounds will help me in that endeavour."

"I'm sure it will," Davison said, confident he would get his man.

"Now drop me off, but firstly, I need you to be tied as I can't trust you not to interfere with my escape, which if you do, will turn instantly violent."

***

Davison and Watkins sit tied to their chairs as Soames stands at the cockpit door, looking in on the pilot and co-pilot.

"We are making our final approach," the pilot explains to Soames' gratification.

"Land then slow at the end of the runway. Once there, I'm going to get to the door, and as you increase take-off speed, I will jump out, and you can go and land where ever you want."

"I can't take off with the door open," the pilot said, concerned.

"He can close it," Soames said, looking at the co-pilot. "You can do that, can't you?"

The co-pilot doesn't like what Soames is doing, which shows in his tone. "If you say so," he mutters, but Soames doesn't like his attitude and menacingly points his Sig Sauer hard into his face.

"If you fuck about and hinder me in any way and attempt to be the hero, I'll put a bullet in your fucking head," Soames said, and the co-pilot, sensing the intensity of the threat, nodded. "Then we have an understanding."

***

Ashley and Conners relax in the plush leather seats of a Bombardier Global Express private jet as it heads at its cruising speed of 560mph toward the United Kingdom as he lounges back with his feet up on the luxurious leather enjoying the flavours of the many alcoholic beverages on offer, but she doesn't mention her concern of his bad manners and greedy nature to indulge.

Having never sat in such luxury, he speaks excitedly. "They've come up trumps here," he said but can see her disinterest. "Come on," he adds with a significant smile. "When have you ever travelled like this?"

"Every time I have flown with the director."

"Of course," he said ironically. "It's an American thing. I haven't travelled in the agency jet."

"Well, we don't want any Limeys stinking it up."

"I get lifts in flying buckets," he whinges, and she snipes instantly back. "I can't think of a better place for you," she said, looking him up and down.

"Don't forget we pay towards this A.A.A. shit."

"Yeah? About two cents on the Dollar."

Aware she speaks the truth, he fidgets his patriotic uncomfortableness and looks away as she bursts into laughter.

"You bite so easily, Jimmy."

"With good reason having to put up with your, we are mightier than everyone, American shit."

"I suppose the truth hurts."

***

Davison's agency jet flies over Bamburgh Castle on the Northumberland coastline and banks on its descent toward Tod Hills to land without complications. It moves to the end of the runway and turns to face the direction of take-off as the co-pilot makes his way to the door, followed by Soames.

"Looks like we are at the end of our journey together, Director," Soames menaced, but Davison called back with dignity and calmness. "We'll meet again, but it will be on my terms."

"You bring the party food, and I'll bring the beers," Soames mocks, and Davison adds bitterly to his amusement.

"That's for when you are no more."

The co-pilot opens the door allowing the warm Northumbrian air to enter.

"You need to go," Davison said, feigning defeat as Soames moved into the doorway.

"Goodbye to you all!" Soames said as he drew his Sig Sauer and put a bullet into Davison's leather seat, just to the left of his face, but the director remained calm and didn't flinch. "It would have been just as easy to kill you, Director, don't forget that," he adds, then taking advantage of the commotion, he jumps to land on the tarmac and rolls back on himself to point the gun at the open doorway.

As the Gulfstream powers up, the co-pilot turns to a unit at his side and opens the drawer to produce a Glock 17 to capture their kidnapper and as the engines roar their acceleration. He leans out, ready to wreak revenge on the traitor, with Davison's voice resonating for him to let him go, and Soames shoots him in the chest to fall back inside as the jet races off down the runway. Realising the danger and gasping for air, the co-pilot closes the door and locks it in one last movement before falling back onto the floor, writhing in pain.

***

Keeping the plane in sight, Soames races along the runway as it lifts off and flies into the distance. Having achieved his goal, he holsters his Sig Sauer and then runs into the surrounding area to exit onto a small country lane where a Range Rover and driver sit waiting for him.

***

Once the autopilot has taken over, the pilot exits the cockpit in shock at his friend.

"How's Young?" Davison shouts, concerned, but the pilot's solemn face answers as he steps over the body to untie him. "Take your time, Captain. There's no rush."

"Sorry, Director, I had to get the jet into steady flight before I could come back," the pilot explains, looking at the bullet hole in his chair. "What the hell."

Davison smiles. "If he'd wanted me dead, I would be."

"What are we going to do, Director?" Watkins enquires as Davison smiles confidently.

"He's going nowhere," Davison answers, then turns his interest onto Watkins. "How are you feeling?

"Not too bad, Director. Thank you for asking."

"Good," Davison adds as he picks up the phone and dials. "Now, let's get the ball back into play."

***

Conners' phone rings and she looks at the screen. "It's the director," she said excitedly as she answered. "Good to hear from you, sir."

"Where are you, Colonel?" Davison questions, apprehensively concerned that they would still be in Bermuda.

"Somewhere over the Atlantic."

"Is everything alright?"

"Apart from Jimmy's constant bitching, yes."

Davison laughs. "Well, it wouldn't be right if he wasn't. Look, this is an open line, so I will keep it to a minimum. I need you back at HQ ASAP."

"Yes, Director."

"I will see you there," Davison said, putting his phone down.

Conners turns curiously to Ashley. "Something's off. He sounds way too calm, considering what has happened for my liking."

"Did he mention Mile End?"

"No, but the back to HQ ASAP has his name written all over it."

***

CHAPTER 27

***

Temporarily situated above an old barber's shop on Old Queen Street in Central London, the English office of the Anglo-American Anti-Terrorism Intelligence Unit had been set up to cover the United Kingdom and Europe. Sipping a large glass of Jack Daniels, Davison sits at his desk with Ashley and Conners sitting on side chairs, uncomfortably unsure what they are waiting for as they hadn't been offered any refreshments.

The door opens, and Lawrence enters without permission and looks around with the conceited arrogance he is notorious for. "Screwed up again, Director?" he said, amused, but Davison didn't stir to welcome his second in command.

"No thanks to you."

Lawrence turns his irrational stare directly onto Davison. "I hope you can explain yourself."

"Let's start with what annoys me the most," Davison said calmly.

"Why didn't your man in Bermuda back up my people when required?"

"My man?" Lawrence feigns. "I take it you mean Chaucer? He wasn't my man, and I don't understand how you could think he was."

"Is that so?" Davison said serenely, which unnerved Lawrence as to where the line of questioning was heading

"I can't answer for him," Lawrence explains with a sadistic laugh that shows he cares nothing for the loss of the operator. "And now he can't even answer for himself."

"You ordered him to monitor the Morrisons?"

Lawrence shakes his head in arrogant denial as he moves to the drinks cabinet and pours himself one of the director's Jack Daniels. "You'll find that's untrue, and you'd better have hard evidence to back your scurrilous accusation."

"Your man informed Colonel Conners that you gave the order."

Lawrence's unnerved glance shifts between Davison and Conners, who feigns a smile to back up her director's words even though she has no idea where they are heading.

"And when the shit hit the fan, you ordered him not to intervene," Davison adds as his tone angrily increases.

"And you can prove that?" Lawrence said confidently.

"Considering the man's dead, that may be hard."

Lawrence grins and then laughs, believing his deceitfulness could never be proven. "You've accused me in front of these people, undermining my reputation with no evidence to back you up. This will go further!" he growls as he places the untouched Jack Daniels down and turns for the door, but Ashley moves in front to prevent him from passing. "I would move if you know what is good for you, Sergeant."

"Hold on," Davison said, and Lawrence turned back. "Finish your drink. I'm not finished!"

"I think you are, Director," Lawrence said, using a derogatory tone on the American's title as he turned his ire back onto Ashley.

"You dealt with the money transfer for Soames?" Davison questions, making Lawrence snap back.

"Under your instruction! You sent the details, and I dealt with it!"

"Personally?"

"Of course."

"And nobody helped you?"

"That's what you requested?"

Davison picks a piece of paper off his desk and moves to Lawrence to hand it over. "Do you recognise that?"

"Looks like the bank account number for the transfer of the money," Lawrence answers as he looks around at all the attention fixed on him. Curious about where the questioning is heading, he looks the paper over again. "For Colonel Soames," he mumbles but stops in thought but still can't make out any irregularities.

Davison presses the intercom on his desk. "Watkins, can you come in?"

Almost instantly, Watkins knocks and then enters with his injured shoulder in a sling.

"Do you recognise the paper in Admiral Lawrence's hand?" Davison said, and Watkins looked it over.

"The bank account number for Colonel Soames, Director?"

"And the writing?"

"Colonel Soames', Director."

"And you witnessed him write it?"

Becoming increasingly unnerved by the line of questioning, Watkins answers as if he is guilty of wrongdoing himself. "Yes, Director, I was sitting by his side."

"And where did this happen?"

"On the agency jet, Director."

Davison picks a piece of paper off his desk. "This is the original e-mail I sent Admiral Lawrence, which he received in his office." He hands it to Watkins. "Look them over."

"May I, sir," Watkins said politely as he took the paper off Lawrence. "What's this all about?" Lawrence demands, but Davison ignores his pleading as he awaits Watkins' reply.

"The numbers aren't the same, Director," Watkins said, bewildered, and Lawrence snatched the pieces of paper off him to compare them. "Is there something wrong?" Davison questions, and Lawrence looks hesitantly up.

"I take it you can't spot the deliberate mistake?"

Lawrence looks the paper over again.

"You heard the admiral say he dealt with the transfer personally," Davison adds turning his determined stare onto Lawrence, who looks confident in his innocence. "How could the money have gone into Colonel Soames' account when the number had been deliberately written wrong."

"Deliberately written wrong?" Watkins questioned, unable to grasp what was happening as Davison smiled broadly.

"I wrote the e-mail, and Soames confirmed the number before pouring me a Jack. In that time, I deleted one digit, as you can see, fourth from right, the number seven and then I sent it on. For that money to go into that bank account, it had to have the right number." He turns on Lawrence. "I knew you were involved but couldn't prove it. Then the overconfident colonel gave me the opportunity for you to give yourself up."

"What if he wasn't involved, Director?" Conners interjects, concerned it may have all fallen by the wayside, and Soames would have retaliated at the money not being deposited."

"I never doubted it, Colonel. There was something in the way Soames protested his dislike of the admiral. You see, through this shit, there has been one constant. The Brits have backed the Brits." He looks at Ashley, but the non-plussed sergeant doesn't respond. "I knew if I dealt him the cards, he would play his own without checking them over. I knew if he was involved, he would transfer the money without taking a serious look at my e-mail and for him to do, he would have to know the number."

"You can't prove any of this," Lawrence defends. "It's an attempt to put your failure to capture Colonel Soames onto me."

Davison presses the intercom on his desk. "Come in," he said, and the door opened for two mean-looking operators to enter but remain in the doorway. "Place Admiral Lawrence under arrest and take him to the secure holding location."

Conscious of who they had been ordered to take into custody, the British operators hesitate.

"This is hogwash!" Lawrence shouts. "I'll have your balls for this, Davison."

"Do we have a problem, gentlemen?" Davison snarls for the operators to come to attention. "The admiral is under arrest, and as your director, you have been ordered to carry out my command."

The operators remain hesitant, and Ashley draws his Walther in a show of threatening intent.

"You'd better do what he says, lads, or you'll have me to deal with," Ashley snarls and without delay, the operators escort Lawrence out as he pleads his innocence.

"This shit will never work if you Brits keep second-guessing my orders!" Davison snarls as he turns to Ashley. "Isn't that right, Sergeant?"

"We Brits have the same problem with you clicky Yanks," Ashley said, and Davison nodded his appreciation of his backing as he exited.

***

Handcuffed, isolated and embarrassed by his rapid demise from power, Lawrence sits in front of a table within the secure holding area as an uneasy operator stands guard.

The door opens, and Davison enters and nods for the operator to exit as he rounds on Lawrence to tower above. "How are you keeping?" he enquires, only to receive a look of contempt. "I hope you're being well treated?"

"When the PM finds out about this, you'll be deported back to the colonies where all you fucking Yanks belong."

Davison laughs at his Imperialistic references. "That's not the words expected from a deputy director of an Anglo-American anti-terrorism task force. Surely you should be more diplomatic than that?"

"Hogwash!" Lawrence shouts impotently.

"If we go, that will greatly save the American taxpayer."

"You can shove your arrogant blood money up your fat American arse!" Lawrence shouts in frustration, showing Davison he is ready to be interrogated after hours of sitting in the claustrophobic room to contemplate his actions.

"But I believe your Prime Minister values his friendship with the President more than yours."

"When he has been informed of what you have done, you'll be

deported with the shit you are trying to pull jammed up your arse."

"I feel sorry for a man who believes he has friends when he doesn't," Davison adds with a wide grin. "Well, let's get back to the business at hand. I have questions for you."

"Good luck with getting any answers from me."

Davison takes a handful of bullets out of his pocket and throws them on the table with a clatter as he pulls over a chair to sit in front of Lawrence. "I can't blame you for not wanting to speak to me, but I'm afraid for you; you ain't got a choice." He draws a Smith and Wesson 36 revolver to Lawrence's panic.

"How did you get that in here?"

"If you don't tell me what I want to know, you're not getting out of here in the best of order."

Lawrence laughs unperturbed as his eyes fix on the bullets. "Idle threats don't scare me, so why don't you take them somewhere else and piss off."

"There's no idleness about this."

"I know my rights," Lawrence interrupts, but his naivety makes Davison laugh.

"Nobody knows you are here. Your office thinks you're on your way to Geneva to recover the fifteen million Pounds from the bank."

"My office knows I had no plans to visit Geneva."

"Not until my office informed them, that is. Oh, and by the way, more bad news. I'm afraid your plane is about to blow up over the North Sea with you on board," Davison said, looking at his watch. "You have about thirty minutes before I make that call, but I could defer it if you tell me where Soames is?"

"What makes you think I would know where he is?"

Davison points the revolver into Lawrence's face. "Because I know you do."

Unimpressed by the threat, Lawrence speaks with disrespect in his tone. "So, you're going to shoot me? We've all done the training, and being the person you are, interviewing a man of my standing is never a good idea."

"The person I am? I don't get you," Davison said, and Lawrence shouted.

"A fucking pussy!"

"You think I'm a pussy?" Davison adds humoured. "And a fucking one at that." He animatedly loads the Smith and Wesson, pulls the hammer back, and shoots Lawrence in the thigh to vault him out of his chair and onto the floor in agony.

Lawrence touches his blood covered leg. "You bastard!" he shouts, but his discomfort makes Davison laugh more.

"That's just a graze. The next one's going in your kneecap and won't be as nice."

"You're fucking mad!" Lawrence screams as tears roll down his cheeks.

"Keep that thought. You know I've dealt with treacherous bastards throughout my intelligence career and was tied by some rule or another, but now I'm in command; I can do what the fuck I want," Davison said, and Lawrence saw the madness in his eyes as confirmation, he means business. "There's nobody to condemn me or my actions, but let's get back to why you are in this room. Don't get me mixed up with the mild-mannered diplomatic ass you've been playing since this shit was set up. This is the real me, and I won't hesitate to kill you if you don't tell me what I want to know." He looks at his watch. "You don't have the time to piss about, so the next shot's coming fast." He taps Lawrence on the knee with the revolver. "I may even let you choose which one. The problem is that you will walk with a limp after you have given me the information."

"You're a fucking animal!" Lawrence screams, and Davison laughs with eerie hilarity.

"Keep that in mind as if you don't give me the information required, the next shot after that means you will spend the rest of your life in a wheelchair. Then I have numerous more places I can hit until I take the end of your dick off."

Shaking at the thought, Lawrence speaks in terror. "I get the fucking picture!"

"So which knee do you want to lose first," Davison adds as he glances at his watch. "The clock's ticking before your plane goes down."

"You mean this?"

"I'm trained in the art of torture, and this day, my weapon of choice is this revolver. My favourite gun is John Browning's 1911 Colt automatic but I've always loved the revolver, and the Smith and Wesson 36 is a great gun," Davison said calmly. "As you can see, I have plenty of bullets, and my knowledge of anatomy gives me plenty of targets to hit depending on how quickly you bleed out, that is."

Keeping his hand over his blood-covered thigh as he worries for his life, Lawrence shuffles into the corner and leans awkwardly against the wall. "I don't believe you will go through with it," he adds with misplaced bravado.

"You came to this shit from the Navy, right?"

"You know I commanded a destroyer."

"So, this underhand shit is new to you?" Davison said as he paced. "You see, I've been a sneaky bastard for," He pauses. "Oh, well over forty years. Probably since birth," he adds with a laugh.

Lawrence is confident he won't go through with his threat. "Then you'd better get on with it because I am telling you fuck all!" he shouts in anger, and Davison shoots him in the right knee, making him grimace in horrified pain as his body is vaulted across the floor into the opposite corner where he hunches into a tight ball sobbing in pain.

"You had the choice, but you left it to me," Davison explains as he points the revolver at the admiral's left knee and Lawrence's terrified glance shifts between his bleeding leg and his tormentor as tears well in his broken, bloodshot eyes. "Don't go to sleep, or you will wake without a dick," he adds, amused. "You do remember the initial question?"

Lawrence's stare fixes on his bleeding knee. "Soames, Colonel Milton Soames," he mumbles as the pain takes over his sensibilities.

"The choice is a wheelchair or tell me where he is."

Lawrence choked, unable to catch his breath as his treason became a reality. "What will happen to me?"

"If I were you, I'd worry about the next few minutes."

Dazed and failing, Lawrence sits against the wall, desperate to faint.

"I need that answer before you pass out."

There's a knock on the door, and Conners enters in mortified shock. "What's going on, Director?" she questions, but Davison is annoyed by the interruption and shouts, stopping her in the doorway.

"I need that fucking answer, and I need it now!"

"The South of France. Monte Carlo. The Hotel Metropole, room one, three, two," Lawrence explains, then takes a deep, exasperated breath. "He's waiting for me there." Feeling desperately sorry for himself, he rips a hole in his jacket and pulls out a piece of paper to hand to Davison. "I was to meet him on Thursday night," he adds as he catches his breath. "This had better help my plea."

Davison looks at the blood-covered paper. "What's this?"

"The passcode for the account where the money ended up."

Davison laughs. "That's not required. We have it already."

"What? How come?" Lawrence shouts shocked.

"You didn't think I was going to sign over fifteen million Pounds to a terrorist, did you? We also confiscated the funds already in your account. I believe that was just shy of five million Pounds."

"You can't do that," Lawrence pleads. "Not all was ill-gotten."

"There goes that ill-gotten again. Surely all money gained illegally is ill-gotten?"

"It wasn't all from illegal activity," Lawrence explains.

"You, of all people, shouldn't be surprised at what governments can do these days," Davison said as he turned calmy to Conners. "What can I do for you, Colonel?"

"It can wait, Director," Conners said, impressed by Davison's guile in getting the knowledge required from the British intelligence chief, who should be tougher.

"You said some of the money in the account wasn't from illegal activity," Davison adds sarcastically. "Can you tell me how much that was, and I'll have it sent to your checking account?" He laughs, but Lawrence doesn't see the funny side. "You've got four days to pull yourself around before you meet him."

Feeling solemnly sorry for himself, Lawrence looks at his bleeding knee. "I don't think I'm going anywhere."

Davison beckons for Conners to cover her ears then pulls back the revolver's hammer and fires at the wall for a large bang and splattering of red to cover it.

"What the fuck!" Conners shouts with the noise still penetrating.

"It's just a powerful blood-coloured paintball," Davison laughed as he took out his earplugs. "Well, there's more to them than that, but they are fucking effective." He looks at Lawrence's traumatised face. "Fucking hurt, don't they? Designed to give you the feeling of being shot without the internal damage. Just a lot of pain and bruising."

Aware he'd been duped, Lawrence rubbed his aching leg awkwardly and grinned, relieved he won't spend the rest of his life in a wheelchair.

"You bastard! What makes you think I'm going to help you now?

"That's up to you," Davison said calmly. "You hold your future in your own hands. The hole I can throw you in has many levels. Some you don't want to end up in. Makes Guantanamo Bay look like a Disney hotel."

"And if I help you?"

"Let's see what happens on Thursday," Davison said, but Lawrence didn't see any hope in his words. "Look I'd better go. I have an urgent phone call to make," he feigns as he exits, leaving Conners staring at Lawrence in amusement.

***

CHAPTER 28

***

The Hotel Metropole in Monte Carlo is only for the elite of society as they are the only ones who can afford its comfort and luxury. Still pained, Lawrence limps through the lobby, looking coyly for the man he knows will be watching his entrance. He gets to the lift, rises one floor to alight, and moves along the corridor to room one three two, whose door lies ajar and enters its emptiness.

As if a father and daughter were on a family holiday, Davison enters the lobby with Conners, and he stops to look around as she carries on toward the lift and moves to the bar to smile at the bartender. "I'll take a Jack Daniels, please."

The bartender sets about pouring the drink. "Ice sir?"

"No, thanks," Davison answers as Soames sits beside him, and he turns to look.

"I'll take one of those," Soames said with the broadest of smiles.

"Hello again, Director," he adds sarcastically.

"If it isn't my second favourite bad guy," Davison said making Soames laugh.

"Surely you mean number one?"

Davison remains straight-faced and emotionless. "That distinction goes to your cohort Lawrence."

"Really," Soames said, shocked. "I take it you have the pussy under your control?" he adds, and considering Davison knows he would already have witnessed what was going on, he doesn't reply. "I told Shirlow not to bring him in, but it seems they were old buddies and went to the same school or some shit like that."

"So, he goes that far back?"

Soames grins. "I take it you've emptied the account?"

"All twenty million."

The sound of his disappearing retirement grinds into Soames' soul but he doesn't show the distress caused.

"You'll be surprised what countries or banks will do not to be associated with terrorists."

"Terrorists?" Soames said, shocked at being called such. "What I did was for the."

"Good of the union," Davison interrupts with a giggle. "Maybe someday you can explain that one to me."

The bartender places two glasses of Jack Daniels on the counter, and

Soames takes a drink, but Davison pushes his aside.

"What's wrong with your Jack, Director?"

"Nothing. I'm just particular about who I drink with."

"But we shared one on your jet."

"Ulterior motives," Davison explains with the most crook of smiles, which Soames understands.

"Of course. The sleight of hand I shamefully missed for the second time. The data discs being the first."

Davison glances at his adversary with the understanding that even though he's a fugitive, he will still have contacts within the intelligence community. "No doubt there are many of you still active?"

Soames laughs, with no intention of answering what at some point may be part of his cover story, then empties his glass with a gasp. "As you can see, I don't care who I drink with as I would always be drinking alone if I thought like you. I take it my being here is pointless?"

"Not really," Davison said confidently. "You need to be here for me to capture you."

Soames laughs self-importantly. "Good one." He draws his Sig Sauer to prod into Davison's side. "Why don't we see how your favourite bad guy is getting on." He stands and lifts Davison's Jack Daniels to down in one. "Now pay the man."

Davison smiles at the bartender and pulls out some notes to place on the counter, and Soames shouts for him to keep the change, and the bartender nods his appreciation as he moves off.

"Very generous of you," Davison gripes.

"Well, as you have all my money, I thought you could at least pay for the round."

"But you still have the spoils from the Morrison robbery," Davison adds to Soames' mischievous delight. "Estimated at three point two five million Dollars. Undoubtably a little less as you'll have to fence some of the more obscure items."

"Enough to keep me going until I get back on my feet."

"That's good to hear," Davison said. "And you didn't share it as we found the bodies of Klaus Holzmann and Claude Daniau under the jetty of the villa you rented in Bermuda with a single bullet in each of their foreheads." He moves toward the lift, followed by Soames, who keeps the area under surveillance. "You seem worried?" he adds with glee. "Nervousness getting the better of you?"

"I've been in these spots before, and a little apprehension never hurt anyone."

"Then you should be nervous."

"Hardly," Soames said confidently. "The colonel is with the traitor, and James Ashley is." He looks around. "I haven't seen him, so I assume another bar must be nearby."

"But you're in his sights."

Soames looks directly into Davison's eyes and then laughs. "You took my advice and sacked the arse. Can't blame you for that."

As the lift door opens, they step inside, and a man attempts to follow, but Soames pushes him harshly back.

"Sorry, sir, but I have business with my friend here. Get the next one."

The Frenchman uses profanities which neither Davison nor Soames understand, as the door closes and the lift sets off.

"What now?" Davison mutters, and Soames relieves the American of his Browning to place in his waistband.

"Very nostalgic, Director, but I thought it spoilt the line of your suit?"

"It was my father's and has great sentimental value, so treat it well."

"I will see you get it back," Soames adds genuinely, but Davison believes it will be the last time he sees it.

***

Conners draws her Colt Mustang as she moves hesitantly toward room 132.

Having expected her arrival, Lawrence calls out. "Come in, Colonel. I'm afraid our bird has flown."

She enters to find him sitting on a chair facing her. "What's going on?"

"How would I know that? I'm just the stooge in Davison's game."

"You've got that right!" Davison calls out as he enters. "But you'll find it isn't a game." He stands aside to reveal Soames, unnerving Lawrence. "Not a very good one anyway," Soames adds as he points his Sig Sauer at Conners, but she has no intention of relinquishing her Colt. "Drop your gun, Colonel." He turns the Sig Sauer into Davison's neck as she looks at the director for instructions, and he nods his approval, and she throws the Colt onto the settee.

Believing Soames was there to rescue him, Lawrence grimaces, relieved. "Thank God, Colonel," he said, but his optimism was short-lived as Soames laughed.

"You've got it wrong, Admiral. I'm not here to save you."

"But we," Lawrence starts standing, and Soames shoots him in the forehead, shocking Davison and Conners with the unwarranted shift into violence as the admiral slumps back into the chair.

"What was that all about?" Davison questions, but Soames laughs off the attention. "There was no need to kill him."

Soames speaks with calm. "You don't think so? He was a snide, and that's a shite in my world."

"He didn't have much choice," Davison explains.

"A good operative would rather die than turn on his friends?"

"All evidence to the contrary," Davison said, and Soames looked at him bemused.

"All your cartel has done is turn on each other."

Soames understood and nodded his agreement. "Well, you don't want to leave un-familiars behind to testify against you to save themselves?"

"Don't give him another reason," Conners said, but the threat didn't faze Davison.

"What are your intentions?" Davison presses. "Are you going to kill us all?"

"Well, I know I ain't going to get my money, even if I ransom you," Soames said calmly. "So, I think I had better go. I know you'll keep coming for me, but that adds to the fun."

"We will catch you," Conners said, determined, as Soames confidently backed to the door.

"But not today," Soames said, exiting into the corridor, and closed the door, then putting a bullet into the electronic locking mechanism and jamming it. He turns to move off but is stopped by Ashley standing ten feet off with his Walther pointing directly at him. "Sergeant James Ashley. I thought you'd been sacked."

"Colonel Mile End Soames," Ashley said with menace as he moved closer. "Now you remember me?"

Annoyed by the reference to the nickname he hates, Soames grins but doesn't rise to the intended slur, "How could I ever forget you? Now you have me at a disadvantage." He looks at his Sig Sauer hanging harmlessly by his side. "What can I do for you?"

Conners and Davison shoulder smash the door, but it won't give way, which unnerves Soames at the thought that he will soon be outnumbered.

"Give yourself up."

"I've come a long way just to roll over without a fight," Soames said, then added with intent to upset. "Now piss off before I put a bullet in your head, arse wipe."

"You'll have to do it fast," Ashley said as an adjacent door opened, and a woman stepped out and he called for her to get back, but seeing the possibility of escape, Soames grabbed her by the neck and forced her into Ashley, knocking him off balance and allowing him to enter her room. Unceremoniously, Ashley pushes the woman aside and onto the floor as two shots ring out, followed by breaking glass, and Soames crashes through the window and falls the single story to the ground below to land in a crumpled heap injuring himself.

Soames limps off a short distance, then instinctively turns to put two bullets through the broken window above, and Ashley enters the room as they make contact with the ceiling to stop him dead. Ashley moves tentatively to look out to see Soames limping off as fast as he can when Conners breaks the door to room 132 down, and she and Davison exit into the corridor, looking up and down but their attention is taken by the woman on the floor, and Ashley standing motionless at the broken window.

"Where is he?" Davison shouts, and Ashley turns to see him.

"He jumped."

"Then fucking follow him!" Davison commands angered that hadn't already been carried out.

Having an injured leg that doesn't do what he wants, Ashley sighs heavily as his solemn glance shifts between Conners, Davison and the outside, and he holsters his Walther and jumps out of the window to land on the pavement and commando roll onto his feet awkwardly then move off a few paces to recompose himself as he draws his gun. Conners lands next to him, and Commando rolls to her feet with her Colt drawn and ready for action.

"Did you see which way he went?" she questions as he rubs his aching leg.

"Yeah? That's exactly what I was doing on the way down."

"I wonder about you, Jimmy."

He smiles pointing. "He went that way."

"Split up!" she shouts as she runs off, leaving him to limp in the opposite direction as he takes out his pain medication and swallows two with a mouthful of whisky.

***

Soames holsters his Sig Sauer to conceal his threat to polite society. Conscious he is injured, he rounds a corner into an alley and keeps his rear under surveillance as he limps. Feeling the strain and pain, he stops and sits on the parapet to look over the sheer drop into the choppy Mediterranean Sea below. He sees Ashley nearing offensively with his pointed Walther and sighs, rubbing his aching leg. "Wait until you've had it for years," Ashley said with knowledge.

"How often do I need to tell you to piss off?" Soames shouts.

"I wish I could, but I have to go around killing shitbags like you."

Soames laughs. "You couldn't kill yourself." He reaches inside his jacket.

"Don't try your luck, Mile End."

"Shut the fuck up with this mile-end shit, arse wipe. I outrank you and always have."

Ashley laughs after getting a rise out of the man he has never got along with. "You did until you betrayed your country. Now you'll be remembered as a traitor."

"A traitor my arse."

"That's right. I forgot you're saving the union," Ashley said as Soames stared his discomfort. "Not that it's worth saving."

"Exactly, arse wipe. So how did you get into this shit?" Soames questions calmly. "You were burnt out in the SAS." He laughs. "I heard you bottled a mission and fucked it up, and that's why you ended up at a desk in MI5 and why Shirlow picked you to investigate the arms deal with the Irish."

Conners steps from the side with her Colt offensive, and Soames turns, amused to see her.

"Not the other fucking idiot set up to fail."

"You're wrong," Conners defends. "I was brought in because of my efficiency as the director knew Shirlow had picked Jimmy in the belief he would fail."

"Even the Yanks think you're an arse," Soames adds, but Ashley is unperturbed by the opinion he holds in himself.

"I can live with that."

"But you don't have to, Jimmy. You showed them they had you wrong," Conners explains, but Ashley still doesn't understand.

"He's a fucking idiot! I should have put you both down when you turned up at the barn in Northern Ireland."

"You were there?" Conners said to Soames' gloating.

"I was!" Soames shouts as he draws Davison's Browning, but Ashley puts two bullets into his chest, and he falls over the parapet into the crashing waves below.

Ashley and Conners move to the parapet and look over the significant drop toward the water without intending to follow.

"Can you see anything," she questions, to his amusement.

"Not with these eyes," he answered. "There's too much surf for me to pick anything out." Sober to his ability, he adds. "He had me well tagged."

"You knew Shirlow picked you because he thought you were a soft touch, but you proved them all wrong."

"Did I?" Ashley mumbled solemnly.

Davison walks up from behind, making the sound of a bugle playing the cavalry charge.

"Once again, Custer's too late," Ashley moaned, but Conners loved the humour.

"I don't need to be the cavalry when I have capable operators working for me," Davison said as he looked around. "Did he drop my Browning?"

"No, sir," Conners explains, aware of the director's mental attachment to the gun. "He went over with it in his hand."

Davison looks annoyed, but there is a bigger picture at stake.

"Jimmy's on a downer, Director. Feeling sorry for himself again." Ashley looks at Conners and grins awkwardly.

"What's new? Come on; I need a drink," Davison said, expecting Ashley to be enthused by the thought.

"What about Soames?" Conners questioned, and Davison had another look over the parapet but couldn't make anything out.

"Leave the piece of shit for the French to mop up when he comes ashore."

Davison adds as he walks off, followed by Conners, but Ashley remains still as he looks at his Walther in shame before throwing it over the parapet into the sea and walking off in the opposite direction. Conners notices his actions and calls out, but he carries on, and she moves to follow, but Davison prevents her.

"He'll come around when he's ready, Colonel," Davison adds solemnly. "Come on let's go. We have a lot of work ahead if we are going to clean house."

"Looking forward to the challenge, Director," Conners muttered, unable to take her eyes off Ashley until he rounded the corner and disappeared.

***

CHAPTER 29

***

Reading from a file of ongoing operations being carried out worldwide by the Anglo-American Anti-Terrorist Intelligence Unit, Davison, sits in the rear of his agency Suburban as it travels through the streets of London en route to his official UK residence.

"Twenty minutes until we arrive, Director," Bruce said, but Davison wasn't hurrying to get home.

They move through the busy streets, congested with cars parked along either side, but Davison pays the outside world no attention when an almighty explosion catapults the SUV into the air and then onto its side to slide along the tarmac and smash into several stationary cars before coming to a halt. Luckily for the occupants, the SUV had been strengthened in case of an attempt on the director's life, but the interior is in chaos as the driver groans in severe pain.

Davison comes around, and even though he's in pain, he unclips his seat belt to drop with a crash, then produces his phone but struggles to see the screen through his blood-covered eyes. "Siri, call Watkins," he said, and the phone rings until Watkins answered. "The threat's real," he said as blood trickled down his face, and he wiped it away. "Track my car. I've been hit, and Bruce sounds in a bad way." Sirens can be heard nearing as people on the street attempt unsuccessfully to open the doors to get them out. "The emergency services are on their way, but send our people to protect the scene," he adds, then drops the phone as he falls unconscious.

***

Every day she's at home, Conners runs along the streets of her nation's capital to keep fit as she listens to classical music on her headphones, but this day, things seem different, which unnerves her. She stops to check her pulse and catch her breath as she runs on the spot so as not to lose momentum and uses the time to help ease the suspicions of her surroundings in the belief that she is under surveillance. Having taken in the scene and seeing no threat, she runs off at speed, but after a short distance, using every trick in the intelligence book of how to witness being followed, she edges up to her front door and stops as she glances into her living room window to see if its reflection shows her anyone behind. She takes her headphones off and stretches to cool down, but all she can see is a delivery van and a man moving toward the front door of her neighbour's house, which doesn't concern her. She enters her well-presented house into the hallway to take her trainers off and discard them into the corner, then moves along surreptitiously glancing out of the hallway window as she enters her living room and calls for Echo to play music, she has no taste for, and Ozzy Osbourne screams out the 1970 classic Paranoid as her eyes shift between the windows in sight to see if anything is moving outside. She moves upstairs, undressing in an over-the-top display of flamboyant sexuality, until she reaches the landing window to glance out before entering her bedroom and moving into the en suite to turn the shower on.

The delivery van pulls up outside, and a man gets out carrying a parcel and makes his way up the path to the front door. He looks at the parcel as if checking the address, then reaches to find the door surprisingly open and steps inside. He closes the door cautiously, then draws a Smith and Wesson Magnum revolver as he discards the box to the floor as the shower upstairs catches his attention over the loud music, and he moves stealthily up, looking lecherously at the clothes strewn all over. Stopping on the landing, he moves into the bedroom and then bursts into the en suite to fire several rounds through the steamed-up shower but on hearing the bullets hitting the tiles behind, he knows his target isn't there and turns just in time to see Conners dressed in a black training suit, as two bullets smash into his chest, and he slumps to the floor no longer a threat. Unsure how many assassins there are, she can see the name of the delivery company printed on the dead man's chest and moves to the window to see a van below with the same markings. She moves to the top of the stairs and then down as she searches for any threat to find none. Having found the house empty, she moves to a window to see a man sitting in the driver's seat of the delivery van, but as she exits onto the path, it accelerates off at speed, leaving her annoyed at not being able to gain the intelligence as to why she had been targeted.

***

Showing his money troubles since leaving the agency, Ashley's flat is small and dingy due to his uncaring of the creature comforts of life. Having qualified for the role of a driver on the Tyne and Wear light rail Metro system that services Newcastle upon Tyne and the surrounding areas, he exits his bedroom in his uniform and moves to his sideboard to lift a bottle of the cheapest blended whisky and takes the lid off to fill his hip flask and take a gulping mouthful, along with his pain medication before pausing in melancholy. He looks at the company logo on his jumper with the realisation he needs to keep his job and the company's policy on alcohol and drug abuse and places the bottle down as he moves to put the kettle on and set himself up a mug of strong coffee.

***

Driving his beaten-up Ford Focus, Ashley parks at South Gosforth Metro station and looks solemnly out of the window as several drivers pass but pay him no attention. Dreading every day, never mind those he has to work, he doesn't miss the life he had left behind and alights into the headquarters building with little haste and moves into the staff canteen where numerous staff from different parts of the company sit around paying each other little attention which he ignores as he makes his way to the vending machine to get himself a cup of the cheapest most tasteless subsidised coffee before taking a seat. He looks at the time to realise, he is late and leaving his coffee untouched, he moves to a monitor to check where his train is and seeing it nearing, he picks up his bag and exits through the throng of passengers waiting for the next Metro on Platform 2 that will take them the long way around toward Newcastle city centre via the coast. He positions himself at the leading end as the Metro car drives up and stops for the driver to alight, who, on seeing his replacement is Ashley, moves off without a word passing between them. The ex-soldier gets into the cab, carries out his pre-departure drills, closes the doors and moves off at a meandering speed. Bored with his long shift at the helm of the antiquated train, he drives along, passing many stations, until a loud bang gives him a start, and he looks to see a large crack in the ballistic glass that is designed to protect a driver from anything thrown at the train head-on. He pulls into Howdon station and opens the doors to allow passengers to get on and off, but his eyes remain fixed on the damage to his windscreen. Needing to look closer, he alights the cab to stare at the damage, then gets back in, closes the door, and lifts the radio mike. "Control, this is the driver of one zero five stopped at Howdon," he said and the radio crackled, but he received no reply and had to repeat his words until a response came back in an uninterested tone.

"Come in one zero-five."

"Reporting a smashed driver's windscreen received between Percy Main and Howdon," Ashley explains to hear the largest sigh coming from control as if he was making up a fault to get off the system.

"Can you carry on?"

Ashley's glance shifts from the damaged window to the driver's mirror, situated on the platform, to see if there is any threat. "That's a negative control. The glass has been smashed and looks like it could come through any time."

"I see," the controller said, unnerved. "Drop your passengers off and bring her home," he adds, and Ashley repeats the message, then switches the radio off and turns the internal intercom on.

"Metro apologises, but this train has developed technical problems and has been withdrawn from service," he said, aware of the upset his scripted announcement would cause. "Could all passengers please alight and wait for the train behind." He puts the intercom down and looks at the driver's mirror to see the disgruntled passengers alighting. Aware he has to check the train for stragglers and left luggage, he alights onto the platform to be confronted by the discontented members of the public, who have to put up with a great deal from the local service, then gets onto the rear carriage to do his checks. He can see a man sitting at the far end of the train and approaches him.

"Excuse me," he said in the politest of terms, but he ignored him until he increased his tone enough for the well-dressed man to turn.

"Apologies, but I must ask you to leave the train as this one's going out of service."

The man smiles and then speaks in French that Ashley doesn't understand, apart from the odd word, and he grins his discomfort as he explains in the most basic of school French their predicament, and the Frenchman's eyes shift to the passengers staring their interest and smiles his awkwardness then nods and alights.

Ashley makes his way through the train and into the driver's cab to close the doors and lock. Being in front of a road crossing with the lights flashing for some time, he blows the whistle and moves slowly forward as he looks at the cars waiting impatiently and sees the Frenchman get into an Audi Q7, which catches his attention as to why he had been on the train if he had a lift in such comfort. Still, he carries on paying the unusual observation no more interest. He drives into the Gosforth depot to pull up alongside a technician awaiting his arrival. He switches the engine off, then takes a sly mouthful of whisky from his hip flask before getting out onto the gangway as the technician looks at the damage.

"What the fuck!" the technician grumbles. "That must have been some rock."

"I didn't see it hit; I just heard it."

Having spent numerous years in the REME as a territorial soldier, the technician closely examines the damage. "If I didn't know any better, I would say that was a bullet strike," he said, and Ashley laughed awkwardly. "Who would want to shoot you?"

Ashley's face turns serious. "They're all in Metro HQ."

The technician looks at Ashley in bewilderment of his educated concerns. "We need to get the law involved."

"It wasn't a bullet, for Christ's sake," Ashley explains, playing down the incident. "I saw the little shit throw the stone."

"Thank god for that," the technician said, relieved, having forgotten Ashley's initial words. "I've seen the damage bullets do, and having served in Iraq and Afghanistan, I've seen it a lot," he adds with pride in serving his country.

"I'm lucky as I've never been to war," Ashley said, feigning solemness and grinning discomfited as he walked off.

***

Heavily monitored, Davison lies in his hospital bed at St Bartholomew's Hospital, in London, as Watkins sits on an armchair to his side without a word passing between them. An armed SCO19 police officer opens the door and looks in, followed by a concerned-looking Conners but Davison ignores this and gets straight to business. "Watkins informed me of what happened, Colonel."

"DC Metro believe I thwarted a robbery," Conners explains, but Davison isn't convinced.

"And you don't believe that?"

"The way he entered, he was there for me."

"And you made it easy for him to find you?" Davison adds with pride.

"I sensed their presence before they made their move."

"Their move?" Davison questions intrigued.

"There was at least two of them," Conners adds. "They followed me on my run, but all I could see was a delivery van with a man delivering parcels."

"But you sussed them out?"

"I wish I had, but I saw nothing until I got home. By the time they had finished, it was meant to look like a robbery gone wrong."

"Who would want you dead?"

"The assassin hasn't been identified, but more importantly, Director, who would want you dead?"

"That list is endless," Davison answered, amused. "But my interest lies with the attempt on you. I know you're important, but to the outside world, you're just a normal member of the public."

Conners sits with the intention of staying, but Davison doesn't want visitors as his silence with Watkins has already proven.

"Your presence isn't required, Colonel," Davison adds, and Conners looks at Watkins and smiles. "I wish he would go, but we have a business to attend to."

"Anything I can help you with, Director?" Conners said, displeased to be left out in the cold, but Davison feigns it is mundane day-to-day business she wouldn't be interested in.

"No. Get yourself away, but now they know who you are. Be on your guard."

Conners moves for the door. "I always am, Director. I will visit you later."

"Tomorrow morning at seven sharp in my office."

"But you're in the hospital," Conners said, shocked. "Receiving treatment for your injuries."

"I don't have time to be injured," Davison said fearlessly. "We don't know if it was an assassination attempt or whether I was just passing an explosion."

"Surely you don't believe that?"

"My liaison at MI5 said that may just be the reason."

"Cars don't just blow up, Director."

Davison smiles with knowing. "Well, as soon as my car arrives, I will be out of here."

"I hope with extra security."

"I don't need any with Watkins at my side," Davison jokes and Watkins looks over, nonplussed.

"As if I have any say in anything he does," he said, and Conners laughed as she exited.

***

Carrying his briefcase, Watkins exits St Bartholomew's and moves along, enjoying the peacefulness of the night. Unknown to him, a scooter drives up slowly with two masked occupants onboard, and the passenger gets off and moves up behind as he turns to see a knife being thrust into his chest, but he pushes his attacker aside with the briefcase and prevents the blade from going in further. Members of the public see what is happening and run over to help and the attacker grabs the briefcase then jumps on the rear of the scooter as it races off with the passer-by's trying to pull them off. In severe pain, Watkins goes onto his knees and takes hold of the knife to pull out and see it hadn't gone in far enough to cause serious damage before collapsing onto the ground bleeding as people attempt to give him first aid.

***

CHAPTER 30

***

Looking dejectedly into nowhere, Davison sits at his office desk when there's a knock on the door, and Conners enters, amazed to see him sitting in complete silence.

"I thought you were joking, Director," she said, but he remained straight-faced. "What's up?"

"Watkins," he answered solemnly, and she looked around in bewilderment at not having seen him. "He was attacked last night," he adds, shocking her. "One of those scooter gangs that carry knives."

"Is he alright?" she adds, concerned, and his face turns into a grin.

"Luckily, his training kicked in, and he turned in time and managed to see them off."

She recomposes herself. "I know these knife gangs are a problem, but this and what else has happened resonates in my mind."

"What are you getting at, Colonel?"

"Someone's gunning for us."

"How could anyone connect any of us?" he said as he sat back, debating her words. "But you have a point. Since the agency was set up, someone has been trying to undermine our good work."

"But who's left that would be against your baby, Director," she said, and he grinned awkwardly.

"Have you heard from Jimmy?" he questions, shocking her.

"Not since he walked away in Monte Carlo."

He looks her over curiously. "Haven't you looked him up?"

"Why would I? I have served with hundreds of people over the years and haven't kept in touch with any of them."

"Then maybe the problem is yours."

She stares, perturbed by the accusation she believes shows her being cold. "He walked away without an explanation and then didn't bother to reply to our correspondence."

"He hasn't responded to anything from the agency, including his severance pay."

"Not my problem, Director," she said, showing she is more perturbed by the Englishman walking out on their short-lived partnership than she is letting on.

"If you knew him better, you would understand why he did what he did," he adds, making her shuffle awkwardly.

"That's not fair, Director," she defended.

"Maybe it's time you looked him up. If we are in danger, he will be too."

"Do you know where he is?" she questions, and not being aware of an answer, he picks up his desk phone. "Put me through to Thames House."

"Do you think that's a call you should make, Director?" she said, and he looked over, concerned.

"Belay that," he says and puts the phone down. "Considering what we discussed, that could have been a self-inflicted wound. Do you know anything about him that wouldn't be in his file?"

"All I know about him for sure is he was born in Newcastle Upon Tyne and loves his soccer team Newcastle United," she said and smiled, remembering his initial tantrum.

"Then we need to find out more."

"How?"

"Are you past being able to do these things?" he said, showing he wasn't in the best of moods, and she exited a little deflated to carry out the task.

***

Ashley limps along the seafront at Whitley Bay, on the Tyne and Wear coastline of North Eastern England, enjoying the early evening sun when a car comes out of nowhere at speed and mounts the pavement in an attempt to run him over. He sees the threat in time and jumps onto a fence as the bumper scrapes along the wall below until it comes to a halt twenty feet off. Believing he was lucky to escape the accident, he jumps from the wall to help the car's occupants when a second car comes out of nowhere and crashes into the rear of the first, shunting it forward before it drives off at increased speed. Bemused about what's happening, he walks to the second car as Conners alights, smiling.

"I told you, you couldn't live without me," she said, and he stared in bewilderment at his ex-colleagues appearance. "I think we should get out of here."

"If you're buying," he said, light-heartedly considering what had just happened. "I could do with a beer."

Conners looks at a crowd of onlookers gathering, most filming on their phones, hoping to sell the action to a national newspaper. "We're being watched and could do without the publicity."

Unperturbed at being the centre of attention, he walks to the people filming, confiscates their phones to their irritation, then throws them over the sea wall to drop the thirty feet into the swirling North Sea below. "Some things aren't meant to be witnessed," he menaced and sensing the threatening tone, nobody argued their side.

"Come on," she insists. "Before others follow in the quest to become internet sensations." She gets into her car, followed by Ashley, who keeps looking back to make sure they aren't being filmed as they drive off.

***

Ashley sits in the Bee Hive public house, Earsdon as Conners buys drinks, then moves over to sit and takes the longest of mouthfuls from his Brown Ale, and then lets out the loudest of sighs, as if it had been an age since his last beer, to her amusement.

"So, Black Widow," he said, making her feel like a female superhero. "Where did you come from?"

"Straight from DC."

"DC. I thought she was a part of the Marvel Universe."

"Washington DC," she said to his mistrust at her lack of humour.

"DC to Whitley Bay? And you landed just in time to save me. Maybe I should have said Wonder Woman."

"You're the wonder to me, Jimmy, but remember what the director said about that?"

"He's not here."

"And I wish I'd thought of that before being the straight man to your rubbish joke. I came from London after seeing the director, not DC."

"Marvellous," he said with a laugh but she remained straight-faced.

"How have you been since you walked out on us?" she said with a hint of bitterness at not knowing the actual reason.

"All the better for it."

She looks at his jacket to see a large Metro logo embroidered on it. "So, who do you work for now or does it stand for M at MI6?"

"It's M for muppet, but as you're concerned, it's nobody now as they are sure to sack me for bringing the company into disrepute."

"That's a big word, but maybe that is for the best."

"Oh yeah, how come?

"Where can I start," she said, sipping her wine but not taking her eyes off her old friend and smiling, pleased to see him looking so well.

"There have been several attempts on the lives of our operators," she said, and he interrupted his concern. "Nobody has died, but that hasn't been for want of the bad guys trying."

"Who?"

"We don't know, but they attempted to blow up the director and sent assassins to kill me in DC."

"You said several but that's two."

"Watkins got stabbed, but the Metropolitan Police believe it was one of those moped gangs in London, so the director has just put it down as such."

"But you don't believe it?"

"Too much coincidence for my liking."

"I agree, but why come for me?" he questions, intrigued.

"That's what we need to find out."

"And for that, who would come for me?" he adds, believing his past doesn't warrant such attention.

"Same answer."

"And how would my enemies know where to come?"

"Easily as it happens. I found you without any help."

"But you're in the intelligence game and can use many agencies."

"I didn't use any, I just typed in Geordie Dick on Google Earth, and it took me straight to you."

"Good one. You seem to be getting better at the sarcasm lark."

"We don't have any friends in your government. We couldn't go to MI5, MI6 or the police," she said to his amazement. "We can't trust anyone because we don't know who wants us dead. We still don't know if MI6 ordered Soames' mission."

"What a fucked-up world, but as for attempts on people's lives, I believe that one was the second," he explains, catching her attention. "A sniper's bullet hit the ballistic glass at the front of my train."

"Well, that makes it imperative we return to London at the earliest."

"I don't get the we," he laughs. "I don't give a flying fuck about what has gone off. If someone comes for me again, I'll be waiting."

She can see he speaks with bravado and cares about what happens to them. "Well, I have got to go, so you have to come with me."

"Oh yeah?"

"Yeah, because next time, there'll be nobody here to save your ass if I go," she said, determined, and he laughed.

"Didn't see you at the first attempt."

"No, but the ballistic glass saved you then."

He shuffled awkwardly as the truth hit home about his vulnerability.

"And you may be able to help us sort this out."

"I'm well out of the game and no use to you."

"You're never out," she explains. "Your reactions to that car bearing down on you shows you haven't lost any of your skills."

He debates her words and what the future holds for him as he sees it as a chance to get away from the mundaneness of driving a train and nods his reluctant agreement.

***

Ashley and Conners sit in Davison's office when the director enters, looking battered and bruised, followed by Watkins, looking equally dishevelled and still in pain.

"Good to see you, James," Davison said as he shook Ashley's hand with genuine friendship.

"We've just been discussing who is trying to kill us, Director," Conners said with humour that Davison appreciated. "Any ideas?"

"How many names did you come up with?" Ashley said as he shook Watkins' hand.

"Who could it be?" Conners adds. "Since you set up the agency, there's been a few contenders."

"And before," Davison adds with a knowing grin.

"Shirlow's dead," Conners carries on. "Soames is dead. Bright, Westwood. Caine."

"Kilbride?" Ashley questions with a need to know about his old colleague.

"Imprisoned in the deepest hole," Davison explains. "There was the IRA connection?"

"Flynn's dead along with his sidekicks Robbie and McInley," Conners adds. "And Stephens, the inside man on Mill Island."

"What about the Wessex's crew?" Ashley questions.

"Cleared by MI5 and reassigned," Davison adds, having already been briefed.

"The Russian connection. Klamenkovich?"

"Found dead by Russian intelligence."

"No doubt two seconds after the bullets made their mark," Ashley said ironically, and Conners made the sign of a throat being cut, but Davison remained quiet.

"If you live by the sword," Conners interjects. "Faisel, err Sokolov of the SVR, dead."

"What about General Reynolds?" Ashley questions and Conners laughs at the humour.

"In the same hole as Kilbride and all his mercenary accomplices are dead."

"Maybe Charlie and Gordon want revenge for the killing of their nephew."

"The surveillance they are under, I can't see it being them. So, what are we missing?"

"Well, if it's not from our time since the AA, whatever shit was set up," Ashley adds, looking at Davison to see if his slur hits home. "Maybe it's from whatever you did prior?"

"Don't leave yourself out," Davison said as he glared at Ashley. "But I believe all the attempts point at the agency as it's only been against those in this room."

"That we are aware of," Ashley adds confidently.

"We need to bring these would-be-assassins out of their holes."

"Why are you looking at me, Director?" Ashley moans. "I'm not a part of this."

"Then maybe you should recall yourself to active duty until we find out who wants us dead."

"And you think I can help?" Ashley adds in disbelief at his own abilities.

"As always, you're the ideal man for the job."

***

Keeping Oxford Street, London, under surveillance, Ashley walks along, feigning shopping, but nothing moves. He stops in a shop doorway to look at his reflection, but nobody pays him attention. "Looks like I'm not a big target for you assassins," he whispers, and Conners' voice comes into his ear bug.

"You're forgetting what happened at Whitley Bay, Jimmy."

"Thanks for reminding me," Ashley said as he moved off, looking at the traffic. "I was trying to erase that from my mind." He stops at another shop window and looks at an elderly lady walking twenty paces off. "I've never seen you looking so good."

"Yeah, well, I thought I would disguise myself as one of your old girlfriends to reassure you," Conners adds to the humour as she steps into view twenty metres behind, and Ashley smiles on seeing her. "Sorry, I mixed you up there, but she could have been your twin sister."

***

Ashley sits in his hotel room in the Tower Hotel, London, paid for by the agency, drinking whisky when there is a knock on the door. He moves to look through the spy hole, then opens it for an armed man dressed like a bellboy, who pushes him aside as he enters. Conners sees the commotion and draws her Colt to be confronted by a gun pointing at her, but Ashley kicks the would-be assassin behind his knees which buckles him. The shot goes past her head into the plasterwork as the killer turns to shoot Ashley but Conners puts a bullet into his back, knocking him against the wall. Still, he turns to shoot her and Ashley jumps in front, and the bullet grazes his shoulder as he flies through the air to land in a crumpled heap, and Conners puts two more shots into the assassin's chest, killing him as he crumples to the floor.

Conners moves to Ashley to find him holding his bleeding shoulder. "Are you alright?" she said, but the ex-soldier played down his injury. "You could get a job with the secret service protecting the President," she adds with a laugh to his disdain.

"Fuck that! I said I would take a bullet for the Queen, but she's the only one."

"All evidence to the contrary, Jimmy. You've just taken one for me." Ashley looks at his blood covered hand. "I fell over trying to get out of the way and got shot by mistake."

"Yeah?" she said with pride in their renewed friendship. "Of course, Jimmy. You are my hero."

"Then you don't have much expectancy from life."

"Just to serve my country," she said to his amusement. "Yet you would take a bullet for your Queen?"

He smiles mischievously. "Not these days. Now I only consider myself."

"Well, thank you for your consideration during your fall," she said with a large smile, but he was desperate to change the subject.

"He must have followed us and waited for a chance to strike," Ashley said, searching the assassin to find no forms of identification on him. "He's a pro. He doesn't even have a phone."

"It will be hidden outside for him to get after killing us."

"That's no good to us; we'll never find it."

"But we've got the confirmation we are on someone's hit list," Conners said, then added on seeing Ashley's discomfort. "Come on; we need to get you to the hospital."

"Fuck that. You'll have to patch me up."

"Do I look like a nurse?"

"Today, you do as we don't want to bring any attention onto us, so if you can put an Elastoplast on my shoulder, it will save us a lot of shit. Anyway, we need to wait to see if anyone else turns up."

"I don't see them being so stupid now they know we are onto them,"

Conners reasons, but having been on several similar OP's, Ashley knows when it comes to acting on intelligence, there isn't a great deal of reasoning considered.

Several hours later, having reported to Davison about the attempt on their lives, they sit relaxing when there's a knock on the door, and he moves cautiously to look through the peephole.

"Don't forget what happened last time, Jimmy," she said as she drew her Colt, and he smiled his understanding as he opened the door to find Watkins outside.

"How are things going?" Watkins knew what had happened, but Conners was more concerned for his well-being.

"Never mind us; how have you been?"

"Not bad considering," Watkins answers unconvincingly as he looks at the dead assassin. "The director wants to see you back at the ranch."

"Why didn't he ring?"

"I don't think he trusts anything or anyone now."

"Can't blame him for that," Conners said, looking at Watkins. "But surely that doesn't include you?"

"No one is excluded," Watkins said with an amused grin, even though being Davison's right-hand man, he's more than trusted as one of the director's oldest and best friends.

Ashley and Conners exit, leaving Watkins alone as he makes his way to the drinks cabinet to pour himself a whisky as he looks at the dead assassin. After several sips, there is a knock on the door, and not being in the best frame of mind, he opens it to find the Frenchman standing in the doorway with his silenced Ruger LC9 outstretched.

"Aren't you going to invite me in?"

Not recognising the armed man, Watkins sees the threat and lifts his hands as he backs inside.

"I take it you are alone?"

Watkins nods, but the Frenchman checks the room as two operatives enter.

"I will leave you to it," the Frenchman said, then nodded and exited, leaving Watkins looking nervously between the two menacing men.

***

CHAPTER 31

***

Davison sits at his desk with two men sitting patiently by his side. Ashley and Conners enter, and the men immediately take Ashley's attention as Conners turns on Davison.

"What's going on, Director?" Conners enquires as the men stand looking threatening.

Ashley remains calm as his eyes shift between all present. "What's with the clowns?" he enquires on recognising the type and Davison grins, amused.

"This is Captain Emerson and Lieutenant Gibbs from MI5, James. They are here for you."

Ashley's curious glance shifts between the MI5 men. "Is that so?" he questioned, aiming his words at Davison.

"They found a Walther P22 at the scene of a murder of an MI5 operative," Davison said flippantly as his attention fixed on Ashley in the expectancy that his mannerisms would give him the answer to a question he knew not to ask.

"And it was traced to me?"

"You've got it in one."

"How convenient," Ashley said, looking at his holstered Walther. "I can't see how it could be traced to me saying it is there."

Davison moves to Ashley with his hand out and his Walther is surrendered to him. "You have a point, James," he said, looking at Emerson. "Out of curiosity. How do you know the gun is James'?"

"Serial number, sir," Emerson answers.

"This is bull shit, Director!" Conners shouts, but Davison calmly lifts his hand to stop her.

"You got that information quick."

"We are the intelligence service of the UK, sir," Emerson explains. "All information is on file."

"Then your information is wrong!" Ashley snarls, but the MI5 men are having none of his attitude as they move forward.

"You have to come with us," Emerson said as Ashley looked at Davison, unsure what to do.

"Go with them, James."

Ashley debates whether to give in or put up a fight which Davison notices.

"James!" Davison shouts. "We will sort it out."

Ashley looks at Conners to see if she is on his side, but her face looks unimpressed by what she is witnessing. Emerson spins Ashley around, places him into handcuffs, and then searches, relieving him of his hip flask, pain medication, and phone to place on Davison's desk.

"I need them," Ashley whinged, and Emerson picked up the pain medication and handed it over. "And the flask," he adds, making Emerson laugh to his irritation, but it remains on the desk.

"Is that necessary?" Conners questioned, unhappy at the treatment of her friend, but the MI5 men ignored her concerns as they escorted him to the door.

"You'd better make it quick, Director, or I will end up in the same hole as Kilbride!" Ashley shouts.

Conners turns on Davison for an explanation, but he stops her speaking as he closes the door and moves back to his desk.

"You were about to say, Colonel?"

"This is bull shit, Director. James hasn't left my side in days."

Davison pauses in thought. "How could they have his gun considering we allocated him with the weapon before you went to Scotland, which was picked up by my operatives from the car you left in Cairnryan."

"And it was on his hip?"

"We can't even be sure that gun has ever been his."

"I'd say it hasn't."

"Maybe you should do something about it," he adds to her bemusement.

"What like?"

"If you need me to explain, you're no good to him," he said as he opened the door. "That will be all, Colonel," he adds as she stares at him, unsure what to do. "Surely I don't need to repeat myself?" He hands her Ashley's Walther, and she grins uneasily, picking up the hip flask and phone and exits.

***

Conners steps out of an exit onto the street, which the agents use to furtively enter and exit further down, but she can't see anything moving. A van pulls over at the main entrance and a side door opens for a well-dressed man to alight as Ashley exits, followed by the two MI5 men. "Hold up there!" Conners shouts as she moves toward them, and Emerson draws his sidearm to point offensively.

"Keep back from the prisoner."

"Prisoner?" Conners said traumatised by the thought. "He's a bloody war hero who served his country with distinction."

"Was! Now he's just a cold-blooded murderer under arrest."

"Don't worry," Conners said with calm. "If he killed anyone, I hope he gets what he deserves and they drop him head first into that deep hole he dreads."

"Cheers for that," Ashley said, demoralised, as he is bundled into the van.

"Where are you taking him?" Conners questioned to be ignored until she impresses Emerson to find out.

"That's none of your fucking business!" Emerson shouts as she moves closer. "Back the fuck off, or I'll have to use ultimate force!" he adds more aggressively.

"I told you!" Ashley shouts. "The same hole as Kilbride!"

Without warning, Conners disarms Emerson and sends him sprawling across the ground, then turns aggressively onto the others who are unperturbed by the threat, and Gibbs goes for his sidearm, but not wanting to take his life, she smashes him in the face with his gun to vault him onto the ground out cold. "Next to try anything won't get off so lightly," she said as she turned offensively between them. "Un-cuff Jimmy!" she said, and Emerson reluctantly carried out her demand.

"Disarm yourselves," she adds, and the third MI5 man looks at Emerson, unsure what to do.

"Do as she says," he said, drawing his Glock to throw aside.

Ashley looks at Conners. "What now?"

Not thinking that far ahead, Conners looks at the van, "Now we take their ride."

"Nice one, but what about them?"

"If we kill them," Conners said unnerving the MI5 men as she disarmed the unconscious man and threw his Glock aside. "We won't be the heroes."

"We can't have that," Ashley said with a laugh.

Conners takes Ashley's hip flask out and hands it over for him to take a swift mouthful of whisky, followed by the broadest smiles of thanks before he takes the phone. "You know the shit in that hip flask is going to kill you one of these days."

"If I live long enough," Ashley replies solemnly as they enter the van and drive off, leaving Emerson and the third MI5 man staring in disappointment at what will happen when their superiors discover their failure.

***

Davison sits at his office desk writing a report when there's a light tap on the door but it takes several seconds until Watkins enters nervously. "What is it?" he said impatiently, and Watkins shuffled awkwardly as the words he desperately needed to say won't come out. "I am rather busy," he adds, wanting to finish his boring report.

"I've been compromised, Director," Watkins said, and Davison giggled at the thought. "They've threatened me."

Davison pushes the report aside as the significance of his colleagues' words hits home.

"I must kill you, or they will hurt my family."

"I see," Davison said calmly. "So, what are your intentions?"

Watkins looks around, demoralised. "I'm informing you of the threat."

"I am pleased you have come to me with this, as we will be able to make it right."

"I can't see how. What about my family?"

"I promise you they'll be alright," Davison reassures as he moves to the window. There's a slight pause as he turns to be confronted by Watkins pointing the Glock 19; he had only just signed out of the armoury. "It's not like you to be armed and threatening someone," he said casually, but his words didn't calm his would-be assassin's demeanour.

"I'm sorry, Director, but I have no choice."

"We always have a choice," Davison explains as Watkins switches the Glock between his sweating hands as he attempts to get the weapon which he is unaccustomed with, comfortable. "Explain what's going on?"

"They have photographs of my boy going to school back in the States, for fucks sake."

"I've told you we will protect them."

"The photographs show they were within reach of him," Watkins panics. "How long will you be able to protect them?"

"As long as it takes," Davison reassures.

"You can't watch them forever."

"We'll only need to do so until we have closed down whatever threatens us."

"And how long will that take?"

"You know I don't have that answer, but we can put your family into protective custody until it's over."

"My wife won't accept that after her life with me."

"Then I will reassure her on your behalf."

"That will only make it worse as she blames you for my failed marriage. I apologise, Director, but I can only see one way out of this," Watkins said, turning the Glock onto his temple. "They want me to kill you, but I believe they will leave my family alone if I die." He looks at his director to see if his eyes give him the answer to his query.

"There's a better way than this," Davison explains, but Watkins can't see it.

"The simplest way to explain is it's either you or me who has to die, and my loyalty won't allow it to be you."

Davison moves forward, but Watkins pulls back the hammer to cock the already-loaded chamber. "This isn't the way it needs to end."

"I'm sorry, Director, but I can't see any other way," Watkins adds, to Davison's distress, as he closes his eyes with the inevitability of death and Ashley smashes through the door, shoulder smashing him sideways as a bullet discharge into the wall, just past the director's face and Conners enters to disarm him.

"Looks like we got back just in time," Ashley said, picking himself off the floor.

Davison looks at his old friend as Conners releases her hold, and he reaches to help him stand.

"I'm desperately sorry, Director," Watkins explains solemnly as Davison grins back unperturbed. "I didn't know what else to do."

"So am I," Davison said, turning to Ashley. "Take him to a holding cell until we have neutralised the threat."

"What about my family?" Watkins pleads as Ashley leads him out.

"They'll be fine!" Davison shouts, but Watkins looks unconvinced.

"What do you intend to do?" Conners questions, and Davison laughs, then turns straight-faced.

"I intend to send my best team to the States to protect his family."

"But we're wanted by British intelligence," Conners said jokingly, but Davison explained, and she realised he meant them all along.

"You'll be safe in the States, Colonel; I guarantee you that."

***

CHAPTER 32

***

Keeping their distance from each other and communicating via ear bugs, Ashley and Conners walk across the car park of Florida Mall in Orlando. Watkins' wife and thirteen-year-old son walk several paces ahead as they venture out for a day of shopping.

After following for a considerable time, Ashley stops as a familiar face appears. "Hold on," he said, seeing Emerson walking a short distance off. "MI5."

Conners' head spins in all directions as she looks for the threat. "How do you know it's MI5?"

Ashley's mind races back to the day of his arrest. "One of the goons that took me from the director's office."

"Which one?"

"The one you put on his arse."

"Emerson. He's followed us here," she said as her mind raced over the MI5 operatives she had encountered that day.

Well aware the man he had identified could just as easily do the same to him, Ashley races forward, keeping the area under surveillance. "Keep with the family, and I will find him." He moves to where he had witnessed the MI5 Man standing, but nothing can be seen. "Why would they risk the vengeance of US intelligence for acting here?"

"Think about it, Jimmy. All the bad guys we've come up against have either been MI5 or MI6."

"Don't forget the SVR," he said.

"And the SAS," she adds, and he mumbled under his breath with the sadness of the betrayal of some of his military colleagues.

Conners follows Wilkins' wife and son into the shopping mall, but the crowds make it hard for her to keep tabs on them alone. "Jimmy, I'm going to have to identify myself."

"Don't do it! We don't know who they are after!" Ashley calls out, stopping shoppers who turn their bewilderment onto him as if he is talking to himself. "If they're here for her, they're probably just tailing her, and if you do anything, they will find out that Watkins hasn't done what was expected, making them viable targets."

Conners moves as close as she dares to Watkins' family but comes almost face to face with Emerson, who instantly recognises her. "I've been compromised, Jimmy!" she shouts as Emerson runs off with her in hot pursuit. "I'm following him towards the blue carpark," she adds, reading a notice directing her, but she frustratingly calls out several more times after hearing no reply.

Emerson exits into the blue car park to get his bearings but sees Ashley nearing with his Walther offensively pointing as the crowd of shoppers part in all directions to get out of the firing line.

"Stand down, Captain; you've been caught."

"Doing what?" Emerson said innocently. "I'm here on my holiday shopping."

"Who for?" Ashley shouts as Emerson looks bemused but doesn't answer. "Disarm yourself, or I'm going to put you down!" he adds, but his words hasten the shoppers to scream in terror as the MI5 man smiles, showing he has no intention of carrying out his command.

Conners exits the mall behind and draws her Colt offensively. "There is no way out!" she shouts, and Emerson turns on her.

"You have no jurisdiction in the United States."

"You'll be surprised what we can do," Conners explains, then adds for the ears of the public brave enough to remain and film the action.

"You are under arrest on the charge of international terrorism!"

Hearing the words international terrorism, the shoppers instantly turn their ire onto the MI5 man.

"Bull-shit!" Emerson calls out confidently when a sniper's bullet hits him in the head, and he crumbles to the ground in a pool of blood. Ashley and Conners take up offensive positions that affords them no cover and would be useless if the sniper has them zeroed in. The shoppers dispersed in all directions, terrified for their lives.

"Get Watkins' family," Ashley shouts. "And take them into protective custody if that shooter has them in sight."

Conners runs in the direction she had last seen them as Ashley looks down on the dead MI5 man, wondering why his life had been taken. He looks around, unaware that the cross hairs of the sniper's rifle are firmly fixed on his forehead as he moves aside.

***

CHAPTER 33

***

Ashley, Conners and Davison sit relaxing in Ashley's new room in the Tower Hotel, London, enjoying a few drinks.

"What happened to Watkins, Director?" Conners questions, but Davison is unsure whether to answer. "I assumed that with him threatening you' he would be under arrest."

"Couldn't be further from the truth," Davison explains calmly. "He had no intention of hurting me. Sadly, he was going to take the heroes way out."

"Suicide isn't the hero's way out, Director."

"The way he was going to do it was most heroic," Ashley adds to Davison's nodding agreement.

"I couldn't see my friend in a cell, so the details of the incident are confidential, and not to leave this inner circle."

Conners needs clarification as to why such a thing happened.

"He's doing something important."

"What's that?" Conners asked, only to receive a mischievous look in reply. "Apologies, Director; I thought I was Jimmy for a second."

"But you asked," Ashley said with a mischievous smile.

"What of his family?"

"Some friends of mine caught up with them later that day, and they are now under my protection."

"And Watkins is aware of that."

"Yes, and after he visits them and all going to plan, he'll be back doing my bidding."

"Hold on, friends?" Ashley said, bemused, and Davison grinned his answer.

"We were stooges to bring out the bad guys again," Conners said, and Davison grinned knowingly. "But this time, we were unaware of it?"

Ashley looks at Conners. "Did you know what was going on?"

"No, and I must say I'm as pissed as you, Jimmy."

"Your acting skills last time weren't up to scratch, so I thought I'd put you in the field without your knowledge of why you were truly there."

"Brilliant to be trusted."

"It had nothing to do with trust. You're more than capable of coping with any eventuality," Davison adds confidently. "So, I didn't see a problem with any of it."

"Knocked down, then picked straight up," Conners said laughing.

"Ever the diplomat, Director."

"Let's get out of here," Davison said. "We have work to do back at the ranch."

They move to exit and open the door as the Frenchman comes from the side with his Ruger pointing offensively.

"Disarm yourselves," he demands and Ashley and Conners draw their guns slowly to throw aside. "Inside."

They back inside as the Frenchman's Ruger follows their every move.

"And you," he demands of Davison, who informs him he is unarmed, but he doesn't believe he is telling the truth and searches him in bewilderment, then Ashley and Conners to see if they have any other weapons on them before removing Ashley's hip flask and opening to take a sniff before smiling and placing it in his pocket to Ashley's disdain.

"We've met," Davison said in recognition to the Frenchman's amusement as he closed the door.

"I'm surprised you remembered, Director."

"I can't seem to recall where," Davison adds, and the Frenchman goes to answer, but the American carries on without taking a breath. "In the foyer of the Hotel Metropole in Monte Carlo."

"You have a good memory."

"Give it time, and anything will come back. You wanted to get on the elevator?"

"He must be one of Soames' goons," Conners interjects to the Frenchman's increasing amusement.

"So, what were you doing there?" Davison questions, but Ashley interrupts.

"I remember your face."

"You kicked me off your smelly tram after a bullet hit your windscreen and put it out of service."

"You tried to kill me?"

"No, but the intention was to get you back in the game."

Ashley's bemused stare shifts around the room. "Why involve me in this shit? I was well out of it."

"Does that include the attempt on my life?" Conners interrupts, and the Frenchman answers without looking at her.

"Your attendance wasn't required, but your life was."

"That's nice to know."

"The Director's bomb was large enough to cause damage but not strong enough to damage an armoured SUV."

"So, I was meant to be here?" Davison said, angered, and the Frenchman nodded. "What about the civilians killed?" he adds, but the Frenchman shrugs his shoulders, uncaring for the innocent.

"This must be a sexist thing where the woman doesn't count toward the story."

"So, where do you fit into all this? Davison questions. "Are you a stooge or a commander?"

"That information is above my pay grade, but my boss will be able to explain," the Frenchman said as he moved to the door and opened it for them to stare in shock at the man believed dead and had fallen into the Mediterranean Sea.

"Am I your favourite bad guy yet, Director?" Soames said as he entered.

"Mile End Soames!" Ashley said with a laugh. "What a lovely sight."

"Watch your mouth, arse wipe. You're not in a position for anyone to appreciate your bile."

"If it helps your vanity, you always were my favourite," Davison said to Soames' amusement.

"Now we know why your body wasn't found," Conners adds.

"My friend here," Soames said, smiling at the Frenchman. "Was waiting for me on a boat just offshore."

"You had it planned?"

"Every eventuality and when I saw you at the bar, I knew I had to go to my escape plan."

"And as he went to get on the elevator, you gave him the signal, and I missed it?" Davison said, annoyed at having been played.

"You could say that," the Frenchman explains. "Two blinks for plan B."

"So, what's this all about then, revenge?"

"You could say that."

"But why did I need to be killed?" Conners interrupts, and Soames looks at her.

"You're not important to this, Colonel, as the others are."

"I'm starting to feel underappreciated."

"Just starting," Ashley jests, then turns instantly serious. "But I don't understand the playing up of my minor role?"

"Just hatred on my part, Jimmy," Soames adds to Ashley's amusement.

"But he said I was needed at the end, but your goons tried to kill me in Whitley Bay."

"My goons, as you put it, were there to get you back in the game.

That's all," Soames said as he turned to Davison. "You cost me a lot of money, Director."

"¬I did," Davison said confidently. "Hopefully, you aren't after me signing you another cheque, as surely you remember it didn't work out too well for you last time."

"I thought I killed you?" Ashley adds with hope, and Soames grins his discomfort as he points at his chest.

"Your bullets hurt, but ballistic armour is excellent these days. You can hardly see it through your clothes."

"But why was ¬I meant to die?" Conners insists on an answer.

"Don't put yourself down, Colonel; your death was important at the time," Soames said as he turned to her. "But seeing you alive isn't upsetting."

"You knew I would put my bullets in your chest?" Ashley said to Soames' nodding amusement.

"I knew you'd double-tap me as your training dictates."

"So predictable," Ashley adds, unperturbed.

"You were led there to back up my escape which my friend here made sure of."

"You're welcome," the Frenchman adds in perfect English.

"And he's not French?" Ashley said with a laugh.

"He certainly fooled me," Conners adds.

"And me, but then I wouldn't know one frog from another," Ashley adds humoured.

"You can't say that these days," the Frenchman grumbles. "It's racist."

"No doubt SAS?" Davison questions showing his deep mistrust of the regiment.

"I wasn't part of those arse holes," the Frenchman argues, insulted. "I was SBS! Special Boat Service. A Marine, not one of those nancy boy soldier types."

"So, you've attempted to kill all of us in this room and have only succeeded in taking the life of Watkins?"

Soames looks at Davison as if disturbed to hear about Watkins' demise.

"It was you who made it personal, Director," he said to Davison's added interest. "After my death, it should have been all over, and I could have disappeared, never to be seen again, but you went after my family, who I might add are all innocent to the life I lead, so I decided to come for you."

"If someone went after your family," Davison explains with calm. "I assure you it wasn't my organisation or me."

"You instigated it, and MI5 carried it out."

"I have no sway over MI5 or MI6, but you forget in your narcissistic world, you betrayed them and your country. You committed the crimes with your treason."

"Crimes? Treason? After all our countries have done in the name of democracy."

"You sound like Shirlow."

"I hope not. He was a snobby bastard, and I was more than pleased when Caine killed him."

"As you didn't come in guns blazing and kill us all, why don't you cut the crap and tell me what you want?" Davison demands.

"Maybe I wanted to tell you why I'm going to kill you all."

Davison stares at Soames with knowing as he grins back. "You needed your stage?"

"I have never wanted you dead," Soames explains. "This has never been personal. I need you to do a little job for me."

"And what would that be?"

"I want you to find General Klamenkovich."

"He's dead," Davison said making Soames laugh.

"Are you telling me you believed what the Russian intelligence service said about his death?"

Davison looks awkward. "I have no reason to disbelieve the intelligence on my desk."

"I take it; it's beginning to dawn on you; you've been sold a pup-."

"Just say he's still alive," Davison said, and Soames interrupted, determined.

"He is. Sokolov told me."

"And you killed him?"

"Before he killed me."

"What makes you think I can help in your hunt for the general?"

"Let's just say professional courtesy," Soames said as he moved to Ashley, but Conners stood between them.

"You could also save your operative's lives."

Davison's eyes shift between Ashley and Conners.

"Don't do it, Director," Conners interrupts. "He's going to kill us anyway."

"You know there are many ways to die, Colonel," Soames explains. "And if my plan hits a roadblock, your deaths won't be by the easiest route."

"If you don't help him, it will just fuck up his plans. Put up those roadblocks, Director."

"What makes you think I can help?" Davison adds ignoring Ashley.

"You know all the right people, so all you have to do is ask them."

"As easy as that?"

"If he's still alive, someone has gone to great lengths to hide him."

"You know these people; all you have to do is ask them, and they will tell you. Call in some markers if need be."

"If he's alive, he'll know we are onto him."

"You've been in the game long enough to know how to track a person without them knowing," Soames praises. "Look, I'll give you one minute to decide." He nods at the Frenchman, who points his Ruger into Conners' temple.

"If you were a gentleman, you'd shoot me first," Ashley said to Soames' amusement.

"But you aren't as important as the colonel now."

"Now I'm important?" Conners interjects to be ignored.

The Frenchman grins at Ashley. "Don't worry, I'm not a gentleman, but I guarantee you you'll die before her body hits the floor."

"I'll help you but must have guarantees on the safety of my people," Davison demands to Soames' increasing amusement.

"If they behave themselves, I will let them go after I've received the intelligence," Soames said as he looked between Ashley and Conners. "Do you understand? I've already proven I have a long reach and could have taken you out anytime."

"They'll behave themselves," Davison reassures.

"I'm not sure about that," Ashley adds, determined to irritate Soames.

"You'll do as ordered, Jimmy!" Davison said, then turned to Soames.

"I will do as you say." He turns to Ashley and Conners. "I would also like to see if the general is alive, so behave yourselves." He turns back to Soames, leaving Ashley in Conners without doubt about what they should do. "So, what now?"

"Now, we will go to your office and get the required information."

"It won't be instant."

"I have plenty of time."

"What about my people?" Davison questions, concerned.

"They can wait here with my friend."

"And you guarantee their safety?" Davison insists resolutely, and Soames turns to the Frenchman with a knowing look.

"Nothing is to happen to them unless they misbehave. I will call when I have what I want," Soames said, leaving the Frenchman in no doubt

about what he wanted him to do. He moves to the door and opens it.
"Shall we go, Director?" he adds, and they exit.
"I'd get comfortable if I were you," the Frenchman grumbles. "This is going to be a long wait."

***

Davison and Soames exit the hotel to find a Range Rover waiting with its engine running, and they get in to drive off.
"You're very thorough," Davison said, impressed to Soames' amusement.
"I've had plenty of time to prepare, so stick to the plan, and it will be over quickly."

***

CHAPTER 34

***

Davison and Soames enter Davison's office, and the director moves to his desk and picks up the phone to dial to Soames' distrust.
"What are you doing?"
"Calling Langley."
"That's not a good idea and not what I want."
"Well, I can hardly go online and Google General Klamenkovich's hideout."
"I suppose not."
"How do you think I will find out if he's still alive?"
"I believe you already know the answer, but I see your point."
"You'll be able to hear everything I say," Davison reasons to Soames' increasing mistrust.
"Any code words, and I will."
"You'll what?" Davison interrupts aggressively. "You'll shoot me? Listen and listen well. If Klamenkovich is alive, I want to know as much as you."
"And why would that be?"
"Confirmation that I have been lied to by people I believed I could trust."
"Carry on with your call," Soames said, drawing his Sig Sauer. "But I will be listening."
"How professional," Davison sneers as he puts the speaker on. "Put me through to Langley!" he shouts, then listens. "Put me through to Delaney in C7!" He waits for an answer. "Director Davison here. Listen, Major, I've been reliably informed that General Klamenkovich is still alive and is in hiding." He looks at Soames. "I need you to find him and report back to me. I'm in my office in London. I'll give you an hour, and if I haven't heard from you in that time, my jet will be heading toward Virginia, where you will have to explain in person," he adds not giving Delaney a chance to speak, then slams the phone down and turns to Soames. "Make yourself comfortable this will take a while. Someone in Langley will know where he is if he's alive."
"As we've renewed our friendship, Director," Soames said, smiling as he reached around his back to produce a Browning 1911 from his belt line, which Davison instantly recognised as his father's. "I'm a man of my word, and I told you I would return it." He ejects the magazine to show it empty of bullets, then cocks it to show nothing in the breech

before handing it over for Davison to gaze at, emotionally moved. Still, he regains his posture not to show the weakness already recognised. "I don't know how to take you."

"I could just as easily kill you. Now drop the relic in your drawer for safe keeping as I would hate to see it used in anger, and keep your hands where I can see them."

Davison moves to his drawer and unlocks it, to Soames' amusement that such a thing would be required in the secure building, then places the gun gently inside before closing it. "Even though I thank you for its return, it doesn't change anything between us."

"I hope not," Soames adds as they both sit and stare their contempt of each other.

***

Ashley and Conners sit on a settee as the Frenchman sits aside, drinking Ashley's whisky from his hip flask with animated delight. "Is that nice?" Ashley snipes with a thirst to partake, which only adds to the Frenchman's amusement.

"It's not bad, but not what I am used to."

"International arms dealing must pay pretty good, Jimmy," Conners snipes, aiming her words at the man holding his gun on her. "You can only afford the blended shit, but he drinks Dalmore like Shirlow."

"Honest money makes it taste better no matter what the cost."

"Bull-shit!" the Frenchman shouts with a laugh.

"Whisky's whisky," Ashley reiterates. "I could do with a drink," he adds, looking at Conners, who is shaking her head at how many times he had said such. "What about you, Colonel?"

"I could do with a dram or two to pass the time."

"Well, you can both fuck off because you ain't getting any."

"Didn't your parents teach you how to share?" Ashley said sarcastically, and Conners added to the humour.

"That's right, Jimmy, I would have been told off for being rude to guests."

Ashley points into his own mouth. "Gobi Desert in there. Come on, just a couple of mouthfuls."

"No way," the Frenchman adds, deadly serious. "You killed some of my friends and deserve to be parched."

"You have friends?" Conners said, and the Frenchman stood aggressively with intent to hurt.

"I love these hard men with guns," Ashley said. "Don't you, Colonel?"

"They are my heroes."

"Mine too," Ashley adds. "So, who did we kill that was so close to you, you are so unsociable you won't share?"

"Reynolds."

"The general?"

"What the fuck are you going on about?"

"The promotion hadn't been made official, Jimmy," Conners jests. "He'd only just told himself and hadn't bought the badges of rank."

"But that's how he became a captain," Conners interrupts.

"I take it there's some sort of an internal joke going on here?" the Frenchman said bemused.

"No joke," Ashley adds. "When I knew him, he was a sergeant, but he'd promoted himself to captain, and we thought he should at least be a general."

"If you remember, you thought commander in chief of the world?" Conners adds to Ashley's nodding amusement.

"Funny, but when Soames gives me the nod, you'll both be dead."

"So, Mile End does want us dead?"

"Mile End?" the Frenchman questions, and Ashley informs him of the slur, but he doesn't see any amusement in it. "I'll wait for the call."

"So, we are pencilled in for death?"

"Just waiting for that call," the Frenchman adds arrogantly.

"And you're going to kill us for no other reason than the words of a madman?"

"Wouldn't be the first time," the Frenchman said with a menacing grin.

"I take it there's nothing in this for us?"

"You've just answered your own question."

Conners grins at Ashley, then launches herself into the Frenchman, and a fight ensues with several shots being fired into the air. Ashley picks up a chair and smashes the Frenchman across the head to knock him to the floor, and Conners scoops up the Ruger to point offensively at the defeated man.

Ashley moves to pick the hip flask off the floor and takes a large mouthful. "Now you get none," he said as he smiled at Conners. "Oh, and by the way, Reynolds is still alive and in a deep shit-filled hole but don't worry; you'll see him soon. Now we need to help the director."

"He doesn't need our help," Conners explains. "Have you ever seen him give in so easily? He's up to something."

"Isn't he always?"

"Tie this bastard up; then we can get on with our jobs."

***

Davison and Soames sit staring at each other with mutual contempt.

"Don't you have a drink in here, Director?" Soames said in the hope of gaining a much needed one.

"Plenty, but the bar is closed," Davison answered, making Soames laugh. "Are you going to tell me where you come into this?" he questions, but Soames ignores him. "I knew about Shirlow, then my people found out about the Dimitri Rossakovich and Kilbride and Caine selling arms to the Irish Republican Army," he adds, and the Englishman shuffles uneasily. "You look annoyed, but at some point, you must have known about the IRA involvement as you used Stephens during the Morrison robbery."

"You're right, Director, used," Soames calmly explains. "I knew about the robbery, and that arse of a Scotsman had been one of Flynn's men at some point. I also knew Grant had sold military intelligence to Klamenkovich because of my connections to the general, who wanted me to check him out. All I had to do was put them together, and I alone would get the data discs the Morrisons kept in their safe for the Russians, and then I would reap the rewards."

"Treason," Davison adds with a broad convincing smile. "After Russia invaded Chechnya, Georgia and Crimea, you were still ready to help them gain military technological advances."

"Say it as you want, but it was purely business. I approached Grant through Klamenkovich then he approached Stephens and Adler separately. Adler believed it was a genuine business opportunity, but after he told Grant the twins wouldn't deal, I had no choice but to send in a team."

"Which my people dispatched with ease," Davison adds with pride. "I had no intelligence that the Morrison's were being guarded so well."

"How did you sell the robbery to hardened mercenaries?"

"Money," Soames answers with the obvious making Davison laugh.

"Money they were never going to collect."

"Obviously. And did they know it was you pulling the strings?"

"Reynolds did. I'd used him numerous times but wanted to remain anonymous to the others this time."

Davison's phone rings and carries on ringing, to Soames' irritation.

"Aren't you going to answer it?"

"That depends," Davison said. "What if it isn't what you want to hear?" he questions, and Soames grins with arrogance. "I take it you won't believe anything until you set your eyes on the general?"

"Would you?"

Davison picks up the phone but doesn't put the speaker on. "Yes?" he shouts, then listens. "What do you have for me?" He looks at Soames. "I see." He takes a pen and paper out to scribble a few lines. "I won't put you in this position again unless you've lied, but then we'll be speaking in person." He puts the phone down and then pushes the paper to Soames to read.

"You're shitting me?"

"Direct from Langley."

"Do you believe it?" Soames questioned, and Davison shook his head in answer as he stood ready to exit. "Where are you going?"

"With you."

"Are you shit," Soames said but Davison wasn't in the mood to be left behind and spoke determinedly.

"I want my eyes on the general as much as you do."

"You get lied to daily, so why would this upset you?"

"That's between the man who told me of his demise and me."

"You've got me interested," Soames adds with an air of mistrust. "I'll let you tag along, but if you step out of line, I will kill you."

"I wouldn't expect nothing else, but like you, I'm not that easy to kill," Davison adds, and Soames grins his intent as they exit.

***

CHAPTER 35

***

     Davison and Soames drive through Hutton Grange and up to the gates of Shirlow's cottage to alight with a mistrust of their surroundings. They walk up to the cottage, and Davison tries the door to find it open, and they enter its desolate shell.

Soames places his hand onto his Sig Sauer as he moves to the window to look out as two cars arrive with Klamenkovich and Rosstof in the first and four SVR agents in the second, and he notices them alight aggressively. "He's here and brought along four bodyguards and his sidekick." He looks at Davison. "Is this a set up?"

"Don't put any of this of me," Davison said as he moved to the window. "You're outnumbered."

"Wouldn't be for the first time, but you've got this wrong. I'm not here to kill the general. We have unfinished business to attend to."

Klamenkovich, Rosstof and two SVR agents enter casually, unaware of whom they will meet.

"Colonel Soames?" Klamenkovich said. "Is it you who has called me here?"

"I asked the director to find you."

Klamenkovich's mistrusting stare shifts between Davison and Soames. "Why would that be?"

"We have unfinished business," Soames explains, and Klamenkovich grins to play down the tenseness of the situation.

"And you thought you'd bring the Central Intelligence Agency along?"

"I'm not with the CIA, General."

"Once CIA, always CIA, no matter what it says on your business card today."

"Leave me out of this," Davison mutters, amused. "I had no choice but to re-introduce you two old friends."

"And I am to believe that?" Klamenkovich snaps as he turns on Soames. "Why have you called me here?"

"To start where we finished, General."

"But I believe your friend has destroyed your organisation."

"My organisation has many guises, General," Soames explains as Klamenkovich's mistrusting glare shifts to Davison, who grins broadly as he digests the intelligence at hand.

"Not me, General. I stay on the right side of the law."

Klamenkovich laughs. "The ever-delusional CIA."

"Anglo American Anti-Terrorism Intelligence Unit, General."

"Of course," Klamenkovich said, mistrusting an organisation he hadn't heard of.

"What do you say, General?" Soames questions in the hope of a positive reply.

"I'm not sure I can do business with you, Colonel."

"Before you carry on, General," Davison interrupts. "Can you explain to me how you're still alive?"

"Always a good idea in my line of business to not exist in the real world."

"Your fellow countrymen said you were dead, yet here you are with three of your SVR goons."

"What makes you think they are SVR?"

"Major Vitaly Rosstof, Lieutenant Dimitri Gavrikov and Lieutenant Josef Naumenko," Davison explains, making them uncomfortable at being named.

"You're well informed, Director."

"It pays to be in this game."

"Yes, it does," Klamenkovich adds, disinterested.

"Surely getting back in bed with the colonel would help Mother Russia in her help towards rearming for the future."

Klamenkovich gives Davison a curious stare as to where that question was meant to take them but instantly chooses to ignore it. "Back to you, Colonel. I know I said I'm unsure if I can do business with you, but I don't want to."

"For what reason?" Soames questions solemnly. "We've worked well together over the years and have both made a great deal of money."

"We have, but other than your CIA friend seeing me alive and your organisation being compromised, you betrayed our cause when you killed a dear friend of mine."

"And who would that be?" Davison said stoking up the mistrust.

"Colonel Sokolov."

Soames laughs. "You can't take that personally, General. It was business. Him or me."

"Really?"

"Was it you who ordered me killed?" Soames questions, but Klamenkovich isn't in the mood to be interrogated and nods at the SVR agents who go for their Makarov pistols, but Soames beats them to the draw and shoots the three of them dead to heighten the intensity in the room.

Hearing the shots, the other agents enter, and Soames takes out a grenade, primes it, throws it into the hallway, and steps aside as it explodes, killing them.

Soames points his Sig Sauer between Davison and Klamenkovich with the realisation that he doesn't have any allies in the room. "You thought they would kill me," he said, and Davison grinned, amused. "I assumed you would kill them, but that's why you have contingency plans."

"And one of those was to get intelligence from the general about the build-up in Russian armaments."

"Russia has a right to build up arms against the forward aggression of NATO!" Klamenkovich argues, but no one pays him any attention.

"You seem to have more information on their future intentions than anyone."

"I don't give a fuck for the future," Soames adds. "I'm living for today."

"You don't care that one day your country will be at arms with the bear, which will result in the deaths of your fellow countrymen?"

"Why should I care for a country that cares nothing for me."

"That's a pretty selfish attitude to have," Davison adds, making Soames laugh at his attempt to gain any favour from him.

Watkins exits a side room carrying Davison's Browning and puts a bullet into Soames' shoulder, knocking him to the floor, writhing in pain with blood seeping through his fingers. "Bloody hurts, doesn't it?" he said, picking up Soames' Sig Sauer and handing it to Davison, then turned the Browning to point at Klamenkovich.

Soames grins with betrayed delight. "I see the reports of your demise have been greatly exaggerated?"

"You could say that," Watkins said, pleased to have got one over on him.

"You've helped me no end," Davison said with glee.

"You used me to capture the general?"

"So, this charade was about capturing me?" Klamenkovich said. "Why? I'm not that important."

"Don't put yourself down, General. You're more important to us in the intelligence game than you think."

"How come?"

"You sold armaments to terrorists worldwide and were a major part of the cartel involving the previous owner of this house. You'll be a font of knowledge to my friends in Langley for many years as they question you on Russia's intentions in the future."

"Good luck with that," Klamenkovich said, confident that he would never give away intelligence to an enemy.

"So, you're still in the CIA?" Soames said, pulling a grenade out and pulling the pin showing intent which unnerves everyone in the room. "You look like you didn't expect this, Director."

"Grenades always make me feel this way. Such an indiscriminate weapon."

Soames turns to Klamenkovich. "Are you sure we don't have any business to attend to?" he questioned, making the Russian shuffle uncomfortably.

"Maybe something can be done, but I will need to speak to my superiors."

Soames turns to Watkins, who is still pointing the Browning. "I'll give you that shot, as that makes us equal, but you'd better put your gun down."

"I don't think so. You threatened my wife and son."

"I knew you wouldn't kill the director, but I needed him to think you might. Anyway, I saved them by taking out the MI5 assassin before he could kill James Ashley."

Watkins turns his bemused stare onto Davison.

"So, now you and James are friends?" Davison adds, humoured as Soames shakes his head.

"All I wanted was him here at the end," Soames explains, turning his bemusement onto Watkins. "I see you have the director's gun. I thought you didn't carry one?"

"You changed my mind at our last meeting. I didn't want to feel vulnerable again."

Davison moves to Watkins and relieves him of the Browning. "He isn't an agent and doesn't need to be armed."

"But, sir," Watkins pleads, desperate for justice.

"You can't shoot him. If you did, he would drop the grenade, and we'd all die in the explosion but I don't think he'll do it on purpose."

"I've done many mad things in my years of doing this shit, Director, and self-survival is strong in me, so I'd appreciate it if you throw your guns aside."

Davison hands Soames his Sig Sauer, then throws the Browning into the corner, and they look at Klamenkovich, who draws a Tokarev TT30 to toss aside.

"What now, Colonel?" Davison questions.

"Now I'm no longer in business with the general."

"But we could strike up a deal," Klamenkovich said, but Soames is aware his changing attitude is due to him being in a tight spot and is having none of it.

I think I will leave him to you," Soames said, approaching the door. "But on the other hand," he adds on looking back. "He knows a great deal about my organisation and me, and I know you still want to retrieve the Morrison's goods."

"We can leave that for another day," Davison adds.

"This isn't personal, Director, but survival is paramount in me," Soames said, dropping the grenade, then exited, closing the door as panic ensued and with no other option but to save his director, Watkins dived onto the grenade to take its full blast as it explodes, taking his life. Davison rubs his ringing ears as the mayhem disperses in a cloud of dust, and he looks in shock at Watkins' decimated body as Klamenkovich takes the solemn moment to pick up his Tokarev to turn onto him.

"Looks like you've lost out, Director."

"You think so?" Davison said confidently as he turned his angst onto the Russian.

"Your man's idiotic self-sacrifice has all been in vain, as you are now at my mercy."

"You know, General," Davison adds with calm. "I wanted to take you prisoner, but your unfeeling words have reminded me I have had enough of dealing with the scum of the world."

"You hurt my feelings," Klamenkovich said sharply. "Shame they are to be your last."

Davison nods, and a sniper's bullet smashes through the window to hit Klamenkovich in the shoulder, knocking the Tokarev out of his hand and him onto the floor, screaming in agony.

Davison picks up the gun as Klamenkovich rolls over to face it being aimed at him. "I had hoped my man's bullet would kill you, but he's a brilliant shot and managed to carry out his orders and injure you. I'm not displeased with this outcome as I look forward to finding out what you know about all the traitors in this game."

**

CHAPTER 36

***

Davison sits solemn-faced at his desk in his office when Ashley and Conners enter.

"How are you feeling, Director?"

"Not good, Colonel. I've just got off the phone with Watkins' wife."

"Did you inform her of what happened?"

"Of course not, James. She's been informed in person by some colleagues of mine, but I wanted to tell her how sorry I was."

"The truth or an agency lie?"

"She believes he was killed in a car crash," Davison adds sadly. "How could I tell her he sacrificed himself to save me?"

"To die so heroically," Ashley said with a romantic notion of such. "Wouldn't we all take that over the mundaneness of life?"

"Why did you allow Soames to escape, Director?"

"Because he'll take us to the millions he stole off the Morrison's."

"Is that important?" Ashley adds as his mind stays on Watkins. "You said Watkins was doing something for you; you must have planned this for a while."

"I had him follow me. He heard everything in my office with Soames, and I left Shirlow's address written in plain view on my desk, and he got my father's gun and followed. He must have got to Shirlow's cottage before we arrived."

"So, what was this all about, sir?"

"Originally, the Morrison's robbery, as it was done on my watch," Davison answers, depressed at the thought. "But now I want justice for my friend. We also need to find out if what he'd hinted at with Klamenkovich that his organisation is still running is true." He takes a deep resentful breath. "I believe he was blustering, but I can't take that chance."

"Do you think he is still acting under the instructions of MI6?"

Davison grins ominously. "That I would like the answer to."

"What about Klamenkovich," Conners questions. "Won't the Russians want him back as they know he was still alive?"

"Was he? Because they assured us of his demise."

"What about the men Soames used?" she adds.

"Surely the Frenchman or Klamenkovich will be able to answer those questions?" Ashley adds disinterested.

"He's been using connections within MI5 and MI6, but my intelligence believes they were unaware they were working for him. The man he killed in the US was there on his orders, including those who arrested James on those trumped-up charges to set him up."

"But those charges were sure to be quashed after Watkins had done what he was meant to," Ashley said innocently.

I believe he was playing for time."

"How will you find him?" Ashley presses.

"I had a drone follow him from Shirlow's cottage."

"That was your plan all along? This had nothing to do with Klamenkovich."

"I knew where he was from the very second the Russians said he was dead. He's been hiding at a pro-Putin oligarchs' mansion in London as he negotiates with others for military equipment, so it took him no time to get to Shirlow's cottage. He was to have his day, but Soames brought him to the fold earlier than anticipated."

"How did you get him to break cover?"

"How do you get a greedy man to do anything? Offer him something out of his control?"

"And what's that?"

Davison grins but doesn't answer.

"Some things you aren't meant to know, Colonel," Ashley said sarcastically.

"Of course," Conners adds. "I got lost in the moment and started to believe I could be trusted."

"You're trusted, but there are some things your best not knowing about."

Ashley takes out his pain medication to Davison and Conners' bewilderment, then places it on Davison's desk.

"What are you doing, Jimmy?"

"Giving up the meds."

"What about the hip flask?"

"I don't think I'm ready for that. Maybe I should take baby steps and do one at a time."

"I've told you it will kill you someday."

Ashley grins awkwardly, then exits, leaving Davison and Conners looking at each other in bewilderment.

"What's going on, Director?" Conners questions, but he has no inclination to explain what they had witnessed as they exit.

***

CHAPTER 37

***

Soames relaxes in his safe house situated in the heart of the Hertfordshire countryside just outside the village of Bassingbourn as he enjoys the anonymity the location gives him. The door smashes in, and Conners and Ashley enter with their guns offensively drawn taking him by surprise.

"If it isn't my two favourite agents," Soames said without moving. "The angel and his bait."

"Not expecting us, Mile End?" Ashley said triumphantly, but Soames looked unfazed by what he was witnessing.

"I knew something was wrong when I couldn't get in touch with them," Soames starts, but Ashley finishes his sentence.

"MI6 agent, Sergeant Major Jonathan Botham."

"So, you got the better of him. How clever of you."

"He's waiting for you along with Kilbride, Reynolds and Klamenkovich in that shit-filled hole that never sees the light of day."

"So Klamenkovich still lives?" Soames said with a deep interest. "How come?"

Neither Ashley nor Conners wants to answer.

"I knew you would come for me, but I never thought it would be today," Soames said as Davison entered, and he turned his stare onto him. "You've brought the big guns with you. You seem to be getting out of your office a great deal more of late, Director?"

"A lot needs to be done to clean the world of scum like you."

"How rude," Soames jests. "I've never personally attacked you but saying you are here, you do know your presence undermines your goons' roles."

Davison looks between Ashley and Conners, then laughs. "I don't think so."

"I take it you had me tailed from Shirlow's cottage. They must be good as I never noticed anyone."

"It was a drone."

"Well, that makes me feel better. I thought I was losing my touch."

"You were never going to notice that," Davison adds with arrogance.

"I keep walking into these situations, so I must be losing something."

"You've come up against your betters, Mile End," Ashley evaluates, and Soames turns angrily onto him.

"I hope you don't mean yourself, arse wipe?"

Ashley laughs as Soames recomposes himself.

"Hold on," Conners interjects. "Where does this Mile End name come from."

"Not from any form of humour," Soames grumbles, making Ashley laugh.

"Everyone posted to my outfit in the SAS was given a pet name. Hopefully, one that irked like Mile End. You know his name is Milton, so we started with Mil Ton, then that changed to My Ton, then My Elton, but we got no response, so one of the lads came up with My End, which ended up as Mile End."

Conners looks at Davison, bemused by the long story for such an unamusing ending.

"Like I told you, it only matters if I'm laughing inside."

"Fucking idiot," Soames said, unimpressed.

"I never thought I would agree with him," Davison interrupts. "But I can't see the funny side of your story."

"You're not meant to, Director; that's the point."

"All this shit with the Russian was a ruse to track me down," Soames adds to change the subject.

"You're overplaying your importance."

"I think not. How did you get out of Shirlow's cottage unscathed?"

"Watkins threw himself on the grenade before it exploded," Davison explains with pride-tinged sadness.

"What an idiot," Soames disparages, and Davison lunges at him, but Conners holds him back.

"You piece of fucking shit."

"There you go with the insults again. Me getting one over on you in Bermuda has cut deep into your narcissistic soul, Director and in the end, it got your man killed."

"By you."

"The grenade killed him, not me."

"You pulled the fucking pin."

"I never thought you would take this so personally. You didn't seem to be that type to me."

"You made it personal by killing my friend."

"You ordered many of my friends killed, but I haven't made it personal," Soames explains calmly. "So, we have a stalemate again?"

"Hardly!" Davison shouts. "This time, you have been captured with your hand on your dick and will lead us to the monies stolen from the Morrisons and the closure of your organisation once and for all."

"I think not."

"You will in the end," Davison adds confidently, but Soames draws his Sig Sauer from the inside cushion of his chair and stands to point it at Conners.

"Say hello to my dick, Colonel."

"You're outgunned."

"I always am, but if you shoot me, I guarantee she will die too!" Soames said with calm. "We may even land on the floor together." He grins menacingly at Davison.

"All in the line of duty," Conners said unperturbed.

"Only death is guaranteed. Your users will forget your duty, but you'll get your star on the wall at Langley that no one will pay any attention to."

"That will also result in your death."

"I'm gambling you'll want to save the colonel, and I will be able to walk," Soames adds with reason.

"Why don't you give in, Mile End," Ashley adds to Soames' irritation.

"Piss off, arse wipe."

"I'm happy with that because a wipe for your arse is important, but people like you never know when you're beaten."

"I'll never accept defeat as long as I can breathe, but you wouldn't know that, Sergeant, as your life is mired in it."

"I haven't been a sergeant in years, and I'm not an officer who carries their rank like a badge of honour," Ashley said as he winked at Conners. "Sorry, Colonel."

"I don't carry my rank around," Conners explains, bemused. "It's others, like you, that keep reminding me of it when the shit hits the fan, Jimmy."

"Being beaten is part of everyday life, and I couldn't give a shit. I don't have an ego," Ashley said, pointing his Walther at Soames. "You lose, Mile End."

"I don't give in that easy," Soames said, but Ashley stepped between Conners and the barrel. "So why don't you just fuck off and get yourself pissed or high?"

"I've given up the drugs," Ashley said, feeling the initial effects of cold turkey, but he is confident in himself to Soames' laughing amusement as he can see the sweat covering his face. "They don't work."

"Since when?"

"A couple of hours now," Ashley explains, making Soames laugh.

"What are you doing, Jimmy?" Conners questioned as she tried moving him, but he remained rigidly still.

"He's being a hero," Soames interjects. "How sweet, but you'll find the calibre of my Sig will go through you both. Two for one, you might say, but your attempted heroics keeps me in a favourable position as the bullet after that will be for your unarmed director."

"Why don't you pull the trigger, and we'll find out," Ashley shouts, but Soames remains resolute.

"That's enough of that, Jimmy," Davison said, attempting to calm the situation.

"Come on, Mile End, you piece of shit. Let's find out what a cold-blooded murderer you are."

"Name-calling doesn't bother me."

"We're aware of that, Mile End!" Ashley said, increasing his tone as he shouted the name the MI6 man hates. "It never seems to upset you when I say it," he adds sarcastically.

"You know, Sergeant, I will take you up on that offer."

"That's enough of that," Davison mediates. "Let's calm things down."

"Do it as the next bullet will be in your head," Soames snipes. "A brilliant end for such a miserable piece of shit, but I won't be going to jail," he adds, and Ashley glances at Davison, who grins with the understanding that the intelligence the rouge MI6 agent has would be vital to them. "I have far too much information for your users to waste."

Angered by such an outcome, Ashley moves toward Soames, and they fire simultaneously to each go down with gunshot wounds. Soames screams in pain as he attempts to turn his gun onto Conners, but Davison stands on his arm as he draws his Browning and beats her to put a second bullet into his head, killing him.

Conners dives next to Ashley and pulls open his shirt to see he isn't wearing a bulletproof vest. "What the hell, Jimmy!" she screams. "What were you thinking?"

"Are you alright?" Ashley groans to her increasing distress.

"Thanks to you."

"At last, I can be proud of myself," Ashley adds but takes a deep, pain-fuelled breath.

"It wasn't your job to take a bullet for me."

"Wasn't it?" Ashley groans. "You're the only one I would do it for," he adds as his breath whines.

Conners looks at his chest to see heavy bruising and a trickle of blood diluted by liquid pouring out of his jacket over him. "I don't believe it."

Ashley pushes himself against the wall, grabs his chest, and breathes heavily, pained. He pulls out his hip flask and smiles at the dent in it with a bullet caught between the two sides of Kevlar, making him laugh. Conners and Davison follow suit as the director takes the hip flask to look at in amazement.

"I don't believe it."

"You bloody idiot, you could have been killed."

Ashley grins, unsure in himself if that was what he truly wanted.

Davison explains. "You need to give James his moment."

Tears well in Conners' eyes that her friend was millimetres from death and that if he didn't have the hip flask, that would have happened.

"Why did you kill Soames when you needed his information on MI6, Director."

Davison's stare shifts to Soames. "I'm tired of playing to his type. The world will be a better place without them, no matter what intelligence they have."

She looks at Soames, staring at the ceiling with his mouth open. "He looks like he is about to say something."

Davison grins amused. "Yeah. He had a lot to say, but I like this outcome better." He walks over to Ashley and helps him stand.

"What about the Morrison's millions?" Conners questions.

"Fuck them," Davison adds with the broadest of smiles. "They can afford it. You know, Shirlow and Co mentioned that what they were doing was for the good of the union, but I believe what you two uncovered throughout this was for the good of both of the unions. American and British."

"Maybe you'll get the Congressional Medal of Honor," Ashley said, and she added to the humour.

"And you, the Victoria Cross."

"As if," Ashley adds as Conners moves to his side and gives him a hearty cuddle. "What we've uncovered won't be appreciated by anyone."

"Don't ever do that again."

"I won't, but you must admit you were wrong about the flask killing me."

"Not the flask, I said the contents."

Ashley looks at Davison. "Talking about my depleted flask, I could do with a few drinks. How about you?"

"I'm always open for a Jack or two."

Ashley smiles, pleased with the thought, as he exits, holding his aching chest, and Davison puts his arm around his shoulder to help him out, leaving Conners following and shaking her head in bewilderment that alcohol is always their first thought.

THE END

Printed in Great Britain
by Amazon

26718218R00172